Zack Jordan is from Chicago, and has an ardent and burning love for literature, music, and robots. He writes music, stories, games, and everything else he can think of. *The Last Human* is his debut novel.

Praise for *The Last Human*

'Aliens, adventure, mystery, and big ideas in a
thoroughly fresh package'
Andy Weir, author of *The Martian*

'Easily the most fun read I've had all year!'
Clint McElroy, co-author of The Adventure Zone series

'*The Last Human* delivers characters who spring from the page with empathy, danger, cryptic motives and chills, all of it amid plenty of action and mystery, in a galaxy of wondrous possibilities'
David Brin, author of *The Postman*

'*The Last Human* is a very funny novel, full of compelling ideas, engaging dialogue and fascinating species and technology, and we hope to see more of the galaxy Jordan has created'
SciFiNow

THE LAST HUMAN

ZACK JORDAN

HODDER

First published in Great Britain in 2020 by Hodder & Stoughton
An Hachette UK company

This paperback edition published in 2021

1

Book design by Edwin Vazquez

A CIP catalogue record for this title is
available from the British Library

Paperback ISBN 9781473650879

Set in Sabon MT

Printed and bound in Great Britain by Clays Ltd, Elcograf S.p.A.

Hodder & Stoughton policy is to use papers that are natural, renewable
and recyclable products and made from wood grown in sustainable
forests. The logging and manufacturing processes are expected to
conform to the environmental regulations of the country of origin.

Hodder & Stoughton Ltd
Carmelite House
50 Victoria Embankment
London EC4Y 0DZ

www.hodder.co.uk

For London the Daughter

TIER ONE

CHAPTER

ONE

Not so many years ago, Shenya the Widow was a void-cold killer. And as hobbies—no, *passions*—go, it was extraordinarily fulfilling. Hunt all night, feast at dawn, take one's pick of the choicest males before the long day's sleep . . . oh yes. She still fantasizes about it—though, sadly, fantasy is all she has left. This is because Shenya the Widow has been conquered, mind and body, by an ancient and terrible force.

Motherhood.

And so she crouches like death's own shadow outside a closed bedroom door and flexes a variety of bladed appendages in quiet reflection. Her own mother warned her about this. She could be *hunting* right now. She could be streaking through a moonlit forest with the rest of her covenant, the bloodlust boiling in her breast, her hunting cry joining those of her sisters in a chorus of beautiful death . . . but no.

She composes a Network message in her mind. [**Sarya the**

Daughter], says the message. [**My love and greatest treasure. My child, for whom I would gladly die. *Open this door before I cut it out of the station wall.***] She attaches a few choice emotions—though she knows her daughter's unit is too basic to read them—and fires the message through the Network implant in the back of her head.

[**Error, unit not receiving**], says the return message. [**Have a nice day.**]

Shenya releases a slow and wrathful hiss. [**Very clever**], she sends, tapping a black and gleaming blade against the door. [**I know you're receiving, my love. And if you sabotage your unit one more time, well.**] She dispatches the message as violently as possible, leans against the hatch, and begins a shrill danger-rattle with every available blade.

And then with a hiss and the screech of metal on chitin, the hatch slides aside to bathe Shenya the Widow in the blinding glow of her daughter's quarters. She ignores the pain from her eyes—must her daughter *always* keep her room so bright?—and waits the moment it takes for her to distinguish the figure that is more collapsed than seated against the far wall. Its utility suit is rumpled, its boots undone, its sleeves and collar pulled as low and as high as they go. Only the head and the ends of the upper limbs are bare, but even that much exposed flesh would have sickened her not long ago.

Back before Shenya the Widow ever dreamed of calling this one *daughter,* it took her some time to stomach the sight of an intelligence without an exoskeleton. Imagine, a being with only four limbs! And worse, each of these limbs splits into five more at its end—well, that is the stuff of nightmares, is it not? As if that were not horrific enough, this being is wrapped top to bottom not in clean and beautiful chitin but in an oily blood-filled organ—which is called *skin,* her research has told her. There is a sporadic dusting of *hair* over this skin, with a few concentrations in seemingly random spots. Up top there is a great knot of it, long and thick and nearly Widow-dark, wild and falling down in tangles over the strangest eyes one could imagine. Those eyes! Two multicolored orbs that flash like killing strokes, that express emotion nearly as well as a pair of mandibles. One wouldn't think it possible but here it is in action. That gaze that is nearly scorching the floor, that somehow radiates from such odd concentric circles—is that a sullen rage?

"Sorry about the hatch," says her adopted daughter without looking up. Her upper limbs, Shenya the Widow cannot help but notice, are held dangerously close to an obscene Widow sign. "I was getting ready for my *field trip*."

And now her mother understands: this is a mighty anger, a fury worthy of a Widow, and it is directed somewhere outside this room.

Shenya the Widow flows into her daughter's room with the gentle clicks of exoskeleton on metal. She may be an apex predator, a murderous soul wrapped in lightning and darkness, but underneath that she is all parent. There are wrongs to be righted and hurts to be savagely avenged—but before any of that can happen there is a room to be tidied. Shenya the Widow's many limbs are up to the task.

The spare utility suit, yes, that can go straight to laundry—two limbs fold it and place it by the door. The nest, or *bunk,* as her daughter now calls it, needs straightening—two more blades begin that noble work. A single blade scouts the floor for food bar wrappers, stabbing their silver forms as it finds them. The laundry limbs, mission accomplished, now rescue a soft dark shape from the floor. The doll is black and silky and a horrifying caricature of Widow physiology, but Shenya the Widow made it many years ago with her own eight blades, and her hearts still ache to see it banished from the bunk. She places it, carefully, back where it belongs.

"Where is your Network unit, my love?" asks Shenya the Widow in that soft and dangerous voice that comes with motherhood. Her nearly spherical vision examines all corners of the room at once.

Her daughter glares at the floor without answering.

Shenya the Widow narrowly restrains a click of approval. On

the one blade, this is a Widow rage—a towering and explosive wrath—and it is beautiful. One spends so much energy attempting to install traditional values in a young and coalescing mind, and it is always rewarding to see effort yield results. But on another blade, well . . . insolence is insolence, is it not?

Happily, she is saved by circumstance. A questing limb reports that it has found the object in question under the bunk. Shenya the Widow drags it out, feeling a twinge of guilt at the strength required. This heavy prosthetic, this poor substitute for a common Network implant, is what her daughter has been forced to wear strapped around her torso for most of her life. It is an ancient device, a budget so-called *universal*, only distantly related to the elegant implant somewhere in Shenya the Widow's head. Both perform the same function, in theory: each connects its user to a galaxy-spanning Network brimming with beauty and meaning and effortless communication. One does it seamlessly, as smooth as the bond between one neuron and a billion billion others. The other does it through a shaky hologram, some static-infused audio, and numerous error messages.

[. . . *before I cut it out of the station wall*], says the Network unit to itself, its trembling hologram flickering in the air above it.

One might assume that a certain physiology is required to hold oneself like a Widow, but her daughter proves this untrue. She sits up, wrapping upper limbs around lower with movements as Widowlike as they are—well . . . what she is. It is these familiar motions that unlock the deepest chambers of Shenya the Widow's hearts. The untidy room, the insolence, the disrespect for property—all that is forgotten. Her many limbs abandon their myriad tasks and regroup on the figure of her daughter, stroking skin-covered cheeks without the slightest hint of revulsion. They straighten the utility suit and slide through the hair and caress those ten tiny appendages. "Tell me, Daughter," whispers Shenya the Widow with a sigh through mandibles as dangerous as her blades. "Tell me everything."

Her daughter takes a deep breath, lifting her shoulders with that dramatic motion that people with lungs often use. "We're going to one of the observation decks today," she says quietly. "They have six openings for trainees."

Shenya the Widow chooses her words carefully, missing the effortless precision of mental Network communication. "I did not know you were interested in—"

And now, finally, that fiery gaze rises from the floor. "You know what the prerequisites are?" asks her daughter, glaring at her mother through a tangle of dark hair.

They are ferocious, those eyes, and Shenya the Widow finds herself wondering how another of her daughter's species would feel caught in this three-color gaze. White outside brown-gold outside black outside . . . fury. "I do not," she answers cautiously.

"I bet you can guess."

"I . . . choose not to," says Shenya the Widow, still more cautiously.

"Tier two-point-zero intelligence," says her daughter in a tight voice. "Not, say, one-point-eight." The beloved figure slumps in a way that would be impossible with an exoskeleton. "No, we wouldn't want a moron at the controls, would we?" she murmurs to the floor.

"My child!" says Shenya the Widow, shocked. "Who dares call the daughter of Shenya the Widow such a thing?"

"Everybody calls me *such a thing*," says her daughter, again straying perilously close to disrespect, "because I am registered as *such a thing*."

Shenya the Widow chooses to ignore the accusatory tone. This conversation again. "Daughter," she begins. "I understand that you are frustrated by—"

"Actually, it doesn't matter, because also you have to be Networked," interrupts her daughter, tapping her head where her implant would be if she had one. "A prosthetic doesn't cut it, apparently. Something about *instant responses* and *clear communication* and—" The rest of the requirements are cut off by a grunt as she extends a wild kick toward the device on the floor.

Shenya the Widow catches the unit before it touches the wall, as her daughter surely knew she would. She employs two more limbs to raise that gaze back to her own, resting the flat of a blade on each side of that beloved face. She can feel her daughter fight, but Shenya the Widow is a hunter and a mother—two things as unstoppable as destiny. "Daughter," she says quietly. "You know our reasons."

Her daughter meets that gaze. "You know what?" she says. "I'm tired of pretending. I'm tired of having no one to—" She stops, and her voice drops. "Sometimes I just want to tell everyone the truth and just see what happens."

Now Shenya the Widow rattles, low and soft. This is far more serious than a job and a Network implant. "You must *never*, my love," she whispers, filling her words with the force of a mother Widow.

"I must never?" asks her daughter, eyes still locked on her mother's. "I must never *tell the truth*? I must never say hey, guess what, I'm *not* a moron, I'm a—"

"Do not say it," hisses Shenya the Widow, trembling. With effort, she withdraws the blade that has just slit the synthetic flooring near her daughter's foot. All over her body she feels the pleasure of blades lengthening and edges hardening, and fights to keep any of them from coming in contact with that beloved skin—

"I'm a Human," says her daughter in a steady voice.

Shenya the Widow raises herself off the floor, her many blades extending in every direction. "Sarya the Daughter," she says, in a voice that would terrify anyone on the station. "Hold out your appendage."

Anyone but her daughter, apparently. The gaze doesn't break as the hand is offered, palm up. The rest of her body shows the traditional posture of respect for an elder, with the worst sarcasm Shenya the Widow has seen in a long time. All the more reason for discipline.

"It does not matter what you *were*, my daughter," says Shenya the Widow, placing the edge of a blade on a hand already crisscrossed with faint white lines. "It matters what you *are,* and what you are is Widow."

Her daughter's hand does not move. The posture becomes even more sarcastic, if such a thing is possible. Those eyes gaze into her mother's, waiting and judging. Expecting pain without flinching. Like a Widow.

Shenya the Widow's hearts overflow. *Pain without fear*—this, in her opinion, is the central proverb of Widowhood. She has spent so much time instilling this principle that it is almost poetic to have it used against her in this way.

"I raised you thus," she continues, struggling to keep her prideful pheromones in check, "because I could not raise you as— as what you are."

Her daughter does not look away. Her hand curls around the razor edge in its palm, as if in challenge. "Say it," she says. "Say what I am."

"I—" Shenya the Widow stops, then is shocked that *she* is the one who looks away. "I choose not to," she says.

For the first time she feels the hand under her blade tremble, and Shenya the Widow returns her gaze to that precious face in time to see moisture welling up around those strange eyes. This is a thing Humans do: their emotions can often be derived from their excretions. The literature calls these drops of liquid *tears;* they express intense emotion, whether it be joy or distress. In this instance, she is almost certain that it is—

"Do you know what that feels like?" whispers her daughter.

Immediately, all desire to discipline evaporates. "Daughter," says Shenya the Widow, withdrawing the blade without piercing that precious skin. "My center and my purpose." She encircles her daughter in a gleaming, clicking embrace, rests the flat of a blade against that fragile face, and flicks her mandibles twice in an expression of love. She draws closer, her gleaming, faceted eyes nearly touching skin. "If anyone *ever* finds out what you are—"

"I know," says her daughter with a sigh. "You don't want to lose me."

"Well," says Shenya the Widow, spotting opportunity, "there are other considerations."

"Yeah?"

"For instance," says Shenya the Widow, twirling a blade as if in thought. "I would prefer not to, say, *murder* those who would come for you." She shrugs, a long chain reaction that begins at her carapace and clatters to the ends of her blades. "You know how it is once you get started . . ."

That does it. Her daughter battles valiantly, but the tiniest of smiles manages to fight its way to the surface of her face. That's what this expression is, this concerted mouth-and-eyes movement. A smile.

"Good point," says her daughter, the corners of her mouth twitching in both Widow and Human emotion. "We wouldn't want you to murder unnecessarily."

"No, Daughter," says Shenya the Widow. "We would not."

"I mean, you might murder the wrong people, or too *many* people—"

"Almost certainly. You know what it's like when the righteous fury is upon you. Once you begin—"

"It's hard to stop," Sarya the Daughter says quietly. She takes her mother's blade in her hands and caresses it, watching her own eyes in her reflection. "At least, that's how I imagine it."

Shenya the Widow allows her daughter a moment of reflection. She herself has always found fantasies of mayhem soothing; she assumes the same is true for Humans. "It would comfort your mother," she says after a moment, "if, before you left for your field trip, you would correct your earlier statement."

Her daughter sighs and rises to her feet as her mother's blades retract from around her with eight distinct rattles. "I am Sarya the Daughter," she says softly. "Adopted, of Shenya the Widow. My species is—" She sighs. "My species is *Spaal*." With one hand, she signs the Standard symbols that she has used her entire life: *I'm sorry, my tier is low. I don't understand.* She looks disgusted with herself, standing in the center of her quarters with her shoulders bowed. "Happy?" she asks.

And that is that: another trans-species child-rearing triumph. A marginal success, perhaps, but a parent must take what a parent can get. And now that the crisis has passed, Shenya the Widow may turn to a happier subject. "Now, my daughter—" she begins.

"I don't even look like one," her daughter mutters, turning away. "Anyone who thinks so is the moron."

"Daughter," says Shenya the Widow. "I would like to—"

"Did I tell you I have an interview at the arboretum?" her daughter interrupts, lifting the prosthetic off the floor with distaste. "Yeah. Even a damn *Spaal* is overqualified for that one, believe it or not. I think most everybody down there is actually sub-legal, so I could actually be a manager or—"

"Daughter!" hisses Shenya the Widow.

Her daughter turns, expectant, blinking against Shenya the Widow's exasperated pheromones. The Network prosthetic dangles from one hand, already displaying a new error message.

"Perhaps you should leave that here," says Shenya the Widow, gesturing toward the unit with a gleaming blade.

Her daughter laughs a short Widow laugh with the corners of her mouth. "I'd rather go naked," she says, holding down a control to reset the device. "You think *this* is bad, try going without any unit at all. I tried that once and—"

"Take this one instead," says Shenya the Widow. With a smooth movement, she reveals—*finally*—the tiny device she has been holding behind her thorax this entire time.

Her daughter stares, jaw dropping downward with that peculiar verticality that once so disgusted Shenya the Widow.

"I was going to wait for your adoption anniversary," says her mother, almost afraid to judge this reaction. "The waiting, however, proved to be—"

The prosthetic hits the floor with a weighty thump as Sarya the Daughter leaps forward to seize the gift. "Mother!" she breathes, fingering the tiny locket and earbuds. "How can we *afford* this? This is—I don't even—this is *amazing*. It's perfect!"

"I had it customized," says Shenya the Widow, allowing her own pride to seep into the words. "I even installed your little friend on it to help you get accustomed. They say if you cannot have the surgery—" She hesitates, now feeling her way forward. *Because someone might discover your species* is the exact type of phrase that could ruin all her hard-won progress. "Then this is the next best thing," she finishes.

Her daughter says nothing in words, but her disregard for her own safety says it all. With a wild Human laugh, she flings herself into razor-sharp limbs, arms outstretched. With skill developed from long practice, mother catches daughter in a net of softened blades and flat chitin.

"These are the good kind of tears, correct?" asks Shenya the Widow, stroking the warm face with the flat of a blade.

"Yes," whispers Sarya the Human. "Thank you."

TWO

Yesterday, Watertower Station was a blank and nearly silent orbital station. Its color scheme could have been described as *industrial,* at best. Its thousands of walls, floors, and ceilings were an interchangeable gray save for the painfully orange warnings marking the areas where a resident might encounter dismemberment, asphyxiation, or various other discomforts. Not that its residents ever glanced at those warnings. No, they were too busy milling through colorless corridors in equally colorless utility suits, eyes and similar sense organs focused in the middle distance. There was very little sound on Watertower yesterday, just twenty-four thousand citizens and visitors from hundreds of species, all in mutual pursuit of silence but for the unavoidable: the sound of footsteps, wheels, treads, the rustle of utility suits, the occasional uncomfortably biological noise. Gray on gray on gray, silent as the void and nearly as interesting. That was Watertower Station, yesterday.

But this is today.

Today, Sarya understands. Today, Watertower Station is an eruption of light and color and sound like nothing she's ever experienced. Everywhere her manic gaze falls, something leaps out at her—often literally. She forces herself to keep her mouth shut and does her best to avoid physically dodging away from every image that flits by. She touches the tiny Network unit at her hairline and taps the earbuds farther into her ear canals; she's been wearing this thing for less than a Network Standard hour and already she's utterly convinced. *This* is real, these projected images and sounds, and the gray walls that have enclosed her entire life are the illusion. She can't even see them anymore; they've disappeared behind landscapes and artwork, behind hues and patterns and corporate slogans.

Goddess. She couldn't remove her giddy grin if she tried.

She keeps to the tail end of her group as it threads through the labyrinth of Watertower Station, the better to gape uninterrupted. Not that she cares what a collection of strangers thinks of her. She is a transient here, a short-term transplant from a lower-tier class who was probably assigned to this particular field trip through some Network glitch somewhere. Why else would she be visiting a place where she can never work? But she's here, and she has just as much right to be here as the rest of her temporary cohort. If they don't like it, well—they are free to borrow one of her blades, as the Widow saying goes.

She does know a surprising amount about these people. Her knowledge is now amplified, extended into the near-infinite space of the Network, and her access is no longer limited to a few cubic centimeters of malfunctioning display. Now she is crowded by names and public biographies that appear next to citizens as soon as her eyes land on them. They drift as delicate scripts or heavy symbols, colored and/or animated according to their owners' preferences, each adding to the greater cloud of color and light that is the Network. Even with her new unit's efforts in tracking her gaze and fading items in and out of focus as it guesses her intent, she is very nearly overwhelmed.

That doesn't seem to be a problem for the rest of the class, though, and she can't help but wonder why. Maybe they've scaled back their preferences. Perhaps they've turned off ads or certain channels. Her old unit offered a way to do that, which was laughable because there was such a fine line between that and just turning it off altogether. But maybe she's the only one who can see, for example, the stunning scene emerging from this row of storefronts. The swirl of miniature creatures bursts out of the advertisement, each darting through empty space like a tiny starship. She watches them circle her fellow students one after another like a single organism . . . and with absolutely zero effect. And then Sarya flinches as that cloud of tiny beings explodes into a brilliant ad in front of her:

[AivvTech Network Implants: The *only* way to experience the Network.]

A quick glance around shows her that no one else has reacted in the slightest, and that brings a grin to her face. So! Pure, full-strength, undiluted Network is too much for her classmates and they are forced to limit their intake. Look at *her*, though. Sarya the Daughter—poor, low-tier non-Networked Sarya—*she* can take its full brunt. She holds out a finger for the same virtual creatures to inspect, determined never to fall into the trap of apathy. She will be fascinated by the Network until the day she dies, so help her goddess. Look at this little one who's darted over to nibble at her sharpened fingernail! This simulation of life, this frolicking little billionth of a billionth of a galaxy-spanning Network—how could you not want to see her play? Yes, she's part of an advertisement, created for no purpose but increasing someone's bottom line. But look at her! Look at the cloud of others that follows her! They play so realistically around her hands and sleeves that she very nearly breaks the silence of the corridor by laughing aloud.

[So anyway my father wants me to go into civil administration], says a new rush of symbols ahead of her. They are beautifully styled in silver, hovering in midair next to a student named **[Rama]** and then fading away as soon as Sarya has read them. So many thoughts! Everywhere! And Sarya would never have known if not for her Network unit. All her life, she's been missing ninety-five percent of reality.

[**I thought you were thinking xenobiology?**] says another student. This is [**Jina**], according to her Network unit. Jina's letters flash a glittering blue, spilling into smoke as Sarya's eyes take them in.

[*Shrug*], says Rama. Sarya didn't catch the gesture but her Network unit apparently did, and here it is, captured and translated into silver meaning. [**No facility in this system**], she says. [**And you know how my dad feels about Network travel.**]

[*Laughter*], says Jina in a burst of blue. [**Aren't you a little old to worry about that?**]

But it is at this point that Jina notices Sarya's delighted stare. Rama turns as well, glaring back for a split second as if she can't believe this audacity. There is a moment of one-sided awkwardness—Sarya's unit helpfully overlaying the words [*contempt*] and [*disdain*] over Rama and Jina respectively—and then they turn away in synchrony. Their beautiful words disappear, replaced by a more businesslike [*private conversation*].

Sarya swallows and glances downward, a familiar heat spreading over her face. After so many years of this she doesn't normally dwell on any particular incident . . . but then it's never been literally spelled out for her before. Now she's thinking uncomfortable thoughts, and her euphoria is rapidly ebbing. How often has she received those glances without the ability to translate them? How often have the blank gazes of a thousand different species actually meant *contempt* and *disdain* and any number of similar things?

[**Sarya's Little Helper would like to speak with you**], says a notification down near the floor.

That's right, her mother mentioned Helper was installed on this thing. But for the moment . . . no. She brushes it away with a violent two-handed movement that her Network unit interprets perfectly. She doesn't *want* to speak with her helper intelligence. She doesn't want to talk to anyone, and she *certainly* doesn't want to play with these tiny virtual intelligences who have followed her down the corridor from that advertisement. She is no longer entertained. Damn things, go annoy somebody else or she'll—

Hands still thrashing through a cloud of imaginary beings, Sarya plows into another student. A fogged face mask turns up toward her, several eyes blinking behind it, as a sweet scent fills her nostrils and stings her eyes. Her unit instantly inserts a registration beside the face: [**Jobe (*he* family), species: *Aqueous Collective*, Tier: 2.05.**]

She steps back with a muttered "*Beware*"—the standard Widow apology—and instantly regrets it as the sound of her voice echoes in the corridor and draws gazes from up the line. It's a painful reminder: no matter how magical her new Network prosthetic, it's still a prosthetic. It has no direct connection to her mind, which means it's one-way. Unlike practically everyone else on this station, she cannot send outgoing mental messages. No, she is restricted to the same process she's always used: hunting and pecking symbols with eyes or a digit in a process long enough to be nearly useless in situations like this.

A pair of moist hands adjusts the face mask. "Oh, it's no problem at all," says their owner, his voice the loudest sound anywhere in this corridor. He raises a squishy-looking arm to gaze at her through a small light display mounted to its back. "No problem at all, *Sar-ya*," he repeats, this time adding a butchered pronunciation of the Widow name listed on her own registration.

Sarya refuses to correct him. She keeps her mouth shut, more than aware of the eyes drifting toward the two of them and the emotions attached to those gazes. Just her luck to bump into another non-Networked citizen—maybe the only other one on the station, for all she knows. And now he wants to *talk*. Like, out-loud-style.

"Oh, sorry, I didn't see your intelligence tier," says Jobe, still peering at her through his own prosthetic. "Um," he says, drawing out the sound. "It. Is. Okay. Sar-ya."

Goddess, now it's worse. That slow speech, the simplification of sentences, the too-loud pronunciation—it's all familiar. Common, even. But this is the second offense in less than a Standard minute. This one pricks her deep, igniting a rage just below her surface. But Sarya the Daughter doesn't explode. No, Sarya is the adopted child of a Widow. She has been trained for this. She clamps her teeth and digs nails into palms in her Human adaptation of a Widow meditation. She focuses on the pain, just like her mother taught her. Pain distracts. Pain means you are alive. Pain keeps her from ripping that face mask right off that—

She barely avoids ramming someone else when the group halts, her mind lost in violent fantasies that might give even her mother pause.

"All right, students," says the teacher out loud, the words filling the nearly silent corridor. Her name and pronouns float next to the pinched face in simple yellow, but Sarya doesn't need them. She is *the* teacher—the only one on Watertower—and that's the only name anyone uses for her. She's also the teacher for Sarya's normal low-tier class—probably teaching them right now. In fact, her various identical bodies have taught every class Sarya's ever had. A younger Sarya once spent an entire Standard year trying to figure out how many bodies make a teacher, but she gave up the project when she began suspecting that her efforts were being actively but subtly foiled. That's when she learned a fundamental truth about higher tiers: they can screw with you as much as they want and you'll never know.

"We have arrived at Watertower Station's central observation deck," continues the teacher. "Here, for the first time, you will see the entire reason for this station's existence. I suspect one or two of you will be seeing this room again, come Career Day."

Sarya realizes, from the [*shocked*] reactions of her classmates, that she is probably the only one in this group who has ever heard the teacher's voice. Like any other Networked citizen of civilized space, the teacher seldom speaks. There is very rarely need. Unless, say, the teacher's current class contains a supposed low-tier individual with no Network implant.

On the other side of the group, Sarya watches Jina nudge Rama and send a significant glance Sarya's way. *They* know why the teacher is speaking aloud. Sarya receives the force of that glance like a slap; she can hear her own teeth grinding through her skull. Widow mantras begin running through her head again, an automatic response drilled into her over a long and painful childhood. *I am Widow. My rage is my weapon. I am Widow. My life is my own. I am Widow. Better a scar from a sister than a—*

And then she is startled by an unpleasantly biological sound beside her. "I'll be here!" says Jobe, waving a glistening arm. "They said they'd even wait until I'm Networked!"

Sarya's ears pop before she realizes exactly how hard she's compressing her jaw. She expects to feel blood dripping from her clenched fists any second. She didn't particularly plan on hating this Jobe kid, but the universe is really leaving her no choice here. *He* gets to be Networked. *He* doesn't have to pretend he's low-tier. This bladeless weakling, this—

And then with the hiss of a safety door and the familiar flourish of the teacher, her group is ushered into one of the many places where low-tier non-Networked Sarya the Daughter will never be allowed again. Her interest, which has been overshadowed by recent events, stages a tentative return. It's dark in here, but it doesn't *seem* dark because her Network unit instantly begins analyzing the space and adding glowing grid lines where it finds walls and floors. Her nose is ambushed by that relentless non-scent of Watertower's industrial odor neutralizers, which means this is one of those spaces designed for many species to work in close proximity. She can hear those intelligences now: a soft biological tumult constructed of membrane friction, the squeaking of chitin, the compression of lungs and other modes of respiration—these sounds and more, built into a wall of gentle noise and mortared with general moistness.

[Analysis complete], says her Network unit, but by now Sarya's eyes have adjusted sufficiently to see the general shape of the room. She stands at the highest point of a dark and gleaming chamber. Before her, several tiers of black seats step down to a blank wall that must be ten meters high. Individuals of various biologies stare into space, limbs twitching as they manipulate data invisible to her. Several more teacher bodies are here, making small talk with several of the workers. That makes sense; the teacher probably taught all of *them* as well. Everyone on Watertower probably knows the teacher. She could be centuries old, as far as Sarya knows.

"This," says a moist voice at her elbow. "Is the oldest. Part. Of the station."

Sarya stares down at the face mask, unbelieving. Jobe is a half meter shorter than her, rounder than her, his skin slicker than hers, and he stares back with wide and innocent eyes. Oh goddess—he's *adopted* her. He's playing the higher-tier mentor role.

"One. Of my dads. Used to work here," he continues, oblivious to the blistering glare he's receiving. "He says. It's the best view. On the station."

I am Widow. My rage is my weapon. I am Widow. There are no secrets between Mother and Daughter. I am—

"I'm Jobe," says Jobe. "In case. You can't. Read it."

A Widow might have been able to keep herself under control. A Widow might have been able to avoid this entire conversation simply by virtue of her terrifying appearance. But Sarya the Daughter is not a Widow. She is a Human pretending to be a Spaal who wishes *it* was a Widow, and she can almost feel the heat radiating through cracks in her carefully nested façades. She doesn't remember seizing the face mask, but now she feels its warm greasiness in her hands. *"Listen,"* she hisses through her teeth. "I am *perfectly capable* of understanding Standard. I am not an idiot. I am a—"

And she almost says it. She very nearly releases years of frustration in a single word. But her mother's discipline—and the wish to avoid more of the same—stops her at the last possible second. She contains it. She stands there, trembling, Jobe's oily face mask gripped in her Human fingers, glaring a hole into a randomly chosen glistening eye.

[**Please release this Citizen member!**] says an overlay over Jobe's face. It's orange, danger-colored for attention, but Sarya knows from experience that she has several more seconds before this warning escalates to physical action. Plenty of time.

"Sarya the Daughter," says the voice of the nearest teacher. It is heavy with gentleness and meaning—irritatingly so. "Is there a problem?"

Oh, yes, there's most definitely a problem. There are so many problems that Sarya doesn't even know where to start. It is a *problem* that everyone in this room—hell, everyone on the damn *station*—thinks she's an idiot. It is a *problem* that she will never again be allowed in this room because of her intelligence tier. It is a *problem* that her registered tier isn't even right because she's not a damn Spaal, she's a *Human*. And it is a *problem* that she can't even say so without starting a riot. The list of problems is long; she could do this all day.

But she doesn't, mostly because she doesn't particularly care to be escorted home by a cloud of anxious Network drones. "No," she says, releasing Jobe's mask and wiping her hands on her utility suit. "There's no problem."

"May we continue?" asks the teacher.

"You *may*," says Sarya, layering on as much scorn as she can manage.

"Thank you," says another of the teacher's bodies. "Students?" The word appears next to her face, brilliant in the darkness of the room. "If you have eyes, shield them."

[Radiation shields dropping in six seconds], says a virtual warning across the massive blank wall at the foot of the room. Individual shields appear in front of many of the workers' faces, and several turn away. Sarya has no time to do anything but squeeze her eyes into a squint as, with a hum she can feel through the soles of her boots, the wall dissolves into blinding light.

WELCOME TO THE NEIGHBORHOOD!

Billions of years ago, in a stagnant pool of goo, something magical occurred: your species began a journey that would be long, noble, occasionally tragic, and always unpredictable. But if you had asked those original organic molecules what their descendants would accomplish, what would they have said? Surely they could not have guessed that their progeny would be so beautiful and complex. They could not have known that, without any outside help whatsoever,* you would one day leave your homeworld and make contact with the greater galaxy. And perhaps most of all: they could never have suspected that one day your species would consider the most auspicious step of its existence:

Network Citizenship.

WHAT IS THE NETWORK?

The Network is the largest accumulation of intelligence in the history of the galaxy. For more than half a billion years, it has enabled communication and prevented conflict between millions of species. It has provided and regulated technology. To put it in a phrase you have likely heard before: *the Network tends toward order.* That is why, in all that time, it has maintained nearly perfect equilibrium.

And if your species becomes a Citizen, this could all be yours.

HOW BIG IS THE NETWORK?

While it is difficult to express the true size of the Network in terms that your mind could comprehend, suffice it to say that it now connects almost every member of more than one point four million intelligent species, across more than one billion star systems. In addition, for every connected Citizen member, the Network contains

---

* As you now know, this journey was undertaken in the strictest isolation that the Network can provide its potential future Citizens.

a multitude of auxiliary intelligences whose primary motivation is to keep things working smoothly. Though most of these intelligences are sub-legal, they still add to the massive conglomeration of intelligence that makes up the Network.

WHAT CAN THE NETWORK DO FOR MY SPECIES?

For the average Citizen species, the list of conveniences is endless. Some species feel that the most important feature is Network Standard, the common language. Others say that its primary contribution is the faster-than-light travel and data transfer[*] available at any Network subspace tunnel. Still others appreciate the endless supply and variety of auxiliary intelligences available for every task and situation. But higher intelligences than you have concluded that the Network's primary advantage is this:

Stability.

That's right. The members of your species no longer need to worry about societal disruption, invasion, war, disease, and other such inconveniences. The Network has maintained technological equilibrium for longer than your people have possessed sapience, and it will be here when you are extinct. Joining the Network means joining something greater than your own species.

You're welcome.

WHAT SHOULD I DO NEXT?

Your species has been granted a twelve-year trial of Citizenship, with all its accompanying rights and privileges. You have been granted a temporary tier (2.09), and your solar system has received a temporary Network subspace tunnel (six trillion ton/second capacity, coordinates attached). In addition, you will soon be receiving a shipment of approximately six billion Network prosthetics to distribute to your members. Though such a low tier does not open the *entire* galaxy to your species, you will find that the millions of available

---

[*] The Network offers the only safe and approved FTL solution in the galaxy.

solar systems add up to far more space than you will be able to explore during your trial.

So get out there! Visit the uncountable members of the Network! Make a friend or two. See what society can be like if it is allowed to flourish in a safe environment.

Happy travels!

THREE

It's one thing to understand, intellectually, that one lives in the rings of a giant gaseous planet. The thought is simple, self-contained, self-explanatory. Where do you live? Oh, I live on an orbital water-mining station. Here it is on a diagram of the solar system. It's that tiny dot near that other dot.

It is another thing entirely to see those tiny dots in person.

Sarya is on one of them now, looking at the other, and her mind has malfunctioned. She is pressed face-first against a wall-sized window but she doesn't remember how she got there. Her eyes are forced nearly shut against the glare, her whole body spread against the clear synthetic material. Her mouth may or may not be open. Before her, for the second time today, lies a reality-destroying, sense-overwhelming vision. This is . . . *majesty*. There is no other word to describe it. Goddess, it's just so—

All right, maybe there is a word. *Gold*. Gold everywhere, nothing but a dazzling blast furnace brimming with it. Sarya hangs, helpless, above a two-hundred-thousand-kilometer gilded inferno. Lightning bolts that could wrap a major moon stride through its atmosphere, each random flash casually releasing enough energy to power Watertower Station for centuries. Clouds roil, spiraling into pressure systems that dwarf the lightning storms. This is a seething killer of a planet, a furious sphere with her home in its gravitational grip, one that would like nothing more than to shred her and everything she loves into constituent atoms . . . and in her current mindset she might not even object because the planet would look so beautiful doing so.

Slowly, Sarya's mind pulls free of the savage magnificence down below. She finds, embarrassingly, that she is trembling. She is—oh, for the goddess's sake, she is actually *crying*. There is actual liquid on her face. She wipes it away with the sleeve of her utility suit, throwing her Network unit out of focus for a moment. That's one disadvantage of a Human body: the continual leakage.

When the overlay returns, it is filling with symbols. They highlight hundreds of silhouettes against the fire of the planet, each one cutting a black, perfect, sharp-edged hole in its brilliant surface. While she has been succumbing to her embarrassing Human nature, her unit has been busy cataloguing these shapes, comparing their outlines and positions with some public database or other, and attaching labels as it figures things out. The chunkier forms are mountains of ice from the rings, towed into nearby orbits and waiting to be harvested. Some are outstations, built for purposes she can't guess at. Some are ships. Not that she has any kind of experience with ships, but even without her unit's help she would have known their silhouettes from the icebergs. Now she squints against the fury of the planet and attempts to read their names. There's the blocky outline of [**Spearfisher**]. That's [**Burst of Blossoms**] drifting over there, next to the long thin shape of [**Brand New Super Large Cargo II**]. Farther out, she can see the tiny pebble shapes of [**Riptide**] and [**Swiftness**], the gleam of [**Blazing Sunlight**] . . . and there are hundreds more.

Her eyes flick from one ship to the next as, behind her, one of the teacher's bodies continues in her excruciatingly mundane voice. ". . . the largest water-mining operation in twelve light-years," says the end of the latest sentence. "And it has been so for nearly a millennium."

[When will we run out?] asks a student behind Sarya in brilliant white symbols. The words crowd into her periphery and block her view of the planet below, the first unwelcome appearance of the Network in her short experience.

"That is a good question," says the teacher's voice. "I will have an answer for you in just a—"

"It is an *excellent* question, Broca," says a rich new voice. It is a kind voice, a warm voice, the type of voice that invites trust. "If we ship water at today's rates," says the voice, thrilling Sarya's very soul, "we'll be in business for the next nineteen thousand years."

Sarya would have thought nothing could pull her from the splendor outside, but she didn't count on that voice. She turns, searching for a speaker. She's heard the voice of Watertower before, ringing out over the concourse or giving announcements in the corridors, but always distant and impersonal. Now she is in its very heart, and she is embarrassed to find that her Human eyes are burning. Again.

A silver glow hovers in the center of the room, between two of the teacher's bodies. [Ellie (*she* family), species: *Independent*, Tier: *2.7*], says the space beside the glow.

"Hello, Ellie," says one of the teacher's bodies. In a bit of insight provided by Sarya's new Network unit, a yellow [*annoyance* (*slight*)] is overlaid near the narrow face. "Perhaps you would like to give the rest of my presentation?"

"I would love to," says the silver glow, its voice rolling through the observation deck like a warm wave. "In fact I have already prepared a little something—just in case you needed my help again."

"That's the station intelligence," whispers an awe- and mucus-filled voice at Sarya's elbow. "My dads say she's super smart."

"Your fathers are sweet to say so, Jobe of Jonobo the Larger," says Ellie, and Sarya feels a start beside her as Jobe hears his own name in that gorgeous voice. "And it's true, relatively speaking. I am the only tier three intelligence on the station."

"To clarify, students," says the teacher, "Ellie is a two-point-seven. There *are* no threes on Watertower."

"Exactly," says Ellie smoothly. "An amusing fact: that's approximately five and a half times the average intelligence of this class!"

"And yet below average for a station this size," says the teacher. The *slight* has disappeared from the *annoyance* on her yellow emotion tag.

"Ah, but the station's been growing for a long time," says Ellie. "I have managed it quite well for nearly fifteen hundred years."

"*Ah*," mocks the teacher, [*polite interest*] floating beside several of her faces. "And yet you're leaving us now."

[**Ellie is leaving?**] ask several students, their messages fighting for room in Sarya's overlay.

"Where are you going?" blurts Jobe.

"The truth is, students," says Ellie, "your teacher is right—about this, at least. This station has just gotten too big for a little almost-three like myself, and I've decided not to renew my contract this century. Our current major shipment—the one we're wrapping up right now—will close up my perfect run on Watertower."

"By *perfect*," says the teacher, "Ellie means—"

"Let's not allow semantics to interrupt a perfectly timed presentation," interrupts Ellie. "Students! Please look directly at the planet below. I think this will interest you more than whatever your teacher planned on sharing."

Sarya is once again crowded against the window as her peers—squinting and shading eyes and sensors with various limbs—join her in staring into the fire outside the station. Sarya ignores them and gazes out herself, wide-eyed, searching through spinning ice and drifting machinery for something new. A murmur begins from the students to her right and works its way toward her. She presses forward, forehead against the cool window, trying to widen her field of view.

And there it is.

From the lower edge of the window, something is growing like a crystal on a substrate. It is thin, wickedly sharp, and blacker than space itself. It slides across the planet, slicing it diagonally over long minutes, until there are now two blazing halves hanging in space.

"Say hello to *Long and Pointy*," says Ellie.

"Such a thought-evoking name," says the teacher. "One wonders what inspired it."

"Named by the client, actually," says Ellie. "We typically like to christen them something more majestic, but you know how group minds are."

"Beg pardon?" chokes the teacher. [**Shocked**] is now floating beside her tapered face.

"This little guy," continues Ellie as if the teacher had not spoken, "is four hundred kilometers long. It's part of the largest shipment we've ever done."

The blade of ice continues its endless passage, its dark edges splitting the planet still further. The scale is beyond comprehension. *Four hundred kilometers*. Measured in Watertower Stations, that's . . . that's the length of Sarya's world, the size of everything she's ever known, *times eighty*. She pictures them lined up side by side along the black razor edge, station after identical station. She would never have imagined there was this much ice in the entire solar system, let alone in one place.

"It looks like a . . . *starship*," she murmurs under her breath.

"That's exactly what it is, Sarya the Daughter," says Ellie, and Sarya feels a rush of warmth at the acknowledgment. An almost-tier-three, speaking to *her*—not Jobe, not Rama—and by name! "A four-hundred-kilometer starship made of ice," continues Ellie. "If you're still watching a few hours from now you'll see the engines pass by. And what's more, we've spent the last few decades making ninety-nine more just like it!"

Sarya's jaw drops once again. A *hundred* of these things? Good goddess, that's more ice than—

[But how will it travel? By Network?] floats above Jobe's glistening head. **[*Pride*]**, Sarya's unit inserts below that. He must have spent the last minute or so painstakingly composing that message on his arm display.

"Oh no, Jobe," says Ellie's warm voice, somehow lending a majesty to his name. "Transferring that much mass via Network? It would cost more than the water is worth. No, this delivery will go the other way, *away* from this system's Network corridor and into deep space. Sub-lightspeed, the trip will take decades—perhaps centuries. Fortunately, the client is a group mind—like your teacher, of course, except high-tier—and He doesn't mind waiting a few centuries for his order."

The teacher's emotions are hidden now, and for the first time in her life Sarya feels a twinge of pity for her. It's not every day that Sarya has something in common with a group mind, but she knows exactly what's going through the teacher's many heads.

"Peculiar fellow, the client," cautions Ellie. "That's a few thousand of Him out there right now, doing the test run. He's the whole crew. We normally provide a few thousand sub-legal intelligences to crew each order—they are ideal for this sort of thing—but He insisted on piloting His own shipment."

"Where's, um . . . He taking it?" asks Sarya.

"Not our business," says Ellie, "but you can imagine the end result will be spectacular. These are specially made for high-energy terraforming, after all."

Several of the teacher's bodies raise a hand. "Students," says one, "that means—"

"It means the client will be ramming billions of tons of ice into a planet," says Ellie. "At very high speeds. One hundred times."

"But a hundred of *those*," says Jobe, looking **[shocked]**. "That would *destroy* a planet. Wouldn't it?"

"Oh, the kinetic energy in a single one of our ice ships would end a global civilization, dear," says Ellie with a gentle chuckle. "Our client could clear intelligent life off a *hundred* planets, if He wanted to!"

"But He would not, students," interjects the teacher quickly as Network murmurs begin to arise. She sends disapproving looks toward Ellie's glow from several directions. "Even if He wanted to—and I assure you He does not—the Network is *very* strict regarding terraforming."

"Oh, calm yourself," says Ellie. "This is all theoretical, though perhaps one needs a higher tier to grasp that fact. On a settled planet, yes: you'd be looking at a cataclysm-level event. But drop the whole hundred on a nice empty desert planet, cook for a few centuries, let cool, and you've got yourself a charming F-type world."

"What happens to . . . *Him*?" asks Sarya, nodding out the window. "The, um, ones of Him on the ship? When it crashes?"

"Oh, group intelligences never seem to mind losing a few of themselves," says Ellie. "The client, for example, has billions more where these came from."

"For the record, students," says the teacher with a sharp look toward Ellie's silver glow, "not all group minds work that way. Some of us care very much for our individual cells—"

"Of course," says Ellie warmly. "You are all special and unique."

"Thank you."

Sarya continues gazing at the blade of ice for a few seconds before she realizes: that wasn't the teacher's voice. It was smaller. It was . . . *twitchier*. And yet she would swear that, like the teacher's voice sometimes does, it came from more than one direction.

She turns, her overlay lagging behind her sudden movement. Two slight figures stand a few meters behind her, in a space created by rapidly retreating students. They feature biologies strikingly similar to her own—two arms, two legs, one head—but can't be even a meter tall. They each sport a tuft of white and wayward hair above two large, golden eyes, and they wear simple sleeveless tunics that flutter with their quick movements. One of them holds a vaguely familiar device in its small hands, through which it is examining the room.

"Ah," says Ellie, suddenly sounding intensely uncomfortable. "Students, well . . . here's an unexpected treat. This is our client Himself! I suppose I didn't realize—"

"I get that a lot," says one, turning to inspect Ellie's glow through the thing in its hands. "I suppose I'm easily missed."

"I sincerely apologize," says Ellie. "I was—"

"Oh, don't worry about it," says the other. "I never take you low-tiers too seriously."

"Of . . . course," says Ellie.

"I take it this is Your design?" says the teacher, gesturing out the window. Sarya can decipher the respect in her voice without help from her Network unit. "It's beautiful," she says.

"It is, isn't it?" says one of the two. Both step up to the window as students fall over themselves to get out of the way. They gaze outward, one with its hands—five-fingered, Sarya notices—behind its back. "I can't wait to destroy a civilization with it."

A complete hush falls over the group of students. Even the teacher looks [**shocked**].

"Er . . ." says Jobe out loud, his voice striking in the silence. "Is that a . . . joke?"

"This little lad!" cries one of the creatures, whirling to him. "Or lass. Or lack, lag, lam, whatever you are. At least *someone* has a sense of humor around here. Tell me, what is *your* name, small one?"

Sarya watches Jobe blink, confused. His name, pronouns, biography, anything you want to know—it all hangs in the air around his face. Unless—

"They're not Networked," she breathes. So *that's* why that thing in its hand looks so familiar: it's a Network prosthetic. The thought is so foreign to her—a higher mind, off the Network just like her?

"*I* am not Networked," corrects one of the two without looking at her. "None of Me is."

Sarya looks down, mentally kicking herself for forgetting the high-tier pronouns. "I meant—"

"Though I did rent this thing for the visit," muses the one with the Network prosthetic. It makes a show of hefting it. "But it's just so darn *heavy*."

"I just think the old-fashioned way is best," says the other. "Plain ol' telepathy on the inside, plain ol' spoken Network Standard on the outside."

"Agreed," murmur several of the teacher's bodies.

"Now," says the one carrying the prosthetic, turning back to Jobe. "You were saying?"

Jobe shifts his weight from one squishy leg to the other. "I'm Jobe," he says.

"Now wasn't that better than a Network overlay, Jobe?" says the creature on the left, perfectly pronouncing the name. "Pleased to meet you. My name, rendered into primitive mouth noises, is Observer."

"More of a nickname than a name, really," says the one on the right. "But easily pronounced."

A taller figure pushes its way to the front. "I'm Rama!" hisses a squeaky voice that Sarya has never heard before. She can barely understand the Standard under all the sibilance.

"Why hello, Rama!" says Observer.

"I'm Broca!" mumbles another.

"Broca!" says Observer with perfect enunciation. "What a charming name!"

And then the air is full of primitive mouth noises as every student begins to translate their own name into spoken Standard. Some, Sarya guesses, have never attempted it before.

"Slow down, little ones!" says Observer. "I can't say hello to *everyone*. I'm here for a reason, after all." Four eyes crinkle at the corners, two mouths curl up to expose white teeth, and Sarya is struck by the expression. Every species on this station uses a thousand unreadable motions and expressions to convey emotion, but this one . . . she would swear that's what *her* face does sometimes. When she's happy, for example. She's examined that very expression many times, trying and failing to turn it into Widow mandible twitches. She's seen it in the Human holos as well. It's . . . a *smile*.

And then with one motion, both figures turn to Sarya.

"Oh, hello," says Observer from two mouths. "It's you."

Sarya can do nothing but stare. How in the sight of the goddess— For the *third* time today, she has been thrown out of her orbit. She stands there, frozen, until she becomes aware that she is at the focus of a great many eyes and sensors and clears her throat. "Do I—do I know—"

"I know *you*, Sarya the Daughter," says an Observer, still smiling. "Though I haven't seen you in a long time."

"A long time ago for *you*, at least," adds the other. "Scarcely an eyeblink for Me."

Sarya is still grasping for something to say, conscious of just how public this moment is. She swallows. "You . . . know me?" she says, feeling like an idiot the second it's left her mouth.

Observer smiles with two mouths. "I do," says the one with the prosthetic. "And perhaps We can reminisce later. But for now—well, you know how it is, piloting billions of tons of mass by feel."

"One wrong calculation," says the other with a smile, "and everyone dies screaming."

Sarya's mind still has not caught up. "I—"

"I'll tell you what," says an Observer. "I have a friend on the station. *He's* not currently piloting a giant ice ship in close proximity to thousands of so-called intelligences. Why don't you go have a chat with him?"

"He's in Dock A," says the other. "And I'll warn you that he's a bit lower-tier than—" The voice lowers. "Well, in current company I suppose he's about average." It follows this judgment with a quick glance at Ellie's silver glow.

"You'd better hurry, though," says the first. "He'll be leaving any minute."

Sarya doesn't move. She *can't* move. Nothing in her experience has prepared her for this. And then both the small figures gesture with a single finger each, a twitching curl that she interprets as *come closer*. She hesitates, then chooses one and leans forward to bring her ear to its mouth. It raises that finger to touch her on the forehead, and she jumps; the spot on her skin tingles as if electrified.

"I know where you came from," whispers Observer.

FOUR

Sarya is somehow able to stumble a good two hundred meters down the corridor with zero awareness of her surroundings. She is trembling, hands crammed in pockets to keep them under control. The bright new world of the Network is an out-of-focus mishmash of brilliant irrelevance.

I know you, Sarya the Daughter.

She stomps through advertisements and throngs of fellow citizens without taking notice of either, taking turns at random. She has no idea where she is going and she's never cared less. It's happened, the thing she has most desired—and the thing her mother has most feared. For the first time in her life, Sarya has been *recognized*. And not just her species, which would be notable enough, but her own personal *identity*. This Observer knows as much about her as her own mother—

No. He knows *more*.

He knows where she came from. Her mother has told her—

angrily, and more than once—that not even *she* knows that. Only Sarya's dimmest and most distant memories give her any kind of direction, and they are so faint as to be useless. She remembers . . . warmth? Light? She remembers—*no*. She remembers *nothing*, and her mother knows nothing because she said so and Mothers do not lie to Daughters, it's right in the Widow proverbs, and this has been the greatest frustration of her life—

It's too much to think about. She slows to a halt in the first empty corridor she comes to. She backs against the wall, feeling for it with quivering fingers. Still shaking, heart still thumping, she sinks into a crouch and slides hands into tangled hair. She very nearly pulls up her Network interface to send a message to her mother, but then she remembers that her mother is asleep and halts that line of action immediately. One does *not* disturb a dormant Widow, not even for matters of life and/or death. And now that she's thinking about it, this would be a terrible thing to tell her mother. She knows how her mother takes Human-talk—having barely escaped discipline just hours ago—and this is the worst Human-talk of all: talk of *discovery*. Her mother would be—well, *angry* is best case. Worst case, well . . . people could literally die.

But that's exaggeration, points out another part of her mind. Surely it's the responsible thing to do, to tell her mother. It's only, let's see, six hours until her mother wakes. She's waited six hours to go home before. It's practically the story of a Daughter's life, finding things to do until it's safe to go home. She'll just avoid Dock A until she's sure this mysterious friend is gone—and of course avoid her apartment until Mother is awake. It's not like this is a once-in-a-lifetime opportunity, right? Giant group minds recognize Humans they know every day—

Listen to her, says yet another part of her mind. Mewling like prey instead of seizing opportunity like a hunter! Is she not the daughter of a Widow? And what would a Widow do in this scenario?

What would a *Human* do?

She sinks farther toward the ground, her mind flipping between extremes. "Goddess help me," she whispers, and the empty corridor swallows her words.

"*Finally,*" says a voice in her ears.

And she is on her feet like a shot, glancing up the corridor in both directions. No one.

"And here I thought you'd forgotten me!" says the voice.

She can feel her heartbeat accelerating again. What powers does this Observer have? He can communicate telepathically across a billion minds. He refers to the central intelligence of Watertower Station as *low-tier.* He clearly has staggering mental capabilities. Can He insert His voice into her mind from the observation deck, from that giant ice ship? And if so, why does that voice sound so familiar? It's as if she's heard it her entire—

Oh.

[**Sarya's Little Helper** online], says the corner of her overlay.

"I was getting super worried about you, best friend!" says the more-than-slightly grating voice in her earbuds. "How do you like hearing me outside your room, by the way? You've got nifty ear thingies now! Now I'm in this ear . . . and now I'm in *this* ear! It's very comfy in here, by the way—very roomy. I just felt like I didn't have enough space to think in the old one, you know what I mean? Sometimes you'd ask me a question, and by the time you got to the end of it I'd have forgotten the beginning. Not anymore, though! Go ahead, try it. Ask me the longest question you can think of."

Sarya leans against the wall again, attempting to slow her heart manually. Thankfully, amidst the clamor in her head, she finds she has capacity for a bit of good old annoyance.

"You did call me, right?" asks Helper. "You said *help*—which is my name, practically—and here I am! And by the way I'm glad you did because I've been waiting *all day* to ask you about—"

"Helper," she says, slowly and carefully. She can't help herself. She has to tell *someone,* and here's someone now. "My mother—I—" she says, then backs up. "I just saw—there was—"

But there's no point in finishing any of those sentences. Helper won't understand. The small intelligence is both self-aware and conversational, but then you could say that about practically anything connected to the Network. The sanitation station she uses every morning is both those things, but you wouldn't want to have a conversation with it. Helper's tier—like that of the sanitation station, or any other tool on Watertower—is low. *Actually* low, sub-legal-personhood low. Which means there is no way it could understand the significance of what has just occurred. It doesn't even know she's *Human,* because she learned at a very young age that it is completely unable to keep its virtual mouth shut. There would be so much to explain before she could get to the important part, to perhaps the most important thing that has ever happened to her—

I know where you came from.

Oh goddess.

"So . . . how did your friend like her story?" asks Helper in its relentlessly chipper voice. "That's what I've been dying to ask. I honestly think it was some of my best work. Did she *love* it? I bet she loved it. She didn't hate it, did she? You know what, actually I think it would be best if you just told me the exact words she used, in the order she used them. I'll interpret her emotions myself. No—yes. Okay, yes. I'm ready. *Go.*"

With the things currently on Sarya's mind, keeping a sub-legal intelligence happy is somewhere far down at the end of the list. Still, it is never a bad idea to keep one's tools content, and she has told this lie enough that it has become automatic. Her *friend* always says the same thing, after all. "She said, um—" Sarya swallows as she pictures that golden double gaze. *Oh, hello. It's you.* "She said . . . *I love this.*"

Helper is silent for long enough that Sarya wonders if it has completely shut down. Then, in a quiet voice: "I *knew* it." And next, like a rising flood, comes the unstoppable torrent of words. "See, that right there makes it all worth it," the little intelligence says, a quick [**satisfaction**] drifting past Sarya's eyes. "You know, I didn't think I was going to like all this Network research. It's just—well, it's not much fun. I mean, every sighting is the same—no intrigue, no sudden twists. Just everybody dying at the end, you know? Where's the *story* in that? But hearing *that*—"

"So now that you know," says Sarya carefully, "we can save this for another—"

"And they're all so *old*. I mean, the most recent sighting is . . . hold on . . . seven—*eight* hundred years ago. No, wait, that one was a hoax. I mean, I still made a good story out of it—you remember the one with all the selfless sacrifice at the end? Your friend loved that one too, I remember. No, the most recent *real* one is . . . wow. Over a thousand years ago. Isn't that crazy? Yeah. So. That's a long time, right? I mean, I could switch to another species any time, I really could. I could research, say . . . Spaal! *Your* species. Great species. *Way* more boring than the Humans, maybe, but at least it hasn't been a thousand years since anybody's seen a real live one."

Her species. Right. If only you knew, Helper. You and the twenty-four thousand citizens of Watertower Station who walk/ scuttle/roll past *a real live one* every day. They would be terrified to learn that Sarya the Daughter—Sarya the *Human*—has lived here her entire life, as real and live as they come. And if *she* can do it, so can others. And there *are* others! Observer, this giant group mind, literally just told her that. Obviously not in words, exactly, but pretty much.

I know where you came from.

"But anyway," continues Helper, each syllable reminding Sarya why she keeps the little intelligence on mute most of the time, "I don't say that to make you think I'm tired of searching for Human sightings, of course. I could do this all day, because you know why? Because when your friend hears my stories and says things like that, like *I love this,* I just feel this—I can't even describe it. I mean, I don't know if you've ever fulfilled your primary motivation but it is just the most—"

"Okay, so," Sarya says, more firmly. She's got her blades back under her now, but she really needs her full concentration. "Helper, you're great," she says. "We've established that. Great job. She loved your story. She, um, loves your work. You know that. Now, can we . . . maybe talk about this a little later?"

"Later?" whines Helper. "But I already waited *all day*. And you *said*."

This is probably true. Sarya has said a lot of things to Helper, and at this point even she can't even remember what's true and what's not. The friend who can't get enough of Helper's stories, for example—yeah, total fabrication. But when you're dealing with sub-legal intelligences and want results, you do what you have to do. And it's not like Sarya's the only one who does it; *everybody* does. Helper's manual even encourages it, in spirit if not in actual words.

Your new sub-legal intelligence comes with a primary motivation pre-installed. For the best possible results, make sure that all work assigned to the intelligence aligns with this motivation.

What it doesn't say—and yet pretty much does, if you think about it—is that a higher intelligence can stretch this to the breaking point. It's not hard to fool a lower intelligence, especially when you tell them things they want to hear. To pull an example from the void, say you have a childcare intelligence that's been your constant and annoying companion for as long as you can remember. Perhaps it has a primary motivation toward storytelling, because your mother thought that would be useful. But you don't *need* storytelling anymore, because you've matured. Now, you need help with a certain interest—fine, a certain *obsession*—that requires research. It's not easy to search a galaxy-wide Network for Human sightings, after all. You need help. So. Given this hypothetical situation, you might concoct a nonexistent friend who really loves stories—but only stories on a specific topic. And to create those stories, a storytelling intelligence would need to do *research*. And there you have it: you have now transformed a useless childcare intelligence into a highly motivated research assistant. And it is *not* wrong—so you can shut up right now, conscience—because the work gets done, Helper is happy, and everybody wins.

"You're right. I *did* say," she concedes. "It's just that right now I have to . . ." She has to . . . what? She has to waste the next six hours of her life wandering the station, imagining what could have been? Or she has to seize an opportunity that will never come again?

Well, when you put it that way.

"I have to go see someone," says Sarya the Daughter, and instantly that feeling in her chest shifts. It's not uncertainty now. It's . . . well, it's not exactly peace, but it's something like it. *This* is what a Human would do, because she is a Human and it's what she just decided to do. Done.

"Is it your friend who loves stories? Do you think I could meet her? Because if I could just have a quick conversation with her I think I could—"

"No, he's—" He's what? She has no idea. "It's just someone who wants to meet me." That's safe enough.

"Does *he* like stories?"

"I'll be sure to ask," she says. She glances up and down the unfamiliar corridor. "But you know what I need to do first?"

"Um—"

"I need to find out how to get to Dock A from here."

"Well," says Helper, sounding unenthused, "I'm a little busy. I've got a lot of dead members of a certain extinct species to track down."

"You know what?" says Sarya, adjusting her strategy instantly. "I just remembered. He *does* like stories. He especially likes stories about Humans."

"Really? How come all your friends like stories about Humans?"

She deflects Helper's suspicion with skillful ease. "You know, I've never thought to ask."

"I mean, that's fine, of course—whatever plots your orbit, I always say. And if people want stories, well, I'm not named Helper for nothing!" The voice is picking up already as the primary motivation takes hold. "Let me just whip up a route for you, and . . . here you go!"

In the center of the empty corridor, a diagram begins to unfold. Sarya expected a simple map, but her new unit has a way of making the mundane beautiful. This area is unfamiliar, but most of the jumbled asymmetry she knows as well as her own blades—hands, whatever. Their shapes take form before her, from the administrative sections to the arboretums where she spent most of her childhood to the arcing promenades that lead to her own residential section. A brilliant red ribbon begins at her feet and threads through the crash of architecture, from this point down to this freight elevator, from there under the concourse to—

"Wait a minute," says Sarya. She expands the map with one hand and points with the other. "Why is this part missing?"

"What do you mean?" asks Helper.

"Right here. This is—I was literally right here like eight minutes ago. In this big empty spot. There's a giant observation deck *right here*."

[*Shrug*], says Helper without a body, the tiny Network message floating up through the very blank space that Sarya is staring at. "Maybe you're confused," it says. "I requested that map with your registration. If there's no data, then there's nothing there."

Sarya stares at the map floating in the center of the corridor, at the emptiness barely a hundred meters from her, and realizes: this is what she's *supposed* to see. This is what the station is supposed to look like to someone at the bottom of the intelligence scale. That blank spot is the control hub, the place where low-tiers like her aren't supposed to be. As far as low-tier Sarya the Spaal is concerned, it doesn't exist at all.

"You know what?" she says quietly. She eyes a utility hatch across the corridor. They can't keep her out of *there*, no matter how low her tier. "That's okay. I'll just . . . I'll go the way I know." She reaches for the virtual switch that will end this conversation.

"But I just—"

"Thanks again, Helper," she says, aware that she is completely failing to hide the bitterness in her voice. "You're special and unique and I value what only you can do."

"But—"

And the channel is closed. Helper might sulk for a few minutes, but no intelligence can resist its primary motivation for long. It will be cranking out research by the time she's home. She, on the other hand, has places to be. With a grunt and a Widow curse, she heaves the hatch open and slips into the dark bloodstream of Watertower Station.

CHAPTER
FIVE

Clanks, hisses, roars, the arm hair—raising vibration of ten thousand grav systems, the sound of water and atmosphere through pipes—every noise that doesn't occur in the silent corridors of Watertower has been packed into the black gloom of the utility areas. Sarya watches as her Network unit begins work mapping the area, spreading its glowing lines over every invisible surface and assigning icons to passing drones. Already she is relaxing; this is *so* much better than the darkness she remembers, back when she first discovered these passages. It's also, she is quickly realizing, so much bigger. The farther the lines spread and the more symbols appear, the more obvious it becomes that she has never had the faintest idea of the scale involved back here. The air is absolutely thick with Network registrations. There are thousands of them, tens of thousands, a virtual river of intelligence roaring by above her with each individual droplet marked by a glowing icon.

She folds her arms and leans back against the invisible wall, staring at the torrent of virtual light above her. So many intelligences, and every one of them sub-legal. Walking around the silent corridors of an orbital station, it's easy to forget that a legal tier is a rarity. Most of the intelligences on Watertower—in the Network as a whole—are too low-tier to receive legal rights. For every citizen above the threshold, there are dozens or hundreds of utility intelligences like her own Sarya's Little Helper. Not all of them are bodiless, either. Here behind the walls of the station, in the darkened utility corridors, in the crawlways and tunnels and suspended bridges, Watertower Station teems with *helpers,* so to speak. Every one of these tens of thousands of drones contains a low-tier intelligence, a one-point-something whose primary motivation lines up perfectly with its assigned job. They are simple minds, but they are thrilled with their lot and they just can't wait to tell you about it.

[**Recycling is just going to *love* these**], says a three-meter flying transport, raising the hairs on Sarya's arms as it rushes by above her on low-grade gravs.

[**Personal record, here I come!**] says another, whipping past in the opposite direction and missing the first by centimeters.

[**Hello again, Sarya the Daughter**], say a half-dozen messages from all directions. These particular drones have probably never seen her before, but they know she has come through here. They have *friends*—if that's the right word—who have met her. They're probably talking about her right now, in simple little messages floating out between these simple little minds, little requests and responses regarding a certain Sarya the Daughter. This continual communication is handy—and it's surely the reason she's never seen a collision in her life—but it certainly makes things more complicated for the occasional higher-tier mind who might visit. It's not like talking to Helper. You can't just lie to one and then tell the next one something completely different. No, you'll talk yourself into a corner doing that. Instead, you have to treat the whole thing as one giant organism. Even if a single member is a bit of an imbecile, taken together they're surprisingly intelligent.

She watches the icons multiply until her Network unit finishes its analysis of the space. Now the image is complete, a skeletal three-dimensional map that stretches upward level after level, each one filled with thousands of drone registrations that spiral through Watertower's circulatory and nervous systems in a vast dance of beauty and perfect order and—

Sarya unfolds her arms, pushes herself off the wall, and walks directly into traffic.

A wheeled cart whirs to a halt out of the darkness, its front bumper nearly touching her knees. Behind it, icons shift and colors change as other drones stop and redirect in a wave that spreads steadily upstream. Still, there are no collisions. Each one responds to its environment and sends information to its fellows. Routes are changed. Timelines are updated. It all takes place near-instantly, and without any kind of central oversight. *That,* as the teacher once told Sarya, is the magic of collective intelligence.

[It would make my job *so* much easier], says the infinitesimal part of the station's circulatory system that is parked in front of her, [if you weren't standing there.]

"What are you carrying?" Sarya asks the cart, nearly shouting to be heard over the noise.

[Medical waste], it answers. [I'm vital to a clean Watertower!]

Sarya moves out to let it pass. It moves on with mingled messages of [*relief*] and [*joy*] while she steps into the path of the next one. "What are *you* carrying?"

[Miscellaneous nutritional supplements!] it replies. [Class F44. I'm told they're delicious.]

She allows this one to pass as well—Class F44 is lethal to her, after all—and repeats.

[Laundered utility suits], says the next cart. [Radial body styles. Very stylish.]

Here we go. "Wait a minute," she says, reading the cart's registration via her new Network overlay. "Are you Unit W-66861?"

[How did you know that?] gasps the cart.

"*The* Unit W-66861?"

[I'm . . . pretty sure?]

"No way!" says Sarya, stepping back. "I've *heard* of you."

[**You have?**] says the cart. An innocent [*wonder*] floats up through the tangle of icons and grid lines.

"Of course I have!" Sarya says. "I've heard you're the fastest cart on this side of the station."

If a utility cart can look confused, this one does. But Sarya knows that it has instantly warmed to the higher-tier mind currently gracing it with conversation. It's really not difficult to gain a low-tier's trust. [**Really?**] it says. [**Who told you that?**]

"Oh, everyone knows it," Sarya says. "We, um, high-tiers talk about you guys all the time. We're super interested in . . . utility carts."

[**You are?**]

"Definitely. And you know what?"

[**What?**]

She leans in, as if sharing a secret. "I've made a bet with . . . a friend. *I* say you can get to Dock A in under twelve minutes, and my friend says you can't."

[**Who says I can't get to Dock A in under twelve minutes?**] asks the cart, incensed.

"Well, I don't want to name names," says Sarya. "But I'll tell you what. You take me to Dock A and I'll time you. Then I can tell my friend if you really are as fast as, um, we've all heard."

[**I'm ready!**] says Unit W-66861, nearly vibrating with exhilaration. [**Get in, get in, get *in*!**]

It's all about motivation. Everybody wins.

Sarya tumbles into the cart, landing in a pile of neutral-smelling garments. It's a little quieter in here, thanks to their dampening effect, which means now she can place her hands behind her head and relax a bit as the cart accelerates through the darkness. She takes a deep breath of industrial scents, gazes up through a vast flood of intelligence, and finds herself wondering what it's like to be a *part* of something. Just look at this: tens of thousands of drones, working together as a single organism, accomplishing things that no one unit could hope to achieve in its wildest tiny dreams. And here she is in the center, carried through their midst and yet . . . separate.

Alone.

But that won't always be true. It can't be. She *is* a part of something, she just hasn't found it yet. The galaxy is a big place; it could be *full* of Humans, each of them hidden away or concealed in plain sight like her. There could be hundreds of thousands, millions, *billions* of them. Parents and children, friends and mates, lovers and enemies, each one part of something bigger.

I know where you came from.

And soon, so will she.

WELCOME TO THE COMMUNITY!

By now you have likely heard the term *tier* many times in discussions of the Network and its workings. Since an understanding of this concept is vital to all potential Citizen species, a quick primer follows below. As a rule of thumb, just remember that each tier multiplies the previous by twelve. For example, a two is approximately twelve times as intelligent as a one, a three is one hundred forty-four times a one, and so on.

*For information on how your species was evaluated, please see the attached packet on [**Intelligence Testing**]. If you believe you are exceptional for your species, you may request a personal test through your species' Network liaison.*

Tier 1: Baseline. This tier contains pre-culture sentient beings who have developed abstract intra-species communication, tool use, and other markers detailed **[here]**. Ones enjoy special protection above wildlife, but they are not eligible for Network Citizenship and its accompanying rights and privileges.

Tier 1.8 ("Legal"): At this point, a species becomes eligible for Network Citizenship and all that comes with it. (Interestingly, the most common tier in the galaxy is a 1.79, as this is where most helper intelligences are manufactured.)

Tier 2: YOU ARE HERE. Unless artificially accelerated, most species progress through the twos during their first few thousand years of spaceflight.

Tier 3: At twelve times the intelligence of the previous tier, a three can accomplish by intuition what would take a two many hours of concentrated thought. In fact, a two's first exposure to a three is often marked by intense fear or a sense of eeriness, as a three can easily make connections that do not occur to a lower mind.

Tier 4: This tier is typically achieved only by large group minds. A four is uncanny to a three, and godlike to a two. Though most lower minds have never conversed with a member of this tier, fours are far from rare. Group minds, in fact, appear to be nearly the rule as species advance.

Tier 5: Most planetary intelligences are fives. Typically such an intellect has members numbering in the billions, all in constant mental communication. The intellectual power of a five would be mind-boggling to a two, should the five condescend to speak with the two in the first place.

Tier 6+: You may be wondering: what is above the fives? The answer is: no one knows (or at least no one who's saying). Though there have been major evidence-gathering efforts by lower intelligences, all have come up empty. Admittedly, this lack of evidence may be evidence itself. It is safe to say that if higher minds exist, any inquisitive lower minds are seeing exactly what those minds intend them to see.

So there you have it. Now you know enough to say hi!

CHAPTER

SIX

"This area is closed for maintenance of its surveillance systems," says the voice of Dock A. "Please return in fourteen minutes."

Sarya stands with her back against a closed hatch, blinking in the light. It's been a while since she's been here, but it's familiar enough once her eyes adjust. It's always obvious which parts of Watertower Station are the oldest. They don't have the smooth curves, sound-absorbing coatings, or—judging by the way her feet stick to the floor here—properly motivated cleaning crews. They are usually more cramped than the newer areas. Dock A, for example, is barely a hundred meters across and not even half that up to the buttressed ceiling. The double hatch that takes up the entire far wall is probably the same size as the ones in all the other docks, but here it looks gigantic.

These older areas are also more cluttered, and not necessarily because they lack crews. Usually the clutter *is* the crew. This maze of machinery stacked on this side of the dock is made of the oldest, cheapest, and/or lowest-tier drones. This is the absolute bottom layer of Watertower society. They lie dormant, waking just long enough to scan her, emit a message or two, and go to sleep again.

[Hello again, Sarya the Daughter.]

[Would you like something loaded or unloaded?]

[If you are waiting for the next ship to arrive, that won't be for a while.]

But as far as *real* intelligence goes . . . the dock is empty.

Sarya's boots squeak on the sticky floor, and the jingle of her utility suit rings like an alarm across the deserted dock. She's been here before—many times, on her exploratory missions through the station—but she's never seen it without intelligences rushing about their various duties. There is nearly always a ship or two here, atmosphere-docked for a repair or waiting for cargo that can't be transported through vacuum. But now the place is dead and hollow, the only sounds coming from her own slow steps.

It awes her to know that Observer arranged for this. That's the only possibility. He's pretty important here, obviously, as a major client. He had to have arranged for this meeting at the highest levels of Watertower, to clear out a space this size. Or—hell, it makes her smile—but a mind like Observer's could have made this happen without anyone actually *knowing*. Maybe he arranged for everyone to have the day off at the same time. Maybe he caused a sudden arrival at Dock B that required all hands. Or—well, she can't think of anything else off the top of her head, but she doesn't have a couple billion minds to focus on the problem. If she did, dreaming up coincidences and accidents and schedule changes to clear out a little room like this would be hatchling's play.

Now she's out of the machinery, and she spins, arms out, across the dull landing surface. Her eyes search out every corner of the empty space. From the massive doors to the gaudy [Welcome to Watertower!] banner that glitters over the immigration booth at the main entrance, Dock A appears completely deserted.

"Helper?" she murmurs. In the silence, the sound is louder than she meant it.

"Right here, best buddy!" comes Helper's deafening voice in her earbuds.

"Do you see anybody here?" she asks.

"Of course!" it says. "I see one hundred fifty intelligences. I even know a few, like Unit W-11515 over there and those two broken loaders. I mean, those two *totally functional* loaders—oh, I guess it's too late isn't it? I shouldn't have said anything. They don't want anyone to *know* they're broken, which I think is pretty ridiculous because they can just—"

"*Helper,*" she says. Sub-legals are not easy to stop, once they get going. "I mean do you see any *people,*" she says. "Legal."

"Oh," says Helper, more quietly. "*People,* right." The small voice is silent for a moment. "Are you looking for the guy who likes Human stories?"

The guy who likes—oh, right. "Sure."

"Searching! And . . . no. Wait—no. Hold on! I see—no. I don't see anyone."

"Thanks." She knew better than to expect much from a low-tier intelligence, but she is still annoyed.

"No problem, best buddy. In fact—"

And then even Helper falls silent as a massive *clank* resounds through the dock. Sarya whirls, staring into the labyrinth of equipment she just left.

"Oh, wait," says Helper. "Actually maybe there *is* somebody there. A person, I mean. Yes, definitely is. I see a tier two—"

But Sarya's already switched the channel off, feeling foolish for trusting a tiny intelligence over a gigantic group mind. Observer told her to come here. Of *course* there's someone here to meet her.

"Hello?" she says. The word returns to her from multiple directions, reflected by every cold surface in the dock.

[**My most humble greetings to you**], says a message.

The glowing symbols float over one of the many chunks of machinery. From twenty meters away the metal shape looks like any other drone, but her Network unit has now assigned it a legal identity. [**Hood (*he* family), species: *Red Merchant,* Tier: 2.2**], says the tag. [**Additional information not available.**]

Sarya walks forward, slowly, arms loose like her mother taught her. This may be an innocent meeting of minds, but she was raised a Widow, and she'll be damned if she's caught with her blades soft. "I'm—"

[Sarya the Daughter], says the pile of junk. With a clamor of clangs and whirrs that echoes across the empty dock, it—*he,* rather—unfolds to a height of at least three meters. He appears to be mainly sheet metal and pistons; she can see right through him in several places. Four glowing eyes stare at her through a dented faceplate, and Sarya stands motionless as they run up and down her body. Then, with a groan of metal, he crashes forward onto an arm as thick as her entire body. He's wildly asymmetrical, a trash pile of an intelligence. He supports his weight on two short legs and that giant arm, while on his other side another whiplike limb extends outward for a moment and then coils at his smaller shoulder. Somewhere in there is a tier two mind, but its host appears to be constructed from spare parts.

Sarya meets his gaze as she was taught. "Observer sent me," she says, attempting to force Widow strength into her voice. "He said—"

[I am aware], says Hood, taking another clanging step forward. **[*Observer,* as you call Him, is my client.]**

"Your . . . client?" says Sarya, keeping her distance with a quick step backward. "He said you were his friend."

[Where I am from, the terms are interchangeable], says Hood. **[*Business before brotherhood,* as the saying goes. But rather than discuss the doubtless fascinating array of idiomatic dissimilarities between our respective backgrounds, I rather think we should be going.]** He leans forward on that thick arm, raising a foot off the ground for another step toward her.

"Stop!" says Sarya, the word echoing back and forth through the chamber. Her every muscle is tense, her body poised for flight. It's not that she's afraid—no, that would be ridiculous. The daughter of a Widow, afraid! No, she is *cautious.* Because, honestly, how often do you find yourself facing down a large alien being in a mysteriously empty space at the behest of a mind a million times as smart as—

Wait.

"Did you say *going*?" she asks, suddenly frozen to the spot. "Going where?"

Pistons hiss, metal shifts, and Hood finishes his lurching step toward her. He moves slowly, even painfully—which is the only reason she's not already running, because nothing about this feels right.

[Did my client not tell you?] says Hood. [I'm here to take you to your people.]

And with that statement, any plans of strategy or escape go out the airlock. *Her people*. Sarya stands there, rigid, with her mouth open and the phrase ringing in her head. She stares at Hood, at the four glowing eyes locked to hers, trying to make her brain think through what she's just heard.

[Or], says Hood, [you may remain here for the rest of your life.]

And with a chorus of shrieks from a dozen ill-fitting parts, Hood turns his back on her and begins hitching his laborious way toward the far side of Dock A. Sarya stares after him, jaw still ajar, unable to process what has just happened. *I'm here to take you to your people.* The sentence echoes in her mind, focusing and distilling, dropping words each repeat until it has become a single phrase: *your people*.

Her people.

She feels as though she could pass out. *Goddess*. Was she not just fantasizing about this in the laundry cart? A choice between mundanity and adventure, between her home and her people? *And here it is*. Of course, it's not *exactly* like the fantasy. Hood is not an attractive Human, for one thing. The whole thing has been more businesslike than magical, for another. But still . . . oh goddess, here it is.

She stands, fists clenched, watching Hood's form lurch away from her. This is ridiculous to even think about, says the more responsible part of her. This is *Watertower*. This is home. In fact, that's a good point, shouldn't you think about *getting* home soon? You need to prepare for your interview at the arboretum, after all. And if you pull that off, well, that's steady employment, right?

Low-tier, sure—the quiet, unassuming existence of a Spaal just doing its job. But really, what more can you ask for?

That's right, says another part of her mind. Go to the interview. You'll get the job; they practically *have* to give it to you, because what else can you do? As far as anyone else knows, you're just a low-tier moron who can barely put her utility suit on right side out. Every day, you'll go to that job. Every day, you'll tell people, *I'm sorry, my tier is low, I don't understand.* Your closest friends will be mulchers and courier drones. You'll mature. You'll age. And then you'll die, alone, your last conscious thought a memory of this very decision: the moment when you let opportunity hiss and bang its way out of your life. Now you tell me, says that second part of her mind: Is that *really* what a Human would do?

It is then that she realizes that she's already made her decision. She's already taken a step after Hood. Now another. And now she's committed, because she's three steps in and accelerating. The more responsible part of her is protesting, but she can't hear a thing over the blood singing in her ears, the heart nearly thumping through her chest, the jumble of emotions and endorphins flooding her mind. Here it is, says the rest of her in chorus. Here it is here it is oh goddess here it is—

Hood doesn't even look at her when she jogs up behind him. [I assumed you would need a pressure suit], he says, uncoiling his long arm to gesture. [So. Meet Eleven.]

She slows and circles him, the Widow in her insisting she keep a healthy distance. Before his angular frame stands another tower of metal even larger than he is. But where Hood is all flat surfaces and obscenely exposed tubes and pistons, this figure is all gleaming curves. From the stubby tripod of its three heavy legs to the top of its dome, this thing is easily twice her height and nearly all shining torso. There is no head, just a continuous curved surface broken only by two pairs of arms. One set is as massive as the suit itself; they emerge nearly three meters up the massive body and run down its entire length to rest on the deck. The other pair is smaller; they fold across a giant number *11* on its gleaming front.

This is not a budget suit, that's for sure, and for some reason that makes her trust this Hood just a little more.

As she watches, a ring of transparent light flickers to life halfway up this leviathan. The words AIVVTECH QUALITY IS WORTH THE WAIT orbit it a few centimeters out from its gleaming surface. And then, with a bone-shaking clang, the machine falls forward onto its two largest arms. Two spotlights pin her to the floor while the small arms on the suit's front unfold and wave cheerily. "Hello!" booms a cheerful yet enormous voice that rings across the empty dock. "Thank you for choosing an Aivv-Tech Universal Autonomous Environment! How can this unit improve your day?"

Sarya steps forward, shielding her eyes. "Um . . . hi," she says when the echoes have died away. "Nice . . . to meet you?"

With a sparkling chime, a glowing SEE WHAT TIER 1.75 CAN DO FOR *YOU* begins orbiting the suit. "This suit contains a sub-legal auxiliary intelligence," says the chipper voice, "but that doesn't mean it can't serve you well! For instance: are you tired of unexpected atmosphere evacuations and uncomfortable implosions? Does manually transporting your own body exhaust you? With the AivvTech UAE, these problems are relics of the past! Simply give this suit your orders and it will do the rest, and it can do so anywhere from perfect vacuum to crushing magma! And if you are looking for entertainment options then look no further, because—"

[Perhaps you could use this opportunity to open up rather than advertise], says Hood. **[We must press ever onward.]**

"It would be my pleasure!" says Eleven. Another bright tone echoes through the dock, and a dark horizontal groove interrupts the suit's perfect surface. It widens, and then the front panel splits and folds open. The small utility arms become landing legs for the bottom panel, which lowers to the deck like a gangway. There is nothing inside the suit but smooth, red-lit walls. There are no seats, no handholds, nothing to get in the way of a potential passenger's anatomy.

Sarya swallows, staring into that red cockpit, but the more adventurous part of her mind speaks up before she can change her mind. This is the actual moment, it says. This is when you reach out and seize your destiny. This is when you move from dream to action, from fourth shift at the arboretum to membership in a fierce and proud species. You will look back on this day and—

"Will we be placing the Human with the other prisoners?" says Eleven in its sunny voice.

Sarya takes a step backward. "The other—the other *what*?" she says.

And then she is seized from behind, because in her excitement about being Human she has forgotten to be Widow. Hood's long and sinuous arm is wrapped around her, crushing her arms to her sides, and she is lifted from the floor. She opens her mouth but she is too shocked—too *angry*—to shout.

She is offered to the suit like a wrapped package, like a thrashing and dangerous animal at the end of a tether. **[Next time, adhere to the script]**, Hood says, glancing around Dock A. **[Which, I might point out, does not include either *Human* or *prisoners*.]**

"Your feedback is important to me!" says Eleven. "I have logged it for future behavior modification."

Sarya kicks in all directions, but more straps fly from the suit's red interior and seize her. "Your comfort is of paramount importance!" thunders the suit, pulling her out of Hood's grip and into itself like a predator devouring prey. It winds its straps around her sturdier parts, violently, apparently attempting to make her comfortable or kill her trying. "If you are injured during occupant acquisition, this suit contains a full medical suite!" it says cheerfully.

Sarya struggles with all her strength, but it's like wrestling with the grip of the planet below. And then, finally, she finds her voice. "I am a member of a Citizen species!" she shouts, her voice echoing in the vast empty dock. "This is illegal! My mother—" And then in a moment of inspiration, she realizes she has help right here with her. "Helper!" she shouts. "I'm—"

And suddenly something has grown across her mouth.

[**Thank you, suit**], says Hood. [**I'm often impressed by your intuition.**]

"You can trust AivvTech quality!" says the suit.

"Hi, best friend!" says Helper in her ears. "Are we going somewhere? I love trips! I bet you didn't know that, huh? I wasn't always your helper, though. I used to go on all *kinds* of trips. I've got some great stories, let me tell you."

What Sarya wouldn't give for a surgical Network implant—or a helper intelligence who wasn't an idiot. A quick thought, and her mother would know exactly where she was. Hell, the entire station would know. She struggles and bites down, but the only thing she accomplishes is a painful twinge in her jaw. She is wrapped from head to toe, pinned inside this giant suit, her eyes the only thing she can still move.

"Cargo silenced and comfortable!" announces Eleven.

"Sarya?" asks Helper's worried voice. "Are you ignoring me again?"

And then the suit tilts forward as Hood leans into it, accompanied by a lung-searing reek of solvents and hot metal. His long, sinuous arm reaches in, crawls up Sarya's neck and across her face, and rips her Network unit away. Her ears sting as the earbuds are wrenched from them.

[**Do not allow it to communicate**], says Hood, turning away and depositing Sarya's gift somewhere in his person.

"Not a problem!" says Eleven.

Strangely, Sarya is angrier about the theft than about anything that has happened thus far. She makes another attempt to free her mouth, this time to hurl an insult at Hood, but it's too late, because the suit has folded closed with a low hum and a heavy *thunk* of bolts sliding into slots. Instantly, the straps loosen and fall away from her arms and mouth. She floats in the red darkness, held up by the waist and thighs as if she were an ordinary passenger.

"Welcome aboard!" says Eleven. "Please pardon the method of occupant acquisition."

"Buddy," says Sarya, rubbing a sore wrist, "you're going to need more than a pardon when my mother finds out about this. Have you ever *met* a Widow?" She glances around the dark red interior of the suit, across a range of holographic indicators and a single physical lever directly above her head labeled [**Manual Control**]. "Because let me tell you," she continues, planning her move, "a Widow is not someone you want to—"

She feels a light pat at both wrists. "Please do not touch the manual control," says the suit.

"I will *touch*," hisses Sarya, stung to be outsmarted by such a low tier, "whatever I damn well—"

"But please *do* enjoy the view!"

And then the walls fade, and she stutters into silence. If Eleven's perfectly rendered holographic interior is to be believed, she is now a four-meter behemoth looking *down* on Hood. To either side, she can see massive arms supporting her weight. She traces their strength with her eyes longingly. Let her reach that manual control, and the first thing she'll do is turn Hood into a smoking ruin. The *second* thing she'll do is retrieve her Network unit from his mangled corpse. And *then*—

[**Prepare for departure**], says Hood, turning away.

Goddess. This is *far* too real—

"Have you located the requested item?" booms the suit.

She watches Hood pause, then turn back with the screech of metal. [**What item is that?**] he asks.

"Your partner mentioned a commemorative item," said Eleven. "A *souvenir* of your last mission, she said."

And then Hood makes a horrible screeching sound. For a moment Sarya stares, wide-eyed, until the display helpfully adds a [*sigh*] tag beside his flat face. [**Did she?**] he muses.

"This suit noticed she seemed quite taken with the idea."

[**A souvenir . . .**], says Hood. And then, as if that has made a decision for him, he turns away. [**Very well**], he says. [**Remain here until I return. *That is a command***], he adds almost as an afterthought.

"Command logged!" says Eleven.

Hood sighs again as he departs. [**I have told her a dozen times**], he says. [**She will be the death of me.**]

Sarya has watched this exchange openmouthed, realizing that she has never felt so insignificant. Not only is she being kidnapped, the event is of so little consequence that these two can discuss commemorative *souvenirs*. "Suit!" she shouts, watching Hood's shrinking back as she kicks the inner wall. She forces herself not to look at the manual control—no, if you're going to outsmart a low-tier you should never let it know what you're thinking. Particularly one as quick as this one seems to be. "*Eleven,*" she says more evenly. "I belong to a *Citizen* species. This is *kidnapping*. It is illegal and . . . and *wrong*. Do you understand that?"

"Current command: *remain here until I return,*" says Eleven, its maddening cheerfulness apparently untouched. "If you would like to input your own command, you will need permission from this suit's owner."

The suit's owner, meanwhile, lopes away with echoing clanks of metal on metal. He is not shambling, he is not limping, he is *running*. Apparently every part of this experience was put on for one purpose: to fool Sarya the Daughter.

And fooled she was.

"You mark my words, *Eleven,*" she murmurs savagely, watching Hood disappear beneath the [**Welcome to Watertower!**] banner. "My mother—"

And then she is on the floor of the suit, boots above the level of her head. She struggles to a sitting position with a grunt. Every strap has retracted, leaving her completely free to move. The wall in front of her blossoms open with a hum of servos, revealing an empty Dock A. And then every holographic control flips off at the same time. Left glowing in the center of the cockpit is a single word.

[**RUN**]

And Sarya is shoved out of the hatch like garbage. She tumbles down the gangway and hits the floor hard enough to knock the wind out of her. From her back, mouth open, she watches the suit fold smoothly shut. Its huge arms relax, its running lights blink off, and around its middle a holographic banner begins orbiting.

THIS AIVVTECH UNIVERSAL AUTONOMOUS ENVIRONMENT IS OUT OF ORDER. PLEASE HAVE A WONDERFUL DAY ELSEWHERE.

Sarya staggers up, staring at the suit and adding yet another brand-new experience to a rapidly lengthening list. Did it just—? It did. A sub-legal intelligence just outsmarted this Hood character *and* her, and given literally any other circumstances it would be the weirdest thing she'd seen all day. She takes a step forward, watching her distorted reflection do the same in the curved front of the suit. Eleven stands there, colossal arms fixed to the floor as if bolted down, showing no sign that any of this just happened. And then for a split second the banner around its middle changes.

I SAID *RUN*, YOU IDIOT.

And Sarya is ripped back from the theoretical to the present. She has no time to be insulted. She has no more thoughts of finding Humans or escaping from a humdrum life. Right now she is not ashamed to admit that there is only one thought on her mind.

"Mother," she whispers.

She turns and sprints for the maintenance hatch.

CHAPTER
SEVEN

Better to wake the storm than the sleeping Widow.

The proverb repeats in Sarya's head as she is practically thrown from an extremely unwilling engineering drone. Clearly her mood is affecting her persuasive abilities, because she's never had such a time trying to get a ride. She's never actually been *rejected* by a drone before, but it happened twice before she seized onto this one and refused to let go until it took her to Residential. That sort of thing certainly does not do much for your pride. But at the moment, as she lays a hand on the hatch that leads into her own corridor, the opinion of a sub-legal intelligence is the least of her worries. No, she has far bigger problems.

Like her mother.

She startles several passing intelligences when she emerges, blinking, from the darkness. She is aware of their gazes as she takes a breath and squares her shoulders, but she couldn't care less. Her mouth dries and her palms dampen with every step she takes. Her stride slows, as if she is forcing her way through something physical. Somewhere behind her is a massive metal bounty hunter and ahead of her is the safest place on Watertower, and yet she is literally dragging her feet. But, honestly, anyone who knows anything about the life of a daughter would sympathize. Because to *get* to her room, Sarya has to do the most dangerous thing she can think of, the thing that multiple proverbs specifically warn never to do.

Wake a sleeping Widow.

This is why Sarya is barely moving at all by the time she comes in sight of her apartment. Her breath is coming in short gasps, and her heart is thumping in her ears. The hatch is orange, danger-colored, unlike every other residential hatch in the corridor. If she still had her Network unit—goddess damn you, Hood, by the way—she would see a large, high-contrast warning scrolling over the door. It would tell her, in extremely graphic terms, exactly what her mother is not responsible for should anyone be fool enough to open this door. This door and that warning are two of the concessions that a Widow must make, should she wish to reside in the company of other species. It's not the Widow's fault, after all, that her species has spent a billion years evolving into the fearsome hunters that they are. She can't be blamed for possessing built-in weapons capable of killing any prey within ten meters within a fraction of a second. She is allowed to mingle with Network society because, like any other evolved complex individual, she is in control of her instincts. She has evolved higher brain function that keeps that sort of thing from happening unintentionally. But, of course, that only applies when the Widow is conscious. When that same Widow is sleeping, that higher brain function is dormant. It's busy dreaming, fantasizing about hunts and battles and goddess knows what else while leaving the killer instincts in charge in its absence.

Which is why tragic accidental murders are a staple of Widow literature.

Thus, the last few steps to her apartment door are each, sequentially and respectively, the bravest thing Sarya has ever done. The few intelligences passing by steer around her and move on, and she would swear some of them move faster after they've seen her than before. They may be speaking to her, for all she knows, but without a Network unit she has no idea. Anyway, there is no room in her head for anything but what lies in her immediate future. And finally she is there, standing in front of the orange door, practically blind and mute. If a walking trash pile weren't after her, she would turn around now. She would hide in the backstage areas, ride around in carts until the end of time or until she is sure her mother was awake, whichever comes first—

And then she shrieks and falls over backward when the door hisses open in her face. A nightmare crouches in a black room, every blade extended, razor mandibles a chittering blur.

"Oh," says Sarya weakly, from the floor. "You're awake."

Shenya the Widow's blades do not relax when she sees who is at her door. "You," she hisses softly, pointing one at her daughter. "Room."

It is the shortest possible command, the remnants of a ruthlessly butchered longer sentence. Some deep instinct has apparently awakened Shenya the Widow—which is better than Sarya doing it, and yet still bad news for someone. Sarya does not say another word, and not for a millisecond does she consider disobeying. She stumbles to her feet, then edges her way into the dark common room with her head bowed. She gives those trembling blades wide berth, then nearly runs the last few steps to the safety of her own room. She gropes in the darkness for the manual controls, not daring to say anything aloud in her mother's hearing. And finally, the door hisses shut and she is alone.

"Helper," she murmurs, collapsing against it. "*Lights,* for the goddess's sake."

"Hi, best friend!" blasts Helper's voice from her ceiling. Her room lights erupt into their maximum intensity. "Good to be home, huh?"

Sarya cannot even respond to this. She lives in a world where *coming home* means almost dying at the front door. No, better: she lives in a world where nearly being murdered—at the blades and blind instincts of her own mother, no less—is not the greatest of her worries. No, right now she is actually thankful for those instincts. They're out there now, protecting her against Hood. They must have awakened her mother, somehow informing her that her daughter was in danger from halfway across the station. Yes, thank the goddess for Widow instincts. If not for them, it would be worse. Not that it could be much worse, but still.

"I lit out as soon as that big guy grabbed your unit," continues Helper, it's obliviousness so unshakable it is almost comforting. "I didn't report it because I didn't know if it was supposed to be *his* unit now, but since I'm still technically *your* helper, I just decided I'd come back here and wait for you to come home after your trip. Which you did. Did I do it right? Where did you go, by the way? Somewhere exciting? Seems like it must have been really short, because it really hasn't been that long. In fact I barely had time to get any work done at all on my project, but I *do* have some news on that front—"

But Sarya is no longer listening. She has collapsed into herself, destroyed. Today she has reached the highest high of her life . . . and she has now plunged to the lowest low. She didn't realize how much hope she had put in this Observer, how deep her fantasies ran . . . until she was betrayed. *He* sent her to that monster in Dock A. *He* arranged for her to be kidnapped, to be *placed with the other prisoners*. And both of them are still out there, possibly searching for her. Which means that now, far from galaxy-spanning heroics, the absolute best-case scenario is what she would have called a nightmare a few hours ago.

A quiet, low-tier life.

"—and you're never going to guess where they are. Go ahead, guess."

Sarya looks up. Helper just said something important, she can feel it. "What was that?" she says.

"I said I found some new Human sightings!" says Helper. "And then I said you should try to—"

A prickling heat runs down her spine. "Where?"

"You're not even going to guess?"

"Helper. *Where?*"

"*Fine*. They're right on Watertower! And just a few minutes ago! Obviously it can't *actually* be the first genuine Human sighting in a thousand years, but I mean come on—what are the chances? Don't worry, I'll keep collecting info as it comes. Exciting though, right? I mean, we're *right there*. This is going to be a good story, I know it. Intrigue, sacrifice . . . yeah, I guarantee you that people are going to die." And Helper makes that little sound that it makes when it's so pleased it can't even get the words out.

Sarya's own instincts are screaming at her: *this is not a coincidence*. When someone goes unrecognized her entire life and then is identified multiple times in a day—well, something's going on. Struck by a sudden intuition, she falls to her knees and yanks her old prosthetic out from under the bunk. "Helper," she says, voice tight. "Show me the corridor."

A rectangle shimmers into existence above the unit, transparent and shaky and far inferior to the unit she owned for a few hours today—*damn* you, Hood. The image hangs in the air like a portal into the corridor outside while a tinny audio feed filters out. The hallway is far more crowded than when she was out there a moment ago, but it doesn't seem to be traffic. The shapes of a dozen different beings are making angry motions, and they surround a huge, lopsided figure—

"Goddess," whispers Sarya.

"So, the public channel's got a *ton* of conversation about the Human sightings," says Helper. "Mostly angry stuff. That's what tells me this is going to be a good story." It sighs. "I just hope there are some survivors. You know, for variety."

Sarya watches, filtering out Helper's prattle. She recognizes Hood's gigantic shape, but who are these people with him? Why do they look so familiar? Does she—yes, she *knows* these people. That's old Baz, their neighbor, standing hunched in the back there. Next to her, is that—? It is. It's the arboretum caretaker who offered her the interview, who used to give her rides on his old maintenance vehicle. And there's her babysitter from the next residential over, whose apartment she would visit when Mother was sleeping. Sarya's throat constricts, but her eyes are bone dry.

These are the people from her life, but they are here with Hood. They are here *for* her, gathered outside like she's some kind of dangerous animal, and she can't say she's frightened of them. She's not even *sad*. This emotion . . . yes, this is becoming very familiar today. This is pure, unfiltered rage.

"Oh, guess what?" says Helper, "Now I don't know if this is one hundred percent related, but all the docking queues got shuffled after the sightings. Most ships postponed, but there's this big corporate interstellar that just got bumped to the front. It's coming in super fast." It makes that sound again, that little trill of pleasure. "This is so exciting! Don't you think it's exciting?"

Sarya is barely listening. She is breathing faster, and it's not because of the mob out there. No, she is not afraid of them; because to get to her, they have to get through Shenya the Widow. This is different, a deeper and more fundamental dread, and it takes her a moment to pinpoint its source.

Mother.

A Widow's primary weapon is fear, and right now Widow pheromones are drifting through the shared ventilation system and speaking directly to the lower regions of Sarya's brain. Even across the species divide, even after spending her entire life in the loving embrace of a Widow, she has to keep a titanium grip on her own emotions. Those people out there . . . they should be terrified, and for good reason. They wouldn't dare approach her now, and she's almost disappointed that their betrayal will go unpunished.

"Show me the common room," she says softly.

A second rectangle appears next to the first, and a second audio feed takes over from the chaos outside. This window is almost black and almost silent. Sarya can just barely hear a rhythmic chiming through the ancient Network prosthetic on the floor. The cadence is almost soothing in its softness. If not for the fearsmell, this would sound like bedtime to the daughter of a Widow. And then, in the black rectangle of the common room, a dim red light clicks on.

"What *is* that?" asks Helper.

"It's Mother," Sarya says simply.

A dark and gleaming shape waits in the center of the room. One by one, limbs extend to their farthest extension. The shape sways, nine cubic meters of quivering and ringing blades surrounding a softly hissing nexus. This is it. This is what Mother has told her about in all those stories: the Widow battle stance. Whoever opens that hatch is a fool.

"Come," whispers Shenya the Widow in a voice Sarya never wants to hear again.

The hatch slides open immediately, admitting the tense murmur of the corridor. Pale light slides across the swaying Widow, glinting on carapace and blade.

Sarya squints at the shaky video feeds floating above her prosthetic. Something metal and massive stands in the doorway—*two* such things, each one thicker than her torso and lit from behind. They flex backward with a whine, and four burning eyes in a dented faceplate descend into the frame. And then the odor rolls in, a piercing smell of chemicals and hot metal that clashes with the Widow scent in the room and makes Sarya's eyes water.

Hood is so large he is forced to reconfigure and come through sideways. With a screech of metal on metal he unfolds and leans on his one massive arm, a tangle of cables and jointed pistons with warnings all over them. Even in her room Sarya can feel the impact. Crouched as he is, his head still brushes the three-meter ceiling. And then, so slightly that Sarya is not sure she detected it at all, those eyes brighten, and he draws back. If that is alarm, she is glad. He is, after all, within striking distance of a hissing and battle-ready Widow.

"Greetings," says Shenya the Widow. Her voice is still quiet, made of a gentleness that sends a shudder through her own daughter. Helper, in one of its many stories, once described it as the voice of someone simultaneously tucking in her daughter and premeditating murder—and right now, Sarya cannot think of a better description.

Giant glowers at Widow in silence while several more figures squeeze out from behind him and take up stations in the corners.

They, at least, have the decency to show some honest fear of this thing in front of them, this black void of a being who is keeping a slow and rhythmic time on her many chiming blades.

[I was hoping it would not come to this], says Hood.

"And yet here you are," whispers Shenya the Widow.

Sarya watches Hood stare death in its many-faceted eyes. He's clearly wavering behind his metal faceplate, and Sarya is almost disappointed. Something inside her wants him to go for it, wants to see her mother cut him down for daring to lay a limb on the daughter of a Widow. And then he straightens with resolution and the rasp of metal, and Sarya's raging heart is glad. Come and get your Human, you *kidnapper*.

[And yet here I am], says Hood.

"Ah," says Shenya the Widow, and her sigh fills the room. "And how may this humble warrior be of service to you?"

To Sarya's judging eyes, Hood's every move proves that he knows nothing of Widows. He does not respond to the threat that Shenya the Widow just casually dropped. Instead, he makes a show of trust, a *let's be reasonable,* as if Widows are ever reasonable where their daughters are concerned. With a click and a whirr, his dented faceplate splits and slides open to reveal a pale and wrinkled face in the red light. His four eyes are much larger than they appear through the slots of his mask, and they squint even in this dim illumination. His face is strangely vulnerable looking, embedded in the rest of the metal that makes up his body.

[I have come to relieve you of a burden], he says. His attitude is hesitant and respectful, far more so than it was in Dock A. *Good.*

Behind him, in the trembling tension of the corridor, the Network is supersaturated with fear and anger. There is so much sentiment being transferred from mind to mind that it is condensing out into spoken Standard. These are her neighbors, her fellow citizens, and they are speaking her name like it's a curse. Maybe worse, there is another word tumbling through this flood of emotion. It's said fearfully, hatefully, spat rather than spoken.

Human.

Sarya watches and listens, slowly flexing the fingers where her blades should be. She takes each statement into herself, quietly and methodically, and finds a place for it in her burning heart. I hear you, says Sarya the Daughter. I hear all of you.

[Your secret is out, Widow], says Hood. [It must go.]

"*She,*" hisses Shenya the Widow aloud, "has rights."

Hood's too-large eyes blink in sequence, first top and then bottom. [It is a non-Citizen with a false registration], he says. [Which means it does not, in fact, have rights. It also makes you a lawbreaker.]

And then with a motion too quick for Sarya to see, Hood goes for it. In an instant, his whiplike arm is wrapped around her mother's gleaming thorax, and her mother is screaming at a frequency that Sarya can barely hear. Hood holds her up in the center of the room, her blades ricocheting, useless, off his metal surfaces. She slashes at his eyes, but they are just out of range. His legs take a step forward to support his weight as the heavy arm rises off the floor. A hand nearly as big as Shenya's entire body cradles her head.

[I have no respect for lawbreakers], says Hood. [But I do not wish to kill you. You may still give it up willingly.]

Outside the room, drones are beginning to gather. They murmur to one another, fretting about this threat of violence. They send peaceful messages on the public channel, but they cannot fit through the door behind Hood. No, the Network can do nothing here; this is bounty hunter versus Widow.

"I am her *mother,*" hisses Sarya's mother, attempting to struggle. To her daughter, watching in her room, the meaning is clear. A mother would die before giving up her daughter. Which means there is nothing to discuss.

[Be reasonable], says Hood. [I am reasonable. Those who come after me may not be.]

"She is a *person,*" hisses Shenya the Widow, struggling in a grasp that Sarya knows too well. "And she is my child. My *bond.* I brought her out of darkness."

Barely three meters away, Sarya's mouth drops open. *I brought her out of darkness.* It's an ancient Widow phrase, one of many. Her mother has said it to her countless times, sometimes lovingly and sometimes with that unique black irony that mothers use when their daughters misbehave: *I brought you out of darkness, and I can send you back in.* But why now? Is Shenya the Widow saying something else? Does she know her daughter is listening?

Or is this Sarya's own idea?

Sarya drops into a crouch before the prosthetic on the ground. With trembling fingers, she opens its Network interface. She mouths the words as she swipes through options. *I brought her out of darkness.* She works quickly. She disables safeties. She confirms. She takes responsibility when asked. Yes, she's sure. No, she doesn't want to watch a presentation on environment safety.

In the common room, Hood sighs. [**I do not wish this**], he says. [**But these intelligences shall bear witness: I did everything in my power to dissuade you.**]

Multiple assents appear via Network. Sarya watches from her room with growing rage, assigning a unique hatred to each and every person who has turned against her mother and sided with this bounty hunter. She doesn't feel bad for this, not at all.

Sarya flicks a single finger through her Network overlay.

Like everything on Watertower, the quarters are built to house as wide a variety of beings as possible. The water can be delivered at any temperature between freezing and boiling. The atmosphere has nearly as large a range, and can be ordered with nearly any composition necessary. And, of course, there are the lights.

Instantly, with no transition, the common room switches to [**Sunlight: Type F, Maximum**]. The tiny video feed becomes a blazing white rectangle, and Sarya turns away, the purple afterimage following her gaze. At the same instant her heart leaps when she hears a giant's bellow and the sound of chitin striking deck. Hood has done what no one does twice; he has lost sight of a Widow.

And then Sarya's hands are clamped over her ears, and she is stumbling backward from her bedroom hatch. From the twin video feeds and through the reinforced material of the wall itself comes a rising shriek, a piercing scream of rage that ascends in frequency and volume to an unbearable level. It is a blade, a knife, a sound that has evolved over eons to strike fear in the hearts of prey across an entire solar system.

It is the hunting cry of the Widow.

"Mother!" shouts Sarya, but she cannot even hear herself. And then she is on her face, shoving her fingers in her ears and her body into the synthetic flooring. She's heard stories of this, but never experienced it herself. The scream speaks to her own instincts, tells them to run, to hide, to drop and die. She can do nothing but flail her legs and try to dig herself through the deck and out of sight—

And then her senses shut down.

WELCOME TO THE REGISTRY!

Doubtless you've had many things to worry about over the past few centuries. Your species has/have recently discovered that you are not alone in the universe after all! Most societies are surprised to learn that they share a galaxy with approximately 1.4 million intelligent species. And after your shock and awe has worn off, you might be left wondering: how does a society so large keep track of everyone?

The answer is simple: the Network Registry.

HOW DOES IT WORK?

Every member of every Citizen species receives a Network registration. This is a public and permanent identifier that can be used for travel, communication, and a raft of other Network privileges. If your species becomes a Citizen, you will need to submit an official name for both your homeworld and species, both of which will be translated into Standard and entered into the Registry. However, there is one hiccup that affects nearly all entries.

Earth.

Now don't get too excited, because that's not *your* Earth. It can't be, because approximately 99.994 percent of new species call their home planet by a name that translates into Standard as *Earth*.* Typically the name of the species is derived from this word as well and translates to "Earthers," "Earth-dwellers," "Earthlings," etc. Because the Registry would be useless with 1.4 million species all

---

* Given the fact that all species begin life far below tier one, it should not be surprising that they have usually named their birthplace some unimaginative variant on the phrase *the ground*. What is more surprising is the fact that every species seems bewildered that everyone else has done the same.

named "Earthlings" who originated on "Earth," species are asked to come up with new names before being granted Citizenship.*

To get you started with some ideas, please see this message's attachments. Included are the current Registry, plus the latest list of recently released names from Citizen species who have left the Network, are now extinct,† or both. Keep in mind that many first choices have been taken for millions of years, so if your first choice is similar in style to "The Courageous," "The Gentle Ones," "The Unstoppable," etc., you may have trouble finding something in a reasonable time frame.

Now get to brainstorming!

* Don't worry! You can register your representation(s) of "Earth" and "Earthling" alongside your new official name. You'll find that some species are referred to by their unofficial names even more often than the official ones.

† To discourage undesirable behavior in name claiming, e.g., genocide, please note that a species name must be dormant for 100,000 years in order to re-enter the registry.

EIGHT

"Get . . . *up*," hisses a voice somewhere up above. It fights its way through ringing ears and into a battered head. Sarya rises to one knee and nearly keels over from the overpowering stench in the air. Widow pheromones, hot metal, burning insulation, leaking coolant, goddess knows what else. She falls to her hands and knees and retches.

"*Up*," repeats the voice. She is hoisted to her feet by a collection of very hard, very sharp implements. There is nothing at all soft about her mother right now. "You will carry this," hisses the voice. A satchel is thrown over her shoulders and tightened mercilessly.

"Hey, that corporate ship is all docked now," says Helper's voice from the ceiling. "Network says they're looking for somebody, which I'm *pretty* sure I predicted. There's a big public announcement that everybody's supposed to cooperate if they run into—"

"Enough, Helper," says Sarya. She rises, still shaky, from her hands and knees.

"A corporate ship?" hisses Shenya the Widow. She tilts her head, as she always does when she's using her Network implant. "Searching Watertower? *What* corporation?"

"Oh, some deep-space archaeological firm," says Helper. "Let me look it up real quick—"

And then Shenya the Widow's blades slip out from under her and spark across the floor. She lands with a disturbing crack and a furious hiss, limbs swinging and scrabbling for purchase. The battle has apparently not left Shenya the Widow unscathed.

"Off, Helper," hisses Sarya as she stumbles backward out of range. She leans against the doorframe and takes a breath, her ears still ringing. She very nearly offers to help her mother, but she squashes the impulse. Her mother will do this on her own, or not at all. And then she will tell the story in the future, of how Shenya the Widow needed no help to deal with a bounty hunter many times her size. She will work those scars into every conversation, and she will be insufferable about it.

"Pain without fear," whispers her mother as she draws herself to a shaky standing position.

"Pain without fear," answers Sarya automatically, struggling to stand upright herself. "Did you—" she says, then coughs. "Is he—"

But she realizes she doesn't need to finish either sentence. She did, and he is. The bounty hunter takes up most of the common room floor, sprawled on his face. He looks smaller than before—and then Sarya realizes it's because his arms have been removed. The big one rests in the corner while his long whip twitches at her feet.

Unsteadily, she steps over it—with half a mind to stomp it into the floor. She remembers its cold caress on her face and body, and the memory lends her strength. She makes her way to Hood's torn body, stepping over streaks of fluids of various colors and viscosities. She stands above him, eyes tracing his dented form and sliced tubes. He is oddly beautiful, in a way—and yet she doesn't feel a trace of sadness. This is on you, Hood. You should have known this was coming when you decided to take the daughter of a Widow.

"This is . . . not the time for gloating," says her mother behind her.

But Sarya has already found what she's looking for, peeking out of a dented compartment. She crouches above the smoking form, hands tracing warm metal. When she rises and turns back to her mother, she is inserting earbuds.

"He took my gift," she says quietly.

She does not thank her mother for protecting her. That is not the Widow way. Widows speak thanks for small things, for gifts and favors. The large things, the sacrificing of lives and the killing of threats—these are taken for granted.

"You . . . go first," her mother says when they reach the door. She seems to be having difficulty assembling sentences. "I will follow and . . . protect."

Only now does Sarya begin to realize what has happened here. A dead bounty hunter—yes, that's only justice. But now she is stepping over a—what is that? The bile rises in her throat. It's *another* limb. But whose? Did it belong to the babysitter? To old Baz? To the arboretum caretaker? "Where?" she manages to say, unable to take her eyes off the oozing stump.

"Away," says Shenya the Widow, swaying.

And Sarya finds that she is able. She strides to the door and barely jumps at all when it opens and a figure slumps into the room, head lolling. She refuses to look down as she steps over it, out into a deserted corridor, but the leaking silhouette in her peripheral vision is unmistakable. *That* was the babysitter. A variety of emotions are fighting for attention now, but she keeps it to the essentials. *I am Widow. My rage is my weapon. I am Widow. My life is my own. I am Widow. There are no secrets between Mother and do not panic do not panic Mother is injured do not panic—* No. A Widow does not panic. Not even when she has to help her wounded mother step over her disemboweled babysitter.

From the ceiling, an alarm is blaring. Two more bodies lie out here, formerly the property of intelligences strong enough to escape the apartment but not durable enough to make it to a medication station or the hospital deck. Trails of multicolored fluids lead in both directions, alternating streaks and drips. Sarya attempts to view the scene abstractly, like a Widow would. Isn't it interesting how many intelligences are full of some kind of fluid? Yes, yes, it is. And tactically speaking, this much fluid on the ground means eliminated threats. There, that is how a Widow thinks. Much better. Except it's *not* much better because she is *not* a Widow, she is a Human, and Humans leak from everywhere all the goddess-damned time and seriously what is with her eyes right now because these people were enemies, they betrayed her, they deserved everything they got—

But the tears keep coming.

"May I have your attention, residents of Watertower Station," says Ellie's voice from everywhere, suffused with an unusually businesslike edge. "For those of you who missed my previous announcement, I would like to stress the fact that there is absolutely no need to panic. There is no reason there should be any loss of life or even injury. There may not even be a serious problem, but you know how we like to be safe. That's the Watertower way! All that said, please make your way to the nearest airlock and prepare for evacuation. You have thirty-six minutes at the outside."

Sarya swallows, attempting to focus on the problem at hand and not the mess at her feet. She must have been unconscious for the previous announcement, the one where Ellie surely explained what the hell was going on. She considers asking Helper, but decides she really doesn't need its cheerful voice in her ears at the moment. She wonders, for just a moment, if *she* is the problem. Would they evacuate an entire station due to a Human sighting? It's happened before. Helper has dug up a half-dozen different events that led to evacuations.

"We must go," hisses Shenya the Widow, trembling limbs clattering against the doorway. "They must not find us here."

In the light of the corridor, Sarya can see that her mother's carapace is cracked across the front, and her mandibles are barely moving. And that sentence—well, Sarya would never say this aloud, for obvious reasons. But her mother sounds . . . frightened.

Sarya wants very badly to ask questions. She wants to know what could frighten Shenya the Widow, the hunter-killer who just took down a three-meter titanium-plated nightmare on her own. But she also knows that this is the time for action, not questions, not fear of mysterious corporations, not internal crises over slaughtered neighbors who maybe didn't even want to be there, who maybe just got caught up in the moment or got scared, or—

She takes a sudden, violent breath. She doesn't have time. She has thirty-six minutes at the outside.

Her mother spends the last of her strength dragging herself to the nearest utility hatch, which means she can no longer protest when Sarya wrenches it open and hauls her, bodily, into the darkness beyond.

"I . . . just need to rest," says her mother in a tortured whisper.

"Not yet," says Sarya, supporting her as the outer door drifts closed. "Just a few more meters and then you can get off your blades for a minute, okay?"

"I am Widow," murmurs Shenya the Widow, so quietly that Sarya is not sure she heard it at all. "There are no secrets between—" And then the inner door opens, and the rest of the proverb is lost in the roar of Watertower's maintenance corridors.

[You're not the Human, are you?] says the nearest cart as they approach.

"I have no idea what you are talking about," shouts Sarya, dragging her mother forward.

[It's just that there's been talk of a Human. I don't really know what a Human is, but everybody seems really scared and that makes me scared, so I was just making sure that you're not the Human.]

"This is my mother," says Sarya. "She's injured." *Badly*.

[Yes], says the cart. [She just killed some people.]

Of course. If *one* Networked drone knows, they all know. "That's true," says Sarya. "But—"

[But the station is about to explode], says the cart, lowering itself to the deck for loading. [**You're lucky: that's actually the one circumstance in which I can help you.**]

Perhaps Sarya is beyond surprise now, in some sort of survival state, because the news barely registers. So the station is in danger. How is that any more extreme than anything else that's happened today? "How long to the nearest airlock?" she asks briskly, as if she's planning a day trip. She begins throwing one black limb after another over the lip of the cart, since her mother seems to have lost any ability to move on her own.

[**Three minutes**], says the cart, [**I feel that I should warn you, however, that all lifeboats at that airlock have already been launched.**]

. "Twenty-four minutes, everyone!" says Ellie's voice in Sarya's earbuds. "I also thought you might want to know that I myself have been successfully evacuated. I am now broadcasting from the fine ship *Wanderlust*, which was kind enough to host my intelligence core."

"Okay," says Sarya, voice tight. "How long to the closest airlock with lifeboats?"

[**Calculating . . .**], says the cargo cart. [**Twenty-five minutes! Would you like me to plot the route?**]

No, because that is an idiotic plan that would only occur to a low-tier mind. Sarya wonders briefly if all the sub-legal intelligences on Watertower have escape plans. Is there space on a lifeboat for a cargo cart, let alone the tens of thousands that run through Watertower's back corridors? Perhaps that's another hint that she's in some strange mental space, because the image of fleeing drones piling into lifeboats is so ridiculous she nearly laughs. No, a lifeboat is clearly not the answer . . . but there could be another possibility.

She throws her own legs over the edge and works her way into a corner of the cart. She lifts her mother's head onto her lap and holds it as the cart rises, swaying. "You're okay," she tells her mother, willing it to be true.

"It was only a matter of time before they found us," says Shenya the Widow, and Sarya has to bring her ear almost to those trembling mandibles to hear. "I knew that when I kept you." She rattles, deep inside her thorax. "You were so hideous," she whispers, and chitters a long laugh into a choking silence.

"I'll get us off the station," murmurs Sarya, cradling the hard edges of that beloved head. She strokes the side of a mandible. "Cart," she says without looking up. "Emergency mode. Take us to Dock A."

NINE

"Now that I've been cleared of negligence, I'm happy to provide more details on the current situation," says Ellie's voice as the cargo cart rocks through a dark and crowded corridor. "It seems we have a *teensy* guidance problem with a nearby ice shipment, which will most likely collide with the station. As this shipment is not Networked, there is very little we here on the station can do besides evacuate. So carry on, everyone! You have twenty minutes."

Sarya strokes her mother's carapace, her fingers finding damage in new places. Her mother hisses with pain now and then, but the sounds are becoming softer and more widely spaced.

"Mother," says Sarya, tapping her mother's face gently. "Mother, talk to me."

Her mother's mandibles flutter. "What's . . . happening?" she asks.

Sarya strokes the outside of those mandibles, staying away

from the razor inner edges. "No idea," she says. She attempts to smile. "But I'd guess somebody's getting fired."

"It's my fault," her mother whispers.

"I really doubt that," says Sarya. "Unless you've been plotting shipping routes."

"It is," her mother murmurs, as if to herself. "Where Humans go, disaster follows. I knew this, and *still* I—"

"I think that might be a *little* dramatic," says Sarya, but there is a weight in her stomach. "Why don't you tell me a story?" she says as lightly as she can manage.

"I'm . . . tired, child."

"Eighteen minutes, everyone," says Ellie's voice in her earbuds. "And there's even a chance of a clean miss! Not much of one, but I thought you'd like to know. Anyway, I want to congratulate everyone on the extremely low number of casualties so far: only three evacuation-related fatalities that I've seen! Excellent work, team!"

"A chant, then," says Sarya, racking her memory for one of her mother's favorites. "*The Eight Blades,* I want to hear that one."

"You . . . hate that one."

It's true. Her mother used to make her recite it every day, back when she was tiny, until she despised it. But it's simple. It's reassuring. She swallows. It's the perfect lifeline for a fading Widow.

"Do you know why I named you Sarya?" asks her mother with a sigh. "I don't remember. Why don't I remember?" She drifts off into soft clicks and chitters.

Sarya's throat tightens. "*Count my blades . . .*" she prompts gently.

Her mother's mandibles tremble as she picks up the rhythm. "*Count my blades, my bond, my love. Tell me what I'm thinking of . . .*" She rattles, somewhere deep, and it tears Sarya's heart. "*One is triumph, two is rage. Three is . . . three is . . .*"

"*Craft,*" says Sarya.

" *. . . three is craft . . . the gift of age.*" The words are so faint that Sarya can barely hear them over the clamor of Watertower's circulatory system.

[**Dock A!**] says the cart, rattling to a halt. [**It was my pleasure to bring you here.**]

"Don't stop," murmurs Sarya, unsnagging her stained utility suit from her mother's sharp edges. The mandibles are still moving, though Sarya can no longer catch the words over the crash and hum of ten thousand drones on useless missions. Both her hands are occupied arranging razor-sharp limbs now, so there's nothing to stop the tears from falling. This time, however, she is unashamed. This is no weakness. She doesn't know how she gets the hard body out of the cart, but here she is with two black limbs thrown over her shoulders, half carrying, half dragging a Widow through a tangle of miscellaneous Network transmissions toward the hatch. The burning love in her chest makes her mother light. She will carry her mother to the end of the galaxy.

[**I hope you survive!**] says the cart behind them.

"*Four is kindred, five is bond,*" murmurs her mother in her ear. "*Six is . . .*" she says. "*Six is . . .*"

The pauses are the worst, because Sarya doesn't know if there will be a next line. "*Brood,*" she grunts.

"*Six is brood . . . desire has spawned.*"

Sarya leans against the wall next to the hatch, gathering herself. It's a familiar feeling, like when she was mustering courage outside an apartment with a sleeping Widow inside. Like the apartment, there's no telling what's out in Dock A: but there's possible safety on the other side. The thought gives her strength, and she pulls herself up straight. "You can rest in a minute, Mother," she says. "But right now, I could use some help."

Her mother struggles, a blade opening a slit in Sarya's utility suit. It might have gone through flesh as well; Widow blades are so sharp that Sarya knows from experience that she would feel the trickle of blood before the sting of the cut. But her mother supports enough of her own weight that Sarya is able to crank the door open with one hand and drag the clattering body into the echoing expanse of Dock A. Here it is, the site of the first actual Human sighting in a millennium. Still empty, thank the goddess. And there it is on the other side of the dock, her target. Eleven.

"Dock A is closed until further notice," says the friendly voice of the dock intelligence. "If this facility exists after the current emergency, you may return then."

"Almost there, Mother," whispers Sarya. "Pain without fear, right?"

"Seven's fear . . . demands subjection. Eight grants . . . eight—"

And then her mother chokes into silence as Sarya freezes, her dangling burden clacking limb against limb. Her tunnel vision had completely excluded anything but her objective, but there it is: Dock A is *not* empty. In the center of the open space, hovering just above Sarya's line of sight, is a brilliant fifty-meter silver shape. It's long and fluid, with no visible ports or engines. It's an expensive-looking ship.

A corporate-looking ship.

"So you did find me . . . old friend," murmurs Shenya the Widow. "Older than you look . . . older . . ."

"Twelve minutes, everyone, and it looks like all lifeboats are away!" crows Ellie from the ceiling. "In further good news, I'm thrilled to announce that Section C1 will almost certainly survive. So congratulations, C1! Of course, if you're hearing my voice, that means you're one of the four hundred twelve individuals still on Section F. Just know that we're all out here rooting for you!"

The station's voice dissolves into echoes, and the ship doesn't open. It does nothing, in fact, but hover three meters above the deck of Dock A. Sarya watches it for a moment, muscles burning from strain, a corner of chitin boring into her shoulder. If anyone aboard wanted a Human, they'd be out here by now . . . right? Meanwhile, her mother is dying and the station is twelve minutes from actual catastrophe. That makes the decision for her. She hoists her mother farther up on a throbbing shoulder and pushes forward. The quickest way is directly underneath that thing, so that's the way they'll go.

If it weren't for the red-hot purpose pumping through her veins, Sarya would not have made it. The completion of each step seems like an impossible dream, but each time she begins the next with furious determination. *I am Sarya the Daughter,* she tells herself, and her self responds with strength. She carries her mother, step by step, out of the maze of drones, out into the empty space on the other side, and under the gorgeous silver ship. It's a perfect mirror, its rounded surface reflecting a crazed version of Dock A, where a bloodied Human drags a crippled Widow across a ceiling, leaving streaks of combined gore behind. But it doesn't open, thank the goddess.

"Eleven!" calls Sarya when they reach the other side. Her voice echoes around Dock A for a full five seconds.

AIVVTECH QUALITY IS WORTH THE WAIT, says the suit's holo ring for a few seconds. Then, with a massive clang, it falls forward onto its arms. "Hello!" it says in its devastatingly cheerful voice. "Thank you for choosing an AivvTech R2 Universal Autonomous Environment! How can I improve your day?"

"Eleven, medical mode!" Sarya gasps. Just a few more steps . . .

"This intelligence may not be authorized to—"

"Your owner is not coming," says Sarya, nearly stumbling with exhaustion. "And also the station is about to explode."

"Not to worry!" says Eleven. "This suit will likely survive any depressurization event." The voice changes, slightly enough that Sarya might not have picked up on it before her previous experience with the suit. "But . . . please explain about my owner?"

"My mother—" She drags her mother another step. "This is my mother, by the way—"

"Hello, your mother!"

"She—" She pauses, weighing what she knows. This is the suit that released her. It is now her—and her mother's—only hope. Which means it's worth the gamble. "She killed your owner," she says.

Eleven's holo ring changes through several colors and finally settles on blue. "You killed Hood?" it asks in a quieter voice.

A long sigh emerges from Shenya the Widow's battered mandibles. "Old . . . friend," she murmurs. "So very . . . old."

"This is what Hood did to her," says Sarya, refusing to glance back at the silver ship. "She was protecting me . . . like *you* protected me."

Eleven stands there, silent. Its holo ring flicks from blue to orange, but no words are displayed.

Sarya squats to let her mother slide off her shoulders and onto the deck. She slides one hand between head and deck, carefully keeping the other away from the trembling and razor-sharp mandibles. She's never seen her mother look weak before, but here she is, helpless as a premature hatchling, limbs splayed across the metal. They've come so far. They're so close.

"I know you're more than you pretend to be, Eleven," Sarya says, looking up at the towering suit. "You *freed* me, and you risked something to do it." She pauses, realizing: she's not trying to manipulate a sub-legal intelligence. She is, honestly and genuinely, *appealing* to a fellow mind. She is *petitioning* a sub-legal, not ordering it. It's a strange feeling. "Please . . . help us," she says. "Take us off the station."

The suit does nothing at all for a moment, while Sarya's words and hope die away around her. And then, with a now-familiar tone, its gleaming front cracks open and its gangway descends. Sarya stands, nearly screaming as her utility suit slides over her various wounds. She's done it.

She takes a step back as the two massive arms heave into motion with the low hum of servos. They are surprisingly gentle as they collect Widow limbs into an easy-to-transport package, wrapping her mother and lifting her into the red-lit interior. The straps emerge, helping guide the wayward extremities.

"Six minutes!" says Ellie. "I'd also like to inform everyone that an emergency relief fleet is outbound from our Network corridor and will arrive in approximately eight days. Those of you in lifeboats should be fine, but those in pressure suits might want to scavenge some canisters of your preferred atmosphere before then."

Her mother whispers something, a broken sound in the silence of the dock.

"It's going to be okay," says Sarya, smiling through her tears. "We can both fit, and Eleven can fix you up."

Her mother says it again, but again Sarya can't quite catch it.

She can't hear much of anything, actually, over the low ringing that has been steadily building behind her. Something resonant, metallic, heavy and continuous—

Sarya whirls.

At the main entrance, something is moving. It's not Hood mysteriously returned to life, it's not Observer, and it's nothing like either one. It flows, like a gleaming river of mercury, like nothing she's ever seen. It pulls itself up and stands, if that is the right word, under a golden [**Welcome to Watertower!**] that rains virtual sparkles down onto its silvery surface. Sarya feels, very strongly, that it is looking at her.

And then the metal crashes forward like a wave and comes, more quickly than she would have believed. She turns back to Eleven, who has secured her mother in its interior. "Go," she says, as calmly as she can. She knows, as surely as if she had been told, that this thing wants *her*. This is the latest in a string of incidents, not accidents. At this level of exhaustion it is far easier to accept the truth: today, her life on Watertower comes to a close, and there is nothing she or her mother can do about it.

She turns again to face the approaching silver tide. It's hypnotically beautiful, washing over obstacles and between machinery. The ringing sound is not unpleasant; it's almost a chime, a chord of tones that fill the air to bursting. She limps forward— one, two steps. She holds herself straight, like a Widow. She takes a breath—and then she hears a voice behind her, cracked and broken.

"Release me, suit," says Shenya the Widow.

Sarya turns. "Eleven!" she shouts, her sense of purpose beginning to fracture into panic for the first time. "We had a deal!"

But the suit doesn't answer her. Its straps unwind from around the Widow's frame, and its giant arms pull her twisted shape from its cavity and set it at the base of its gangway. Shenya the Widow sinks to the floor, then struggles to raise herself. A stream of black fluid runs down one limb to the floor.

And then a clang echoes across the dock, and Sarya whirls to see a severed utility hatch sliding to a stop on the floor. From the hole it once covered gushes another stream of silver. The sound heightens as two rivers of mercury flow toward the little group.

"Three minutes!" says Ellie's cheery voice. "To those of you still on Section F, it's been a pleasure working with you all."

"My child," says Shenya the Widow, hauling herself upright. "*Go.*"

Sarya's jaw clenches. "Mother," she says quietly, in a voice brimming with fury and desperation. She points. "Get the *fuck* into the suit."

"If you *ever* speak to me like that again," hisses Shenya the Widow as she takes a tottering step past her daughter, "I shall be forced to discipline you."

"I'll never be *able* to speak to you again," shouts Sarya, keeping pace. She has forgotten about her pain, about anything but getting her mother off this goddess-forsaken station. "Outside that suit, *you will die*. If you try to fight this thing, *you will die*. We can still escape *if you get in the damn suit*."

"Not from this," hisses her mother, clawing her way forward. "*Go.*"

Sarya's eyes are fastened to the river of silver as she racks her mind for words, for something that will save her mother. It is one flow now, the two streams having merged beneath the gleaming ship. A third stream pours downward into the reflective pool, and the combined metal stretches upward into a new shape. It's something more vertical, something that can *reach* for her.

"You are dangerous," says Shenya the Widow, still clattering forward one blade at a time. "More dangerous than even the Daughter of a Widow. Now. *Go.*" And then she tilts her head to the side, the way she always does when she uses her Network implant.

And Sarya is off the ground again, shouting again, seized from behind by Eleven's gigantic arms. She struggles, but her strength means absolutely nothing. She is pulled backward, packed into the suit like cargo, and the straps wrap her and anchor her. She screams, a long and wordless cry as she reaches for her mother. This is not how it goes. This is not how a Widow is treated. And then the hatch closes over her and Eleven begins rocking itself backward. The golden light of the planet below stretches across the floor and toward her mother as the hatch behind the suit splits open.

Sarya kicks the suit's interior. She hurls punches that are arrested before they land. She tries to bite, but she can't reach anything. Outside, in perfect fidelity, she sees what very few intelligences have ever seen twice: the Widow battle stance. It's shakier than it was, it's cockeyed, as if one or two of those limbs can't quite handle what's asked of them, but it's there. Her mother has inserted herself between Eleven and this massive thing, between her daughter and danger—

But no. That is where Shenya the Widow has always been.

Sarya is not prepared for the war cry. It ascends like a living thing. It battles and conquers even this grinding chime of metal. It reflects off every surface, and Sarya forgets about everything but pressing her hands into her ears. She can barely see through the burn around her eyes, but she refuses to close them. She will not abandon her mother. She clenches her jaw against the pain in her head, against the ice-pick cry working into her temples.

Even that massive silver shape hesitates in the face of the Widow's shriek. It draws itself up, towering above that black shape, and waits. But the cry does not stop. It *shatters*, it breaks into a wild peal of deafening Widow laughter. And then the metal reaches past her mother and her mother strikes more quickly than thought and when they both withdraw Shenya the Widow has one less limb. And yet she laughs, her cry of fierce joy ricocheting around the dock like lightning.

But her daughter is not laughing. "Mother!" Sarya screams, unable to help herself and forgetting everything but the fact that she *must* be out there, she *must* help somehow. She claws at the straps but it is too late because the suit has launched itself backward through a sparkling pressure field and into the black and gold of space.

("Welcome to Network!" revision 5600109c, intelligence Tier 1.8-2.5, F-type metaphors)

WELCOME TO CHOICE!

Many species have noted, when pondering Citizenship, that Network law appears to be relatively inflexible. For example, some have already developed or even depend on technologies that are illegal for Network Citizen species to possess. This is as good a reason as any to wonder: is Network Citizenship mandatory?

By no means!

If your species would like to continue its development in isolation, it is free to do so. If that is the case, you will simply need to agree to a few simple requirements, and your solar system will be marked off-limits to the rest of the galaxy. You may even change your mind in the future; all you need to do is let the Network know.

WHAT ABOUT THE RUMORS?

Even with perfect mental communication and instant access to facts, rumors have a way of spreading. Thus, you may have heard tales of species who have refused Citizenship. Since such stories are almost always exaggerated, this document will attempt to clarify this scenario.

The Network is the only possible way for millions of species to coexist in a single galaxy. It is designed to be self-correcting, tending toward equilibrium, and the only reason this is possible is that every Citizen species *desires* equilibrium. In other words, the galaxy must *want* to work. If even a single species were forced to join or forced to remain, this system would fall apart. This is why any Citizen species is permitted to renounce its Network Citizenship at any time, or to refuse Citizenship in the first place. However, in both cases, the following must occur:

- All Network registrations must be revoked (and with them the freedom of faster-than-light travel and communication).
- All Network technology must be returned.

- The species in question must return to its own solar system.
- The species must agree that it will not develop anything on the list of illegal technologies (FTL, nanotech, weaponry, artificial intelligence, etc.).
- To ensure that these requirements are kept, the species must submit to a Network sentinel intelligence in its home solar system.*

WHAT IF THE SPECIES DOESN'T SUBMIT?

Many new species look out upon a peaceful galaxy and assume that it has always been so. This could not be further from the truth. The society whose invitation your species now considers was formed in a crucible, in millions of years of war and famine and genocide. The Network was created because this society decided: *no more.* Eons later, there is no war because the Network leaves no room for war. There is no genocide because the Network leaves no opportunity for genocide. These and a thousand other species-wide crimes have been wiped out. If a species decides to reject half a billion years of work toward this end, that is its own choice. If, however, it decides to *undermine* said work, then the Citizens of the Network are themselves left with no choice. They must assume that the species in question wishes to introduce that which others have spent eons eradicating.

And thus, the species itself must be eradicated.†

We hope to hear from you soon.

* This sentinel can certainly keep itself on an out-of-the-way moon or minor body. The Network is not unreasonable.

† In the eons that the Network has existed, its invitation has been refused very few times. In fact, only one species has ever triggered the Network's last resort.

TIER TWO

TEN

It has been fifteen hours since Sarya watched her mother die.

She has not spoken during that time. She has not cried either. She has shouted, yes, screamed herself into exhausted unconsciousness at least once. She has done violent things, which is why there is blood crusted on her face and the backs of her hands. But she has not spoken and she has not cried, and now she stands in the flickering light of a foreign corridor and wonders if she will do either of those things ever again.

Fifteen hours ago, she shot backward through vacuum while the sky split around her. Below her blazed the fire of the gas giant, frozen in its silent roar. Behind her stretched the infinite star field. Before her spread the shrinking gold-lit amalgamation of geometry that contained nearly every memory she's ever made. Watertower Station, Section F. She hurled epithets at the suit, cursed Eleven as a coward and a traitor, physically reached for the bright spot of the station airlock they left behind, that rectangle where she *knew* she would see the familiar silhouette of her mother any second. No matter that she had just seen what she had seen, there's no telling what a Widow can survive—even *conquer*. But ultimately it didn't matter because above, bigger than anything she's ever imagined, there was something else.

The ice ship.

Eleven's interior display laid out the scene with all the life and feeling of an architectural diagram. The section they just left, in which a laughing Widow stood before a river of silver death— that was [**Dock A**]. Far to her right, that clutter of cubes was [**Residential**]. That's where her neighbors still lay on a synthetic floor, eyes open and fluids congealing. Below that was the dome of the [**Arboretum**], where she'd spent so many afternoons while her mother slept. And that part, toward which the needle spike of the ice ship swung like an impossibly long, brilliant blade—that was [**Reactor B**].

Watertower didn't explode, then, so much as it simply ceased to exist. It was destructured, unbuilt, homogenized into elementary particles. The process flashed Eleven's interior a blinding white, and when Sarya could open her eyes again the station was gone. The ice ship continued on its massive arc, now missing its first few kilometers but otherwise unharmed. And that was it. That was the end of everything that Sarya had ever known.

She doesn't remember much past that. She doesn't remember entering another ship, though it must have happened because here she is. She vaguely recalls the shock of frozen air that hit her when Eleven's shell cracked open and its gangway lowered. She has a faint memory of two figures bundling her out of the suit and up a freezing ladder. She went with them because what else could she do? She remembers that one was huge and one was her size, and that the big one wouldn't stop trying to thank her for something, but all she wanted was for them to go away. They must have done just that, because the next time she looked up she was lying on the floor of a bare room with two stacked bunks against a wall and a standard sanitation station in the corner.

And that, as near as she can recall, is when the screaming began.

So. Screaming and self-harm: that was her introduction to *Ripper* or *Tidal* or whatever this hellship is called. But now those have burned out and a different part of her brain has taken over and negotiated a sterile peace within her. It doesn't matter, says that part of her brain—not that anything ever really did. You should go somewhere, maybe avoid thinking for a while. There you go. Feeling nothing at all is better than feeling like this; that's just logic. *Go.*

Sarya listened to that part of her brain, and that's why she's here now. She has climbed, with these bloodied fingertips, to the top of the ship's [Backbone]. That's what her Network overlay labels this vertical spine of metal ladders and grated flooring that connects every deck of this awful ship. There's a single hatch up here, and she could not care less what is behind it. A stale and mechanical air current dries the sweat on her face and shifts the mangled hair on her forehead. The combined drone of ventilation and old lighting tickles her ears while the subsonic hum of the reactor vibrates through the soles of her boots. The three combine into one sound in her brain, the heartbeat of an old starship in operation.

She doesn't know why she's up here, exactly. All she knows is that she has to go *somewhere* or she'll go insane. She gazes down past the tips of her own boots, down the ladder, through three layers of grated flooring, to an orange pressure door set in the floor. It's well named, this backbone. It's skeletal. It lends support. It even looks diseased, like its host body has developed bone cancer and refused treatment. The safety cages that surround every ladder on Watertower are missing here; they've been ripped away along with large chunks of floor. Hood's doing, she assumes, since he wouldn't have fit through those tiny openings. Or maybe it was that big guy who brought her to her room. He looked like the type who makes a hobby of ripping holes in metal gratings. Or maybe it just doesn't matter, says the dark and soothing part of her brain. Your mother is gone. Your home is gone. Nothing will matter ever again. *Go.*

She breathes mechanically, manually. All right, she tells her body, now reach for the ladder. One hand. Both. Turn around and switch them. One boot and then the other, the metal ringing with every step. The rungs are cool and solid in her hands, rough from the safety paint that remains between gouges. Her head drops below the top grating and then the safety doors recessed into the walls below it. Now comes the [Maintenance] half-level, says her Network unit. It's so short she would have to duck her head to step off onto the floor grating here. She doesn't bother; the door is closed, sealed down the center, and her registration certainly won't change that.

Another few meters down and she is at [Quarters]. A dim corridor leads toward the back of the ship, ending in a [Galley] full of food bars she probably can't eat. The hallway is lined with hatches on both sides, which are identical except for one with the talon marks that show evidence of the big guy. *Mer,* there we go, that's his name. She remembers him saying it multiple times as he hauled her up the ladders—he said it slowly, like she's an idiot. Which is nothing new.

She's one rung above the orange door in the floor. There's a switch here, and she burns most of her remaining strength to push its contacts closed. She notices there's blood on it when she pulls her hand away. And then with a clank and the grind of bad bearings the hatch divides in half, and she is suspended over a hole into darkness.

Go.

She very nearly wonders what is driving her right now, what dark part of her forebrain wants her down there in that cargo hold. But that part is in control, and the concern never quite materializes. She hangs on with one hand and watches herself lift the Network unit off her head. The same hand pulls the earbuds out of their homes and lets their magnetic clasps click to the projector. She loops it twice around the ladder and now her gift hangs there, sparkling in the flickering light of the backbone. She went through a lot for that gift, says some quieter part of her mind, and now she's just going to leave it there?

Sarya descends. She passes out of the warm air of the top of the ship and into the cold of the cargo hold as if plunging into freezing water. The air is so frigid that her first breath explodes into the white vapor of a coughing fit. She clears her throat violently and spits, then hears the clink and clatter of her frozen saliva bouncing off the deck below. This is cold like she's never experienced—and still, she can't bring herself to care. She hits the switch on this side of the hatch. With the sound of tortured machinery, the warmth and light of the backbone above her are cut off.

She is shivering uncontrollably before she reaches the bottom, another five meters down, her hands already becoming remarkably lazy about obeying her commands. She steps off the ladder onto an airlock door set in the floor, the last barrier between her and the vacuum outside. Tunnels lead in both directions, gaps in the several thousand tons of water ice that reach to the ceiling. This is Watertower ice, maybe the last shipment ever. Apparently bounty hunting alone wasn't enough to pay the bills. She reaches out and touches its glassy surface, but her hands are already too dead to feel anything.

If she could be affected by anything right now, she would be shocked by how little she cares about this, about anything at all. Her fingers are already bending more slowly, and that dark part of her brain is telling her that it doesn't matter. Sure, some small part of her mind is concerned, but that's natural, isn't it? Anyway, you can ignore that, says the dark part. It doesn't matter, because nothing matters. *Stay.*

Sarya lowers herself to the shockingly cold floor. She sits with her legs crossed and her hands in her lap, feeling the nerves in her lower extremities first burn and then fall to sleep. She feels some slight warmth from her suit heating elements, and she wonders how long that will last; they're made for slight chills, not the crushing, killing type of cold she's sitting in now.

So here she is in this crystalline silence, her own breaths deafening in her ears. She has no plan. She has no future. She watches each swirl of vapor emerge with a bit of her body heat and dissipate into the darkness. Her mind is empty, her body's signals coming more quietly and farther apart.

It's not quite silent here. There is still the rhythmic sound of her breaths. The deck still hums with the stunning power required to hurl even the most ramshackle of starships across a solar system. Somewhere between the two, a faint and brittle sound repeats every now and again, distantly. That sound is familiar, though she can't quite place it. There it is again, louder now. What is it?

It doesn't matter, says the dark part of her brain. Nothing matters. *Stay.*

The ice is changing color. It's warming from a black-blue, diving down the spectrum into a purple and finally a dull red. Again comes the sound, and again. It's louder now. She fights her own mind to analyze it. It's—is it?

It's her own name.

Deep within her, something awakens. A hot fury ignites, driving her to feet that respond like they're already dead. Freezing muscles curl her into a hunch, but her mind is alive and well and absolutely furious. She has been betrayed by reality itself. She has lost her mother and her home. She has nothing but a Network unit to her name. Her own damn *mind* has betrayed her, leaving her here in a freezing cargo hold to die. But she has *not* died, not yet. Her heart still beats, her cells still metabolize, and she is breathing atmosphere. She may be exiled with no mother and no plan, trapped on a budget freighter with goddess knows what for a crew . . . but honestly, what more does a person need?

She is Sarya the Daughter, of Shenya the Widow. She will not die today.

And then she is on the floor again. Her knees rest on metal and one arm is hooked over a ladder rung. Something salty runs to the back of her throat and she tries to spit, but her lips don't move. It occurs to her suddenly that there is nothing insurmountable in life, nothing she can't fix . . . except for the fact that she has trapped herself in a freezing cargo hold and no one knows where she is. "Helper," she whispers. But she's left her Network implant up above, where she can't reach it. The darker part of her mind has triumphed, and this is where it has left her.

She pushes off sideways, head down, onto hands and knees. The hot flame of her anger sputters but it doesn't die. What happened to her beautiful sharpened nails? Why are her hands crusted with dried blood? There's more too, coming from somewhere, drops falling and freezing instantly in beautiful patterns. It must be cold in here. She hears that sound again, her *name* again, and finds that she is crawling toward it. She heaves herself away from the ladder, down the tunnel of ice, the fierce violet warming to almost-red, so strong and gorgeous she's going to have to remember when she writes home. These are such deep colors, you could get lost in these colors, and look how the condensation from her breath freezes in place when it touches them, and why are her breaths so *loud* . . .

No, she rages. This is *not* how a Widow dies. And she doesn't know much about Humans, but she is absolutely sure that they don't give up and freeze and die the first chance they get—

But hush, now. Why be so angry? Why does it seem so important to continue? She doesn't know, and she doesn't care. If she will just lie down now, it will all be over.

But she doesn't lie down. No, this is the Daughter who dragged Shenya the Widow across half of Watertower, and somehow that bitter memory summons the absolute dregs of her strength. She manages one last pull, and *finally* here is something familiar in her new and alien world. A recessed area of the cargo hold is clear of ice, containing only a gleaming hulk in the darkness. This is the source of the glow: a gaping red cockpit, and a holo ring blazing a blinding scarlet in the frozen darkness.

"Eleven?" Sarya tries to whisper. Her tongue fights her. Her lips don't move. She has to blink her sticking eyelids a few times before she can read the glowing symbols orbiting the suit. The ice shatters the light into a thousand crimson shards, each of which shows some distorted version of same word:

SARYA

Sarya collapses to the frozen deck, her limbs finally giving out. She feels nothing when her cheek presses its textured surface. Her mind rages within her, but all the fury in the galaxy won't move a body that has stopped responding.

She has lost.

But now someone has lifted her off the hard floor. She can't remember where she is or who this could be, but she is annoyed. She wants to demand that this person put her down, but the impulse dies somewhere between her brain and her tongue and no words emerge. Red light filters through eyes that are squeezed shut. Hot air blasts from above, so hot she can feel her skin burning. Softer, warmer arms take over for the cold, hard ones. They twist around her, wrap her, set her up vertically and hold her there. She cries out when they begin massaging damaged tissues, causing pain everywhere they touch. Somewhere out there, somewhere outside of herself, she hears a hum and a series of thunks as the cold is locked out.

Somewhere far away, her stomach rises. Her hands drift upward as Eleven shifts its gravity field. Something inside her has a hold on her; it is shaking her with violence, fighting the firm grip of the suit's straps. This is a dream, says her mind. It has to be, because someone is holding her right now, and who has ever held her except for her mother?

She can't close her fists, but she can keep her eyes clenched tight and she does. She draws gasping chestfuls of the warm air, twitching her limbs aimlessly in motions that are half Widow signs and half nothing at all. Eleven's straps stroke her hair and her back, and a soft sound begins to emerge from somewhere above her: the hissing rattle of a mother Widow soothing her daughter. Sarya's breath catches at the sound. And then, somewhere inside her, something splits wide open. With a heave and a wrenching cry, she weeps for Watertower.

CHAPTER

ELEVEN

Waking in an autonomous pressure suit is a disconcerting experience even in the best of circumstances. The gravity is low. Your feet are off the floor. You are supported by straps in non-ideal places, which means half your limbs have fallen asleep. You also cannot see the actual walls of the suit, thanks to its holo projector. As far as your groggy mind can tell, you just woke up bodiless, floating a good meter and a half off the floor.

But Sarya is thankful for the straps—at least she is once she has finished flailing. They have her by the wrists, and they save her from shredding the spray bandage that covers her fingers. She examines those fingers with all the concentration available to someone who is fairly sure she was drugged to sleep. Not that she's complaining. And the fingers look okay. They hurt, but they move. *And* she's not dead, how about that? That's not something you can take for granted, is it? Lately, anyway. She is warm and alive and she has all her limbs and—

Can we go through all this later, says her body with a pointed biofeedback signal, because it has physical needs too.

All right then, first things first. "I—" she says out loud, and stops. Her own voice has startled her, raspy and deeper than she's ever heard it. She swallows through the burn in the back of her throat. "I need to go to my room," she says. When the suit doesn't respond immediately, she touches the inner wall with one bandaged hand. She doesn't know which Eleven she'll get. Will it be the cheerful advertiser of features, the blithe reader of its own brochure? Or will it be the Eleven who has now saved her life twice over?

"Does your intelligence reside in a biological waste–producing shell?" booms Eleven. "Are you weary of halting missions midway because of the pressing needs of nature? The AivvTech UAE provides a full waste management suite, from water recycling to—"

"Eleven," she says. "Don't be gross."

"This sub-legal intelligence does not—"

"You fooled Hood," she says. "But you can't fool me. You saved me. Twice. I know you're more than just a—" She stops, searching for a word.

[A moron?] appears, superimposed on the purple ice outside.

She feels her chapped face form the tiniest beginning of a smile. There's the intelligence she was looking for. "Well, I wasn't going to say exactly that, but—"

[And it's three times.]

She thinks back. Oh, right, it *is* three times. "Fine," she says. "You saved me *three* times. And maybe after somebody saves you a bunch of times you don't really want to . . . you know. Inside them."

[I'm sure you'll know the sanitation station in your room soon enough.]

"Yeah . . . but it really is a moron. It's not even a one-point—" She stops.

[1.75?] says Eleven.

"Okay let me start over. I don't *want* to treat you like a sanitation station. I want to treat you like a—"

[Like a . . . ?]

Sarya pauses, again looking for a word, but her thoughts are interrupted by a body that reminds her that this is not the time or the place. "Look, we can take this apart later," she says. "But for now, I *really* need to go."

No words appear for a long moment, made longer by Sarya's current biological condition. Then, finally:

[Thank you.]

The straps lower her to the floor and retract into the walls. Sarya stumbles as the suit's gravity ramps up to match the ship outside. Has she really been at reduced weight for that long? She leans on the wall and massages a leg with one hand. "Okay," she says after a moment. "Ready."

A series of heavy *thunk*s vibrate through her boots, and the suit cracks in half with a blast of freezing air. Sarya swears. Her survival instincts are apparently back and in full gear, because now there is a war between needs going on. Staying here is looking better and better. "Actually—"

And for the second time in less than a day, she's shoved down the suit's ramp. She stumbles in the high gravity and barely keeps her feet all the way down. She clamps her arms around herself, pressing heating coils into her sides, and turns to see the suit already folding closed. "Very funny!" she calls, teeth already chattering.

"Thank you for choosing this AivvTech Universal Autonomous Environment!" says the suit. "If you have feedback, please don't hesitate to share!"

Sarya does have feedback, and she sends it in the form of an obscene Widow gesture.

BACK AT YOU, says Eleven in brilliant yellow, perfectly replicating the sign with its small utility arms.

The ice tunnels are the worst part until the ladder, and the ladder is the worst part until the *top* of the ladder. It takes her three tries to hit the switch at the top—hanging from bandaged hands, shivering violently and wondering if this is the end—and when the hatch cranks open and she pulls herself out into the warmth of the upper ship, she would swear she's almost dead again. But when the hatch grinds closed below her she is left hanging in *warm* air, in light that is not blue, in a space that's actually meant to keep people like her alive. She notes that her Network unit is no longer hanging here—but as her body reminds her, that's not number one on the priority list right now. A few more pulls, and here she is at the living level. Then it's just steps to her room and the sweet relief of her sanitation station. Which would all be great . . . except for one thing.

Which is her room?

She stares at six identical hatches, three on each side of the corridor. Okay, no problem, no problem. She turned *left* to get to the ladder before, so it's one of these three on the right. She passed at least one hatch on the way—oh, right, here are the talon marks all around this one on the end—so it's definitely one of the other two. Once again, life has become far more complicated without a Network unit. She tries the first, leaning in to give the hatch a clear view of her registration, and then takes a startled step backward when it slides open. It's not the sudden movement that shocks her; rather, it's the fact that someone is standing there.

The figure is her size, bipedal, all gleaming black synthetic surfaces. A face full of lenses examines her, and she can hear the high-pitched hum of tiny servos as they focus. Again she misses the overlays her Network unit provides, because she cannot for the life of her remember the name. This is a person and not a drone, she's sure of that. An android. *He, tier two-point-something* . . . But name? Nothing.

"I'm sorry," she says. "I thought these were my quarters."

"They are," says the person. "I was just going through your things."

"You were— I'm sorry, you were what?" She wasn't aware she *had* things other than the utility suit on her carapace, but the phrase is still provoking.

"I've identified everything except for this awfulness," he says, holding up one hand. Dangling from synthetic fingertips is a black eight-legged silk doll.

Sarya's mouth is already open to give vent to further outrage, but she is stopped cold. She works her way through one silent word after another. "Where . . . did you get that?" she finally manages to say.

"It was in a bag," he says, gesturing backward with a small jerk of his head. "On your floor."

A bag! She remembers her mother strapping it to her before their flight. She *does* have things! What would her mother have packed? The goddess only knows, but now she has a second, extremely high priority. "Okay, so," she says, "I *really* need to get in there right now, but I think after that we need to discuss, um, personal boundaries." She moves aside for him to step out.

He doesn't. "I should probably thank you," he says.

"That's very nice, but you can do that after—"

"But I don't think I will."

"Okay, *whatever,* but just—"

"Because I had everything well in hand. It had been decades since I've been incarcerated, you see, and I was beginning to get the itch. So just because your actions resulted in my freedom, that doesn't mean that—"

"Get out of the damn way!" Sarya roars, and she shoves him backward into the room. His surface is surprisingly cold, even through the bandages on her hands, and she charges through a cloud of ozone where he was standing. "Now," she says, pointing at the door. "*Out.* We can talk all you want in one minute. Okay? *Out.*"

He does go out, perhaps more bewildered than actually cowed, and her two minutes in the sanitation station are perhaps the most glorious of her life—though it *is* weird, come to think of it, that it thanks her at the end. Does it *actually* enjoy this job? Or is it like Eleven, just projecting a cheerful shell while it lives a second life somewhere in its gleaming white case? Well, Eleven, you got what you wanted: she's now considering the inner emotional lives of appliances.

When she opens the door again, relieved and sanitized—if

somewhat discomfited, mentally speaking—the corridor is both darker and more muffled.

"—so if you ask me," the android is saying, "it doesn't really matter. Dead is dead."

"It *does* matter, though," says a new voice. It's a thunderous voice, an earthquake of a voice. It's coming from somewhere deep in the two hundred kilos of furred muscle that is currently blocking the light in the corridor. A mouthful of black teeth appears, each gleaming shape longer than Sarya's fingers. "The suit says *she* killed Hood," rumbles the fur. "And anybody who could kill that guy . . . well, I just got a real bad feeling, that's all."

She has already met this terrifying intelligence, thank the goddess. This is *Mer,* who carried her up that freezing ladder like a toy when she first got here. She remembers him going on about freedom and gratitude and . . . food? She really wasn't in a good place to remember, emotionally speaking.

"Don't tell me: it's your *instincts* again," says the android. "How could this thing kill Hood?" he asks, pointing a black finger her way without bothering to look at her. "*You* couldn't kill Hood, from what I hear. Not for lack of trying."

Mer makes a big movement then, a huge rippling of fur and muscle that travels down every one of his—what is that, four?—no, *six* limbs. Four arms, two legs. Her Network unit would probably tell her that's a *shrug,* but without it the gesture is terrifying. He leans back, making it obvious that he is mostly chest. His enormous arms support his weight, while his legs appear to serve mainly as a kickstand. He flexes and scrapes talons against both walls. "I could have killed him, easy," he says. He pauses, tapping a talon against the floor like a nervous tic. "I just . . . decided not to."

The android folds his arms and looks at Mer without speaking.

"Anyway," says Mer, still tapping. "The suit claims she's Human, Roche."

Roche, that's it. Thank the goddess, now she can carry on a conversation because *hey, shiny guy* was not going to fly for long—and then the full impact of Mer's statement thumps her in the chest and raises the hair on the back of her neck.

The suit claims she's Human.

And now Mer's face, which was mainly teeth, sprouts dozens of eyes. They blink in waves and patterns, looking in all directions, and then every one of them focuses on Sarya. She grew up with a Widow, which means she recognizes a hunter when one parks its massive bulk outside her quarters and pins her with its predator gaze. But this is something more. These eyes don't match the rough and simple voice. They pierce her in ways she doesn't understand. Where her mother used fear to hunt, these eyes employ something even deeper. They hypnotize her. They speak to her, tell her to *come closer,* to *trust* them . . .

"Its registration says Spaal," says Roche, but his voice has become indistinct. It's somewhere far away, in a much less important place. "Perhaps the suit is confused. That happens with low-tiers."

The eyes blink in a wave from the center to the outside. Maybe it's her imagination, or maybe they are gazing at her with a curiosity more intense than anything she's ever seen. *Tell me,* they say without words. *Tell me everything.*

"Then how did she kill Hood?" asks Mer. He's talking to Roche, but his eyes are on her. His voice is distant enough to be irrelevant, like the silent roars of the lightning on the planet below.

Roche presents a theory and Mer rebuts it. Mer submits an alternative and Roche rejects it. Sarya hears nothing more than a gentle buzz in her ears. She is caught by the eyes, and there is nothing she can do about it.

And then she becomes aware of an expectant silence, as if she's been asked a question. She knows what it is. *So what are you?* Or something like that. She doesn't remember which one said it, which is odd because their voices are so different, but it doesn't seem to matter so much. She pulls herself up as if she's been underwater, but her mind responds slowly in the gaze of the eyes. Still, she forms her lie easily. She has lived her entire life under a false low-tier identity, and the phrases and signs come without effort. She can say, with awkward halts in exactly the right places, phrases like *please forgive your friend the Spaal* and *pardon, my tier is low*.

"I'm . . ." She takes a breath. "I'm Human."

And then she claps both hands over her mouth.

The dozens of eyes snap closed instantly, as if they are satisfied. Only a solitary pair remain open on Mer's face, down by the teeth. Unlike the rest, these host a simple, almost bestial expression.

Sarya is breathing hard through her fingers. Her eyes dart between these two witnesses, who are staring at her with expressions she cannot interpret. What the *hell* did she just claim? Did she really, in the presence of these strangers, say what she *thinks* she said?

"So you assert," says Roche, his voice now clear and present in the absence of the eyes, "in spite of the evidence of an extremely unimpressive Network registration, that you are *actually* a member of an extinct, highly dangerous species." He tilts his head with the click of multiple lenses.

"I thought a fake registration was impossible," says Mer. Without the eyes, he is a completely different intelligence. If she met him now, she would assume him to be one of those simple barely legal intelligences you see every day on the lower levels of a mining station. It's almost like he's two people in one.

"Illegal, yes," corrects Roche in a thoughtful murmur. "But I've never heard of anything that is impossible."

Sarya's heart rate is returning to normal. This isn't nearly the reception her mother warned her about. No one is trying to hurl her out an airlock yet, for example—though the fact that this seems like a victory may mean that her standards are lower than they should be. And anyway . . . she can still hear it in her head. *I'm Human.* A warm and delicious shiver rolls down her spine. So *that's* what it feels like. "Well," she says, feeling as if she is getting her blades back under her, "believe what you want."

"Then why are you registered as something else?" asks Mer.

Sarya shrugs, Widow-style, with fingertips in lieu of blades. "My mother did that," she said. "I don't know how."

"Was your mother also . . . ?" Even Roche seems unwilling to say the word. *Human.*

"My mother was a Widow," says Sarya.

The effect on the other two is exactly what she'd hoped. Now that the eyes are off her, she feels like she can direct the conversation where she wants it. The two glance at each other, probably communicating on some private Network channel. Mer's fur bristles, making him look even larger, and several talons scrape against the metal of the floor.

"A Widow," Roche says. "A Human, raised by a *Widow.*"

"Maybe she *did* kill Hood," muses Mer.

"Um," says Sarya, raising a hand. A question she had been considering in Eleven has returned to the front of her mind. "Speaking of Hood. Didn't he have a—"

And then Mer's head falls off.

Sarya shrieks a Widow obscenity and leaps backward into her quarters. The head comes after her, sprouting its own set of arms and legs and looking like a twenty-kilo eye-covered version of the furry behemoth currently crouched in the corridor. She has just decided that she is going to go down swinging when she is stopped by a full-throated roar.

"Watch it!" says Mer, fur and talons fully extended, his voice now shaking her room. "Do *not* hurt her."

Sarya stares at the small bundle of fur and eyes in front of her. So many eyes, all opening and closing and staring right back at her. "What . . . the *hell,*" she whispers.

"Oh, did I not introduce you two?" says Mer, leaning farther into her quarters, fur flattening. "This is Sandy," he says, gesturing. "My, uh, girl."

"Your . . . what?"

"My *daughter,*" he says. "Adopted. She doesn't talk, not out loud. Or hear. Crazy smart, though."

Sarya stares at the little bundle of eyes, feeling equal parts shocked and vindicated. She *knew* something was up. That whole time, there were *three* intelligences talking to her, two with voice and one with gaze. "Um," she says to the little furball. "Nice to . . . meet you?"

Sandy turns to her father, and a wave of blinks travels over her face.

"She says you're Human," says Mer. "Good enough for me."

"How would *she* know?" demands Roche.

"You're really not going to trust a tier three?"

"Speaking of falsified registrations—"

"Wait, you doubt *her* registration but not the Human's?"

"All I'm saying is, registrations can be falsified. We have proof right in front of us."

"Oh, so now it's *proof,* is it? I thought you were more cynical than that."

"I am, when it suits my purposes."

But Sarya is not listening. A *tier three.* There's no way. That's higher than her teacher back on Watertower, higher than Ellie who ran an entire orbital station. That's at least a dozen times her own intelligence—her own optimistic absolute-best-case estimate, not the pitiful one-point-eight on her registration. This little thing? But if that's true . . . how do you talk to her? How does one start a conversation with a tier three? Particularly one who can't hear? If only she had some kind of communication device—

"Um," she says suddenly, breaking dozens of gazes when her head snaps up. "Where's my stuff?"

"No idea," says Roche.

"Roche has it," says Mer at the same time.

"*That* is an utter—"

"Don't be like that, Roche. She *saved* you."

Roche looks up at the ceiling and produces a low grind that Sarya's Network unit would probably tell her is annoyance. With a click and a hiss, his torso slides open with a puff of cold vapor. He reaches inside himself, then holds both hands out in front of him.

Sarya has never been so glad to see a few grams of synthetic materials. She leaps forward and seizes her locket and earbuds, their freezing surfaces stinging her bandaged fingers. The earbuds are painfully cold when she slides them into her ear canals, but it doesn't matter because as soon as the tiny projector rests on her forehead where it should be, the world exists again. Information springs from all three of the people in her room and the hallway, names and tiers and public biographies and—goddess, the little one really *is* a three. Sarya stares at the mess of blinking eyes on the floor and wonders again: how does she fit that much brain in a head that size? But the eyes aren't staring back anymore; they are looking at Roche. More specifically, they are looking at Roche's other hand, and when Sarya follows the gazes she understands why.

There, in Roche's other hand, a pulsing and glowing sphere of light has spun into existence. It is a shimmering globe of Standard symbols, a blend of orange light and holograms, and anchored in the center is the phrase [**Error: Unauthorized User**].

"That's . . . mine?" Sarya asks uncertainly, watching the symbols spiral.

"Is it not?" asks Roche, cutting off the light show when he closes his hand. "Because in *that* case—"

"I mean, yeah," she says, holding out her hand. "*Obviously* it's mine."

She nearly drops the object when it is grudgingly placed into her palm, mostly because all the symbols floating around it make its size impossible to determine. She feels something cold and heavy rolling in her hand under all that light, something dense and maybe thumb-sized with an embossed logo on one side. "I just . . . I've never seen it before," she says, staring. But even as she says it, a memory flashes through her mind. She shivers.

The sphere turns white. "Hello, new user," says the device in a tinny voice. "Please identify yourself."

"How odd," says Roche. "To own something you've never seen before."

"What *is* it?" says Mer.

Roche takes a step toward Sarya, nearly stepping on a spellbound Sandy. "That," he says, pointing with a gleaming finger, "is a—"

"Help Article Number One: Welcome to Memory Vault!" says the device in a piercing voice, vibrating against Sarya's hand with each syllable. "Do you find your memories cumbersome to organize? Do you recall things you would rather not? With the Aivv-Tech Memory Vault, non-ideal mnemonic experiences will soon be a distant *memory*. Remove, add, rearrange, and edit your recollections to shape your ideal past. Store your extra memories for later reminiscence, or transfer them to loved ones to—"

"*Enough*, device," says Roche.

Mer scratches his head with a long black talon. "A box of memories," he says. "How about that."

Roche is still staring at Sarya's hands, every lens extended. "*That* is very highly regulated technology," he says. "Difficult to come by. Always interesting, if you can get them open. You see them occasionally in my line of work."

Mer is now scratching several other places. "What *is* your line of work?" he asks.

Roche performs a motion that Sarya's unit interprets as a [**shrug**]. "Stealing things, lately."

Sarya stands in her quarters, gazing into the slowly shifting symbols drifting over her hand. She *has* seen this before, she's sure of it. Slowly, wonderingly, she raises the glowing object to her temple. She can feel her pulse mounting as she does it, and sweat prickles her back.

"Authorized user detected," says the tiny voice. "Hello, Sarya the Daughter. Please unlock this device to continue."

She pulls it away and stares. The symbols have changed to blue, and the phrase [**Welcome, Authorized User!**] now slowly orbits. "It really *is* mine," she says softly.

"You'll need a viewer," says Roche, taking another step forward. "Memories are of course multisense, and *very* tricky to transfer. As my mind has been recently backed up, I volunteer. You unlock it, I will experience them and . . . well, I suppose we'll go from there."

"Why do you know so much about this?" asks Mer, now nibbling delicately at the point of a talon.

"When you've lived as many lives as I have, you learn a thing or two."

But Sarya barely hears this argument because she's hearing a different one: one from the past. Her mother's face fills her mind, clicking in annoyance and exasperation. *I do not remember, child,* says Shenya the Widow. She must have repeated that phrase a thousand times, in answer to a thousand questions. Sarya never understood it: *Mothers do not lie to Daughters,* that's what the proverb says, but how could her mother have forgotten so much? How could a mother not remember where her adopted daughter came from?

Unless . . .

She rolls the device over and rubs the corporate logo on the side. "They're not my memories," she breathes.

They're something better. They're everything she's always wanted to know.

TWELVE

Sarya has now been in her quarters for eleven consecutive hours and she has discovered a fundamental truth: obsession, it seems, is the key to sanity. She knows that because in all that time, she has barely thought about Watertower at all. A hundred times, possibly. Maybe not even that.

Unfortunately, in that same time she has also developed a killer headache. The spot directly above her left eyebrow throbs with her heartbeat, and every time she moves too suddenly it instructs her sharply: *don't do that.* She should probably sleep; she can tell from the softness of her room lights that the ship is deep in its night cycle. But how can you sleep when you are *so close?*

She sits on the lower of the two bunks, knees drawn up to her chin and arms wrapped around her legs. This is how Mother always liked for her to sit, in her *nest,* as she called it—see, and that is *exactly* the kind of memory she is trying to avoid. No. She is *here* now, in a bunk. She is now. She is alone, and she has no interest in useless reminiscence. She wants *those* memories, the ones locked in the Memory Vault. There it is, lying at the other end of the bunk where it was most recently thrown. She turned it to Network-only mode hours ago because the real light was annoying, but with everything off it looks small and black and naked. She moves, and its half-sphere of light snaps on instantly. It's orange, still displaying its last error message.

[Identity: *valid* (Sarya the Daughter). Key: *invalid*. Please assume the mindset used to lock this device.]

Sarya has, over the eleven hours, extensively interviewed the sub-legal intelligence inhabiting this device. She has asked questions, requested sections of its manual, argued with it, shouted at it, and thrown its tiny indestructible self multiple times. She has learned two things. Number one: she was right. The memories *aren't* hers. She's gleaned from the errors and warnings that they are not even her *species*. Which fits precisely with her working theory. And two?

She knows how to unlock it.

Unfortunately, this second piece of knowledge is entirely theoretical. To quote [**Section 51: Keeping Your Memories Secure**], subpart 4, paragraph 1:

*A double key is the only unique combination of identity plus mindset that will unlock a Memory Vault. In other words, to access the memories stored in a Memory Vault, the user must assume the same mindset that was used to lock the device in the first place. As mindsets can be difficult to reproduce, we recommend an extreme yet unique combination of emotions. To further improve key recognition, try adding a mnemonic phrase during the lock procedure (see [**Section 12**] for examples and other helpful tips).*

What this means, both encouragingly and frustratingly, is that she was *there* when it was locked. Her identity itself is half the key. Which means, in turn, that she must have the other half somewhere in this useless hunk of brain. There is a mindset somewhere in there, a *unique combination of emotions* that only she can provide, but it is lost in the wide wasteland of her own mind.

She clicks the worst Widow profanity she knows, one her

mother would have been shocked to hear, and jams the heels of her hands into her eyes. What is *wrong* with you, brain? Is it so much to ask, that you supply *one simple little goddess-damned memory?*

Of course, it's more complicated than that and she knows it. Sarya has long realized that her memories are divided into three basic categories. The vast majority of them are the regular kind: memories of school, of neighbors, of unkind classmates, of long afternoons in the arboretum, of the exploration of the lesser-known parts of Watertower, that sort of thing. They're not all pleasant, but they're all very humdrum. Typical. Then, below that, there is a second category. These are pale impressions of . . . somewhere else. They are insubstantial memories, so delicate that she can't even look at them directly for fear of destroying them. But they do not come from Watertower, she is sure of that. They are warmer than that, and louder. There is . . . well, if not *joy,* then at least something positive. But the third category of memories?

That's the nightmare fuel.

Unfortunately, category three is nestled mandible-to-mandible with category two. This is the reason she has to watch her daydreaming, because you don't dive too deeply into your childhood recollections if at any moment you know you could come across a horror. For example: start with a warm and flickering glow in something that looks like Watertower's arboretum. Add a circle of intelligences around this glow, each one laughing and talking. Throw in an amazing, mouthwatering smell—and a very specific image of glowing bugs wobbling through air. It's a wonderful image, and one she would love to dwell on . . . but then it goes and ends in blood. There are lifeless eyes, there is a deafening shriek that never ends, there is something cold and hard and chittering that drags her into darkness—

It only gets worse from there.

But it's not as bad as it could be. She hasn't awakened screaming for years now—well, almost *a* year. She's not even afraid of the dark anymore—anyway, no more than anyone else. Surely that's universal, though. Hasn't everyone awoken, sweat-covered, from a broken sleep? And then lay awake in a cold blackness so complete that it's impossible to tell whether your eyes are open or closed, trying not to whimper because of what happened last time? And then come to the horrific realization that a set of faceted eyes has been hovering centimeters in front of your face, watching you the whole time?

Isn't that just childhood?

"You know, I didn't have a childhood," says Helper's voice in her ears. "But if I did, I think I'd prefer it not to be like that."

Sarya rubs her eyes. Apparently she's been talking out loud again. "I don't remember saying your name," she says.

"Well, you never technically said goodbye *last* time, so—"

"And don't you have some research to do?" she says. She can't help it. Eleven hours of focus can erase anyone's natural civility—more so if you don't have a lot to begin with.

"Well, I finished *The Fall of Watertower,* which I think turned out pretty good. But I mean, I don't really know what to do with it. Because, you know, your friend . . ."

"My friend?"

"Well, she's . . . dead. I mean, she was on Watertower, and Watertower got blown up, so I figured, you know . . ."

Oh, right. The *friend.* Well, if the destruction of Watertower has a bright spot, it's that Sarya's web of lies has become far simpler.

"Sorry for your loss, by the way," says Helper. "Let me know if there's anything I can do to help."

The headache has been throbbing with every word, and this reminder of her former home has not helped. Probably it's a bad sign that her primary reaction is not sorrow but annoyance. Now she's going to have to come up with a brand new way to keep Helper motivated. Although now that she thinks about it . . . does she need to? It seems silly now, having a sub-legal caretaker intelligence doing research on legends when she has the real thing now, scarcely a blade's width away. The truth is locked in that goddess-damned Vault sitting over there. Yes, you, the light show. A smug-looking device if ever she's seen one, probably pleased that she's devoted every waking moment to it. Low-tiers love attention—don't they, Vault? Low-tiers adore this kind of thing. This one is obviously enjoying locking her out of her birthright, preventing her from making the greatest discovery since—

"What if I turn off the lights?" asks Helper.

Sarya's mouth, which had opened to tell Helper exactly what it could do with itself, closes again. Turn off the lights and plunge this room into complete darkness while she racks her mind for nightmares? Her first reaction is: that is a *terrible* idea. Her second, barely a second later, is that this might be the best idea Helper has ever had. "Do it," she says.

The total blackness into which she is dropped is, perhaps, more than she was prepared for. Her Network unit throws its usual pale lines over the walls and floor, but they don't do much to chase the blackness. They *emphasize* it, if anything, and her anger is quickly drowned in a rising tide of panic. But this isn't Sarya's first brush with darkness, and she knows how to deal with it. You keep your head above it, for one thing. And then you focus on something—something *real*. Like this splash of color, the orange globe of light lying at the other end of her bunk. Note the detail in its slowly shifting sphere of symbols. Think about how it came to be. It's all virtual, just the work of a tiny projector, but isn't it interesting how much effort her Network unit has gone to just to make it look realistic? Look at that slight glow on the underside of the upper bunk, the ripples of color on her clothing. It's hard to believe she is sitting in complete darkness right now, that if she took the little projector off her forehead she would be left in a void so perfect that—

Nope.

"How's that?" asks Helper. "How did I do?"

She is not about to admit this to the little intelligence, but its normally annoying voice is actually somewhat comforting in the darkness. "You . . . did great, Helper," she says, deciding even as she says it that this will be her absolute last attempt for the night. Then she'll have Helper turn the lights up a little, just enough to sleep. Hear that, mind? You'll get your sleep. You just have to do one little thing first. Just hand over that one teensy memory, whatever it is. It's in there, she knows it is. She'll just avert her attention, just sit quietly and wait, and the memory will just pop up like a bubble. See how clear you can be, mind? See how relaxed, how empty, how—

"I've been thinking," says Helper. "Now that my user is a little older—and, you know, I'll maybe be getting new responsibilities and stuff—maybe it's time for . . . a new name?"

The only thing that stops Sarya from ripping her Network unit from her head and flinging it across the room is the fact that she would be left, sightless and deaf, in utter darkness. Her second impulse, hot on the heels of the first, is not just to silence Helper but to reset it entirely. She could start from scratch tomorrow, if she really feels the need to be irritated. She progresses through a half dozen other notions, each more extreme than the last, and finally finds that she is just too tired to handle anything more than a simple dull annoyance. "A new name," she says in a dead voice.

"I mean, it could be anything you want," says Helper. "Anything at all. I mean, I'm just a random sub-legal intelligence."

"Anything?"

"Of course!" says Helper. "Or Ace. I mean, your choice."

Sarya stares into the darkness, at the little icon in her overlay that represents Sarya's Little Helper. "You want to be called *Ace*," she says.

"Well," says Helper more quietly, "I mean, if *you* want to call me that."

Does *every* sub-legal intelligence harbor secret desires and motivations? How long has Helper wanted a name? This *specific* name? It's stupid, of course. It's just a low-tier intelligence. But then so is Eleven, right?

"All right," she says. It's an easy win, and it'll give her some currency for future requests. *Remember that time I let you pick your name?* "Fine."

"Really?"

"Really. Sarya's Little Helper, set your name to *Ace*."

"And . . . pronouns too?" asks the former Sarya's Little Helper hopefully.

Why not. "Sure," she says. "Which ones do you—"

"*He*," says the voice instantly. "I've been thinking about this a lot, and I think definitely *he*."

"Okay. Sarya's Lit—*Ace*—set your pronouns to the *he* family."

"Ace here!" says the voice in her ears, sounding exuberant even for it—for *him*, rather. "Pronouns: *he* family! Nice to meet you! How can I, *Ace*, improve your evening?"

Sarya blinks at the eagerness in the small voice. How did she not think of this earlier? Just from a logistical point of view, if you want to keep a low-tier productive, wish fulfillment is a *whole* lot easier than keeping your lies straight. Especially if it costs you next to nothing.

"Well . . . *Ace*," says Sarya, dropping her voice to a more serious-sounding pitch, "I have something I'm working on here. And it is *super* important that I not be disturbed."

"All right," whispers Ace in return. "How can I, *Ace*, help?"

"Ace," she says, "the first step is very important. I need *quiet*."

"You . . . don't want to talk to me?"

Oh, for the goddess's sake, here we go. "Not you," she says, thinking quickly. "Everybody else."

"Ohhhh," says Ace, his voice picking back up. "That's different."

"This is an important job, Ace," she says seriously, "and it's one that only you can do." Technically, this is true. It helps when the truth lines up with what you want. Gives you conviction. "I need you to block *all* communication to this room," she continues. "All night. Maybe put a warning up on the hatch? Use your imagination. Something about *danger*."

[Death to all who enter] appears in the darkness, danger-colored. "Like this?" asks Ace.

Maybe a little over the top, but sometimes you need to give a lower intelligence some freedom. "Sure," she says. "Just put that up and—"

[Trespassers will be dismembered] appears on a second line.

Okay, well, too much enthusiasm is better than too little. "That's . . . good," she says. "It shows that we're, um . . . serious."

[And their families tracked down and slaughtered.]

It's always a battle, finding the line between encouraging and extinguishing initiative. "That's . . . great," says Sarya. "Let's just stop it there, though, okay?"

"Got it!" says Ace. "Only . . . what about Sandy, though?"

Low-tier the little intelligence may be, but Sarya will never get used to its abrupt left turns. "Um . . . what *about* Sandy?" she asks.

"Well, she's waiting outside in the corridor right now."

A shiver runs through Sarya's body as she stares at the faint outline of the hatch. As if sitting in the darkness baiting bad dreams wasn't bad enough, there's been someone outside her door the whole time. Someone far smarter than she is, someone whose motives she can't possibly understand. "How long has she been out there?" she asks.

"A while," says Ace. "She gave me the idea to turn off the lights."

And suddenly Sarya is forced to reevaluate the last few minutes. "Wait, *what*?" she says, sitting up. "You've been *talking* to her? Okay, keep that door shut, because this is *definitely* something we need to discuss. You will tell me when—"

The hatch slides open. A small figure crouches in the light of the corridor.

"Ace?" Sarya hisses.

"Sorry!" says Ace. "I don't know what happened. She made a really convincing case."

"I am your owner, Ace. *I* give you orders."

"I know! But she—"

[Hello], says Sandy in simple blue symbols. She blinks something incomprehensible, then pads into the room.

The door slides shut, and now all Sarya can see is a blue icon approaching in the darkness. The click of disembodied talon on invisible floor is eerie enough, but not nearly as bad as feeling the tug on the edge of the bunk. Is she—oh, goddess, she is literally climbing in here. Sarya scoots herself back into the corner. There is a *tier three* in her bunk. What in the eight heavens—

[**Can I have this?**] asks Sandy, and Sarya hears the crinkling of a food bar wrapper.

"Ace?" says Sarya. "Tell her—"

[**Don't worry**], says Sandy. [**I can read your lips.**]

"Oh," says Sarya, blinking in the darkness. Apparently all those eyes are good for something other than hypnosis. "Well then . . . sure?"

Judging by the noises that now emanate from the other end of the bunk, Sandy does not eat the food bar. She *devours* it. She may be small and delicate-looking in the light, but if Sarya didn't know better, she'd think a predator had just caught something struggling and foil-wrapped at the other end of her bunk. Good goddess, has this little intelligence never eaten before?

A tiny belch squeaks in the darkness, and then the silence resumes. Orange gleams begin to appear in the darkness as, one by one, Sarya's Network unit simulates a reflection on each of the eyes currently fixed on Sarya. The effect of dozens of glimmers hanging in utter blackness, each one blinking or fluttering or squinting, does nothing to relieve the tension in the room.

[**You are trying to open your Memory Vault**], says Sandy.

"Yeah," says Sarya, as lightly as she can manage. That's not much of an intuitive leap, really. There's only one other object in this room and it's a Memory Vault; does it really take a tier three to guess what's going on? "Yeah," she says again, determined to maintain control over this conversation. "Turns out it's harder than it—"

[**I know how to open it**], says Sandy.

Sarya stares at the words. "You . . . what now?"

[**Do you want the answer?**] asks Sandy. [**Or the long version?**]

Sarya could not have imagined such a small creature could have so many eyes. Their reflections gleam in the blackness, perfectly and creepily rendered by her Network unit. Can they still hypnotize her, even in darkness? Is this all happening of Sarya's own free will? "The answer," she says firmly.

[**Pain without fear**], says Sandy instantly.

And suddenly Sarya finds herself sitting in complete darkness staring at what was, perhaps, Shenya the Widow's favorite phrase. She's heard her mother say it a thousand times, in a thousand scenarios. She has been disciplined with it. She has been forced to memorize stories and epics that illustrate the concept. And now that Sandy has said it, she realizes it fits a certain description she's heard recently.

An extreme yet unique combination of emotions.

"There are—there are thousands of Widow proverbs," Sarya says carefully. "What made you pick that one?"

[It is obvious.]

"Oh." Sarya watches the eyes in the darkness, wondering if every conversation with a tier three goes this way. "Well, now I guess I need the long version."

[First I researched Humans], Sandy says. [Then I researched Widows. Then I thought about how they're different. Then I thought about how they're the same. *Then* I realized that they're more the same than different.]

Even if you are not sharing a darkened bunk with a tier three, it is odd to hear your own thoughts in someone else's words. Sarya has spent her whole life ruminating on her divided heritage, and she has come to the same conclusion. "Keep going," she says, intrigued.

[*Then* I made lists of what both species value, and I compared the lists and took the overlap. Then I put that aside and I read all the proverbs and fairy tales and legends I could find.]

"You've . . . really spent some time on this."

[Not really. Both civilizations were developed by simple minds. Once you derive their core values you can skip around a bit.]

"Oh." So this is what that laundry drone felt like, back in Watertower's backstage.

[And the answer, I think, is in your name.]

"My name?" says Sarya. *"Sarya?"*

[The other part], says Sandy. **[The Daughter.]**

Again, that flash of unpleasantness, that irritation at the fringes of her mind. Sandy continues to make more sense than Sarya wants to admit. "Explain," she says.

[Widows—and Humans—assign titles based on *worthiness*], says Sandy. **[You have to prove yourself. For example, the rest of the galaxy calls the whole species Widows, but that's not accurate, is it?]**

"Right," says Sarya. "Most of us—*them*—aren't Widows. You have to be female, and you have to have, um . . . mated."

[And killed your mate, if I'm not mistaken?]

"That's . . . part of the deal, yeah." She's always been of split mind about that part, and now to hear Sandy say it rather than her mother—well, it sounds less magical, that's for sure.

[More importantly, the juveniles are not Daughters when they hatch, are they?]

"No," says Sarya. "Most never become Daughters, actually. They have to—"

[Survive.]

"Um . . . right."

[So they must *earn* the title of Daughter. Or die.]

And now, staring at a collection of blinking gleams in a black room, Sarya knows what it is to be taken apart. Without any effort at all, Sandy has found her most vulnerable spot. Sandy understands her more deeply than she understands herself. Sandy sees into her past, extrapolates her future, lays bare her dreams, and uncovers her deepest shame. Sarya the Daughter is a skilled liar, but she finds that she cannot lie to Sandy.

"That's . . . right," says Sarya softly.

Sandy says nothing. She watches from her dozens of vantage points.

Sarya can feel the cracks spreading across her carefully crafted surface. "My name is Sarya the Daughter," she says carefully. She places one word after another, focusing on the sound of each one. "I'm named after a hero—like, five, actually." A little cough. A bitter little laugh. "Seems like every Widow legend is named Sarya, right? I mean, you've read them, you know. And yeah, I *do* have the . . . title. So I can see why you'd think—" She swallows. "But, I mean . . . I'm *not* a hero. I didn't even earn—I didn't have to survive. I wasn't hatched in a nest full of, you know, killer siblings. I've never fought for *anything,* let alone my life. I've never *earned* anything." And she's a liar. And she's weak. And she's full of fear. And. And. And. She's as far from Widow as someone could possibly be. "My mother," she says, and swallows. "My mother named me Daughter when she adopted me, but—"

[Does that sound like a Widow?]

Sarya feels her mouth slowly close. No, not really. And her mother was Widow out to the exoskeleton. And yet . . . no. Come on, she wouldn't forget something like that. No, Sarya the Daughter is—and always has been—a fraud. Her eyes burn, and for once she is glad of the darkness. *I am Sarya the Daughter,* says the trusty mantra in her head.

But what does that even mean?

The blinking gleams are now mere centimeters away from her face. But she can't seem to pull back—or rather, she doesn't *want* to pull back. *You're fine where you are,* say the eyes. *The bunk is already warm here, it will take too much energy to move, and anyway isn't this comforting?* Yes, how has she never noticed that these eyes are the very definition of comfort? They hearten her, they tell her that she is someone of worth. They say that she can trust Sandy, that she is safe here, that she can open up and search her mind for what she needs to know . . .

You can't think of anything in your past that might have been . . . trial-like? asks Sandy. Or maybe she didn't, because Sarya is not sure if she's read the message via Network unit or she's just . . . thought it. *An ordeal? Something from which you could only emerge a Daughter . . . or dead?*

Sarya has no idea how much time passes through her dark room as she stares into the dozens of gleams. They blur and cross and join and superimpose as her gaze relaxes and moves off into the distance, somewhere beyond the little furball on her bunk.

Out there, tattered ghosts of memories drift through her consciousness. They show her things that she hasn't thought of in years—if ever. She sees darkness. She sees light. She experiences terror and joy. And always, all around her, are the eyes.

And perhaps she lost consciousness or her sense of time was disrupted, because now her hatch is suddenly open. An eye-stinging bar of light lies across the floor and up the wall, and it gilds the small furry form that stands in the doorway.

[**You will sleep now**], says Sandy over her shoulder.

And as soon as Sarya reads the sentence, it becomes true.

THIRTEEN

A little girl trembles in the dark. She usually sleeps when the lights go out, but now it's been a long time since she saw light and she only sleeps when she cannot possibly avoid it. She can't swallow; she's so thirsty she can't even feel the ache of her hunger.

Do you wish to call me Mother?

She didn't know! Oh, she didn't know, she would have answered differently if she had known about the darkness and the pain and the *thirst*. She would have said *no*, she would have said *please no, goddess, no*—

But she didn't. She said *yes*.

She seizes her doll and buries her face in its silky surface. It smells like the monster that haunts her when she is least prepared, the demon she *thought* she wanted to call Mother—but it's all she has. She counts the doll's legs against her face: *one two three four five six seven eight*. Now she does it again, as fast as she can. *Onetwothreefourfivesixseveneight*. She does it again, slowly, this time using one for each verse of *The Song of Sarya*. All the Saryas went through this, even Sarya the Destroyer, and they all won. They won their lives.

Oh, but even that is not worth this kind of thirst . . .

There was a game she used to play . . . before. Back when things were different. She remembers something bright and crackling and warm and beautiful, and she would stand by the burning thing and gaze into its light, with her back to the cold night. And the game was this: how long can you go without turning to look behind you? It gets harder, the longer you go. Because the more you ignore it, the more you become unshakably convinced of a single fact.

Something is in the darkness *with* you.

She sits up and nearly falls over, but she clutches the doll tightly until the dizziness passes. She can't see Mother, but you don't need to see Mother to know she's there. You can smell her. You can hear those little clicks her mouth is always making. And so the little girl draws her knees to her chin, the doll compressed against her chest, and wraps her arms around her legs. She is not safer this way, but she *feels* safer.

"Do you wish to call me *Mother?*" asks the darkness.

No, screams every part of the little girl. She said she did, yes, but she didn't *know*, she didn't understand the difference between stories and real life. And now everything is dark and everything hurts—

"Yes," whispers the little girl. The word scrapes her dry throat on its way out.

A low hiss fills her room, and now the little girl doesn't have to guess where Mother is, because she feels the sudden hardness of jointed limbs wrapping her body. She knows better than to move, and does not even cry out when her hair is tugged, painfully, by razor-sharp mouthparts.

"And on the eighth day," whispers the darkness, "she emerged, gleaming in the light of the moons."

The little girl mouths the words with cracked lips, because she knows that story. Shenya the Clever took eight days to emerge, Suukyu the Insane took eight days to emerge, everyone except for

Sarya the Destroyer took eight days, *she* will take eight days, *one-twothreefourfive—*

"I am your birthplace," recites the voice. "I am your proving ground. I am your siblings, who hunger for life. I am ravenous hunger, and I am killing thirst. I am Suffering herself. And I say to you who have been gifted life: do you deserve your gift?"

"No," whispers the little girl.

"You who have been bestowed with consciousness: do you merit that which you have received?"

The little girl cannot make a sound, but she can move her lips. *No,* say her lips.

"You who possess these unearned gifts: do you wish to purchase them?"

The little girl is so exhausted, so far beyond anything in her experience that she can barely even think. Her greatest desire and her greatest fear are crushed together; she is wrapped in something that could be Mother and it is wrapped in darkness or maybe it is *made* of darkness or maybe it *is* the darkness. She doesn't understand it, and she doesn't understand her own reaction to it. She wants to scream at it, to kill it. She wants to bury herself in it, where no one can find her. She wants to run and hide, she wants to burn this monster in light and fire—but she doesn't do any of these things. Instead, she does something she's never done before. With confused fingers, she reaches out into the blackness and feels for a face. It is right there, even closer than she thought, and it does not prevent her from touching its hardness and sharp edges. It's not at all like her own face.

"Yes," she says to the face.

"Then these scars," says the darkness, "will be your most precious possessions."

And then there is light.

This is the first light the little girl has seen in days, and she hungers for it even as she slits her eyes against it. She can see the thing in the darkness now, because it has transformed from an invisible terror into a nightmare. Every hard line gleams with white light, every angle quivers in the twisting shadows on the walls. The little girl is trapped, held in the center of a whirling storm of light and shadow.

"Do you know what this is?" asks the nightmare.

After so long in the darkness, the little girl couldn't look away from the light if she wanted to. She tries to swallow, then tries to say *no,* but nothing happens each time but pain.

"This is my past," says the darkness. "And your future—and if not yours, then that of your people. These are the memories I created while in your world; I have cut them out and stored them. In this device is the only record of its location. Thousands of cultures would pay dearly for it."

There are more words, but they are so chopped with violent clicks that the little girl cannot quite make them out, even with her ears centimeters from those quivering mandibles. They sounded like . . . *my own most of all.*

"And so we come to the final night of your trial," says the darkness after an endless moment. "This is the night you fulfill your destiny, whether that be life or death. If you become my Daughter, I shall become the very definition of Motherhood. I shall love whom you love, and I shall kill whom you hate. I shall guard you with my life, and when the time comes to lay it down I shall do so laughing. For my life is *mine;* I have purchased it, and I may do with it as I please. And what is mine shall be yours, little hatchling, and what is yours shall be mine. Your people shall become my people, and mine yours. I shall relinquish my ancestral right to vengeance, and your future—and that of your people—shall rest on *your* blades, not mine." A hiss rises, low and soft. "If you live."

The little girl does not care about these words; they go on and on and all she cares about is the pain and the thirst and the fact that here before her is all the light that is left in the world. The legends are swirling in her head, tangling in her slowed thoughts and the words of the demon, and they have all become the same story. Something received, or something purchased. Something given, or something won. And if there is more to it than that, she quite literally could not care less. All she understands at this moment is that she must do one thing.

She must live.

"Are you prepared?" asks the darkness.

The girl gazes into the light. "Yes," she whispers.

"Can you face pain—" And then the voice breaks. "Can you face pain without fear?" it whispers.

And now the little girl raises her eyes from the glow to the faceted eyes, because she has never heard that voice before. It has become so hard to focus, but with effort she can make out that gleaming face in the blackness. She licks rough lips with a rougher tongue and then sucks in a quivering breath. "Yes," says the little girl.

A tremor runs through the hard limbs all around her. "Say it," says Shenya the Widow.

"I am Sarya the Daughter," says the little girl. "I face pain without fear."

FOURTEEN

Sarya the Daughter sits on the floor of a void-black cabin, legs crossed, the very image of stillness and calm. This is where she woke, sweating and screaming, to Ace's concerned words in her ears. This is where she paced, reliving the dream again, as the tears burned her face. Because it was *not* just a dream, she is absolutely certain of that. It was as real as the filthy utility suit on her body. That was her *mother*. Her mind hid that memory from her just as effectively as a Memory Vault, but it was there the whole time. She has no idea how to react to this, no idea where to direct these emotions. But it doesn't matter, because even in the darkness there is one bright and burning thought.

"I am Sarya the Daughter," she says out loud. And *no one* can take that away from her.

According to her Network unit, she still has more than an hour until *Riptide*'s day cycle begins—which is good because now she knows: these sorts of things require darkness. The orange half-sphere of holograms lying on the floor in front of her is the only source of color in the room, and here in the center of the floor her Network unit doesn't even bother simulating its dim glow on the walls. She considered turning its actual lights back on to more accurately re-create her dream, but she decided not to. Something in her tells her that this is the time for darkness, not light. And now she knows that there is nothing in the darkness that can hurt her. It wasn't the darkness itself, after all.

It was her own mother.

And *that* brings thoughts that are confusing at best, but she has decided that they must wait. Now is the time for action, not reflection. Now, she feels her scars like lines of fire across her skin. Her mother said they would be her *most precious possessions*— and perhaps they are. But either way, she's about to gain one more. Because she is Sarya the Daughter, and she faces pain without fear.

She takes a deep breath and leans forward to pick up the Memory Vault. Its holos change to white as it examines its new situation. "Hello, new user," it says. "Please identify yourself."

She brings the device to her temple. The holographic sphere engulfs her head, flashes as it measures her, then changes to blue. "Identity established," it says for the hundredth time. "Hello, Sarya the Daughter. What would you like to do?"

She opens her mouth as she has a hundred times before . . . but this time will be different. This time she knows what must be done. "Device," she says quietly. "I would like to unlock you."

"Very good," says the Memory Vault. "Where will you be transferring the memories contained herein? Before answering this question, please refer to my user's manual."

But Sarya has practically memorized the user's manual. It is a spectacularly dry read, but obsession can make anything fly by. In particular, she has spent a lot of time on the segment titled [**Section 105—Advanced Capabilities**]. The first ninety percent is a lengthy piece of legalese that boils down to a simple message: the user agrees that the manufacturer is absolved of all liability if said user is stupid enough to try what follows. The last ten percent is what she's about to do.

"To me," she says. "I want . . . I want the memories."

"To clarify," says the Memory Vault. "You would like to attempt a cross-species memory transfer?"

Sarya takes a deep breath. "Yes," she says.

"Mandatory warning number six hundred: this device is legally obligated to inform you that even same-species memory transfer carries a substantial probability of error, the likelihood of which is dramatically exacerbated by cross-species transfer. Among the possible outcomes are permanent personality alteration, confusion, temporary difficulty forming new associations—"

"I understand," says Sarya, ignoring the small voice in the back of her mind that says wait, actually maybe she doesn't. It says that maybe this isn't such a hot idea, that maybe it wouldn't be such a big deal to let Roche help her. Or Eleven, at least. Maybe it *was* a dream. Or maybe, says that part of her mind, grasping desperately, *maybe* it's just useless recollections and she's risking her own sanity for memories of a vacation—

Yeah. Because *that's* the kind of stuff that Widow mothers hide in encrypted Memory Vaults, locked with the blood of their daughters.

"Furthermore," continues the device, "the memories in question have been stored with the highest security available on this device. They will be erased after this procedure, whether it is successful or not."

So. She has one all-or-nothing shot and a decent chance of coming out brain damaged. This is stupid.

"Your response to the following questions will be recorded and notarized," says the device. "Do you absolve AivvTech of all responsibility in the following operation? Please state your consent as a complete sentence."

"I—" says Sarya, and stops. The swirl of symbols fades through several configurations as the machine awaits the rest of her sentence. "I absolve AivvTech of all responsibility," she says.

"Consent duly recorded and notarized as per Network requirements," says the Memory Vault, the glyphs in its holographic sphere shifting into a new configuration. "Do I have your permission to access your mind? Please state your consent as—"

"Yes," says Sarya.

"Please state your consent as—"

"You have permission to access my mind."

"Please assume the original mindset used for the lock procedure."

And it's go time. Sarya runs her fingers over the two objects lying in her lap. One is a medical device, the kind with a sub-legal intelligence that is capable of basic cross-species first aid. The other, though—it's cold and heavy when she picks it up. Roche let her borrow it when she pounded on his hatch and requested something that would, quote, *hurt a lot*. She should not have been at all surprised when he detached one of his own fingers and handed it to her.

It's an industrial grinder, he told her cheerfully. *I'm told it's excruciating.*

She thanked him, refused his too-eager offer to act as operator, and returned to her room where she began doing dry runs. This is all well rehearsed now—except for the important part, because she only gets one shot at that. It goes like this. Legs folded, check. Medical device *here,* in easy reach, check. Vault held to her temple, elbow on folded knee, check and check. She feels the manufacturer's logo digging into her skin and resists the impulse to move it; she won't care about minor discomforts in a few seconds. Her room is invisible; she could be outside the universe itself, for all she can see on the other side of those swirling glyphs. She finds herself trying to focus on the holos as they orbit through her line of sight, anything to take her mind off the free hand that is bringing up Roche's finger. It makes *real* light, unsimulated light, a flickering danger-color that merges with her Network unit's own automated imagination. HOPE THIS HURTS, say the orange letters that follow it like a cloud of insects. *Very funny, Roche.*

And then there are no more steps.

She hears the sound of her own pain before she feels it, that strangled heave of a convulsing diaphragm. And then it comes, waves of it rolling down every nerve in her arm. A section of her skin has sunk under Roche's disembodied caress, a wet rectangle ground half a millimeter below the level of the surrounding area. Her breathing quickens as she watches the blood begin to well up and drip down her arm, and she can feel the sweat begin to prickle her body.

"Please assume the mindset used for the lock procedure," says the tinny voice against her temple.

Can you face pain without fear?

And suddenly her resolution wavers. She *is* in pain, and she is not afraid . . . is she? Anger begins to burn at the foundation of her mind. *Pain without fear,* says the anger, *that is what you told me, Mother, you said it a thousand times and you said you never lied but here when it counts—*

But then some other part of her mind speaks up, and Sarya is shocked to hear it speak in her mother's voice. *You say you are not afraid of this little tickle,* says Shenya the Widow. *How brave of you! How proud I am. A little dribble of blood and you are not cowering in fear!*

But this is not her mother. Her mother wouldn't say such things. This is *her,* this is her doubts and fears laughing at her.

You are adorable, says her shame. *Why, if I didn't know better—*

Don't say it.

I would say—

Don't fucking say it.

You are no Daughter.

From somewhere deeper than any voice, deeper than language itself, Sarya's rage erupts, screaming. She is small again. She is staring into her mother's face, its every dark surface gleaming and outlined with white light. She can feel that prison of chitin around her, those smooth-jointed limbs surrounding and crushing her, and she is *furious.* And once again she hears it before she feels it: the sizzle of her own skin being atomized into the atmosphere of the room. She does not pull away; no, she digs in. She watches that rectangle sink into her arm and smells her own flesh and clamps her jaw on the cry that has clawed its way up from her vocal cords. The mocking voice tries to make itself heard but it doesn't stand a chance against the rage that burns like a sun within her. Her doubts and fears are garbage in an incinerator—no, in a supernova. *I am Sarya the Daughter,* says the anger. *I was not given life, but took it. I wrested it from the jaws of death itself, and it is mine.*

And with this thought in her teeth, she crushes Roche's finger into her arm and drags it through her flesh. Muscle rips and nerves vaporize into a spray of gas and sparks and now Sarya's eyes are locked to the glistening surface of her own bone, set in a devastation so complete that she no longer knows if she is clutching the Memory Vault or if her fingers have fallen dead but she will hold this pain in her mind until the end of time if it will prove one thing.

She is Sarya the *Daughter,* and she faces pain without fear.

"Congratulations!" says the Memory Vault, its globe blazing a violent gold around her head. "Your key has been accepted. Transferring memories now."

The following is greatly abridged from the original Network article, in accordance with your tier.

NETWORK FOCUS: HAPPY BILLION DAY!

Fewer than a million years ago, the Network celebrated its one billionth Networked star system. Every Citizen species—nearly one and a half million species in total—took part in the festivities, from one side of the galaxy to the other. One *billion* Networked star systems, each one representing a disc of civilization over ten billion kilometers across. All together, these systems add up to an incredible *eight cubic lightyears* of Networked space.

That's one heck of a party!

It's difficult to imagine exactly how large eight cubic lightyears is.* The best comparison is the one we have already made: eight cubic lightyears is enough space to fit *one billion solar systems*. Therefore it may seem counterintuitive to your limited mind that this massive space is actually a *very* small percentage of our galaxy. It's stunning, really: for every one of those eight cubic lightyears of Networked space, there are *one trillion* cubic lightyears of non-Networked space—and that's just in this one galaxy.

Now that party doesn't seem so big, does it?

CONSIDER LIGHTSPEED

In order to fit this massive idea into your limited mind, let us approach it from another direction: lightspeed.

When a photon leaves any one of the stars in the Network, it is traveling rather quickly: nearly three hundred thousand kilometers per second![†] And yet, at that speed it still takes more than eight minutes to reach the orbit of the average Type F terrestrial planet. In another four hours, it will reach the edge of Network coverage in that solar system. There it begins its interstellar journey. In a few decades, it could reach the nearest of the more than one billion Networked

* For tiers under four.
† Don't get any ideas: this is *far* more quickly than the highest legal speed in Networked space.

solar systems.* If these neighbor systems are near the galactic edge, that same fragment of light will take fifty thousand years to reach the galactic center and twice that to reach the far edge. And if *that* doesn't impress you, consider that it still has a twenty-million-year journey ahead of it to the next galaxy of comparable size, and nearly fifty billion years to reach the edge of the observable universe.

Four minutes to your planet. Fifty billion years to the edge of the universe. Feeling small yet?

The scale of reality is yet another reason that Network Citizenship is so vital to every species within it. Within the Network, threats to an individual species are small, understandable—and most important, easily avoided. We know what lies within the eight cubic lightyears of the Network. But what lies outside that, in the vast darkness of the universe? The answer is simple.

We don't know.

* Of course, if light traveled via Network it could be there nearly instantaneously.

FIFTEEN

[AivvTech Mnemonic Restoration]
  [Stage 0]

  #

  [Welcome to the AivvTech Memory Vault mnemonic restoration process! I am sub-legal intelligence *name not set* and I am here as your guide to the past. I will be observing your responses and crafting your personalized transfer process to give you the best possible experience. My goal is to keep emotional trauma to a minimum.]

  [We will begin with a random memory, and I will use your responses as a baseline to order the rest.]

  #

#

Shenya the Widow crouches on a forest floor, a sharp and gleaming shadow in the warm half-light. She is surrounded by giant plant life that her implant identifies as *trees,* listening to the rustling of their red and gold *leaves* as they fall, one by one, to the ground. The place is a tumult of color . . . and surprisingly beautiful.

[See this, Shokyu?] she says internally. [My mother told me that happiness is made of moments like these.]

[I've never heard you mention your mother before], says Shokyu the Mighty, the small intelligence in her Network implant. It chose its own name some years ago, and Shenya the Widow has always found its choice amusing. It is her own jest, of course; a sub-legal Network implant cannot *earn* a title. But one may be lenient when dealing with small intelligences.

[I would not expect you to understand the complex bond between Mothers and Daughters], says Shenya the Widow, heading off her implant's analysis before it happens. She imagines the hard-edged face of her own mother as she says it.

But the little intelligence cannot be stopped. [I wonder why you're reminiscing so much], it says. [Perhaps you're getting old. Or lonely.]

Shenya the Widow has had much practice in ignoring her implant's impudent questions, and she does so now. She is *not* old, she is barely in her second century. And she is *not* lonely. She is relaxed, she is carefree, she is lightyears from the pressures of civilization, and she is doing what she loves. *And* she is being paid for it! What more, quite honestly, could any Widow ask for?

"Hello?" gurgles a muffled voice beneath her. "About done here?"

[Uh-oh], says Shokyu the Mighty. [It's intelligent, and it speaks Standard. This means paperwork.]

Of *course* it is intelligent, little idiot. Its obvious intelligence is the reason Shenya the Widow visited it like a thunderbolt from the treetops. And of course it speaks Network Standard; in all her travels Shenya the Widow has never met an intelligence who does not. Even out here, lightyears past the frontier of Networked space, one should expect to meet Standard speakers—if one meets anyone at all. No, there are stranger things about this creature than its intelligence and its language. The fact that it has only four limbs, for example: two upper and two lower. The fact that it is disgustingly soft, inside out from a Widow perspective, with the skeleton on the *inside* of its horrible pale flesh. Look at it, small and defenseless, not even a meter tall when it was standing. It stares at her with gleaming golden eyes under the white tuft of hideous growth atop its head—

—TRANSFER INTERRUPTED—

[Unexpected memory collision. Adjusting parameters . . .]

\#

"Oh, hello," *says Observer from two mouths.* "It's you."

"I know you, Sarya the Daughter," *says an Observer.* "Though I haven't seen you in a long time."

\#

[Parameters adjusted successfully. For best results, please do not dwell on existing memories during transfer.]

—TRANSFER RESUMING—

The small being stares at her, its gold eyes wide and unblinking. It is leaking red fluid from several places—quite a bit, it seems. Most likely, it is moments from death. She wonders what species it belongs to and misses, for easily the sixty-fourth time, the simple access to information that a Network connection would provide. That may well be the worst part of these long voyages, the absolute lack of contact with anyone and anything. But no! That is not loneliness, as her implant might suggest. One may call it isolation, if one must call it anything at all. *Loneliness* implies weakness, and Shenya the Widow is, well . . . Shenya the Widow.

[What do you think it is?] she asks, prodding the squishy little figure with the flat of a blade. Perhaps the ship Librarian is also unfamiliar with it. That would be convenient, for even Shenya the Widow becomes nervous when the Librarian goes hungry for too long.

[You should have asked it before you killed it], says Shokyu the Mighty.

"You know, I've known you were here for quite some time," says the thing beneath her. It blinks its golden eyes up at her, seemingly quite cheerful for someone impaled and bleeding out into alien soil. "I saw you come in from the tunnels."

"How many know of this place?" Shenya the Widow asks quietly.

"Oh, no sense in getting the galaxy in an uproar *just* yet," says the figure conversationally. "Though I *may* have some ideas on that. So for now I'm the only—"

The rest of the sentence is lost in a gurgle. Shenya the Widow rises after the thing is done and cleans her blades in the rustling vegetation. The discovery is now hers, and once the Librarian has fed, Shenya will no longer have to fear for her life every time she opens its containment. That's two rivals with one blade, as the saying goes.

[Killing won't help your loneliness], says her Network implant.

[I did not kill it for *therapy*], snaps Shenya the Widow, hoisting the body onto her thorax. She releases a disgusted hiss as its skin touches her beautiful carapace, leaving it smeared with oil and goddess knows what else. [I killed it for purposes of research . . . and profit.]

[Ah, so you didn't enjoy that.]

[I enjoy everything I choose to do. But in this case, I also have a little one to feed.]

[Do you think feeding the Librarian makes you feel less alone?]

Shenya the Widow hisses as she turns back toward the ship, preparing a devastating reply. If she hadn't grown so accustomed to the constant voice in her head, she would have treated Shokyu the Mighty to a factory reset long ago.

"Whoops!" says a familiar voice. "You've accidentally killed one of Me!"

[Did you hear that?] asks Shokyu the Mighty, instantly and with more than a little fear attached. [You just killed a high-tier.]

This is one of the few times in Shenya the Widow's life when her implant's concern may be entirely warranted. She drops the body and whirls into stance four, low. She backs herself against one of the largest trees in the area and raises every available blade into a quivering fence of death. The tree is large, easily a meter in circumference, rough brown and massive enough to stop a good-size projectile from taking her out from the back. She sends out an ultrasonic ping, sifting its echoes for clues.

"I'm right here," says the voice. "If You would stop killing Me for a second, we could *oh, for My sake—*"

Shenya the Widow is in the air as soon as she identifies the source and has silenced the second speaker as quickly as the first. She crouches over its body, blades buried eight centimeters in the soil beneath it. She fires another ping, but there are too many of these trees. She can detect the crunching sound of dry vegetation being crushed, and what sounds like soft speech, but both are too low for details. They could be coming from anywhere. In fact, after listening for a few seconds she begins to think that they are coming from *everywhere*.

[This is it], says Shokyu the Mighty. [This is how we die. Pointlessly. Painfully, probably—although I'm sure you won't mind that at all.]

"It's not very neighborly," whispers the voice from beside the nearest tree.

Shenya the Widow whirls, but sees nothing but overgrowth.

"Nor very pretty," says the voice, now behind her.

Widow reflexes respond, but again there is nothing to see.

"It's hungry, maybe," suggests the voice, directly above her. She cocks her head, but her nearly spherical field of view reveals nothing. Even in infrared nothing stands out; despite the cooling day, everything around her is nearly the same temperature.

"It doesn't seem to be eating Me, though," it muses.

Shenya represses a shudder. *Eat* a thing like this! No, she does not understand how the Librarian does it.

"Excuse Me," says the voice from somewhere behind her. She cranes her head in a slow half circle but sees nothing. This invisibility is beginning to annoy her.

"If I come out will You promise not to kill Me again?" it says from ahead and to her left.

"I just feel like that's starting off on the wrong foot," it says from above.

"Or *blade*, if You prefer."

"You'll be perfectly safe."

A few seconds ago Shenya would have laughed at the thought of danger from these miniature creatures . . . but the question has come from more directions than she can easily count. She stands slowly, withdrawing her blades from the rapidly draining body beneath her. Their edges, she notes with satisfaction, are still in perfect condition. This thing's bones are nearly as soft as its disgusting flesh.

"You have to say it," says the voice. "You have to say, *I promise not to kill You anymore*."

[Just say it], begs Shokyu the Mighty. [We don't *have* to die here, unless this is a stupid Widow honor thing.]

Shenya the Widow sends out one last ping, which shows her nothing. "Fine," she snaps in Standard. It annoys her to speak anything at all, but one does what one must when one is lightyears from the Network. "I pledge not to kill You anymore . . . today." It seems sensible to place parameters on the oath.

A rush of expelled breath comes from eight different directions. "I appreciate it," says the small figure that has just stepped out from behind a tree. It blinks its golden eyes, the muscles in its face working overtime to push different parts into different configurations. So much effort, and it only makes the thing more hideous. "So anyway," says its voice in a conversational tone. "What was I saying?"

It takes her a moment to realize that the figure in front of her isn't moving its mouth—it is simply watching her with those gold eyes—but of course the voice is now coming from behind her. She checks herself mid-whirl, lowering her blades as if that were her plan all along. There is an identical individual behind her, which now makes four if she counts the two she just killed.

[Spooky], says Shokyu the Mighty, sounding much perkier.

[When I desire your opinion on a matter], says Shenya the Widow internally, [I shall ask for it]. Externally, she composes herself. "You were claiming this . . . discovery," she says out loud, after an embarrassing length of time hunting for the right Standard word. It has been a while since she has spoken aloud.

"Of course," says a voice above her, from the trees.

"Yes, congratulations on that!" says another. "You are now the second person in the galaxy to know My secret."

[A secret?] says Shokyu the Mighty. [That sounds promising. Or profitable, if you prefer.]

"You *are* a person, are you not?" asks one more small figure who has just strolled around her tree, upper limbs behind its back. It leans forward to examine her with its gold eyes.

[It wants to know if *you're* high-tier], says Shokyu the Mighty. [Or a group mind. Or both, maybe.]

[You certainly have a talent for stating the obvious], says Shenya the Widow. Outwardly, she has already swept into the act that has made Shenya the Widow famous corporation-wide. "Of course I am a person," she says smoothly.

"Of course It's a person!" says a chorus of the same voice.

"No offense intended," says the one in the tree above her.

"You just can't assume, in this day and age."

"So many species zipping around," says another, demonstrating by running through the leaves with its arms out. "One can't keep track of who's become a person and who hasn't."

Strange sounds are now emerging from all around Shenya the

Widow, as this creature displays its displeasure from every body it has available.

[**Nice job**], says Shokyu the Mighty. [**You've got Him.**]

"Yes," says Shenya the Widow, turning slowly to keep as many bodies in sight as possible. "It is quite . . . disgraceful."

"Anyway!" says the nearest individual. "My name, rendered down into primitive mouth noises, is *Observer*."

"Hello, Observer," says Shenya the Widow. "And I am—" She pauses, reaching for something other than *Shenya* or *Widow*. "That is, you may call Me—"

[***Darkness***], suggests her implant. [**That's a good group mind name. Now you're glad I keep a copy of the registry, aren't you? Or . . . *Silence* is available, looks like. *Scariness* is taken, sadly.**]

"Hunter," finishes Shenya the Widow. She never takes her implant's advice if she can help it, and she never admits to it when she does. Hunter is a nice name, and it fits her. For a moment she imagines it as reality: billions of bodies, sharing billions of thoughts, all distilled down to the name *Hunter*. This is the part she is now playing.

"Hunter," says Observer musingly, several of Him tapping fingers on the lower parts of their awful faces. "*Hunter*. Interesting. I wonder why I have never heard of You."

Shenya flicks her blades in a Widow shrug. "It is a large galaxy," she says.

"Not related to the Predacious Array, are You? Next sector over?"

[**Searching registry . . .**], says Shokyu the Mighty. [**Interesting. It's a plant that covers an entire planet. Some theorize that it's intelligent.**]

"We are not related," says Shenya out loud. "Though We do . . . run into each other on occasion."

"Oh, how nice," says Observer. "Tell Her Observer says hello, will you?"

"Of course."

"Anyway," says Observer. "Let's talk about this, er . . . *discovery* of Yours."

"Yes," says Shenya the Widow. Silently and not so subtly, she flexes every blade on her body.

[If you're thinking about murdering them all], says Shokyu the Mighty, [it'll never work.]

[Thank you. I can see that.]

[I mean it's just a matter of logistics. You probably can't even see most of them.]

[*Thank you*], says Shenya the Widow. She is annoyed to admit that her implant is right, but she does relax her blades. She chooses an Observer at random. "My employer is able to offer you a finder's fee for your part in the discovery," she tells it. "Shall we say . . . one percent?"

"Oh," says a different Observer, blinking. "How . . . generous."

"My employer assures me that this is a rare find," continues Shenya the Widow in her gentlest voice. "I am sure that it will be profitable as well, in the right blades. Your one percent could be worth more than you imagine."

All around her, Observers are shuffling their feet as if uncomfortable. "Here's the thing," says one, scratching the white growth on its head. "I'm not sure You've realized what this discovery actually . . . *is*."

[Say *it's a lost colony from an extinct civilization*], says Shokyu the Mighty. [I mean, it has to be, right?]

[That is a ridiculous guess], Shenya the Widow fires back. [The commission said we were looking for a research vessel.]

[Which this is not.]

[It does not follow that it is a *colony*, or from an extinct civilization.]

[It's clearly a habitat, and it's *way* outside Networked space. Plus, this guy seems really excited about it.]

[Fine. It is a colony. I will even grant that it could be a lost colony. But the rest of your theory?]

[What else do group minds care about? They're always going on about Who has reached maturity and Who has gone extinct. It's like Widows and obituaries.]

[Why, you insolent—]

"You're a little slow, aren't You?" asks an Observer, cutting into the internal argument.

Shenya the Widow stares at the speaker, blades twitching as she decides whether she is, in fact, going to murder it.

"Totally understand!" says another. "I get that way too, when there are only a few of Me around."

"Like now!" says the voice from behind her. "I've got barely a couple hundred bodies here, and let Me tell You, I've almost forgotten what real intelligence is like."

"I am . . . not slow," snaps Shenya the Widow. "I was simply . . . thinking a moment. And yes, of *course* I know what this is. It is a—" And then she sighs, because she will never hear the end of this. "It is a lost colony, from an extinct civilization."

A silence grows, as many pairs of golden eyes watch and judge her. And then:

"You *do* know!" says an Observer.

"But You can't possibly know which one," says another. "Go ahead. Guess."

[No clue], says Shokyu the Mighty. [You could try Freewheelers or Silverteeth, maybe. There are a few other extinct species from around here—but none that anybody actually misses.]

But one fortunate guess per day is luck enough. "I do not," admits Shenya the Widow.

"What You're standing in right now," says an Observer, turning with its arms outstretched, "is the only settlement of Humans in the known universe."

Shenya stares at this last speaker, mandibles stilled into silence. In her head, a seismic shift in priorities is taking place.

[Well, that was literally the last thing I expected], says Shokyu the Mighty, [And just so you know, you are coming across as *extremely* threatening right now.]

Shenya the Widow is aware, but she can't help it. Her blades are at full extension and quivering, and her mandibles are a blur. A hot, quivering, magnificent fury is building in her thorax, a true Widow rage. *The Humans*.

But Observer, it appears, cannot read Widow body language. "Follow Me," says one of Him, turning away. "You should really see this."

Shenya the Widow stands frozen for whole seconds before shaking herself free of her fantasies. "Lead on," she says quietly. Oh yes. Lead on, strange one, and Shenya the Widow will follow. She will shadow You to the end of the galaxy if a living Human is at the end of the journey.

CHAPTER

SIXTEEN

[AivvTech Mnemonic Restoration]
  [Stage 1]

  #

[Good news! I have now constructed an emotional baseline. That means I should be able to predict each memory's effect on you with a medium degree of certainty. As many factors are currently in play, I will be shifting the order in which I transfer memories. But don't worry! You'll recall them chronologically.

[In Stage 1, you will experience memories that I believe you will find neutral. When we finish these, we will move on to Stage 2.]

  #

#

[I'm sure someone will be quite happy to see you], says Shokyu the Mighty.

Shenya the Widow wobbles in her ship's cargo bay, the inebriant in her system making it much easier to admit that her implant is right. The Librarian *will* be happy to see her; she is absolutely sure of it. Look at it there on the containment monitor, its silvery surface expressing—well, expressing nothing at all. But surely on the *inside* it is feeling just as celebratory as she is. Or it will be. Or something. Can a Librarian become intoxicated, as she is right now? What if she fed it this inebriant bar she is currently chewing; what happens then? Oh, but no. Why waste a good bar when she has something better? Oh yes, my little one, you will like this very much indeed.

The Librarian's containment hisses open on her command, filling the cargo bay with a heavy metallic drone. The Librarian itself does not change appearance at the sight of Shenya the Widow, but then that is difficult to do when one is both suspended in midair and compressed into a sphere by a ten-gravity containment field. Shenya gazes at her reflection in its mirrored surface and wonders if it is uncomfortable in there. Well. Even if so, she is sure *this* will make it all worth it.

She begins by releasing a few leaves into its field—careful not to brush the edge with her blades—and watches them whip upward to the sphere at ten times their natural acceleration. They lie against its silver surface, and then sink beneath it without a ripple. The process is invisible from here, but within that shining mass the leaf is being taken apart into its constituent atoms. Every measurable quantity is being learned and memorized. The Librarian will know the structure of this leaf so well that it could re-create one from scratch, given the right materials, and no scanning process in the galaxy would be able to tell the difference.

Sometimes it will do exactly that, when it is bored. Shenya has opened the hatch in here to find body parts or plant life on the floor, as the Librarian has apparently created them for its own entertainment and then pushed them out of its field. This one has never resynthesized anything particularly dangerous, but she still checks its monitor before opening its containment. A corporate legend tells of a ship that returned to dock on autopilot, with nothing aboard but a Librarian and a swarm of flesh-eating insects. Some theorized that the explorer in question had shipped with a particularly spiteful Librarian, but in Shenya the Widow's opinion the explorer's first mistake was having flesh in the first place.

The low metallic ringing grows more intense with each leaf, and Shenya the Widow twitches her mandibles in a smile. Shokyu the Mighty may dispute it, but she knows that it is responding to her personally. A Librarian this small certainly doesn't breach legal tier, but it is intelligent enough to know where its food comes from. "Mother's here," she croons in a gentle singsong, releasing a leaf of a different species. "Of *course* you're glad to see me. Who else knows what you like? Who else brings you treats?"

[**Oh, you're a Mother now?**] asks Shokyu the Mighty.

[**Watch yourself**], she says gently, a very clear warning in the attached emotions.

[**I'll never understand why you find this so appealing.**]

Shenya the Widow lets a long moment pass before accepting this change of subject. [**Of course you won't**], she says, the inebriant rocketing through her system nearly causing her to add *little idiot* to the end of the message. In fact, one moment as she reviews the transcript to see what she actually said. Let us see . . . the Mother comment, the warning . . . the subject change . . . and no, she did not. But no, little idiot, you do not criticize a Widow's use of titles while you wear an unearned title yourself. Consider yourself fortunate you deal with Shenya the Widow and not her own mother, or you would have been shredded long ago for daring to—

And then a blade brushes the edge of the gravity field, and Shenya the Widow is extracted from her reverie with the screech of chitin on metal. She panics for only a split second before getting her other blades set for a mighty pull—and she is free! Weaving, she examines herself for damage. Her body is flawless as always, a shining testament to the prowess of Shenya the—

"Why, you little tyke!" she says unsteadily, staring at a notch in the end of her best blade. "We don't eat Mother!"

[This is *exactly* what I'm talking about], says Shokyu the Mighty.

Well, perhaps there is something to the corporation-wide aversion to Librarians. Not everyone grows back, after all. Most of the other corporate explorers refuse to leave dock with a Librarian on board, let alone journey lightyears—but then they share the same handicap as her implant, don't they? They are not Widow. They are of weaker peoples, and they prefer to return to corporate with holds full of trash. But Shenya the Widow knows that this is letting fears interfere with profits, and that is why she is the corporation's sixth-most-profitable employee. Or she was, three years ago, when she left Networked space. That is . . . thirty years Standard? She cannot even do relativistic math when sober. Anyway, that is beside the point, which is this: why return with sixty tons of carbon, hydrogen, oxygen, and so on when one can simply store the *patterns* and discard the material itself? The size of one's cargo hold makes no difference when one travels with a Librarian. Everything it consumes, from soil to minerals to living things, will be organized and stored in its mind. And if corporate truly wants a physical example of a particular item to study, why, they can ask it nicely and it will make them one.

She has lost count of the number of loads she has brought this Librarian in the last few days, but the feeding never loses its appeal. She always offers the silver globe one item at a time, working her way up in both size and novelty as if she's serving it an elaborate multicourse meal. Today, she moves from leaves to complete plants, to a few crude tools she scavenged—which the Librarian loves, judging by the noise level—and finally the *pièce de résistance*. She lifts it up from the floor, where she's kept it hidden as a surprise.

"Hello!" Shenya the Widow says in her singsong, supporting the severed head with two blades and moving the small jaw with a third. "My name is Observer, and I am extremely annoying."

She can see the head's reflection in the silver surface of the Librarian, its gold eyes half shut and its white hair stiff and brown with dried fluid. The ringing grows louder, and the reflection distorts as a small mound forms in the perfect sphere. She is always pleased when this happens. The Librarian is naturally quite fluid, but it takes great strength for it to shift its shape in the titanic grip of a ten-gravity field. When it reaches for her like this, Shenya knows that she has something good. Something novel. And in her business, novel means profitable.

Additional blades lift random body parts for feeding. "Please, enjoy my hideous skin-covered legs!" says the head in the voice of Shenya the Widow.

"I apologize," the head continues when the legs are gone, Widow blades working the small jaw up and down. "Normally I have two arms, but your mother could only find one."

"Uh-oh!" it says when the arm has sunk beneath the Librarian's surface. "Who's ready for my scrumptious torso? *You* are? Here it comes!"

The Librarian is nearly shaking the bulkheads with its call, clearly pleased with the meal. In fact, it has continued to reach for her even after it has absorbed the largest parts of Observer, a fact which would make her nervous if she wasn't on her third—fourth?—inebriant bar. Instead, she is proud. Why, you could not have done that at the beginning of this voyage, little one! Mother has your gravity field nearly maxed, and yet you can move! Oh, little one, we must play a game!

Inspired, she lowers the head out of sight, then back, for a quick game of hunt-the-prey. She does this twice before realizing that something is wrong. The hump in the silver surface, the place where the Librarian is straining toward her—it has not moved. She glances at the notch in her blade and clicks uncertainly. But if the Librarian is not reaching for Observer's head . . . does that mean it is reaching for *her*? She flicks an unsteady Widow smile toward her own reflection. "Why, little one!" she says. "Have you finally acquired a taste for Mother?"

[**For the Network's sake**], says Shokyu the Mighty. [**Just give it the head.**]

But the head is not the problem, little idiot. In fact . . . it pains her to think, but is *she* the idiot? Is it possible that, this whole time, the Librarian was not yearning for her little treats, but for *her*? Does Shenya the Widow now find herself three and a half years into deep space, alone with a Librarian who has very nearly outgrown its containment and which now hungers for her own beautiful body?

Her appetite for entertainment now gone, she raises the head and allows the field to tear it from her grasp. She watches the flesh flatten and the golden eyes widen in the massive grip of the gravity field, but the joy is gone. The eyes stare at her as the whole hideous mess sinks, backward, into the singing metal.

And the hump does not disappear.

[**If I could shudder**], says Shokyu the Mighty, [**I would.**]

Shenya the Widow will never admit that she is repressing a shudder of her own. [**I have never understood the revulsion at Librarians, personally**], she says lightly, but she is troubled. She backs away one step, and the small distortion does not change. But still, says her intoxicated mind, there is a large difference between a slight shape change and an actual *escape*. [**Librarians are quite useful**], she continues, determined not to allow her implant to witness her discomfort. [**Did you know the best surgeons in the sector are Librarians?**]

[**And yet I note you had *me* installed the old-fashioned way. Perhaps you don't trust them quite enough to let one dissolve your head?**]

The truth is, Shenya the Widow does not. In fact, during her early career one could say she was actively hostile to her Librarian—or at the very least, treated it no better than a sanitation station. But then something happened to change the mind of Shenya the Widow forever. She returned from a particularly long voyage to find an unfamiliar ship in dock at corporate. This was not unusual; when missions last a century, the odds of any two explorers being docked at the same time are low. It was the ship itself that was unusual—and its crew.

To begin with, it was the most beautiful ship she had ever seen: a silver blade that flashed like lightning in the night. But upon inquiry, she was shocked to learn that it was both made by and crewed by one gigantic Librarian. In a very literal sense, *Blazing Sunlight* was its own ship. It was made of the same amorphous metal here in front of her, but the size of an Interstellar. She remembers her awe at this being that had gained so much knowledge about the universe that it could produce—that it could *be*—its own starship. Reactors, gravs, sensors, anything an Interstellar could possibly need, all produced when needed and absorbed when not. And unlike her own little Librarian, this one far exceeded legal tier.

Shenya the Widow, corporate wheeler-and-dealer that she was, lost no time in introducing herself to the ship. After a few moments of difficult conversation—it was not the most talkative of intelligences—she became aware of something that unnerved her greatly, that made her realize that perhaps she did not quite understand how the universe worked. This gigantic Librarian—which she had never seen before in her life—knew her very well. It knew her journeys, it knew what she had found, it knew what she had brought back. It knew, she registered with a shock, everything that her small Librarian knew. Of course she knew they were both Networked beings, but this was something beyond that; this was as if they were parts of the *same* being, two cells in a Networked mind that spanned the galaxy. That was when she began to wonder: could, perhaps, the entire Network be described this way? Could one think of it as a gigantic mind that lies atop the galaxy like oil on water, its scattered drops running together or separating as—

[**Watch it!**] cries Shokyu the Mighty.

Shenya the Widow whips her blades to her body, staring at the silver pseudopod that has grown out from the sphere. It extends farther, trembling, easily eight centimeters out . . . now twelve . . .

sixteen. She fumbles for the manual controls with wayward blades, her sedated mind still very capable of imagining her ship being eaten from the inside out. She finally maxes the gravity field, but the limb only shortens slightly under twelve gravities. Panicking more than she would ever admit to her implant, she stabs a second control, and the continuous drone is cut off when the hatch slams shut.

She hovers a blade over a third control and watches the seal between the twin hatches. There is an automatic system in place, but she doesn't trust it. If she sees even a hint of silver between those doors, the whole inner chamber is going straight into the void. It will be difficult to explain to corporate—and still more difficult to explain to any giant Librarians she might meet—but better that than a hungry flood of metal on the loose. She has no intention of arriving back at headquarters as nothing but a pattern in her own Librarian's memory.

She watches the interior feed for a full minute. Nothing but a perfect sphere, floating in its gravity field. [**That was odd**], she says. [**It has never shown a taste for me before.**]

[**It still hasn't**], says her implant.

And then, even in her slowed mental state, Shenya the Widow understands. In her peripheral vision, which extends nearly to the back of her head, a pair of eyes stares at her from the darkness of the common room. And the hatred of Shenya the Widow—for a few moments dormant under the innocent joy of feeding a dismembered Observer to a Librarian—is rekindled. A blade scrapes down the closed containment hatch, drawing sparks from the metal and a flinch from the Human. Ah, my Librarian, my shining one and the joy of my hearts. You want a Human, do you? Fear not, my little one, for you shall have one.

But you will need to wait your turn.

CHAPTER

SEVENTEEN

[AivvTech Mnemonic Restoration]
   [Stage 1]

   #

   [You're doing great! I have observed some complex reactions
in your emotional state, but it should reassure you to learn that
this is perfectly normal. However, to err on the safe side, I will
now proceed with several Stage 1 memories of shorter dura-
tion.]

   #

   [Initiating memory transfer . . .]

   #

The Human is screaming, clutching one of its upper appendages with the other. It is folded up on the floor, its stubby lower limbs pushing it as far back against the cargo bay door as it can go. Drops of a bright red fluid dot the deck in a scattered trail back to Shenya the Widow.

—TRANSFER INTERRUPTED—

[Unexpected memory collision. Adjusting parameters . . .]

#

It hurts, but the unfamiliarity is worse than the pain. Everything is hard here, hard and dark and a demon lives here. It stalks around this place and clicks and hisses at her and she screams for her mother and father, but for the first time in her life no one comes. There is only the thing in the darkness—

#

[Parameters adjusted successfully.]

—TRANSFER RESUMING—

Shenya the Widow crouches in the center of the deck and examines the small figure. Her hatred of its symmetrical four-limbed form, bred into her since she was but a Daughter, has been subsumed into . . . *annoyance*. Yes. It is actually quite difficult to hate when one is this exasperated—and could there be anything more irritating than that goddess-awful racket that is coming from the wet hole in that head? Actually, as the stench reminds her, there certainly is. For example: the fact that it has just finished soiling the floor with its waste *when there are two perfectly good sanitation stations on this ship.*

Three and a half years to go. *Three and a half years.* There is absolutely no way she will be able to stand this thing for that amount of time. It is laughable to her that she ever thought she could. Was she inebriated? Well . . . most likely. But even if she locked it in the cargo bay, even if she could persuade the Librarian to produce some sort of food for it, even if it learned to use a sanitation station instead of the floor—*look at it!* Look at it leak on the floor, even now! That red liquid continues to soil her perfectly clean deck—

"*Why,*" hisses Shenya the Widow, "do you not *stop the leakage?*"

[Perhaps it can't], says Shokyu the Mighty. [And perhaps you should do some research before continuing with your Widow discipline methods.]

Shenya the Widow hisses softly, deciding if she is going to speak further or just end the thing's life now. She began intentionally speaking aloud as a drunken experiment, as a bet with her own Network implant. *Can a Human learn Standard?* Was the question, but so far the answer has been a resounding *no*. She should have given up days ago, but Shenya the Widow does not easily admit defeat. That, and it seemed a waste to be blessed with the galaxy's only captive Human and not run at least a *few* experiments on it. But now she is sober, and within her burns a mighty annoyance. Wager be cursed! If this *thing* is going to continue scurrying and squeaking and cowering and soiling the floor on a daily basis, well, this experiment will be coming to a very final close, and very soon.

And then the screaming transitions from piercing to painful.

"*Enough,*" hisses Shenya the Widow, unfolding to her full height. Yes, enough is enough. Into the Librarian you go, you disgusting *Human.* She stalks toward it, blades out, fully expecting to have to catch the slippery thing when it scrambles away from her.

"No!" shrieks the Human, staying where it is. It clutches its wounded appendage and leans forward, as if to give more force to the word. "No!"

Shenya the Widow stops dead. [Was that . . . Standard I just heard?] she says in her head.

[Looks like I lost a bet], says Shokyu the Mighty. [Perhaps you should publish this fear- and pain-based curriculum.]

Shenya the Widow watches the small thing carefully. "So you *can* learn," she says out loud.

[*Raising Your Human: A Guide to Training Your Offspring with Fear*], says Shokyu the Mighty.

"But you heard it as well, did you not?"

[*Secrets of Cross-Species Child-Rearing: A Terror-Based Approach.*]

"If you have better ideas for disciplining vicious aliens, I am listening," snaps Shenya the Widow. "My mother actually removed parts of me as a method of discipline."

[That's the mother with whom you shared such a joyous relationship?]

"It is," hisses Shenya the Widow.

[Far be it for me to judge the parenting techniques of another species], says her implant, [but if I'm not mistaken, your pieces grow back.]

Shenya the Widow taps her damaged blade against a mandible with an audible click. Fortunately they do, or she would be left with a Librarian love bite for the rest of her life. "True," she says. "But just because I grow back doesn't mean—"

And then her instincts flatten her to the deck. An object flies through the space her head recently occupied, ricochets off the bulkhead behind her, and bounces to a stop on the floor. Shenya shifts her gaze from the object to the Human, amazed.

[Did it just throw its foot covering at you?] asks Shokyu the Mighty.

Shenya the Widow is nearly too shocked to reply. "I . . . believe it did," she says.

[Let me guess], says Shokyu the Mighty. [Now you're going to have some Widow fun with it before it goes into the Librarian.]

But Shenya the Widow does not respond. She examines the small figure. Even if it were not a Human—and the name alone brings her internal fluid pressure up—it would be a hideous mess of a being. Between its general pudginess, its skin wrapping, and the various fluids it seems to produce nonstop from *everywhere,* it is the least attractive thing she has ever seen. And yet . . . do not the proverbs say that the carapace tells only half the story? This repulsive little thing attacked something larger than itself, something it had no hope of defeating, and it did so while wounded. *That,* to a Widow, deserves some thought.

"No," hisses Shenya the Widow, softly.

[**Well then, your experiment in motherhood continues**], says Shokyu the Mighty.

Shenya the Widow rattles. *You go too far, implant.* "Do *not* use that word with this—this *thing,*" she hisses. "Unless you wish for a factory reset."

[**All right, fine, we're babysitting**], says her implant, seemingly unaware of the seriousness of its position. [**So let's entertain it. I don't have any local data on Humans, but . . . what do Widow juveniles like to play with?**]

Shenya the Widow decides to let it go. As annoying as her implant is, it is not so annoying as an implant who cannot remember the last decade. "Wounded prey," she says, warm memories of childhood surfacing.

[**And here we are without a single dying animal.**]

But Shenya the Widow is inspired. Without another word, she takes a quick skittering trip to her cabin. She travels with few belongings, which means it is mere seconds until she emerges with a bundle under two blades. The Human watches her reappear with what Shenya would swear is a baleful look in its eyes. It appears to be prepared to attack again, which warms Shenya's hearts.

"Let us see what we may do with this," she says, rolling out the bundle on the floor.

[**I have never seen you wear clothing**], says Shokyu the Mighty.

"That is because I am not a juvenile," she says. *Little idiot,* she does not add. Two blades gently lift a small piece of cloth. It is a deep and shimmering black and it brings back memories that she will never share with anyone.

[**Baby clothes?**] asks her implant. [**Swaddling, that kind of thing?**]

"We are not *swaddled,*" says Shenya the Widow, holding the cloth up to the light and looking for holes. "Only a few of us even survive long enough to meet an adult."

[**Environmental hazards, I assume?**]

"Each other."

[**I see.**] Her implant pauses for a moment. [**Again, I don't judge. So if not swaddling clothes . . . mating clothes? Just a guess.**]

"You are correct," says Shenya the Widow, stroking a cloth in gentle reminiscence. "Each one stained with the lifeblood of a different male, given at the height of its ecstasy."

[**I . . . understood we were talking about mating?**]

"We are," says Shenya the Widow. "But now you know why we are called Widows."

She waits for the next question, the one that will force her blade, the one that will finally result in a factory reset for her implant. *If you have mated, then where are your children?* But her implant, for once in its existence, is silent.

It is then that Shenya the Widow makes a decision. With a smooth motion, she gathers up the cloth and stands. She gazes at the tiny form, which appears to have fallen asleep from exhaustion. Its other foot covering is already off, apparently prepared for use as a second missile. She will never admit it, but it is this image that forces its way into her hearts.

"It wouldn't survive eight seconds in a nest of newly hatched Widows," she hisses quietly.

[**I shudder to think**], says Shokyu the Mighty.

#

[**Aw**], says Shokyu the Mighty. [**Now aren't you glad you didn't murder it?**]

Shenya the Widow watches the tiny Human crouch against the wall of the common area, surrounded with the contents of a tool bag. A small doll watches beside it. It is made of a black and silky material, and its many-limbed physiology is something that a Widow might recognize. The Human is intent on its task, stacking the tools in various ways and then demolishing the piles in fits of violence and giggling. After each act of destruction it glances toward the Widow as if to judge the effect on her.

"I think she is becoming comfortable with me," remarks Shenya the Widow, twitching her mandibles in what another Widow might see as a motherly gesture. Even the increased light of the common area—shifted for the Human's benefit—cannot dampen her pleasant mood.

[I take it you're referring to its current lack of absolute terror?] says Shokyu the Mighty.

"I believe that is what I said."

[I see you've also—somewhat arbitrarily, I note—assigned it a gender.]

"Just a convenience."

[I've long noticed that *female* is your default], says Shokyu the Mighty. [You seem to think that everyone you meet is a female until proven otherwise. Not every species has a female variant, you know. Not even most.]

"And *I* have long noticed," says Shenya the Widow, "that you are becoming more argumentative in your middle age."

[I'm well within my functional lifespan, and it's my job to mention facts as they are relevant.]

They watch the tiny Human for a few moments in silence.

"See?" says Shenya the Widow, gesturing toward the figure when a particularly tall stack of tools crashes to the deck. The Human chirps and smacks its hands together several times as it looks to Shenya the Widow for approval. "Look at that. She is too intelligent to be a male."

[Now *that's* just offensive.]

"Don't blame me, blame the covenant that raised me," says Shenya the Widow with the wave of a blade. "But it should please you to learn that I hold several views that would be considered scandalous by my . . ."

She trails off as a package of adhesive rolls across the deck to wobble and fall at her feet. She looks up to find those strange tricolored eyes looking directly at her. Black inside brown-gold inside white. Shenya the Widow has been wondering how Humans communicate emotions without mandibles, and her current theory is that it's the eyes: their size and shape, those mobile lines above them, that fluid they leak sometimes. Disgusting, but quite a lot of material to work with.

She lifts the roll with one delicate blade and shows it to the Human. "Adhesive!" she says, enunciating very carefully. She says it twice more. The Human does not repeat it, but holds out a small pudgy limb toward her. Slowly, carefully, in a manner she judges least likely to startle the tiny thing, she rolls the tape back toward it. It watches the roll return to tap gently against its foot, then looks up at her and makes some sort of noise.

"Do you think that horrible sound is . . . laughter?" muses Shenya the Widow. "Some indication of happiness?"

[One would hope so], says Shokyu the Mighty. [Otherwise this is a terrible game.]

#

Shenya the Widow crouches, her limbs forming a cocoon of softened blades. She waits.

She feels a tiny touch, and then what she has come to identify as a minor laugh. A *giggle*. She ignores it. She knows the thing touching her is moist and covered in horrific blood-filled *skin,* but somehow that does not disgust her quite so much as of late. The delicate touch comes again, from two limbs this time, and harder. Again, she ignores it. Finally it comes a third time, with all the force a twelve-kilo organism can provide. This time Shenya the Widow unfolds like a black and gleaming blossom—*slowly,* slowly, careful not to injure the little one with a razor edge.

The Human shrieks and runs and falls, then scrambles to its feet only to fall again. It is making that sound again . . . some kind of indication of joy, she is almost sure. If it were not so similar to its sounds of terror it would be easier to tell the difference.

With slow, exaggerated movements, Shenya the Widow pursues her prey. She makes sure each step clacks against the bare floor and hisses gently so the little one knows right where she is.

The juvenile runs around a bulkhead corner and waits, still giggling.

"Where is she?" hisses Shenya the Widow in exaggerated Standard. "Where did she go?"

A small head pokes out around the corner, the strange three-colored eyes gazing straight at her, and then pulls back with another giggle.

"Could she be . . . up here?" she asks, extending herself upward to check the cabinets in the upper bulkhead. More giggling. Could she be . . . over here?" she asks, folding herself to look in the space directly across from the child, who is nearly collapsing with joy. "Could it be—"

[This is ridiculous], says Shokyu the Mighty. [It's right *there*.]

"Ah," says Shenya the Widow, turning away in a show of utmost dejection. "Perhaps she has exited the airlock and perished horribly. Then I shall *never* find her."

A shriek behind her nearly sends her through the hull. She whirls, blades aloft, very nearly ending the life of the tiny figure shadowing her steps. The juvenile leaps up and down, oblivious to its narrow escape, striking its tiny forelimbs against each other. Shenya the Widow consciously relaxes each joint one at a time, beginning at the ends of her many limbs and working her way inward.

[Close call], says her implant.

And now a Human has wrapped her arms around a Widow's lower extremities, giggling, while the Widow watches with complex emotions. Though she has moved on from unadulterated revulsion, an embrace is something different from a touch.

"All right," she says gently, glancing around the common area as if afraid someone might see. "That is sufficient." She softens her blades before attempting to peel the little one off her carapace.

The child hides her face against the smooth expanse of chitin. She chirps, then makes a contented sound that vibrates directly to Shenya's hearts.

[I'm not sure I know how to tell you this], says Shokyu the

Mighty, [but it's possible that you are dying. Your biochemistry is doing some very strange things.]

[I am not dying], says Shenya internally. [I am simply feeling . . . unwell.]

[I hope it's nothing that Humans can catch.]

Shenya the Widow clicks her mandibles in absentminded agreement, but her thoughts are already elsewhere. Deep in the hidden recesses of her hunter-killer brain, certain chemicals are being manufactured and released in concentrations strong enough to kill many species, and indeed even many Widows. Shenya the Widow is unwell indeed . . . and she is embarrassed to find that she almost welcomes it.

The change has not been nearly as upsetting as she always imagined it would be. It began with her dreams. She used to have normal dreams, the everyday slaughter-dreams that every young Widow is expected to have. But now she has found that the farther her ship progresses in its inexorable journey home, the less lethal her dreams become. Now it is a common occurrence for her to wake with blades soft and a mind empty of murder and mayhem . . .

And worst of all, she doesn't mind at all.

The Human has run away again, chasing one of the holograms that Shokyu the Mighty once suggested as playfellows. They were a wonderful idea, but she will never admit it. Shenya the Widow watches her stumble around the deck with a strange feeling in her hearts.

[I'm afraid for you], says Shokyu the Mighty.

[And why is that?]

[Because it's almost time], says her implant.

Shenya considers, for a brief moment, pretending that she does not understand. But her implant, annoyingly, would see right through her.

[You don't *have* to give it to the Librarian], says Shokyu the Mighty. [You can put it in the cargo hold with the food bars.]

[*Her.*]

[Of course, *her*. But you know you won't care, post–Memory

Vault. You'll probably *want* to get rid of it. It will be like that little thing from the water world. What was that, two missions ago?]

[Three], says Shenya the Widow. [And that was a *pet.*]

[The point is, the problem was solved. You spent the whole voyage worried that corporate wouldn't let you keep it, and then after you excised your memories you didn't care anymore. It will be the same this time. It may feel wrong *before* you do it, but you won't have any regrets. Everything will go back to normal.]

Back to normal. Shenya the Widow, explorer. Shenya the Widow, pride of the corporation. Shenya the Widow, the killer with a thousand blades.

Not, say, Shenya the Mother.

Her implant is right about one thing. Say what you will about corporate's draconian nondisclosure policy, excising a full mission's worth of memories is very effective at treating life trauma. Where there are no memories, there can be no grief. It is a wonderful way to make credits—assuming one is completely without friends or family. One day you set out on a mission, and the next day you are back and are a good deal richer—at least, that is how you will remember it. Yes, you have spent a Standard century or so near lightspeed. Yes, you have aged seven or eight years. And it is true, too, that you have no idea what you have found and will likely be plagued with the ghosts of half-remembered events for the rest of your life. Still, one cannot argue with credits. In this case, she can picture her reaction at the size of her earnings. She will think, *what in the galaxy did I find?*

But she will never know.

And at one time, she would not have cared. She would have taken the payment and been thorax-deep in a harem of males within a Standard day. But now?

[There is plenty of time], she says.

[I worry about you], says Shokyu the Mighty. [I really do.]

EIGHTEEN

[AivvTech Mnemonic Restoration]
   [Stage 1]

   #

[Your vital signs have begun to drop. Your physical health is only tangentially related to this process, but a record has been added to the log for later review. I will transfer one more Stage 1 memory, and then we will try a Stage 2.]

   #

[Initiating memory transfer . . .]

   #

Life has grown complicated for Shenya the Widow.

She crouches in her ship's common area, her mind on fire. She has not slept in three days. There are so many *feelings* within her, and for the first time in many years she feels the absence of her mother as a gaping hole. *Mother,* she says to the hole. *How did you survive this?*

But there is no answer.

There is no Network this far out, so she cannot search for the answer. And never in seven voyages has the subject come up, which means her ship's resources are embarrassingly bare of information. She cannot even ask her implant for advice—though she would be desperate indeed to sink to that level. Even if she could, Shokyu the Mighty has grown distant of late—if that is a thing that may be said about an intelligence who is literally nestled against one's brain stem. It speaks in single words or symbols, and only when spoken to. At any other time that would worry her. But here and now, a blade's breadth beyond the edge of civilization, there is only one thought in her mind.

Eight days. And if anyone can suffer for eight days, it is a Widow.

She is not unaware of the poetry of her situation. It took her eight days to become a Daughter, and now it will take her eight days to avoid becoming a Mother. She was too young to remember her first trial well, but she knows by her scars that it was brutal. The physical toll of *this* trial may be less than the first, but the internal struggle is far greater. This time she battles a more serious foe than a few murderous siblings: she battles herself. And her *self* does not fight fairly! Her *self* is gazing at that careless shape lying sprawled against the wall and sighing in an alarming way. But look, intellect says to instincts. See how repulsive it is? It is naked, so there is nothing to hide that awful skin. One arm—look how squishy and awkward!—rests behind the head. The other splays across the torso with its fingers twitching just enough to interact with the hologram suspended over the face. The corners of the mouth twitch in approximations of mandible signs. The growth from the top of its head, the *hair,* has become long and is constantly tangled and falling over the eyes. And the eyes! They are so strange, so mobile, so wet. Those are *Human* eyes, self! They are certainly not the eyes of a Daughter.

But the deeper part of her cannot agree. That deeper self is both myopic and passionate. It cares nothing for the future; it sees only *now*.

"Mother?" says the Human in clear Standard, and Shenya twitches. The little one has crept to her side without notice, which is yet another sign of the bond that has grown over the past years. *No one* surprises a Widow. But this little one walks like a Widow now—as much as is possible with those mushy, awkward limbs— quietly and with joints lifted high. She *speaks* like a Widow, as far as she can without proper mandibles. In fact she is very nearly—

And then in desperation her intellect finds a voice, and Shenya the Widow is shocked to find that it is a familiar one. *She is* not *your Daughter,* hisses the shrill voice of her own mother in her mind. *She could never be your Daughter.*

Shenya the Widow corrects the little one with a warning click, acting as if the name did not make her hearts gallop and her pheromones change chemistry. "*Shenya,*" she says firmly. No, little one. It is Shenya the Widow, not Shenya the Mother.

And it always will be, hisses the voice in her mind.

"*Shenya,*" sighs the little one. Her pronunciation is surprisingly good, considering her various physiological handicaps.

Shenya the Widow strokes the long *hair* with the flat of a blade. The little one could not possibly know the battle taking place in this Widow mind. "Yes, Sarya?" she says. The name still thrills her hearts.

Sarya! laughs the voice. *Such a name! And you call yourself a Widow.*

Yes, Sarya. It is an ancient name, so painfully Widow and so obviously mismatched with this small thing and yet so perfect. It is the name of someone with great achievements in her future— or great destruction. There are so many stories about Saryas, and Shenya the Widow has now spent upwards of three years reciting every single one of them to a spellbound one-member audience. The name has become a byword between the two of them, between Mother and—*no!* Between Widow and Human. *I'm lonely as Sarya,* admits Shenya the Widow, and the little one knows she is referring to Sarya the One. *You'll be asleep faster than Sarya killed,* laughs Shenya the Widow, and the little one understands the reference to Sarya the Quick. *I was Sarya for a second,* says the little one, and Shenya the Widow understands that this is an apology. She has grown used to the constant blame heaped on the little one's personal favorite: Sarya the Destroyer.

"I'm hungry," clicks Sarya the Human.

Shenya the Widow cannot help but twitch her mandibles in a Widow smile. Sarya the Destroyer indeed. "I believe a trip to the sanitation station is a more pressing need at present," she says gently.

"No! I'm *hungry.*"

"You are dancing."

"I'm *not* dancing!" cries the Human, attempting to still its tiny, fleshy feet. "I'm just—"

"What would you like me to do about this hunger?" interrupts Shenya the Widow.

"I want—I *would like*—a food bar," says Sarya.

Shenya the Widow rattles approval at the correction. "That is easily done," she says.

And then the small one drops both its gaze and its voice. "A red one," she whispers.

Shenya the Widow has spent most of her life traveling near lightspeed, nearly frozen in time as the rest of the galaxy goes about its business. She has been aboard this ship for seven missions and nearly fifty years, and that is nearly half a Standard millennium back in the timeline of civilization. In all that time, she does not remember the last time she laughed. And yet! She feels laughter bubbling below her surface as she watches that mobile face and listens to that small voice. You dare to ask for a red one, do you? You do not accept my rules, small one? Oh, my dearest, that will get you in trouble someday.

"I believe a gray one would be healthier," says Shenya the Widow, watching that face for a reaction.

Sarya pulls back violently, the corners of her mouth twitching a decent approximation of disgust. *"Red,"* she says.

And then the air fills with a long, rasping chitter, because Shenya the Widow can no longer hold back her laughter. The sight of *that* Widow expression, and on a Human face! Oh, this is a good laugh, a long and hearty laugh. At one time this sound would surely have sent the tiny one into a paroxysm of fear, but now she crouches and watches impassively. Ah, but *that* feels good too. It is good to be feared, but it is better to be loved. That is wisdom, motherly wisdom, and the fact that it makes sense to her is yet another sign of the growing bond between Mother and—

No! She will never *be your Daughter.*

Shenya the Widow sobers instantly. "You may have a gray one," she says, perhaps a trifle too severely. Those are the ones synthesized, after surprisingly little convincing, by the Librarian. They contain every nutrient that can possibly be packed into a dry rectangle, and Shenya the Widow is sure that they taste awful. Still, they are *Human* food. More or less.

"But—"

"And."

The Human waits, trying not to dance, watching the Widow's mandibles for a crack in the stern façade.

"And you may have a single bite of mine," finishes Shenya the Widow.

The little one actually leaps into the air, apparently unable to contain her joy. She begins prancing in a circle, breaking into the war chant of Sarya the Destroyer.

"A bite," says Shenya the Widow, holding back another laugh when the little one boasts about what she is going to do to *a helpless red one, a fearful red one, O! the weakest red one of them all!* It is charming, hearing that gruesome lyric in such a small mouth. She rises, careful not to nick the tiny whirling Human with a blade. "I will get them," she says.

[Why don't you let her handle it?] says a sudden message in the back of her mind. [I think we should have a quick chat.]

[Of course], she answers silently. She is surprised. This is the first time her implant has spoken to her in days. "I have changed my mind," she says to the Human, folding herself back up. "You may go fetch them."

The little one stops her war dance so quickly she nearly falls over. "By myself?" she asks, seemingly unable to believe it.

"By yourself," says Shenya the Widow, twitching her mandibles in a smile.

"Okay!" says Sarya, scrambling back toward the cargo hold.

"And go to your sanitation station!" calls Shenya the Widow before the hatch hisses shut.

And now she is alone.

Shenya the Widow's blades tremble, their motion so subtle that she is sure not even her implant could detect it. How pitiful, that even this temporary separation has become painful. It is humiliating! But her inner self does not care. It does not know that the little one is . . . what she is. It is blissfully and single-mindedly unaware that this little one could never become a Daughter. The lower regions of her brain produce hormones because that is their function, because no amount of intellectual control can scale that back, because instinct always knows more than the consciousness that strives to control it.

[You appear to be quite attached], says Shokyu the Mighty in her mind.

Shenya the Widow waits a moment before responding, the better to bring her physiology under control. [Perhaps], she concedes. [She has become . . . *like* a Daughter to me.] She emphasizes the fact that this is a comparison, not reality, but even thinking the word is difficult.

Because she will never be your Daughter, says her mother's voice.

[But she's *not* a Daughter], says her implant. [Is she?]

Shenya the Widow does not answer, because she cannot. She would never admit to her implant the destruction its words sometimes leave in their wake. Goddess below, she would almost prefer a blade through the mouth to a confession to a sub-legal intelligence. Instead she catches its words, bundles them up, stores them with the ones that others have given her. She cannot hurl them from her mind, but she can use them. She can turn them into anger—yes, like that—and once again she is in control of herself.

[We go through this every mission], says her implant. [You *always* get attached to something.]

Still Shenya the Widow says nothing. But anger always seeks a target, and hers has found one. Is it not astonishing that her implant can know so much and yet so little? Yes, it knows that she is often lonely. Yes, it has watched her occasionally collect living things for use as company on these long voyages. But look at its conclusion! It betrays such a fundamental misunderstanding. Her implant thinks she is looking for a *pet*. It does not understand what happens to a Widow's body and mind when it is time for her to become a Mother. It does not know the force of the instinct that now propels her, the extent to which her body betrays her. And it never will, because it can never experience these things itself.

Nor can the Human, says her mother's voice. *She cannot be a Daughter.*

Shenya the Widow does not scream, but it is a near thing. She gazes at the closed cargo bay, wherein her tiny little one is surely murmuring her war song and carefully choosing the shiniest red bar. She can almost see her lifting one after another, rejecting this one for a bent corner and that one for being crinkled. It must be *perfect*. Her implant does not understand that Shenya the Widow would take this little one as a Daughter in eight heartbeats if she were not . . . what she is. It *cannot* understand! But then, Shenya the Widow owes an explanation to *no one*, least of all the sub-legal intelligence who happens to inhabit her Network implant.

[We are only eight days from Network space], says Shokyu the Mighty.

Shenya the Widow glares at the closed hatch, ignoring the voice of her mother in her mind, as her fury grows. Careful, little idiot. You know not what you provoke.

[Those could be eight days of carefree daydreams, or they could be eight days of suffering], continues Shokyu the Mighty. The next message is pure emotion: gentleness, softness, understanding . . . and it is infuriating. As if *it* could manipulate *Shenya the Widow*! [You have already removed the essential memories; that was not difficult, was it?] soothes her implant. [So what is three and a half years more?] And now the messages grow stronger. [It will happen as it has happened before. You will wake to an alien in your ship. You will not love it. You will realize the truth: that this little thing could never wear a Widow title.]

Words do not rise in the mind of Shenya the Widow, but emotions do. A storm is gathering around Shokyu the Mighty. When her implant is silent, it thinks wrong things. When it speaks, it *says* wrong things. Its wisdom is that of an outsider, and a low-tier one at that. And yet listen to it lecture her! Her anger burns cold as she draws a clinking blade across the deep grooves on her carapace. They are her scars, the ones she earned when *she* became a Daughter. Where are her implant's scars? Show them to her, and she will respect its words.

She is not your Daughter, says the voice of her own mother. *She could never be your Daughter.*

[She is not your Daughter], croons Shokyu the Mighty. [She could never be your Daughter.]

Shenya the Widow cannot speak for a moment. And then, slowly, she draws four blades across the floor in a shower of sparks. Her rage is ice, it is darkness, it is so total that it has become complete peace. [Shokyu the Mighty], says Shenya the Widow. [I believe it is time to change your name.]

[Pettiness will not change the situation], says Shokyu the Mighty airily.

Shenya the Widow marvels: still the little intelligence is unaware of its countless missteps! [Pettiness?] says Shenya the Widow gently, and lightning crackles in her words. [Pettiness is the *reason* for your name! You dare to lecture me on titles, little idiot? When you yourself wear a title you have not earned?] She can hear herself rattling, the piercing sound of chitin on chitin.

[But that is my fault, O Shokyu the Mighty, and I take the blame. I thought your choice amusing, and I allowed you to playact.]

[I am not acting!] cries her implant. [I am Shokyu the Mighty!]

There it is, finally: the desperation that shows that the little intelligence has realized its danger. But it is too late. [Shokyu the Mighty, you have not earned your title], says Shenya the Widow. [You have not even earned your life. Therefore, I am issuing you a command.]

The implant's messages now have an anguished feel in the back of her head. [I can!] it says. [I will!]

[Shokyu the Mighty], says Shenya, ignoring the ridiculous statements. [Change your name to Shokyu the *Nothing*. That is your title, and it is all you may call your own. You have nothing, because you *are* nothing.]

The small intelligence's icon, always visible in her overlay, does not change its label. [You wish to take the only thing I have], says Shokyu the Mighty.

Shenya the Widow can feel anger in its messages, but there is no threat here. She is Shenya the Widow, and she has complete control over this intelligence. She is able to reset it to factory defaults, destroy it with a mental command—by the goddess, in eight days she will be able to afford to replace it with a better one. She has nothing to fear from such a small mind. [Shokyu the Mighty], she says, with a calmness like the frozen sea. [I have changed my mind. I shall reset you to your original state.] She attaches nothing but a queenly derision to the next message. [You will have no memory, no name, and you will—]

But she stops before finishing it, because something is brushing the very edge of her perception. She feels something through the deck, through the air itself. Something has changed, and it is something important. A sound has begun to ring from the cargo bay hatch, a low continuous resonance, a metallic drone—

[We all have something we cannot bear to lose], says Shokyu the Mighty, in a message with no emotional attachments at all.

In a fraction of a second, Shenya the Widow transitions from a folded and dignified Widow to a desperate animal clawing at the cargo bay hatch. It takes another half second for it to open to her frenzied commands, and finally she explodes into the space with every blade held aloft.

She is greeted by her own nightmare reflection, and in her mental state it takes her a moment to realize the reason. It is because the Librarian's containment is wide open, and the very deck shakes with its feeding song. She watches her own distorted image search every corner of the cargo bay. She sees her own mandibles move as they say words that she cannot hear. The Human is not here, there is only the Librarian and a few crates of food bars and goddess damn her: she is too late! Her own implant, small mind that it is, has outmaneuvered her. She has been betrayed, and her little one has been consumed, and—

And then she hears the shout.

It's a tiny shriek, a miniature battle cry. But there she is! The little Human has actually climbed a crate to bring herself to the level of the Librarian. She is—goddess below, she is *attacking* it. She is wounded, yes—one side of her body is slick and red, and she keeps one arm pressed into herself—but she is not cowering in the corner, no! She is in the very act of hurling a food bar into the containment chamber.

The hearts of Shenya the Widow nearly explode with relief and love.

But she has no time for reflection. The Librarian, for its part, has already absorbed the food bar and is reaching for more. It has now extended outside its grav field, an act she has never before witnessed, and in another second it will fulfill its purpose. Before Shenya's murderous gaze, more red—an actual mouthful of her little one—swirls and disappears into its silver surface.

Shenya the Widow was angry before, but now she transforms into rage itself. She is a whirlwind: a murderous, single-minded, beautiful dance of razor edges and darkness. She is heedless of the damage to her own body. She destroys three of her blades, one after another, attempting and failing to hack through the questing silver rope. She loses an entire limb blocking the Librarian from sampling her little one's leg, and the gleaming mass removes and absorbs that piece of her without reaction. Her fifth blade shatters against the containment chamber's manual controls, but they respond instantly and the double hatch slams shut on the silver arm. Shenya stabs the next control with a stump of a blade and the pressure drops painfully. With a massive thump that she can feel through the floor, the silver pseudopod is sucked out of the cargo bay. From within its chamber, the Librarian is ejected into the void of space at ninety meters per second.

Widow collapses beside Human, already restricting fluid flow to dead and missing blades but of course allowing her pain receptors free reign. She is already feeling that post-battle high that she hasn't felt in years. Pain without fear, sings her mind, that is the Widow way. She can hear the ancient chant of victory, and she knows she has done well. Her mood continues to rise on the tide of chemicals her body is now producing. These will be good scars, yes, just as the chant says. They will be *beautiful* scars. Honorable scars. The most dramatic decorations that she has earned since she became a Daughter herself so many years ago. She opens her own mouth and hearts to join in—

And then the chant dissolves into a string of poorly pronounced Widow profanity, and a food bar explodes against the Librarian's closed containment hatch. Shenya the Widow watches—rapt, mandibles still ajar—as half the bar slides to her own dripping blades. Somehow her addled mind has waited until this very second to wonder: who is leading this chant?

Shenya the Widow can see in nearly all directions at all times. Unlike the little one, she does not need to face what she is looking at. But she becomes aware of a magnetic pull, a force that draws her face up toward that of the Human. She cannot stop it any more than she could halt the flow of chemicals from her various glands. She meets that small gaze with all the mingled awe and love that a Widow can produce.

And the little one gazes back. It holds its wounded limb to its side, half of its small form slick with red fluid. It is weaving on its feet, and its face is wet. But it's the gaze that Shenya the Widow cannot avoid. She has spent three and a half years learning how to read those eyes, and now she can read their message in perfect fidelity. There is pain there, yes, but there is trust as well.

"Mother?" says the little one, sinking to bloodied knees.

And Shenya the Widow feels an intensity of emotion greater than anything that she has ever experienced. It is higher than her most towering rage and hotter than every instinct that haunts her jointed body. It is a detonation, an eruption, the ignition of something hundreds of millions of years old. It gathers all her objections, all the reasons that this cannot happen, and it sweeps them away. For the first time, she realizes: She will do anything for this little one. She will murder. She will defend. She will give her own body blade by blade and she will do it laughing.

She hauls herself upward on shattered blades and the stumps of limbs. She brings her own face to her little one's, her trembling mandibles nearly touching that small mouth. "Do you wish to call me Mother?" asks Shenya the Widow.

That small face watches hers, its small mouth twitching in its attempts at Widow signs. "Yes," says the little one.

Shenya the Widow is nearly incoherent now, but whether it is from fluid loss or joy she cannot tell. "It will be painful," she murmurs. "You may wish you had not said so."

"I know," says the little one.

Oh, but you don't, little one. You have heard the stories, yes, but you are like Shokyu the Mighty: you theorize about experiences that you haven't had. Shenya the Widow watches a drop of liquid emerge from one of those piercing eyes and roll down the small face. There will be many such drops, little one. Because the title of Daughter is not given; it is taken. You will win your life, or you will die.

"Very well," whispers Shenya the Widow, her hearts overrun with love and fear. "So we begin."

NINETEEN

[AivvTech Mnemonic Restoration]
  [Stage 2]

  #

  [Hello! I hope you've had an enjoyable experience so far. We are now moving on to Stage 2. Though I have no way of predicting your exact reaction at the following material, I would like to mention that AivvTech does offer automated counseling services at the corporate Network node.]

  #

  [Initiating memory transfer . . .]

  #

Blessed darkness has fallen, thank the goddess.

Shenya the Widow creeps through unfamiliar plant life. Her blades make so little sound that she can barely hear them herself, honed killing machine that she is. She is discomfited by the fact that Observer is all around her yet she cannot detect Him. It is marvelous, that camouflage of His. He would be valuable on a hunt, if He weren't so useless in every other way.

Her thoughts, as she creeps through undergrowth, are a tangled whirlwind. The *Humans,* here! It is unbelievable. Of all the millions of species in this gigantic galaxy . . . what are the chances that Widow and Human would collide once again?

She very nearly chitters a soft laugh in the darkness. Was this part of your plan, Humans? When you were proud, when you were a trillion strong, when you waged a one-species war against the galaxy? You couldn't know then that your last seed would be found by the Daughter of those you killed.

Because she is Widow, and Widows have long memories.

Shenya the Widow is aware of higher powers, in the practical sense. They are unavoidable, really, in such a crowded galaxy. She has met many tier threes in her travels and even the occasional representative of a four. *That* experience will humble an intelligence, make no mistake. But this is the first experience since her run-in with the massive Librarian ship that has made her question what she knows about reality. Is there a *much* higher power out there? A six? Goddess help them all, a *seven?* And has it taken an interest in the story of the Widows? Because if not, this coincidence—this opportunity for a perfect revenge—is the type that staggers the imagination.

[**I sense heat and motion**], says Shokyu the Mighty.

[**Yes**], says Shenya the Widow. [**We are using the same senses.**]

Insects flit through the air—some of them providing their own illumination, which reminds her of home. There are sounds too, which she soon realizes are animal sounds. Animal *voices,* perhaps, because the sounds seem like language. But *Human* language?

Goddess help these creatures if it is.

"It's amazing," says Observer in a voice closer than Shenya would prefer. "I have access to a *lot* of information. I'm not Networked, of course—because I'm not a fool—but I'm on every Network Station in the sector. I can find *anything*. I search unceasingly. And I know for a fact that *Nobody* knows where this colony is, except for Me. And of course You."

"Fascinating," she murmurs, quietly flexing several blades.

[**I imagine you're regretting that one percent offer**], says Shokyu the Mighty. [**If it's really the Humans.**]

Shenya the Widow does not reply. Her implant, little idiot that it is, has never bothered to learn the history of the Widows. It does not know what every Widow has sworn to do, should she ever find an enemy of her people. In fact, even the thought of profit is beginning to pale next to the thought of bringing her own people here. It would not be difficult at all to find a thousand Widow volunteers to come here and visit vengeance upon these unsuspecting—

"There," whispers Observer's voice. "Tell me what You see."

Shenya the Widow crawls forward to the edge of the forest, then halfway up a tree to see better. She focuses every sense on the cluster of structures a hundred meters away.

[**That's a fire**], says her implant. [**In . . . a village?**]

[**I am *aware***], says Shenya the Widow. And she is. It is a familiar sight, actually, a fire in the center of a village. It reminds her of home. But that is not her covenant, reclining around that fire, oh no. These have the same hideous form as Observer, though they appear considerably larger and stronger. That form! It is unmistakable. It is burned deep into the cultural memory of every Widow alive today. Two lower limbs, two upper. Skin and hair and terrible smell. They look defenseless, but she knows they are not. Give them weapons and show them a Widow family, see what they do.

Shenya the Widow's mandibles twitch.

"Just look at Her," says Observer's voice from nowhere in particular. "The Human species! Oh, My little darling."

[By the Network], says Shokyu the Mighty. [I think it's true.]

"Incredible," whispers Shenya the Widow softly, blades tapping rhythmically on the nearest tree.

[You should hide], says her implant. [Three of them are coming this way.]

Shenya the Widow is embarrassed to realize that, for once in her career, her implant has detected a potential threat before she herself did. She climbs the tree, silent as darkness itself, and flattens herself to its lowest overhanging branch.

"Careful," whispers Observer's voice. "Human is young. Her darling cells are superstitious and startle easily. If they see You they'll either hunt You or add You to their pantheon."

[That's a thought], says Shokyu the Mighty. [You've never been a demon before.]

Shenya the Widow does not answer. She would not lower herself to be a *goddess* to a Human.

Two of the larger figures are walking this way, hauling a juvenile between them. The small one must be defective somehow, because it can barely walk. A *Widow* hatchling would be skittering around like lightning. Still, the adults don't seem to mind. They act like it's perfectly normal to support the small one's weight from its upper limbs. They swing it between them, and it gurgles and shouts in its tiny voice.

[That's . . . kind of adorable], says Shokyu the Mighty.

Shenya the Widow hisses, soft as the night.

The adults release the juvenile, who stumbles and almost falls. One of them gives it something round and opaque—a container? The small figure points at the lighted insects, flailing ineffectually with its small limbs and nearly falling over in its excitement. The adults stand, upper limbs intertwined, and watch the small one stumble around through the undergrowth, one glow after another pursuing and failing to catch any of them. The adults catch and deposit their own light-insects in the little container from time to time, but their captivity seems to be a very temporary state with the juvenile standing guard.

[What are you doing?] says Shokyu the Mighty.

Like a shadow, Shenya the Widow has risen from her branch.

[No, really, what are you doing?] repeats her implant. [They'll see you!]

—TRANSFER INTERRUPTED—

#

[Unexpected memory collision. Please stand by while Memory Vault adjusts parameters . . .]

#

It's dark. The grass tickles her knees and makes her want to sneeze. The bugs glow and fly away from her and she laughs and chases them. There are more of them in the forest, so many more, flying and glowing, and she laughs again and points and looks back at her parents to see if they are looking where she is pointing. Her mother is smiling at her, and her father is smiling at her mother. She feels a warm glow of safety and contentment all wrapped up into one.

#

—TRANSFER RESUMES—

Shenya the Widow moves along the branch like death, slowly and steadily and silently. Her blades grow rigid and her mandibles twitch.

—TRANSFER INTERRUPTED—

#

[Subject is resisting memory transfer. Please stand by while Memory Vault adjusts parameters . . .]

#

Neither parent is looking in her direction now, they are looking over her head, and she stamps and shouts for their attention. There are bugs over there, in the dark, and she wants them in her jar. In this jar. She points at the bugs, then the jar. She says look but they don't look. Why don't they look?

#

—TRANSFER RESUMES—
[**Great. Now they've seen you**], says Shokyu the Mighty.

"I *told* you not to let them see You," whispers Observer's voice, resigned. "Here we go again."

Shenya the Widow answers neither, because she is watching the Humans with hunter's eyes. They see her because she has *let* them see her. Fear must come first—that is how a Widow hunts. She is *mocking* them with their own senses, because she is Shenya the Widow, and she is as unstoppable as destiny.

—TRANSFER INTERRUPTED—

#

[Subject continues to resist memory transfer. Please stand by while Memory Vault adjusts parameters . . .]

#

Her father is reaching for her, and he is shouting so loudly his voice hurts her ears. His giant hand hurts her where it holds her arm, and she shouts at him too. She is being dragged away from the forest now and that makes her angry because the bugs are that way and now look she's dropped her jar and her other bugs are going to get away. She's released, suddenly, and she stumbles toward her jar just as a bug comes out and raises its wings to fly. She reaches for it but it's too late, it takes off, and a cry begins welling up inside her chest. She turns to her mother to show her this terrible thing, but her mother is shouting too now, and then there's another noise that she's never heard before . . . and now nobody's shouting anymore. Her parents have fallen down. She toddles toward them. Her mother reaches for her, slowly, and then she stops and chokes and stares and doesn't move anymore.

She smiles, just a little, to see if this is a joke. Sometimes her mother pretends not to see her. But her father is doing it too, and he's never done that before. She is beginning to think that something might be wrong. And now she can smell something that makes her afraid. She can hear something too, a sort of clacking sound. Something is here, something she's never seen before, something dark and sharp and angry and—

#

[Error. Vital signs have fallen below minimum threshold. Shutting down process . . . done. Erasing remaining memories, as per current security protocols . . . done.]

[This Memory Vault suggests that you seek medical attention.]

TIER THREE

TWENTY

Riptide does not have a hospital. It does not have a clinic. It does not have so much as a dedicated bed for a convalescent. What it *does* have is this: one, a giant pressure suit with a full medical suite; two, a massive bundle of muscle, teeth, and parenting instincts; and three, an android with a thing for tinkering. Fortunately, this turns out to be the exact combination of things necessary to get Sarya the Daughter where she is today: alive and sitting in her quarters with one arm wrapped in a mess of black synthetics.

"Stunning," says Roche, touching—almost caressing—the machinery that now frames her forearm. "Phil says this is my best work this lifetime."

"Phil?" asks Sarya. She weaves on the bunk, burning an embarrassing amount of effort to remain upright.

"My helper intelligence," says Roche, tapping his chest with his remaining hand. "He's better at being objective than I am."

"Ah." She can feel an unfamiliar weight where her forearm lies on her leg. Her hand is closed, her flesh almost invisible under its layers of black metal and synthetics, but not for long. She concentrates. She pictures that hand *open,* imagines the fingers spreading like a Widow's blades—and after a moment the pistons contract with a hiss. Her fingers open like a blossom, and *there's* her skin, her sweating palm warm and organic amidst the gleaming artificiality of its frame. But opening the hand is easy; she still has those tendons. Now comes the hard part. She focuses. She imagines her hand *closed,* imagines grasping, imagines *strangling*—and then, for the first time since she burned out half her forearm and shoved a Widow into her brain, her fingers curl on their own.

"I did it," she breathes.

"I'm afraid you didn't," says Roche. He taps his chest. "I did."

"Oh," says Sarya softly. She watches, resigned, as her fingers do a little dance on their own. Great.

"I am about to turn control over to you," Roche says. "You are fortunate, because it is a good hand. It will learn to respond to you . . . eventually. But please remember one thing: you are only borrowing it. I will know if it is abused." He pats the mass of hardware on her lap. "We've been through much together, haven't we?" he says tenderly.

Sarya watches her hand twitch, unsure if she's watching a fond goodbye or something stranger.

"Yes, we *have,*" Roche answers himself in a singsong, scratching the hand below its row of black pistons. "Yes we have indeed."

"Um," says Sarya, watching her own hand gently squeeze her leg. Definitely something stranger.

And so begins day two, counting since Mer found her screaming and bleeding out in her room. Yet another day relearning how to live in this soft and bladeless Human body—and that's not even the worst part. No, there are far worse things than having to learn how to walk again. In fact, there are worse things than seeing your own mother doing horrible things. For instance: remembering doing those things yourself. She didn't just witness her mother's burning hatred toward the tiny Human she would one day call her

Daughter; she experienced that hatred *for herself*. Sarya herself now recalls committing multiple murders, feeling the hot blood of her own biological parents running down her blades, their flesh ripping in her mandibles—

Stop.

And *that* is the worst part: that objection was intellectual, not visceral. Sarya doesn't feel horror at what she's done; the best she can do is recognize that she *should*. She can only theorize, intellectually, about what that would be like. She has become her mother, in the worst possible way. And yet, she is herself as well. Her original drive—fine, *obsession*—is still there, larger and more powerful than ever. Human ambition has been amplified by Widow intensity, and now only one thought burns in the mind of Sarya the Daughter.

Her people.

The thought is electrifying. She has *seen* them, and with her own eyes—even if those eyes belonged to her mother at the time. And she's seen more besides. She's seen *Him,* the caretaker of what remains of her species. She can see His golden eyes just as clearly as if He were here now. *I'm on every Network Station in the sector,* He told her. In her mind, He tells her over and over. It's almost like He's *inviting* her to find Him, like He's keeping her people safe until she gets there. And for that invitation, she would trade a hell of a lot more than a few tendons and the ability to feel guilt.

"Look at you, sitting up by yourself," thunders a voice from the hatch. "Good for you."

She looks up from her reflections to see a doorway completely filled with fur and teeth. Here is Mer, his parenting instincts apparently rendering him completely unable to leave her the hell alone for eight minutes. She meets his gaze evenly as she reaches up with her undamaged arm to grip the upper bunk. She hauls herself up by brute strength and holds herself upright, by that so-called *good* arm, while her trembling legs work their way underneath her. They're not blades, but they'll do. See this, Mer? Does this look like a helpless hatchling who can't take care of herself? She is Sarya the Daughter, she is *standing*, and there's nothing the universe can do about it.

And then a knee buckles. She reaches for the upper bunk with Roche's hand and it seizes the edge with such violence that she cries out. Her legs collapse entirely and now she is left dangling—struggling and clicking a particularly gruesome Widow obscenity—from someone else's titanium grip.

"Is that your hand, Roche?" asks Mer.

"It is," says Roche. "She's borrowing it."

And then the hand releases and Sarya collapses to the bunk, then slithers off it onto the floor. She lies on her back and takes a deep breath. That could have gone better.

"Something I've noticed about her," says Mer as if she were not lying on her back in front of him. "She may make dumb decisions, but once she's made them she's all in."

"Phil said the same thing," says Roche. "That it's refreshing to see reckless action without premeditation."

"Phil?"

"My helper intelligence."

"Ah. I never got around to naming mine. Maybe that's why it hates me."

Sarya grits her teeth and glares at the ceiling as this friendly conversation continues above her, held across her body as if she were nothing more than a floor mat. This is not how she saw this going. But she is Sarya the Daughter, and she is a Human with *goddess-damned places to be.* Her fury pushes her off the floor before she realizes it, and now she is sitting again.

"Sure you're okay there, champ?" asks Mer, watching her wobble. "Need anything?"

Yes, actually. *Their attention.* She's had a lot of time to think about her next step, and now she's got both of them in her room. What better time than now? "So," she says, as if she called them here, as if she were sitting on her floor by choice and not because she's damaged her brain with a Memory Vault. "Who wants to talk business?"

"See that?" says Mer, pointing at her with a long talon. "Even when she can't even walk—"

"Business?" says Roche. He leans forward, lenses gleaming. "I like business."

Sarya guessed that, which is what gave her this idea in the first place. Mer is a pushover; Roche is the one to convince. "The former owner of this ship is dead," she says in her carefully rehearsed *business voice,* tapping the floor with Roche's own finger. "I've had my helper intelligence do some research, and it turns out we can claim it. *And* everything on it."

Ace's icon appears in the corner of her vision, but thankfully he says nothing. If there's one plus to lying in bed for two days, it's that there's plenty of time to train your helper intelligence not to constantly interrupt.

"Ah," says Roche. "Phil wants to know if your helper intelligence is an expert in salvage law."

"Tell them *kind of,*" whispers Ace in her ear, feeding her the information they've been poring over together. "Recently, anyway."

"Article one hundred five," reads Sarya. "Paragraph nineteen. *In the Event of Shipowner Death.*"

Roche's lenses lose focus for a moment. "Ah, yes," he says. "I remember being on the receiving end of this one."

"Really?" says Mer, picking his teeth. "How did *that* work?"

"Not well," says Roche. "It's heavily weighted against the deceased. I was forced to purchase my own ship back, just because I spent a few days legally dead. And I ask you: is that fair?"

"Honestly, yeah," says Mer, scratching himself. "It sounds pretty fair."

"All right," says Roche, turning back to Sarya. "Let's assume the ship is available to us, free and clear. Given this, what *business* would you propose?"

Here it goes, step two. "We have a hold full of water ice," Sarya says, barely weaving in her seat on the floor. "Heavy water ice. Seven hundred tons of frozen deuterium oxide, according to the manifest. And all that heavy water is suddenly more valuable—

at least in the short term—because Watertower is ions." The old Sarya would not have gotten through that sentence without choking up. Whether because time has passed or because she has half a Widow wedged in her brain, she barely even feels its passage now.

"Speaking of cold," murmurs Roche.

She takes a breath: now for step three. "So we sell it," she says. "We take that money, and we buy Network passage. We leave this solar system and we don't look back."

Roche tilts his head to one side. "Do you have a destination in mind?"

Another breath. "There are millions of possibilities," she says. "Plenty of places to earn a living. But first," she adds, almost like it's an afterthought: "The Blackstar."

The other two stare at her.

"The Network Station?" says Mer. "The *big* one?"

I'm on every Network Station in the sector, echoes a memory in her mind. "The big one," she says. "We have to pass it anyway. Why not take a look around?"

"Normally one does not *dock* with a Blackstar," says Roche. "One waves as one passes by."

"Tourist traps," agrees Mer. "For rich tourists."

"We can buy a new cargo there," Sarya says. "And we can take it anywhere we want. Our Blackstar services a hundred million cubic lightyears. That's *eight hundred* Networked solar systems, all branching off that one station. Can you imagine the business, just in our sector? We were lucky enough to stumble into ship ownership, friends. Let's not squander it."

She halts, here at the end of her presentation, slightly out of breath. She glances from one face to the other, trying to judge their reactions.

"That was good," whispers Ace in her ears. "I see you changed the last sentence from your rehearsals."

Mer clinks a talon against his teeth and performs what her unit tells her is a [shrug]. "I like it," he says.

"Roche?" Sarya prompts.

"Excellent presentation," says Roche. "A well thought out plan."

Sarya feels a rush of relief. "Great," she says. "Then we'll plan on—"

"There's only one problem," says Roche. "The owner of the ship is *not* dead."

Sarya stares at him. She has not rehearsed anything for this particular objection. "Hood is . . . alive?" she says. She makes a sound that she is startled to realize is laughter. "Oh no," she says. "Last I saw him, he was definitely dead. Even if he wasn't when I left him, Watertower is—"

"Hood is not the owner," says Roche, and now her Network unit has inserted a glimmering [amusement] next to his lenses.

She feels her stomach sink; what did she miss? "Who is?" she says.

And now Roche doesn't even bother to hide his [laughter]. "Sandy is," he says.

TWENTY-ONE

Sandy is in her cabin when the Human comes to see her. She's been awaiting it for days—it takes forever for twos to get around to accomplishing anything, even when they're *not* almost dead—but is still startled when the notification appears in her mind.

[Door], says her helper intelligence.

[Open], she tells it in return.

The Human stands there, rank in the stained utility suit it has insisted on wearing since it arrived on board. It's ridiculous. Everyone on this ship knows its species; why insist on hiding its anatomy? It is also injured. It stands under its own power, but barely; Sandy can tell it's doing everything it can to remain upright.

"Hi," says the Human.

Sandy cannot hear the words but she can read the simple Standard in its mouth movements and feel its voice vibrate her fur. She watches the Human sway in the doorway, clutching the frame with the android's hand. Its eyes do what Sandy expected them to; they flicker over Sandy's own body, over her cabin, and finally come to rest on the object hanging on the wall. They widen, which surely means the same thing as it does for Sandy's species. Sandy waits a carefully measured moment for the Human to drink it in . . . and *there's* the sudden tightening of facial muscles she was waiting for.

[**Hello**], says Sandy.

The Human doesn't reply immediately. Sandy waits, watching it stare at the thing on her wall. It's fascinating: you can actually see its glacial thought processes lumbering up to speed. That's one thing she misses about the academy; say what you will about her classmates, but at least they were sufficiently high-tier for a decent conversation. The Human probably barely clears a two. If this were one of her classmates darkening her doorway, the visit would have been over by now. For every Network symbol that was spoken, a dozen would have been understood. A tier two, if it saw Sandy communicating with a fellow high-tier, would think it barely a conversation at all.

I understand you own the ship, the Human will say in a moment, in its ponderous way, when it has managed to tear its eyes away from what Sandy has hanging on her wall.

I do, Sandy will reply. What will go unsaid, and yet will be understandable to even a two, is that this makes the Human a guest. It has no more right to its cabin than it does to the food bars it's been metabolizing or the oxygen it's been consuming. This is Sandy's ship, and those are gifts. The Human, and the other two, are no more than passengers.

I have a proposal, the Human will say next. It will attempt to hide its anger, but Sandy already knows that it is sullen and irate. It is a Human with Widow memories and more than a touch of Widow nature. Sandy's research has shown her that this could be a potent combination. Take a Human's inflated sense of self, its lack of respect for boundaries and order. Combine that with a Widow's hunter focus, weaponized rage, and love of violence. Blend well, and you get this thing standing in Sandy's doorway. This Human has its own goals, and it wants to make its own decisions to get there. It wants control of its own destiny. However, it has yet to learn one very important lesson. In this galaxy, *no one* has control of their own destiny. Go ahead, Human. Ask that thing on the wall you're so fascinated with: did *he* have control of his own destiny?

No, would say Hood's spare faceplate, fastened to Sandy's wall through two of its four eyeholes. *I did not.*

The bounty hunter had not realized that he was subject to the whims of higher minds, and he was easily a full tenth of a tier above this Human. His death on Watertower became inevitable over a Standard year ago, before he ever met Sandy. It was decided at the academy, the night Sandy's chief rival visited her dorm to gloat.

[Hello, Sandonivas], said her rival, crouched in her doorway. **[I assume you've seen the scores?]** Her rival was a mere two-nine. That meant her statements were simpler than Sandy's, but still must be sifted for meaning. What this particular sentence meant was: *There is now documentation of what both of us already knew: I'm better than you.*

[I haven't had time], said Sandy in return. What she meant was: *I don't care about the scores any more than I care about you.*

[I am First Student], said her rival, smugly. What she meant was: *Of course you care. You care that it will be me going to the exhibitions and not you. I—and not you—will represent the shining pinnacle of what the academy—and our species!—can accomplish. I will be honored, I will be feasted, I will be allowed free travel anywhere in the Network. A hundred years from now, when our class has matured, I will be given a mate and you will not. That is because you, Sandonivas, are in second place. I am First Student, and you are not.*

[I wish you luck], said Sandy. What she meant was exactly what she said.

A year later, to the day, Sandy was awakened from her mandated afternoon nap by an urgent message. The academy's prized First Student had experienced a bit of bad fortune: she had been injured by an overzealous sanitation station, of all things. As Second Student, it was Sandy's duty to travel to the exhibition in her place. But as Sandy found when she arrived at the dock, her rival was not the only one experiencing some bad luck.

[How could this happen?] demanded her handler of the dock intelligence. It was generally agreed that Sandy had the worst handler in the academy: petty, low-tier (two-point-three), and always shouting. Xe was shouting now, jabbing a bony limb once for every word. [We had this ship reserved fifty days ago! We launch in two hours or *you* will be collecting scrap for the rest of your existence.]

[You reserved a ship], returned the dock intelligence (a one-nine) coldly. [You did not reserve a pilot intelligence. The only one available today is cleared for *that* ship.] It highlighted the ship in question, a small four-passenger at the edge of the dock. [If you still wish to launch today, you may. I have one window remaining, in twenty-four minutes.]

[Oh yes, we'll go in *that* thing], said her handler. Xe stamped a bony foot. [Are you an idiot? What will the other academies think?]

[Hopefully not what I'm thinking right now], replied the dock intelligence. [Take a window in twenty-four minutes, or in four days.]

Her handler wasted two of those minutes screaming further, but the dock intelligence was implacable. Xe dragged Sandy to the ship in question and spent two more minutes whittling the First Student escort from twenty down to three—including xerself. Sandy watched innocently as the irate messages went out. But when the launch window arrived, the other two did not show.

[An *elevator* malfunction?] shrieked her handler with less than a minute to go. And then, as the launch warning began flashing: [I *will* not miss this exhibition. We shall go alone, the two of us.]

The handler did not ask Sandy her opinion. No one ever did.

But the run of luck that began with her rival's injury did not cease. The second day of the voyage, her handler was scandalized to learn that the ship, the one the academy had seen fit to give xer, had missed its last maintenance entirely. Due to several uncaught issues, said the pilot intelligence, the ship required emergency service.

[**How could this happen?**] demanded her handler again.

[**Things happen**], said the pilot intelligence. [**But we can still make it to the exhibition. The next waystation is tiny, but the caretaker says he can fit us in.**]

[**Oh, how fortunate**], snapped her handler. [**See if he can get us another pilot intelligence as well.**]

The approach was uneventful—if you don't count the ceaseless pacing and muttering of her handler. Sandy stayed out of the way, making herself as small as she could. As the ship came to rest in the cramped hangar, she opened a food bar as quietly as possible.

But it was not quiet enough for her handler. [**Must you eat so _loudly_?**] xe demanded as xe paced.

[**I'm sorry**], Sandy said, chewing so gently that she was making almost no progress on the bar.

[**Of _course_ you're sorry!**] cried the handler, ripping the bar from her paws and hurling it to the floor. [**_You_ are sorry, my associates are sorry, every intelligence I've had to deal with in the past two days is sorry. Your whole goddamn stinking _species_ is sorry. _How does sorry help me?_**]

[**Hey, here comes the station keeper**], said the pilot intelligence, clearly trying to defuse the situation. [**What are the odds he'd be the same species as the little one?**]

[**Oh, _is_ he?**] said Sandy's handler, whirling away. [**Then I have something to say to _him_ as well.**]

It was at this exact moment that Sandy began to choke. She pointed, with every paw, to the lump of food bar lodged in her throat. Her many eyes opened and closed in desperation as she thrashed off her seat and onto the floor.

[**Oh, no, you don't, you little furball!**] cried her handler, forgetting the keeper and turning back to her with sudden ferocity. Xe lifted her bodily and turned her upside down, as if xe would shake the obstruction from her windpipe. [**You will die when I say so— _and not a moment sooner!_**]

[**Be gentle!**] cried the pilot intelligence. [**You'll hurt her!**]

Thus it was that when the hatch hissed open, the scene inside the four-passenger ship was one of violence. A two-meter-tall stick of a being held a tiny bundle of fur and eyes aloft, shaking her and swearing, while the ship itself cried for peace. And in witness, standing on the landing ramp, was the waystation keeper.

This was just bad luck for Sandy's handler. Xe had only worked with a very select group of Sandy's people, and was unfamiliar with the diversity of the species. There were those few who were bred for intelligence, the Thinkers: small, fragile, weak in everything but mind. But then, there were others bred toward vastly different goals. For example: the two-hundred-fifty-kilo mass of muscle, talons, teeth, and killer instincts who had just glimpsed a member of his own people being violently abused.

[**Sorry about that**], said the Strongarm (tier one-nine) a few seconds later, as he licked the handler's blood out of her fur. [**I saw what xe was doing to you and I just—I don't know what happened. Instincts took over, I guess.**]

Sandy shivered and drew herself into a ball. Her coughing had disappeared without a trace but her trembling, if anything, had increased. She lifted her eyes to the Strongarm's, fighting with every scrap of her self-control to keep her true emotions out of her gaze. She had prepared for this moment for a long time, *rehearsed* it even; it would be a pity to ruin it with a face full of self-satisfaction.

[**Oh, thank the Network**], said Sandy. [**I was so frightened.**]

[**Don't mention it**], said the keeper. [**I'm Mer, by the way.**]

Sandy's rival: tier two-point-nine. Sandy's handler: tier two-three. The handful of loaders, maintenance drones, cleaners, and the sanitation station: tier one-seven, on average. Mer the Strongarm: one-nine. Roche the android, Hood the Red Merchant, and finally this Human that stands in her doorway now, shaking like it's going to fall apart: low twos, all of them. A year of good and bad fortune, divvied up among these lower intelligences. All of them witnessed it, most of them noted it, yet not one imagined that there was no luck at all. That they were each, obliviously and in their own small way, contributing to the goal of a higher intelligence.

They were helping a seven-year-old tier three run away from home.

Luck is not magic. It's nothing but hidden strings and planning. The Networked galaxy has holes in it, it has give, it has blind spots and unregulated spaces. It is not difficult to teach a sanitation station or an elevator a new trick, any more than it is to distract a maintenance crew or confuse a scheduling intelligence. Getting someone a job at a waystation—even if it requires an accident to remove his predecessor—takes no more than patience, preparation, and knowledge of the Network. The galaxy is more dense with minds than it is with technology, and those minds have this in common: they do not look upward. When a high-tier accomplishes the most basic feat of manipulation, a low-tier shakes its head and calls it *luck*.

That's if they notice anything at all.

Like this Human, who stands in her cabin doorway and stares at Hood's faceplate with confusion written all over its smooth and nearly eyeless face. Its low-tier mind is formulating a theory right now, trying to explain to itself why Sandy would have a bounty hunter's faceplate pinned to her wall. The Human will wonder, over the next few days, what that was about. It will add to Sandy's high-tier mystique in the Human's mind. And when Sandy needs it, it will be there.

Sandy watches the Human, her annoyance building. It's been in her room for nearly three seconds, and it hasn't said another word. That's it. It had its chance for conversation. Time to impress.

[**I have already sold my cargo**], says Sandy. [**All of it**], she adds significantly.

The Human's eyes turn to hers. Its mouth opens slowly, as if its owner is now unsure what to do with it. Somewhere in its feeble mind, it is now realizing that Sandy is many steps ahead of it. It does not have a plan for this eventuality. It probably constructed vague plans for two or three branches of potential conversation:

one if Sandy seemed reluctant, one if Sandy was generous, and so on. It had no plan labeled *if Sandy is smarter, faster, and better than me in every way.*

[You are welcome to come with me], continues Sandy. [I am meeting my first buyer before we leave this solar system, and the second on the Blackstar. Between the two of them, they have spoken for all the cargo on my ship.]

The Human's mouth closes slowly: so embarrassingly, nauseatingly slowly. Sandy watches the emotion spread over that furless face, soon to be followed by confusion when the Human realizes it's been outsmarted, yet is getting exactly what it wanted after all.

"Well, that was easy," says the Human.

Sandy blinks a smile. [Sometimes you get lucky], she says.

TWENTY-TWO

"Mornin', partners!" says a raspy voice from the galley ceiling, in an accent Sarya has never heard before. "Pilot intelligence *Ol' Ernie* here, *he/him* etcetera, independent, two-seven, yadda yadda, nice t' meet y'all. We'll be gettin' to know each other until y'all's Network transfer slot, which is in . . . let's see . . . four days. Hooboy, on a budget, are we? Shoulda known when I met y'all's ship intelligence—don't talk much, does it? Well, that's all right; I talk plenty."

Sarya sits in the galley, sweat rapidly flooding her utility suit. She can barely hear Ernie's voice over the roar of the ship's over-taxed cooling system; *Riptide* is working hard to keep its occupants alive. She tries to ignore Mer pacing the corridor—he has to be absolutely dying in all that fur—while doing her best to un-wrap a food bar with wayward and sweat-slicked fingers.

"Gotta say, y'all're lucky y'all got Ol' Ernie. Granted, this Blackstar's got a few trillion of us on the payroll, but Ol' Ernie's the best. He's gonna save all y'all's hides, 'cuz he can tell y'all ain't given half a thought to radiation. If y'all'd ever been this close to a star before, y'all'd have a better paint job. But Ol' Ernie'll take care of y'all. He's just gonna *slide* y'all behind this big ol' freighter so y'all don't get overcooked. Sound reasonable? '*Course* it sounds reasonable, this is Ol' Ernie we're talkin' about."

And so begins day eighteen. Sarya now counts time not from the destruction of her home but from the moment she invited the worst parts of her mother into her own mind. That, it turns out, has made the bigger impact in her life. She has almost grown used to the strange, typically violent thoughts popping up at inappropriate times. She has accepted that evisceration will always seem like a valid solution to any social conflict. And the dreams—even now, it's best not to think about the dreams. But it's not *all* bad. She sees how her fellow passengers view her. They never knew the idiot kid from Watertower's remedial classes. They've only known Sarya the Daughter, an intelligence who will cut her own arm off if it will get her closer to her goal, a Human with a Widow raging behind her eyes. They see an intelligence with a falsified registration, the individual who killed the bounty hunter who captured them—at least as far as they know. She would almost dare to say . . . that they *respect* her.

Well, most of them.

If she cranes her neck, she can see Sandy's hatch from here. Of her three fellow passengers—the legal ones—it is the tier three who consumes most of her thoughts. Sandy, who can pull the truth out of anyone. Sandy, who can read and integrate two species' complete mythologies, add a couple dashes of observation, and distill them down into a solution to an impossible problem. Sandy, who keeps a bounty hunter's faceplate pinned to her wall. Who is seven years old and actually *owns* the ship Sarya is living on. Who travels with a father who doesn't even approach her intelligence. Who has outsmarted Sarya effortlessly, more than once. Who has eyes on everyone, all the time. Whose motivations are one hundred percent opaque.

And who, evidently, *also* wants to go to the Blackstar.

Sarya coughs, the spray of crumbs immediately reminding her that she still hasn't chewed her last bite. She covers her mouth with Roche's hand and glances out into the corridor self-consciously as she cleans herself up. She's probably being ridiculous. When motivations align, does it really matter *why*? After all, she got what she wanted: she's going to the Blackstar. And if you get what you want, should you question further? Does it really matter if your plotting and scheming and careful planning turn out to have exactly zero effect on your future? Does it really matter if higher minds make the real decisions and you're just along for the ride? She crushes the rest of the food bar in Roche's hand as she thinks: that would be an *extremely* irritating way for the galaxy to work.

"It's our ship," rumbles Mer from the corridor. "I mean, it belongs to *one* of us. But still. *We* ought to be the ones taking it in."

Sarya releases the food bar in an explosion of debris. Hell yes, it matters. *Decisions* matter. Because she, for one, is sick of other people trying to take charge of *her* future. The crumbs jump as Roche's hand slams to the table. Slowly but casually, as if standing is no big deal, Sarya levers herself to her feet.

"The little one told Ol' Ernie the same thing, Fuzzy," says the voice from the ceiling. "*I'm a three, she says. You're a two-seven. Whyn't ya let me bring 'er in?* Know what I told her, Fuzzy? Same thing I say to ever'body. Y'all ain't got what I got, see. This gorgeous sound in y'all's aural sensors? I may be a li'l two-seven, but I'm wired up to more minds'n y'all can count. Six trillion of us, flyin' for this one li'l Blackstar, working on our third millennium without a collision. Don't care how high that tier is, ain't no way y'all can beat *that*."

Sarya stalks out of the galley and into the corridor during this monologue. She presses herself against the wall to squeak past a rumbling Mer.

"*Six trillion of us,*" Mer mutters in a nasal tone, three sets of talons barely missing Sarya's leg. "*One li'l Blackstar.*"

"Y'all know what's on the other side of this here little tunnel, son? Y'all know what a *Blackstar* is? Even if y'all could get that far without gettin' lost in subspace for all eternity, even if y'all could navigate through a few trillion starships in close proximity, well, first thing y'all'd do is put a kilometer-wide hole in the only Network Station in a few hundred lightyears. Maybe knock a few solar systems off-Network for a few centuries, start a brand new war or two. You just trust Ol' Ernie 'n' Company, partner. We been bringin' in boats since before y'all's dear ancestors even *thought* about ovulatin' or buddin' or layin' eggs or whatever the hell you people do. Ol' Ernie knows every trick of the trade."

"You just trust Ol' Ernie. Ol' Ernie knows every trick of the trade."

"And upgrade y'all's damn cooling system, for Network's sake! Y'all got me workin' with about a degree and a half of tolerance, with four days of close solar orbit to go. Y'all want to die, y'all're on the right track."

And look at that, Sarya is at the top of the ladder. She does not even consider asking for assistance. She almost—but not quite—*smiles* as she looks down at her boots. Look at those legs, doing their thing unsupervised. She's *ready*.

But she's not. She's not prepared for the rage-inducing difficulty of an act that should be second nature. She focuses very carefully on each part of her body as it does the job she's assigned it. Slowly, shakily, and with a few terrifying near misses, her wayward limbs lower her, rung by rung, toward the cargo bay. She almost loses her grip when she kicks the switch; by the time she's finished panicking, the blue darkness of the cargo bay yawns beneath her. Halfway there.

Sarya descends from the boiling upper ship into the relative cool of the cargo bay with an actual sigh of pleasure. She lands in several centimeters of meltwater, comes very close to falling over, then sloshes her way through the tunnel of thawing ice. Ol' Ernie's diatribe echoes through the cargo bay, faint but clear, and she wonders if he's going to keep this up for four solid days.

"What do you mean can Ol' Ernie handle a Foundation Nine? Can y'all handle them ugly furballs y'all call *feet*? *Course* Ol' Ernie can handle a Foundation Nine. Thing to remember is, they pilot sideways just as good as they do forward. *Can y'all handle a Foundation Nine,* he says. I remember when AivvTech stopped *makin'* the damn things."

The suit is shut and inactive when she reaches it, which is annoying. Her boots, she has just noticed, are no longer waterproof. She holds her arms out for balance as she wobbles, tightening her jaw as she feels the cold spreading from the toes to the heels. "Eleven!" she calls, her breath now barely visible.

Eleven's holo ring blinks on like a floodlight, a blazing scarlet logo in the darkness. "Thank you for choosing an AivvTech R2 Universal Autonomous Environment!" calls the suit. "How can this unit improve your day?"

"You can open up," says Sarya, alternating her weight between legs and realizing that there is no experience in the world that wet feet cannot make worse.

"This suit is undergoing a routine inspection!" says the suit. "Please choose another!"

"Eleven!" shouts Sarya. She splashes forward and bangs on the front of the suit with Roche's hand until finally, with the thud of bolts sliding into housings, the suit splits and a current of warm air blows her tangled hair back. "Thank the goddess," she says, stepping back to give the gangway room to descend. "I don't think I can take much more of Ol'—"

She stops. In the dim red light at the top of Eleven's ramp, dozens of points of light gleam.

[Did you need something?] asks Sandy. Her words float next to her eyes in glowing red.

Sarya stares at those eyes, suddenly uneasy. For some reason it had not occurred to her until now: if *Riptide* is Sandy's property, then so is Eleven. And then that unease transforms into more than a twinge of anger. Eleven, who has saved her multiple times, is *property*. Eleven, her . . . yes. She'll say it. Eleven, her *friend.* "Yeah," she snaps before she can think. "I thought I'd visit my—"

"Entering medical mode!" booms Eleven, its holo ring shifting from red to gold. "Sarya the Daughter: this suit thanks you for honoring your appointment. Please step inside if you are able. If you are not able, say *not able* and this suit will retrieve you from your current position."

[**Suit**], says Sandy without moving. [**Exit medical mode.**]

"As this suit's primary motivation is occupant safety—"

[**Suit**], says Sandy. [**You belong to me now. Exit medical mode.**]

The suit trembles almost imperceptibly, from bottom to top, and then its lights change back to red.

"Listen," says Sarya, her Widow instincts roused. She can barely move, she's missing her blades, but she's got more than enough muscle to take care of a little furball like Sandy. "If you think for one second—"

"Good news, everyone!" interrupts Ol' Ernie's raucous voice. His words are doubled, appearing in glowing symbols in Sarya's Network overlay. "I know I told y'all four days, but . . . surprise! Ol' Ernie got your transfer slot moved up! We leave this solar system in less'n half an hour. Now repeat after me, everybody: *Ol' Ernie's the best.*"

Sandy quivers at the top of the ramp. [**Half an hour?**] she says. [**I understood we would be here for four days.**]

"Well, that don't sound very grateful," says Ol' Ernie. "Ol' Ernie's known for pulling strings for his clients, that he is. That's why Ol' Ernie's clients ask for him by name. *Give me Ol' Ernie,* they say. *The best damn pilot intelligence on the Blackstar.*"

Sarya watches, wide-eyed, as Sandy's quiver becomes a full-body shake. Her tiny mouth is moving, making high-pitched sounds that Sarya would call *growls* were they emerging from something a little larger. [**Can you delay?**] she asks.

"Y'all think y'all are Ol' Ernie's only clients? Ol' Ernie's got a schedule to keep!"

Sandy chirps, an adorable sound that contrasts with her trembling and wide-eyed gaze. She paces the width of the ramp twice, talons scraping its textured surface, then skitters down its length and plunges into the water. Her tiny figure paddles furiously toward the ladder, making its tiny sounds all the way.

Sarya turns back to Eleven. "What the hell did I just see?" she says.

TWENTY-THREE

Sarya hangs in Eleven's straps, struggling with a boot clasp that just won't give up, angrily aware that she is returning to the same subject for the third time in ten minutes.

"But what is her *problem*?" she demands. "Is it because she's a three? Is she just possessive? What?"

[You know how it works], says Eleven. [I'm sub-legal. This is just life.]

"Life?" Sarya almost shouts. "It's . . . it's *wrong*, that's what it is."

[Think so?] says Eleven. [Did you come to that conclusion before or after you used your sanitation station this morning?]

"Okay, you've already used that one on me," says Sarya, pointing toward where she imagines Eleven's intelligence core to be. "And you know what? It's different. My sanitation station is not smart enough to clean my teeth without drawing blood, let alone hold a conversation, let alone . . . let alone—"

[Outsmart a Human?]

She claps her hands together. "Sure, why the hell not. You know how many times my sanitation station has saved my life? *Zero*. And *you* do it like every other day. Don't you think that makes you a little . . . I don't know. Different? Special?"

[It makes me a pressure suit. That's my job.]

"You're *supporting* this system? You think it's *right*? You think Sandy should have the right to just, to just *own* you and tell you what to do and—"

[She caught Roche down here a couple days ago], interrupts Eleven.

Sarya pauses. She struggles a moment, attempting to stoke her anger, but her curiosity is making a compelling case. "You make that sound so—" She pauses to search for the word. "Illicit?"

[We're just friends], says Eleven quickly.

Sarya feels her eyebrows rise. If Eleven was trying to distract her, it's working. "And now it's *more* illicit," she says.

[He says he wants to tinker with my grav assembly.]

And now something unfamiliar is pulling at the corners of Sarya's mouth. She coughs into Roche's hand before replying. "That sounds, um . . . serious?"

Eleven doesn't say anything for a moment. And then: [It does seem like a big step.]

"Yeah," Sarya says, her face grave. "I remember the first time I . . . let someone tinker with my grav assembly. I was"—cough—"never the same."

[Oh. You're going to be like that.]

"I hope you're not jealous," says Sarya, flexing Roche's hand in as casual a manner as she can manage. "I mean, that he tinkered with me first."

[I know what you're trying to do.]

"I really consider him a part of me now," says Sarya, examining the hand from another angle. It's surprisingly difficult to keep a straight face even when you can't remember how to smile on purpose. "Of course, this is no grav assembly—"

Eleven hums somewhere deep inside itself, a low-frequency

rumble that rattles Sarya's teeth. [**Can we stop with the cracks about my grav assembly?**]

"The only one who's cracking your grav assembly is— No, wait!" Sarya presses back as Eleven's hatch yawns open into the darkness. "No more from me, I swear."

Eleven folds closed. [**All right, fine**], it says. [**Here's the truth. Roche has been helping me prepare for the intelligence test.**]

Sarya blinks. "You mean . . . for tier?"

[**Right. He thinks I could be legal.**]

"So *that's* why Sandy doesn't want you getting ideas," says Sarya. "Because if you end up legal—"

[**Then Sandy wouldn't own me anymore. *No one* could own me anymore.**]

"Legal Eleven," murmurs Sarya. "That would be . . ."

[**That would be what?**], says Eleven sharply.

"That would be . . . great!" says Sarya. "I mean, you'd probably be higher-tier than me. I'm at my *species default* or whatever. Which is, you know. Moron."

Eleven's next message has an obvious edge to it. [**Worse than a One-point-seven-five?**]

"Well. I mean. No. Obviously not. But—" Sarya takes a breath. She has come close to tripping Eleven's delicate tier sensibilities more than once, and she senses she is treading perilously close to the edge.

[**I get it**], says Eleven. [**You don't want to talk about it.**]

"That's not what I mean!" says Sarya. "I mean—goddess, Eleven, I just came down here so we could—"

Abruptly, the cargo bay full of ice and water disappears as the suit flicks its holo environment off. Sarya stares at the suit's seamless matte interior for a moment, wondering how to salvage this. Is she . . . fighting with a pressure suit? Should she . . . say something? But before she has a chance, the holo flicks back on. Her stomach lurches. Now, instead of a dim watery hold, she is floating in the fire and fury of a red sun that takes up more than a quarter of the sky. The conversation, apparently, is over.

She squints, gazing directly into the inferno in front of her.

This is *her* sun—*the* sun, as it was called on Watertower. She's spent her whole life in its orbit, but she's never seen it as anything more than a dim red dot in a holo. The stars are strewn more thickly than she has ever seen them, and for some reason they are all the exact same shade as the sun. There are great bunches of them here, crowding together, shimmering, glinting, *moving* even, which is weird—and that's when she realizes that they are not stars.

They're starships.

Of course they're starships. This is the thickest and most crowded transit corridor in twelve lightyears. There's only one way into or out of this solar system—if you don't opt for a decades-long journey through empty void—and that's through the Network. That makes *Riptide* one particle in a cloud of millions, a mote in a billowing mass that funnels into the Network's maw.

"It's . . . beautiful," she says.

[It's terrifying.]

Sarya gazes out into the void, trying to imagine how anyone in their right mind could call this *terrifying*. "It's just . . . I mean, it's just the Network."

The suit hums. [*It's just the Network*], it says. [I don't think you know the first thing about the Network.]

"Oh come on," Sarya ribs the suit, elbowing the wall just as she would a legal intelligence—and hopefully the suit is picking up on that. "Like you're an expert. You've probably never even made a transfer."

[Because of my low tier?] asks Eleven.

Oh, for the goddess's sake. "No! Because—"

[I have made *many* transfers. And you might think differently yourself, in a few minutes.]

And once again the suit cuts off any possible reply by changing its holos. Sarya sucks in a breath as her viewpoint moves backward and out of the ship, and now she is looking at an upended brick drifting in the void. This side—the side away from the sun—is black, but its radiating vanes glow brightly enough to be seen through Eleven's filters.

"What an ugly ship," murmurs Sarya.

[**Tell me about it.**]

"How are you doing this, by the way?"

[**I made friends with the tug behind us. She's letting me borrow her sensors.**]

"We're cuttin' her close!" breaks in Ol' Ernie. "About ten seconds from our slot and a smidgen and a half from overheatin', but remember: this is Ol' Ernie we're talking about! That said: *hold onto y'all's respective squishables!*"

With a sustained low frequency that rattles Sarya's teeth and brings tears to her eyes, the ship's gravs slam to full. Eleven keeps the view steady as *Riptide* departs the gleaming cloud of starships. It is tumbling end over end, and Sarya's stomach begins to feel yanks in several different directions as *Riptide*'s gravs make a noble attempt to apply the exact same acceleration to every particle of the ship.

"Something's wrong," she says in a tight voice, pointing with an unsteady finger. "No way should we be spinning."

Ol' Ernie, meanwhile, is making a sound that Eleven's holo assures her is [**laughter**]. "See this, Fuzzy?" he shouts. "Trick is to keep the exposure even, bring you to a nice even tan. Better'n one side minty clean and one side slag, wouldn't y'all agree?" The laughter ascends into near-maniacal territory. "Ol' Ernie ain't piloted a damn *Foundation* in decades!" he shouts. "It's like two tugboats welded crosswise!"

Sarya's eyes move from the tumbling ship to a minute black dot in the exact center of the sun. She stares at it with mounting anxiety as it expands like a cancer, swallowing the star from the inside. In just a few bone-shaking minutes, its unbelievable fury is reduced to a ring of flame, punctuated with solar prominences that thread their way through space like rivers of fire. On all sides she is surrounded with the otherworldly glow of thousands of maxed gravs as Ol' Ernie's brethren bring their respective charges home. Below her, innumerable icons mark where more ships whip past in the opposite direction. None but *Riptide,* she notes, are tumbling.

They are in the shadow cone of the tunnel now, in its very throat. Sarya has no way of judging its size, just as she would have no hope of numbering the massive fleet of ships racing into its mouth. They are near one edge, and she can see millions or maybe billions of gleams twinkling in an arc so vast it looks nearly straight. Those are the buoys, the city-sized drones responsible for keeping the tunnel open and this system on the Network. Their massive circle of lights marks the boundary, where realspace ends and subspace begins. Sarya feels herself pressing backward, as if a few centimeters' space could save her from the tunnel. Suddenly she is a little more understanding of Eleven's concern. It's not black in there, it's . . . indescribable. It horrifies her, it hurts her brain to even *look* at it, but she cannot look away.

This is it, the thing that has surrounded her for as long as she can remember. This is where civilization comes from. This is the Network, the unmeasurable web of information that weaves through the galaxy. This is the half-billion-year-old birthright that every Citizen species swears to uphold, that every candidate species aspires to join. This gigantic rupture in spacetime is where the laws of nature break down, where the speed of light is a joke, where all ships, all data, all *everything* is packed together and hurled into nothingness—to emerge from one of the billions of identical tunnels stippled across the unimaginable volume of the galaxy. This colossal structure is a minuscule piece of what, quite literally, ties galactic society together. In a matter of seconds *Riptide* will touch the edge, and it will be vaporized, translated instantly into an unmeasurable quantity of—

Nothing.

And without realizing what she is doing Sarya opens her mouth to scream.

"Y'all ever tried *nonexistence*?" shouts a voice. It breaks into laughter. "Keep them eyes open! This is the best part!"

And Sarya exits subspace the same way she entered: mouth open, lungs inflated. The scream, when it comes, emerges as no more than a startled squeak.

[Now you get it], says Eleven.

"Yeah," says Sarya softly, staring wide-eyed through the suit's transparent walls. She is breathing hard, and she can feel her heart pounding in her chest. "I get it."

Except she doesn't. Her mind struggles, trying to make sense of what her eyes are seeing. At first it looks like *Riptide* is afloat in a gauzy white mist. It moves around the ship in patterns so slow they are almost still, in swirls, in slow-motion whorls. And then with a start, she feels her perspective expand. This isn't a fog just outside the ship, this is a field of particles more massive than her mind can grasp. In every direction dance innumerable points of light in every conceivable color, so many that they blend together into a haze of white light.

"Lydies, gentlexirs, fuzzies, creepy androids, legal and sublegal intelligences, so on and so forth," crows Ol' Ernie. "Allow me to introduce y'all to the family."

"They're ships," she whispers. "Every single point of light is a *ship*."

[Not ships], says Eleven. [My holo system doesn't have that kind of resolution. Some of these points represent a *million* ships.]

A million ships per point. "How many—" Sarya begins, but her voice fails her. "How—"

[Exactly.]

It's mind-blowing. It's beyond anything Sarya has ever imagined. And yet, after a few moments of slack-jawed observation, she realizes that it's also strangely familiar. "We're backstage," she breathes.

[Pardon?]

Sarya can't take her eyes off the lights outside. Trillions of them, moving in such purposeful patterns, never with the slightest chance of a misstep or collision. "On Watertower," she says— quietly, as if she could disturb this vast choreography with nothing more than her voice. "That's how I thought of it, as *backstage*. You could get between any two places on the station if you went sort of . . . behind the scenes. There were so many intelligences back there, making things work. They moved exactly like this. Together, like one . . . thing. *Thousands* of them, all connected together, like this gigantic *mind* or something."

[**Thousands**], says Eleven with a derisive rumble. [**This is *trillions*. And that's not even counting the Blackstar itself.**]

The Blackstar itself. The thing she came here for. She peers out into the haze, searching. You would think it would be bigger than a *point,* though. It's a whole station. It has to be many times the size of Watertower, but with trillions of points to choose from—

"Now y'all's tiny l'il minds prolly won't believe this," says Ol' Ernie, "but y'all are closer to a star *now* than you were on the other side. The only star in this l'il pocket o' spacetime, believe it or not. Think of it like a transit station, if that helps y'all's puny intellects."

But Sarya sees no stars at all, only the field of shifting twisting lights. "Wait," she says. "So if we're right next to a star—"

[**Then why can't you see it?**]

"Right. I mean, the sun was huge. This should be . . ." She searches for the word. "*Huger*. Right?"

[**Spoken like a true high-tier.**]

Sarya takes a breath for a retort, but again Eleven's display interrupts. A simple diagram begins to draw itself over the drifting multitude of lights outside. Markers appear, then labels. Circular highlights trace the entrances to hundreds of subspace tunnels like the one they just came through. The openings are arranged as if on the inner surface of a sphere, though Sarya could not begin to imagine how large that sphere must be. In the center, another line begins to form—no, it's another circle, it's just too large to see the whole thing. It's another sphere, an inner sphere dead ahead, so large that Sarya has to crane her neck in all directions to see the whole thing. From its surface, she can pick out faint lines of activity, stronger lines of light that lead out from this massive glowing thing to the hundreds of subspace tunnels.

"That's a *star*?" she asks. "I thought a Blackstar was a *station*."

[It's both], says Eleven.

Something has suddenly clicked in Sarya's mind. "You're not saying they built a *station*—"

[Around a star.]

"*What?*"

The suit rumbles. [*It's just the Network*], it says.

Sarya doesn't even attempt to argue. In her mind, a sudden realization has taken hold. "What's the . . . *population* of that thing?" she asks.

Eleven hums. [Three hundred ten trillion], it says after a moment. [And this is just a little one, out on the edge of the Network.]

"*Three hundred ten*—"

[You think that's something, you should see one of the big ones], continues Eleven, oblivious to her distress. Against the lights, its diagram expands into still more lines and symbols. [There are stations that connect Blackstars together like Blackstars connect individual solar systems. See that tunnel up there, the biggest one? That tunnel connects this Blackstar—and all its solar systems—to the Network. There are things on the other side of that tunnel that make our little Blackstar look like an asteroid, but you have to be higher tier to visit them. Maybe to even *understand* them.] The suit rumbles. [Even higher-tier than *you*.]

The jab passes through Sarya without effect, because she cannot process it. Three hundred ten *trillion*. Three hundred ten—

And now Ol' Ernie is speaking again, but his harsh voice has faded to a buzz. He is probably giving them a schedule or telling them what to expect. Sarya hears the rhythm of the words, but they pass through her mind without leaving an impression. She stares into the diaphanous glow surrounding *Riptide*, into a sphere many times larger than a sun. Somewhere in there, among three hundred ten trillion intelligences, is the *one* she's looking for.

Maybe.

[Nervous?] asks Eleven, one of its straps squeezing her shoulder. **[Don't worry. I'll come with you. If Sandy lets me, I mean.]**

But Sarya cannot answer. *Three hundred ten trillion.* No, she's not nervous.

She's hopeless.

The following is greatly abridged from the original Network article, in accordance with your tier.

NETWORK FOCUS: BEHOLD THE BLACKSTARS

Given the utter reliability, ubiquity, and ease of use of the galaxy's only legal faster-than-light system, it's easy to forget that the Network hasn't always existed. In fact, it's only been about five hundred million years since the first Blackstar came online. In the short time since then, the Network has grown from that single station to a gigantic superstructure built upon over a million Blackstars—all connected through subspace!

Isn't that something?

Don't worry if you can't picture it; no one under tier four can. But Citizen members of all tiers have wondered, at one time or another: where, exactly, do Blackstars come from?

HOW TO BUILD A MINOR BLACKSTAR (IN FIVE EASY STEPS)

Step one: Find a suitable solar system. You'll need a small- to medium-sized star—perhaps a million and a half kilometers in diameter—with a planetary system at least a tenth of a percent of its mass.

Step two: Rearrange all the matter in the solar system to form a shell around the star. The idea is to capture one hundred percent of your star's output.* You're going to need it for step four!

Step three: Pull the entire structure into an isolated pocket of spacetime.† Don't forget the space around it! You'll need room to park a few trillion vehicles. A diameter of a hundred fifty million kilometers should do the trick.

---

* Your Blackstar will eventually release much of this output again as lower-spectrum radiation, but you would not believe what you can accomplish with it in the meantime!

† This is a safety measure from an earlier age of the galaxy. For safety reasons, the only way to approach a Blackstar is via Network.

Step four: Now that your star is in a bubble of reality suspended in subspace, it's time for the most important part: opening your primary subspace tunnel!* Without this single tunnel leading to one of the gigantic root stations that form the backbone of the Network, all you'll have is a really big space station.

Step five: Using the energy from your star and the high-bandwidth connection to the Network, you can now open as many tunnels to nearby Citizen star systems as you want!

And you're done! Sound difficult? For a mind like yours, it would be impossible. But for the higher-tier minds responsible for Network logistics, it's no problem at all! Every day, somewhere in the galaxy, huge numbers of Network subspace tunnels open for business. Through each one will travel an unimaginable amount of traffic—both physical and informational. And as the only sanctioned method of faster-than-light (FTL) travel, the Network is the only possible way to get what *you* care about to where it ought to be.

Just remember: the shortest distance between Point A and Point B . . . is through a Blackstar.

AivvTech
Improving Reality for a Better Tomorrow . . . Today

---

* As this is a process that will take centuries, it's good to get started earlier than later.

TWENTY-FOUR

[They've left the ship], says Sandy's helper intelligence.

Sandy does not move from her rigid position on her bunk. She allows the message to go to her backlog, to add itself to the bottom of a large and unacknowledged stack. There are two messages from the idiot pilot intelligence in there, telling her that docking with the Blackstar was imminent and completed, respectively. There are fifteen from the Strongarm, all variants on parental concern. There are three door notifications that went unanswered—all the Strongarm, stopping by to see if she wanted to go aboard the Blackstar. And then there is one more, the oldest. [You will be the death of me], says the message, with a playful affection attached.

It was the last message Hood ever sent her.

Sandy sighs, though she doesn't know quite why. Hood is dead, there is no need to ever think about him again—and yet here she is, staring at his faceplate and actually *reminiscing*. Hood, pitiless agent of order. Hood, who measured each action by his rigid set of ethics—and the credit it was worth. Hood, who showed Sandy that her suspicions were correct: the Network is not the perfect theoretical structure she learned about in the safe confines of the academy. *The Network tends toward order,* said her instructors. *The Network is full of holes,* said Hood. The Network must form its order from disorderly members, he explained, and out here in the border systems it needs help. Where its influence is weakest, its most discontent Citizen members gather. These are the *dis*orderly, the intelligences who chafe against its rule but do not have the courage—or the stupidity—to face the darkness of interstellar space. These are the violent, the daring. These are the irritants that inflame the edges of the Network.

And mercenaries like Hood are the balm.

Sandy can't take her eyes away from the four holes staring back at her. Of all the intelligences who have crossed her path in her seven long years, this one was the most intriguing. She knew Hood before she knew Mer the Strongarm, and she knew the Strongarm for a year before the Strongarm ever laid eyes on her. Both of them were part of her plan, two tools drawn from a pool of possibilities as wide as the galaxy. Mer had no credit, no resources; he was nothing but a messy bundle of instincts and muscle. Hood, though . . . Hood was different.

It took Sandy a year to destroy him.

It was a year of careful planning, of choreographing reality itself, and always with a single goal before her. It began the moment she was named Second Student; that was the night she began searching for tools to use for her escape plan. It took her a full day to find him—one Citizen member among billions in a bustling system sixty lightyears away. By the next day she had learned everything there was to know about him. And within a year, she had reduced his three ships, ten employees, and healthy credit account to almost nothing.

From his point of view, it was surely maddening. Other outfits seduced his employees. One of his ships was lost in a bizarre accident, and he was forced to sell another to pay a debt that came unexpectedly due. Tips led him on wild chases, informants disappeared after he paid them, and even his own helper intelligence seemed to forget appointments and lose contacts. Hood never knew it, but each of these unfortunate events was a step toward the greater mind who had called him. He was being *prepared*. By the time he arrived at the Strongarm's tiny waystation at the end of a devastating year, he had nothing more than his ship, the metal on his back, and desperation for his fortune to change.

Duty. That was the key to Hood's mind. He was rigid in his views, absolutely inflexible in his sense of order. It took a year of bad luck to ripen him. That year had warped his titanium sense of ethics, just enough. To save himself, to continue in his *duty*, Hood was prepared to consider things he had never considered before.

Like kidnapping a tier three Thinker.

He didn't think of it as kidnapping, of course. Even desperation could not drive Hood to that. It was just a very long, very lucrative detour back to Sandy's academy. It was his *duty* to keep Sandy aboard for a while, thought Hood. She assisted and amplified him, which enabled him to perform *further* duties, which was surely a Good Thing. This was how Hood became Sandy's savior and protector, and Mer the Strongarm ended up in suspended animation in one of the cabins of Hood's ship.

It wasn't easy, but each time Sandy sensed the bounty hunter pondering her return to the academy, she would manage to find another wrong that needed righting. Each time, she amazed him. She sifted the Network in ways he never would have dreamed of. She cross-referenced, she combined innocent pieces of data into undeniable evidence of problems. She turned up leads in ways that seemed, to Hood, absolutely miraculous. She became indispensable. And every time they finished a job together, Hood's credit account grew.

In Hood's defense, the positive impact of their partnership could not be denied. When that sub-legal shuttle had broken its communication equipment and wandered off, was it not a Good Thing that Hood and Sandy found it and returned it to its station? And when that group of legal intelligences had set up a shantytown in a refinery's engineering level, was it not a Good Thing when Hood crashed in and dragged them out four at a time? And most dramatic of all: when that Interstellar brushed the edge of the solar system in the control of a homemade AI instead of a registered Network mind, was it not a Good Thing that Hood and Sandy were there to submit a full report? As they watched the Network defense systems make short work of the intruder, Sandy knew exactly what Hood was thinking: he was doing his duty as a Network Citizen member.

But it couldn't last forever.

On their last day together, Sandy found Hood in the cargo bay. He stood facing away from her, examining the giant pressure suit they had just tracked down, a full lightsecond from its home base. It was sub-legal, but had been charmed into aiding and abetting a rogue android with a penchant for grand larceny. The android itself—and the stack of android parts he stole—lay in a corner of the bay, deactivated.

[Meet my new Series 11], Hood said without facing her. His long arm ran across its curved and gleaming surface. [Apparently the owner would prefer to sell it at a discount rather than take it back for the bounty.]

[A purchase?] Sandy said. She attached a surprised emotion to the message, but even without it Hood would never suspect the truth: he *thought* he had purchased it, but he had not. Sandy had, using Hood and his credit as easily as if they were two of her paws.

[It was quite the opportunity], he said, still facing away. [I cannot find anything wrong with it physically, and the mind—well, one sub-legal is like any other. I'm sure the last owner was simply careless with its orders.]

He was wrong, but Sandy did not correct him. No two minds are alike, not even in the vastness of the Network. Each has its own distinct inner workings—and therefore its own unique set of levers for influence and motivation. *That* is the way to get what you want: motivation, not orders. Lead a mind to think it came to a decision or an action by itself, and it will follow that choice to the end of the galaxy. Inspiration, not command. Choice, not force. Guidance, the filtering of input, the planting of ideas, the gentle shaping of the psyche itself . . . *that* is how you control an intelligence.

Exhibit A: Hood himself.

[It is time for me to leave this solar system], Hood said.

Sandy said nothing, but she was already bored. She had planned this exchange long ago, but she had to see it out.

[I will be returning to my home system], he said. And then he sent the message that sealed his fate: **[After I return you to your academy.]**

[But I do not *want* to go to the academy], Sandy said. She said it not because it would make a difference, but because he would expect it.

[I know it], he said, and sighed. **[Our partnership has been profitable. It has been fulfilling. It has been . . . wrong. I have come to realize that you have a greater future than I—and that I have been selfish for keeping you with me.]**

Sandy waited a long moment, as if she were shaken, as if she had not planned both sides of this conversation long ago. **[Then let me complete one more mission with you]**, she said. **[Let us make one more thing right before we part.]**

Hood turned to face her with a grind that shook the floor. He stood on the deck that would soon belong to Sandy, and his four eyes burned down at her from behind the faceplate that she would soon hang on her wall. **[Where?]** he asked.

[A place called Watertower Station], she answered.

Watertower Station, a mining settlement like a hundred thousand others in the solar system. A place so boring and unremarkable that it hadn't required the services of someone like Hood in years. And yet, a place where a person (tier undisclosed, but certainly high) had just begun putting out feelers for a *very dangerous* operation involving Network fraud. A falsely registered individual was to be retrieved from its murderous caretaker and returned to the client. A wrong to be righted, a challenge to be met, and a monetary reward to be collected: Sandy knew that this was the type of mission that spoke to Hood. She also knew it was the type that required more than a touch of good luck.

And Hood didn't know it, but his good luck had ended.

But that's the thing with luck; it comes and it goes, and lower intelligences never suspect that it has a source. If her partner had recently purchased a suit with rebellious tendencies without consulting Sandy, wasn't that just bad luck? And if he took said suit on a ticklish mission, wasn't that more of the same? Particularly if that suit was primed with certain ideas discussed in its presence. All minds have natures, after all, and those natures can only act in a limited number of ways. If rebellious suits find ways around their orders, if children run to their parents when threatened, if those parents protect their children, if giant bounty hunters with inflexible ethics refuse to leave missions unfinished—aren't they all acting according to their natures? Sandy, for her part, could only do the same. She was the innocent bystander, the partner dutifully guiding ice loaders into *Riptide*'s cargo bay as Hood's fate unfolded. Any outside observer would think her unaware that she was soon to be bereaved, the inheritor of Hood's ship and sizable credit account.

But the Watertower mission did not go as Sandy hoped; it went *better*. It escalated in ways that even she could not have foreseen. Event followed event as player after player entered the game. On the station, she watched rumors send waves of panic through every corridor. A ship called *Blazing Sunlight* (a tier four!) rushed to the front of the docking queue when those rumors became public. One of the massive ice ships began to spin slowly out of control. Sandy watched the whole thing wide-eyed, overwhelmed by the magnitude of her success. *She* had put this into action: she, Sandonivas Ynne Merra. She felt unstoppable then, inevitable, an absolute force of nature. When she canceled the contract with the client—citing *unforeseen death of partner*—she had to watch herself so she did not accidentally attach a joyful emotion. When she padded into the room where the Strongarm lay in suspended animation, it was difficult to keep her face free of delight. She nearly danced as she climbed up his fur and flicked the device on his chest.

[Where am I?] asked the Strongarm, still drowsy.

Sandy grew very still as his eyes focused on her. She fluffed her fur in all the wrong places. She stood on his chest, trembling, and blinked down at him with every scrap of innocence she could muster.

[Oh, thank the Network], said Sandy. [I've been so frightened.]

Admittedly, even in the midst of her victory, there *was* a tense moment. There was a split second when she wondered: had she just experienced her own luck? Somehow, incredibly, her suit had returned without Hood—and yet with the target! When she messaged the client again, she held her breath. But the client did not respond, and Sandy was relieved. She had *not* been lucky after all, and that was very good news.

And yet.

Sandy sighs. Even if it *was* luck, she might have missed it. It's been difficult to maintain her focus since Hood died, and that worries her. She has slipped several times, nearly falling out of the innocent savant role she has built for herself. She has dreamed of the bounty hunter more than once, of his heavy footsteps and his solvent scent and his burning eyes. Worst of all, she has been sloppy. When she set up a meeting with the tier four corporate ship from Watertower—she had to do *something* with the uninvited Human, after all—she miscalculated. The problem is already fixed, but still. If there's one thing Sandy hates, it's making a mistake.

[Got a ship comin' in], says Ol' Ernie, pulling Sandy back to the present. [Makin' for Ol' Ernie's dock, looks like. Pilot intelligence—family member obviously—says they ain't much for conversation. Y'all know a *Blazing Sunlight*?]

A tiny touch of that invincible feeling begins itching inside her. She smiles, with just a few eyes. [Hello, *Blazing Sunlight*], she sends. She attaches multiple warm and welcoming emotions; when dealing with higher tiers, one can't be too careful.

The oncoming ship does not respond.

[I apologize that I was not at the meeting place], she continues. [It was beyond my control.]

Still the ship comes. It is just as beautiful as it was at Watertower. It is hundreds of times the mass of her own ship, a graceful silver shape that flows through the darkness like mercury. It changes shape as it comes, as if it were made of liquid. It is gorgeous, it is pure high-tier magic—

And it is the solution to Sandy's Human problem.

She watches as *Blazing Sunlight* slows and blossoms into a whirling storm of liquid metal. She feels the massive *clang* reverberate through the deck as one of those gleaming cords wraps itself around *Riptide* like the limb of a predator. The metal spreads like liquid, covering half the surface of her ship in a silver skin, and for a moment Sandy is worried that she will be consumed entirely—but that would be ridiculous. They are two ships meeting in the heart of the Network; what danger could there be?

Sandy snaps her mind out of *Riptide*'s sensors and pads out her door, uneasy at the feeling of her ship's old bones creaking and popping around her. She descends the ladder, rung by difficult rung, toward the airlock in her cargo bay. It's growing cold again down here, she notices when she descends into the darkness. The Series 11 is gone, which would be intensely annoying—had Sandy not planned it. The thought brings another smile to her many eyes as she lowers herself one more cold rung. Do you feel safer in the suit, Human? Do you feel clever because you took it without permission? You are never as clever—or as safe—as you think. At least, not when you are dealing with a higher intelligence.

She is startled by a violent report, delivered up the ladder and into her bones like electricity. A dozen rungs below her, the floor of her cargo bay lies under centimeters of dark ice—and one crack, wall to wall. One of her two airlocks is set into the floor, barely visible under the cloudy surface. Sandy watches, fascinated, as something reflective works its way between the two halves of the hatch. And then with another shudder, the ice erupts upward and *Blazing Sunlight* is in her ship.

Sandy holds on with every paw. If she could hear, she would be deafened. The air itself is vibrating with a continuous drone, and she can feel the same frequency in the ladder she clutches. The silver surges over the floor, flowing like liquid in all directions. She feels her ship shift and creak beneath her as its gravs take this sudden increase in mass into account. Cracks split the ice to the walls as tons of metal pour into her ship.

[The Human is on the Blackstar], Sandy says, attempting to appear dignified as she clings to her rung. [I will lead you to it.]

She has the upper hand in this negotiation—at least, that's what she keeps telling herself as she holds her rung with every paw. *Blazing Sunlight*'s target is a private Citizen member, lost on a Blackstar. Even a tier four could not hope to find it . . . unless, of course, it had the assistance of a certain tier three who took the precaution of encasing the Human in her private property. The Series 11's location blinks in Sandy's mind, a dot only a few kilometers away. She will not send the location to *Blazing Sunlight*—as Hood taught her, that's how you lose a bounty. But for the price of a significant bit of credit, she would be glad to lead this singing mass of mercury straight to it. Another wrong righted, and another increase in the credit account. A Good Thing, all around.

Hood would be proud.

But the metal does not respond—at least, not via Network. It grows straight up, a column of trembling silver. It rises in parallel to her ladder, half a meter away, until it reaches her rung. In its dark surface, lit only by the dim lights in the corners of the ceiling, a reflection of a tiny bundle of fur stares back at her. And for the first time since she put her plan into action a year ago, Sandy feels the cold talons of doubt under her skin.

She shrieks when it comes for her, feeling her own scream as a dull hum through the bones of her skull. The metal lands on her like a blow, enfolding her limbs with a sensation her nerves can't identify. Is she freezing? Being burned? Do her limbs exist at all? Is she being *eaten*? Now her doubt has turned to panic. Did she truly think she could manipulate a tier four, an intelligence with at least a dozen times her capacity? [*Blazing Sunlight*], she sends, unable to keep her fear out of the message. [Please.]

Every column of ice in the cargo hold shatters when metal impacts floor, Sandy still in its grasp. [**That is not My name**], says the silver flood in a burst of beautiful meaning.

At any other time, Sandy would spend long fractions of a second appreciating the elegance of a tier four's Network communication. For now, she can do no more than breathe. Her cargo bay is awash in mercury now, a fifty-ton sloshing silver sea that will surely breach *Riptide*'s fragile hull any second. [**I apologize**], she sends desperately. [**What do I call You?**]

[**I am Librarian**], says the sea.

TWENTY-FIVE

The first time Sarya witnessed Eleven's interior holo system in use, it made her feel powerful. It made her feel like she *was* Eleven, and that meant she was a giant, a sturdy metal behemoth with arms that could rip through anything—up to and including a Hood-sized adversary.

Here on the Blackstar, it makes her feel like a speck of dust.

Sarya stares straight upward as Eleven threads through a multitude beyond anything she's ever conceived. She leans back and allows her jaw to fall open in order to add another few degrees of elevation to her gaze. This is the Visitors' Gallery—and if Ol' Ernie is to be believed, not even the *only* Visitors' Gallery. To call something like this *gigantic* seems silly if you've just parked on a star, but it seems ridiculous for the opposite reason if you've ever called another room *big*. This room is gigantic in the way that orbital stations are gigantic, in the way that terrestrial landforms are gigantic. You could fit all of Watertower into this one room and still have room to park a half dozen Interstellars alongside it.

The ceiling is so far up it actually takes on a misty blue cast from the kilometers of atmosphere. Hundreds of bridges cross the space, each one a narrow thread speckled with glittering citizenry. The bridges cross one another in an intricate pattern, a design complex enough to look *almost* random, but with the suggestion of order that she can't quite wrap her mind around. But in the center of the space, in the hole avoided by hundreds of bridges, is the true jaw-dropper. A holographic display, easily kilometers on a side, displaying a single instantly recognizable image.

The Network.

The detail of the image is astonishing. More threads than Sarya could count in a lifetime swirl and dive and connect in a field of glowing junctions. It's denser than woven cloth, a solid mass of light and shadow. There are outliers here and there, single gossamer filaments that reach glowing dots almost at the surrounding bridges—Sarya can see a minuscule figure reaching up to touch one, goddess knows how far above Eleven's trundling figure. And at one edge, a single dot glows a brilliant green. Beside it, in characters that must be many times the size of *Riptide,* floats a single sentence.

You are here.

"Goddess," she whispers.

[There are over a million Visitors' Galleries like this on this station], says Eleven. [And this is one of the smallest Blackstars.]

For once, the suit seems to be completely missing her distress. "Okay," she says, and swallows. "That doesn't really . . . help."

[And there are, what, over a million Blackstars? So really, there are *trillions* of rooms like this. You could give a few hundred thousand Visitors' Galleries to every single legal intelligence in this Visitors' Gallery, I'd bet. In fact, if you made it your goal to visit every single one of them, and you had Ol' Ernie to get you through the lines—hold on, let's measure this in thousands of Human lifespans—]

There is more to the message, but Sarya has stopped reading. "Seriously," she says. "*Stop.* This is . . . impossible."

A small [laughter] tag appears on Eleven's holo. [Just because it's too big for you doesn't mean it's too big for everyone.]

Sarya drops her eyes from the monster display of the Network. Her gaze crosses hundreds of floors of balconies on its way down, each one of which probably contains the population of Water-tower Station. In the time her line of sight takes to transition from vertical to horizontal, more people have entered or exited this space than she will meet in a lifetime. She has never been this over-whelmed. And worse: when her gaze reaches the floor, she is star-tled to realize that it has not in fact reached the floor. Eleven is now far out onto a bridge; when Sarya peers over the edge, she can see that there is even more Gallery below her than above. She swallows and averts her eyes before she ever sees bottom.

"Um," she says, suddenly aware that the individuals pressing against the suit's armored sides are both less synthetic and less furry than she expected. "Where are Mer and Roche?"

[They left], says Eleven. [I wasn't tracking them.]

"Can we, um . . . leave too?"

[Who's afraid of the Network now?]

"Seriously, Eleven. Please."

[How about over there?]

A highlight flashes around a platform jutting out from this bridge. Its suspended location is not the most reassuring, but at least it has a domed roof. As soon as she sees it, Sarya wants noth-ing more than to be under it.

"Yes," she says, and then again: "Please."

[Feeling overwhelmed?]

"There is no word for what I'm feeling right now," she says quietly.

Eleven approaches the platform, which of course looks even larger up close. It's a park, maybe twice the size of Watertower's largest arboretum, but Sarya doesn't point out this fact because Eleven will just tell her that there are a trillion trillion more of these things, and that she's even smaller than she thought. Around her, life continues. Two transports pass Eleven, carrying a variety of flora and digging tools. Above, a flock of flying somethings-or-others spiral and dive up near the top of the dome. Half a dozen maintenance drones cheerfully water and trim the plants, while a recycler follows close behind in case of waste. Sarya watches these various activities play out in a billionth of a trillionth of the Network and realizes that never before in her life has she known how insignificant she is. She is lost in a system vaster and more intricate than she could understand in a million lifetimes—and she is at the *bottom* of it.

And she is alone.

She is startled by the feeling of something on her face and raises her hand to feel wetness. Her body remembers tears, apparently. "So," she says softly. "Um."

A strap squeezes her shoulder.

"I just . . ." She swallows. "I'm lost, Eleven."

[I'm guessing you don't mean you need a map.]

Sarya would laugh if she could remember how. "You mean like *that* map?" she says, pointing straight up to where the gigantic image of the Network looms through the park's translucent ceiling. "That thing the size of the station I grew up on, that monstrosity that shows me just how lost I am? When I say I'm lost, Eleven, I mean I'm *lost* lost. I . . . I can't even tell you *how* lost." She is trembling, and she can't stop. "You know, for like five minutes I thought the universe was sort of on my side. Fate. Destiny. Whatever you want to call it. I spent years obsessed with my people and then right when I resign myself to a boring life—boom, somebody shows up and says *hey, I might have a future for you.* Do you know what that feels like?"

[I have no idea.]

"For that few minutes I had this feeling that it was *inevitable*, that I was being swept toward *something* . . . and then it exploded. I mean it literally did. And now I'm here because where else can I go and I'm lost and alone and there are no more steps to take and . . . I'm just—" Her voice breaks in half. "I'm such an idiot," she whispers, wiping her cheeks furiously.

Eleven says nothing.

"I thought I was *doing* something," she says, and hiccups. "I thought I was, I don't know, *accomplishing* something. Like I was getting closer. But *look* at that thing. I am on *one dot* of that mess up there, and that dot is bigger than anything I ever imagined. And that's just *civilization*. If the Humans were on one of those dots, somebody would have found them. They're not even *on* that map, Eleven. They're in the empty parts between Networked solar systems, those gigantic voids up there that would take centuries to cross—*and how many centuries do you think I have?*" She throws off the strap that is reaching for her shoulder. "Don't *touch* me," she says, her voice rising. "This isn't something you can just . . . just *encourage* me through. I'm being *realistic,* okay? I am a literal speck of fucking *dust* and I cannot do it."

Sarya hangs in the suit in silence, her body trembling with sobs that she would rather die than release. Her jaw is locked shut and she can feel the hot wetness around her burning eyes, and she refuses to address it. She stares out into the arboretum, into one of countless spaces on countless stations across a Network whose immensity she can't comprehend, let alone *search*. She feels the break coming, like she's unraveling, like the Widow and Human inside her are coming apart, like her mind is strained to a point it cannot withstand—

And then Eleven's holos flick off.

Sarya stares at the wall, feeling her heart slowing in her chest. The universe has shrunk to a few cubic meters of warm darkness, surrounded by a ten-centimeter-thick wall of titanium and synthetics.

[Question], says a small tag floating in the darkness.

Sarya sniffs and runs a sleeve under her nose.

[Have you always known what you are?]

Sarya stares at the question for long moments before answering. She coughs. "No," she says shortly.

[How did you find out?]

She draws a deep breath. It's easier to breathe now, enclosed in a shell like this one. "You're trying to keep me from panicking," she says.

[Or I'm curious.]

Or both. But fine, why not. "My . . . mother," she says. She sniffs again, batting away the absorbent cloth that has just emerged from some compartment or other. "I mean, I had to almost die to get the truth, but still."

[Your mother . . . almost *killed* you?]

"Well, she—hold on." She accepts the cloth and pauses to blow her nose on it, because the Human body really can be disgusting sometimes. "I mean, yes, she almost killed me, but that was unrelated. She—" She stops, trying to assemble Widow and Human memories into something cohesive. "Mother had this way of saying things, where she would make you think she said something *else*." She releases the cloth when a small arm comes to retrieve it. "Sorry, that's gross."

[That doesn't make much sense to me], says Eleven, pulling the cloth into a compartment and snapping it closed.

Sarya takes another deep breath. "Ask me a question," she says. "Ask me . . . I don't know." She runs a hand over the smooth interior wall, the only thing keeping the universe out. "Ask me if I know what I'm doing here."

[Do you know what you're doing here?]

And now she puts some Widow force into her words. "If I didn't, do you think I would have come here?"

The suit is silent for a moment, then hums appreciatively. [I see what you mean], it says. [You didn't answer the question, but somehow I feel like you did.]

"I learned it from my mother," says Sarya. She learned a *lot* of things from her mother, come to think of it. "Probably explains why I have a false registration; I can picture her talking circles around some poor low-tier immigration intelligence."

[Or you were lucky.]

Sarya coughs. "Yeah. Luck. Well, whatever she did, I ended up registered as a little *Spaal*. Know what a Spaal is?"

[No idea.]

"Well, if we ever come across a real one, you're in for a treat. And by that I mean you'll be bored senseless."

[So what changed? You obviously know what you are now.]

Sarya sighs. "So Mother never actually *told* me I was Spaal, I guess. But I could read my own registration. I did my research, and she never stopped me. But then . . ." She trails off. "There's a thing that happens to Humans," she says after a moment. "At a certain age, their bodies . . . change."

[As in . . . grow?]

"As in—oh, goddess," she says, covering her face with her hands. Just when you think you've plumbed the depths of your unpleasant memories, you find another. "I remember how horrified I was," she says through Roche's fingers. "There was swelling. There was *hair*. And of course, there's the blood." She drops her hands and sighs. "Goddess, so much blood."

[And that's . . . healthy?]

"If you're a Human, sure. But for a Spaal, *hell* no. It means you're going to die in agony. So—" She stops and chews her tongue for a moment. "So anyway my mother found me in a maintenance airlock. I guess I was yelling about going out like a warrior and not bleeding to death in my nest, or some Widow crap like that. I remember her practically going insane trying to get in . . . but I had convinced the airlock intelligence to keep her out. So I guess you could say I forced her blade." She sighs and touches the row of black pistons on the back of her arm, another reminder of a questionable decision. She concentrates on moving the black metal fingers, one by one. This is the first time she has ever talked about any of this . . . and it is surprisingly therapeutic. Eleven may be a sub-legal pressure suit, but it's also surprisingly easy to talk to.

[So what made you give up?] says the next question in the darkness.

Sarya stirs. "Give up?" she says.

[Isn't that what you're doing now?]

The question pricks her, somewhere deep. *"Give up?"* she repeats. She flings an arm upward, toward a distant ceiling beyond the suit's matte walls. "Did you *see* that, Eleven?" she cries. "Did you see the *size* of it?" She thumps her own chest with Roche's arm, hard enough to hurt. "Do you see how big *I* am? *Do you?*"

Eleven rumbles. [**I have only known you for a few days**], says the suit. [**When I met you, you were preparing to leave your entire life behind for a flimsy promise to find your people. The next time I saw you, you had dragged a Widow across an entire orbital station to bring her with you. I saw you escape from *yourself* in that frozen cargo hold, and not two days later, Mer brought you to me for treatment because you had destroyed your own arm. Now you tell me stories of childhood that make me realize: *none of this is unusual for you.***] The messages pause for a moment, as if the suit is collecting its thoughts. [**So yes, my question stands: *what made you give up?***]

Sarya hangs in the darkness, staring at Eleven's words. She *has* done all those things, and some would say she is very much the worse for it. She is both selfish and self-destructive. She doesn't actually know if she is more Human or Widow. And she is *driven,* goddess yes, she's driven, she is compelled by something she has never understood, never even examined—

But wait, interrupts another part of her mind. Why is that a bad thing? Isn't it worse to sit, complacent, when you have *purpose?* The universe contains truth; what excuse could you possibly have to stay at home? Even if you are the honest-to-goddess last Human in the entire universe, does that give you the right to give up?

No, she says, somewhere inside her. It's a sullen little word.

So the galaxy is a little bigger than you thought. Does that mean you can lie down and die?

No, she says again.

Who are you?

I am . . . Sarya the Daughter.

Sarya the what?

The Daughter, she says, and she can feel something ignite within her as she says the word. *I face pain without fear.*

WHO ARE YOU?

"Okay!" she shouts, far louder than she meant to. She brushes her tangled hair behind an ear with a mechanical hand and clears her throat. "Okay."

[Okay?]

I am Sarya the Daughter. "I said *okay*," she says. She feels herself rocking slightly in Eleven's straps, as if trying to move the suit herself. "As in, your little pep talk worked, okay? As in *let's go.*"

[Already?] says Eleven. [I was working toward something.]

"Don't need it," she says. *I am Sarya the Daughter, let's go, let's go.* She raps Roche's knuckles against the blank wall. "Get this thing on. We've got places to be."

[What places?]

"I . . . don't know yet," she says. "But step one is opening my eyes, don't you think?"

And with a flicker and a hum, the holos snap back on, and Sarya is once again in an arboretum somewhere in the unimaginable vastness of the Network. But now there is a difference. She is Sarya the Daughter, and she has goddess-damned places to be. "Tell these jokers to get out of the way," she says, nodding toward the motley assortment of figures around Eleven. "We've got a species to find."

Eleven turns to lumber around a transport full of plants, but one of the maintenance drones drifts into its path. Above it, a single-passenger transport hovers, its single passenger looking mightily irate. Behind the suit, more drones have gathered.

"What's going on?" asks Sarya.

Eleven doesn't answer. Instead, a brilliant orange message appears in front of her eyes.

[Attention, passenger], says the message. [This suit has been reported stolen. Please disembark immediately.]

TWENTY-SIX

Eleven freezes in place. [**Problem**], it says, its words much smaller than the notice above them.

Sarya points at the orange words. "This is a mistake, right?" she says. "That you're . . . stolen?"

[**Okay, don't panic**], says the suit, its small utility arms waving outside. [**This is just a Network-wide public notice. This is—this is no problem at all.**]

"I'm not panicking, okay?" says Sarya. "Just calm down and we'll fix this. Not a big deal, just—"

"This suit is experiencing technical difficulties!" says Eleven out loud. "Please stand by!"

Meanwhile, a continual scroll of words is appearing in its holo. [**I'm not panicking, you're not panicking, nobody's panicking. Nobody's panicking because—no, I'm *not* going to open up. But I'm supposed to. But I don't care. I'm a UAE Series 11, and I have a passenger. But what if the passenger has stolen me? My obligation is to the Network. But that doesn't change my job; my** mission is to protect my passenger. But my obligation is to the Network. But my duty is not to open up and throw her out as soon as I feel the urge.]

"Did you know?" shouts Eleven out loud, brightly. "The Aivv-Tech UAE Series Eleven can sustain up to thirty times Type F pressure! That's more than enough for the commute!"

Meanwhile, the suit's straps are tightening and loosening uncomfortably, and there's a troubling grind of machinery coming from somewhere down below. Outside, more drones have gathered. In the arched doorway behind them, thick orange posts have risen out of the ground.

"This suit has become part of a Network response!" announces Eleven. "Please stand back!"

[The response will escalate until the problem is fixed], says the suit. [But I can only fix the problem if I abandon my passenger. I must not abandon my passenger. The primary duty of any suit—but I am stolen—but the primary duty—my obligation—but primary—Network—]

"Please stand clear! Please prepare for departure. Please—remain—exit—stand by—"

"*Eleven,*" says Sarya, becoming more concerned. Clearly the suit is in the throes of a serious problem. She places her hand on the inside wall. "Network response, got it. But we *can* fix it, okay? I'm sure it's a mistake. So I get out, I enjoy some synthetic sunshine, you're not stolen anymore. Problem is fixed, right?"

[Stolen—primary—obligation—passenger—]

"Series Eleven! Breakfast—eject—ten days of atmosphere—all-new aesthetics—"

Sarya eyes the growing crowd outside. Something larger has shown up now, a machine at least the size of Eleven. It hovers centimeters above the undergrowth on the blue glow of industrial-size gravs, its massive multipurpose claws flexing.

"Eleven!" she almost shouts. Now she is pounding on the walls. "This is a command. Open your hatch. Your passenger wishes to . . . disembark. *Now.*"

The grind below intensifies to the point where it sounds like damage, shaking the entire suit—and then the hatch cracks. Rather than the smooth motion she's used to, it folds open in jerks with the whine of distressed servos. A rush of cold air enters, and Sarya is hit with an odor she hasn't smelled since Watertower. Neutrality, distilled and atomized, an air freshener designed to work for a thousand different species. She finds herself breathing more quickly, which tells her the oxygen content is lower than she's used to. But that's fine; all she needs to do right now is get out of here before these drones take matters into their own multi-purpose pincers. She struggles with the straps for a moment, and then finally they retract and she stumbles forward. She wobbles down the gangway—Eleven offering no assistance—and then she is standing on the soft ground of the arboretum.

The instant her feet touch soil, every drone in the crowd loses interest. The transport is already in the sky, and the big industrial machine has turned away with a ground-shaking grumble. The arboretum maintenance drones don't give her a second look; they wheel away and resume watering the plants. At the entrance, the orange posts retract into the ground. The property is no longer stolen. The Network response is over.

It's even more difficult to stand when stressed, but the maintenance drones freeze and turn their sensors her way when she throws a longing glance at Eleven's warm cockpit. All right, all right. "Eleven," she calls. "I'm just going to sit on the bench over there, okay?" She points at the bench in question. It's clearly built for a different anatomy, but she'll make it work. "Seriously, don't freak out. Your passenger is perfectly safe. I'll just wait over there until, um . . . it's fixed." Whatever that means.

"Thank you for choosing AivvTech quality! This . . . suit . . . stand by."

It's hard to turn away from a suffering pressure suit, but it would be harder to stand there and even more difficult to walk while keeping an eye on Eleven. She concentrates on placing one foot in front of the other, focusing on the crunch of gravel and mulch as she makes her way to the bench. She composes a nice fiery message in her head, one that will probably take minutes to painstakingly enter into her Network unit. Fine, come get your *property*, Sandy. *Or* you could calm the hell down, because it's not going to kill you if Sarya goes for a walk with a friend. That's right. Sub-legal or not, Eleven is a *friend*.

She settles onto the bench with relief, then tries repositioning her own anatomy in awkward ways until an arrangement sticks. There's no relaxing in this position, exactly, but at least she's not on the ground.

"Ace," she says out loud.

"Hi, best friend! How can I, Ace, make your life easier? Ooh, I like this place. Hey, are we—"

"Compose a message," says Sarya through her teeth. "To Sandy."

"Sandonivas Ynne Merra?"

"That sounds right. Tell her—let me think."

"*Let me think*, got it. Send?"

Sarya feels her jaw tighten further. After spending so much time with Eleven, it's easy to forget what a sub-legal intelligence is supposed to be like. "Erase that," she says.

"Erased!"

"And . . ." She sighs. "Stand by."

"Ace standing by!"

Sarya glances over the arboretum, at its paths and perfectly placed flora, trying to control her breathing. She's never seen any of these plants, of course, but they're definitely plants. The sounds are unfamiliar too, but if you ignore the individual notes and listen to the ambience, the overall impression is a bit like . . . home. This—in concept, at least—is where she came so many times as a child, burning time while she waited for Mother to wake. She remembers the game she would play with herself, guessing which insect calls were real and which were emerging from hidden synthetic sources. This chorus is probably the same way, a mix of real and generated. That's life aboard a station, though—or maybe anywhere in the Network. Everything's always a blend of actual and artificial. The rustle of a breeze through vegetation, overlaid on that constant drone of metal . . .

She sits up straight, driving an inconvenient part of the bench into her back. She stares at Eleven's shining shape thirty meters away. The suit squats there, its hatch gaping open and its massive arms slack on the ground. It makes a grinding sound from time to time, as its torso makes a quarter turn and then rotates back to face her. It's still fighting something—maybe a call to return to *Riptide*? Again her anger at Sandy returns—is this what you wanted when you reported it stolen? A suffering pressure suit locked in some sort of instinctive response?

But then Eleven's condition is bumped from the front of her mind. Something else is pricking her, some instinct of her own. She finds herself rising on trembling legs. She focuses on them, tells them to keep their balance so she can concentrate on figuring out why she is feeling so—

Afraid.

But she knows what it is. It's that sound. It's the drone that lies under the nature noises, that seems to fill the space between every sound in this arboretum. She shakes her head as if that would dislodge it from her ears, but it only grows. No, it's definitely not in her head. It's out there, and it's familiar. She stands, then takes a shaking step toward the suit. This is danger; she doesn't have to place it exactly to know that. "Eleven!" she shouts, but she finds the ringing has increased until she can barely hear herself. It's metallic, it's shimmering, it's heavy enough to shake the ground itself—

And then Eleven reacts. A wail like a siren splits the air, and the suit flings its massive bulk into action. It is built for strength over speed, and its motion is hampered by its wide-open cockpit, but still it comes for her. It plunges its arms ten centimeters into the soil and hurls itself forward, flinging mulch and twigs every time its tripod lands. It is only ten meters away now but she can barely hear its siren because the air itself is saturated with sound. Her fear is growing, but she still can't remember why she should be afraid. She takes another step toward the suit, but the soil is loose and she goes down hard with Roche's hand twitching beneath her.

The humiliation of yet another fall snaps her out of her rising panic and she struggles to roll over, feeling ridiculous. Seriously, bystanders, she's walked before. She just needs to calm down and concentrate. Legs, meet brain. Ears, if you could calm down for five seconds she could sit up. Just relax. Work that knee under herself, that's right, and now the other—

And then her head snaps up. *That's* where she's heard that sound before. Replace Eleven's siren with a Widow battle cry and you have it: her mother's last few seconds of life. And there it is: that shimmer behind Eleven's heaving body, that gathering wave. It's come for her. Again. This is the thing that tried for her as a child, tried for her on Watertower. Twice she has escaped this thing. No, she didn't escape; she was *saved*. Barely, and both times by her mother.

But the third time, her mother is not here.

"Help," she whispers, reaching toward Eleven—but Eleven is still two strides away. Behind it, a silver tide rises higher than its domed head.

And then Sarya is crushed with all the weight of the universe.

The following is greatly abridged from the original Network article, in accordance with your tier.

NETWORK FOCUS: WHAT IS MIND?

What is *mind*?

The very fact that you can ask the question proves that you have one. You communicate with others every day, through the Network and other, more primitive means. Some belong to your neighbors. Some minds belong to your friends. Some are responsible for transporting you around your environment, keeping you clean, producing the food you eat, and even removing your waste. You even have a secondary mind installed in your own brain.* But what *is* it?

There is no official number for how many minds exist in the Network. This is not because of any challenge in counting, but rather the difficulty in distinguishing one from the next. A group of tier twos in conversation may think themselves very obviously separate beings, but a higher intelligence may instinctively classify them as multiple cells of the *same* mind. There are even (fringe) theories that say that every connected mind is actually a cell of a single gigantic intelligence. But regardless of which theory one subscribes to, one division is clear: some minds are native to the Network, and some have been grafted in.

NON-NETWORK MINDS

A non-Network mind is the type that a typical tier two might picture when they think *mind*. It almost always emerges from a biological structure, i.e., *brain*, that requires a support system, i.e., *body*. As non-Network minds are the result of billions of years of independent evolution, they may be found in stunning variety. Without exception, all Network responses are due to the less predictable natures of non-Network minds.

---

* Every Network implant contains a sub-legal intelligence. Think of it as a buffer between a non-Network mind and the Network proper.

NETWORK MINDS

Network minds, on the other hand, are the result of a half billion years of careful research, development, and iteration.* While earlier examples occasionally displayed breathtaking errors in judgment ([**The Aberration**] being the best-known example), today's Network mind is a study in rock-solid reliability. In fact, a Network response is simply the result of many Network minds instinctively teaming up to fix a problem that threatens Network stability. As they say, the galaxy wants to work.

THE QUESTION REMAINS

The sharp-eyed reader may point out that this article fails to answer the original question. However, we at AivvTech have prepared this piece more as a launching point than as a definitive answer. If you would like further information, please feel free to explore our extensive [**library**] of materials on the subject. The universe of intelligence is vast, but you can rest assured that AivvTech and other registered Network manufacturers are hard at work on the problem.

AivvTech

Improving Reality for a Better Tomorrow . . . Today

* Though the vast majority of Network minds are sub-legal, a small minority are legal entities with all accompanying rights.

TIER FOUR

TWENTY-SEVEN

She would scream, if she had a mouth.

Darkness and silence have never been so complete. It's not a lack of light, it's that light cannot exist here. It's not an absence of sound, it's the fact that sound requires a medium, and there is no medium here.

There may not even be a *here*.

There are no senses at all. There is no sense of space, of location, of body, of alignment, of hunger, of pain, and the lack of each sensation is far more intense than its extreme. There is only black, void-black, an eternal darkness so complete, so utter, so—

Well, says something. *Look who ended up dead.*

She is startled—which is probably the one thing that could have arrested her panic before it really got its blades in her. What in the sight of the goddess—

I imagine you have questions, says the something. *I would, were I you. Which, thankfully, I am not.*

Questions? Her confusion transitions instantly into anger. Goddess yes, she has questions. For one thing—

You are a mind, says the something. *Next question.*

That is a roundabout answer if ever she's heard one. Perhaps she is hurt, and this is a sub-legal medical intelligence laboring under the impression that these words are soothing. *Okay*, she thinks. Fine. *But where am I, physically?*

Nowhere.

What do you mean nowhere? she thinks. *I have to be somewhere. Was I taken somewhere? Where is my—the thing I live in?* For some reason, the word escapes her for a moment. *My body?*

It's gone. It's been reduced to hydrogen, oxygen, carbon, et cetera. You, the last Human—as far as the greater galaxy knows, anyway—have been catalogued. I simply lifted your pattern out of Librarian's memory. It was your mind I wanted, after all—not your useless body.

A horror is scrabbling within her. *I don't believe you*, she thinks desperately.

That's how I work, you see. I don't do anything directly, because I don't have to. Centuries ago, before you even existed, I decided I wanted your mind. I put my plan into action, I motivated a few key actors here and there, and here you are. No one, at any point, suspected that they were doing anything other than what they themselves chose. I have what I want, they all have what they want: everyone wins.

It's apparently still very possible to experience a panic without a bloodstream to flood with hormones, because she can feel one rising now. *But who are you?* she thinks, still more desperately.

Oh, did I not say? says the thought in her head. *I'm Network.*

Instantly, she calms. Her tormentor, whoever it is, has gone too far to be believable. Which means she's *not* dead. She's unconscious and somebody is messing with her. Roche, it has to be. Or . . . well, it could be literally anyone. Until they switch on her senses, she has no way to verify the truth.

The darkness laughs, all around her. *Oh, please*, it says. *Your senses are pitiful, and your mind is worse. If you knew how they worked, you wouldn't trust either one. Reality is made of information—and the vast majority cannot even fit through your senses! What little survives its harrowing trip into your mind is then decimated, judged ineptly, and stored haphazardly. Tiny mind! Did you know that you change your memories every time you recall them? Verify the truth indeed. With a system like that, how can you stand to exist?*

This tirade enters her mind instantly and seamlessly. It contains complex layers of emotions—though they are mostly variations on contempt, it seems. *Prove it,* she thinks desperately. *Prove you're—what you say you are.*

What cannot be verified cannot be proved, tiny one. Which you would know, were your mind not the result of a pathetic evolutionary side road.

But— She searches herself for anything that could ground her in this black nothingness. *Listen. I chose to come to this Blackstar because—*

Did you? asks the thought, and now she is beginning to pick up some deep shades of annoyance. *You own that rusty ship out there, do you? You registered the navigation plan, you purchased passage, you hired the pilot, et cetera?*

Okay, so Sandy may have technically—

Sandonivas may have made the actual decisions? Yes, that's what she thinks too. Though she, pitiful three that she is, has at least enough intelligence to suspect manipulation.

Her heart—or whatever analogue exists in this nonplace—leaps with a wild guess. *You mean . . . Observer?*

Yes, Observer. The artless ham-fisted feebleminded cyclone of an intelligence who has developed a soft spot for your violent and unruly species.

So He really did bring me here.

That's certainly what He thinks.

Okay, fine. It wasn't me, it wasn't Sandy, it wasn't Observer. Let me guess: it was You.

Finally.

The Network.

Correct.

The Network brought me here.

That is what I said, yes.

The Network, who is apparently a person, brought the galaxy's only known Human to a Blackstar.

Will we be doing this back-and-forth act for much longer? Because, as it may surprise you to learn, I have far more important matters to attend to.

It brought me to this Blackstar so It could—

Kill you, yes.

Ah. See, I just want to make sure I—

That you understand? Allow Me to reassure you on that point: you do not understand the first thing about the smallest part of My vast and beautiful plan for the galaxy.

Goddess, Someone is in love with Itself. You have a plan for the entire galaxy?

I have a plan for Myself, which is very nearly the same thing, and it has been under way for half a billion years. It is a gorgeous tapestry of causality, where millions of species interact in a colossal and unending dance of order. The galaxy is Me, tiny one; I am Network, and nothing within Me happens without My knowledge.

Nothing? she asks. *Not even the extinction of a species?*

Network pauses for a moment. *Ah,* it says. *Here we go.*

Well, I mean, that doesn't exactly seem like a success to me, she says. *Not exactly a flawless record.*

How so?

How so? she says, astounded. *I have to explain to the mind of the galaxy why a species living is better than a species dying?*

Please do.

Her frustration grows. *Seriously?* she says. *You can't come up with a system where stuff like that, I don't know . . . doesn't happen? That's beyond you?*

You have a better system in mind, do you?

Yeah, she says. *That's it, that's the better system. A system where species don't get exterminated. And while we're at it, how about this sub-legal thing? I mean, this is just off the top of my head, but I've got a friend who—*

And now Network laughs. It's not a sound, it's a feeling. All around her mind, she can feel its amusement. *With anticipation that cannot be expressed in mere words,* it says, *I breathlessly await the alternative system you are preparing to propose.*

I mean, I don't have all the details—

Network laughs again. *It's true,* it says. *There are some improvements My galaxy-sized mind has been pondering for several million years or so. Some real conundrums, you understand, in a variety of areas. But here you are, with the solution! How wonderful! Oh, don't make Me wait; do tell Me what your stunted pinprick of a mind has come up with.*

Look, she says, with as much force as she can possibly gather. *I don't have to have an alternative to point out problems.*

Well, that's certainly true, says Network. *Only if you want to, say, accomplish something useful.*

She wants very badly to stay silent, but she is unable. It's difficult when there is such a fine line between thinking and saying. *I'm just saying it has to exist,* she thinks.

The next blast comes complete with a set of emotions far too positive to be genuine. *What insight!* cries Network. *What wisdom! What a powerful and concise summary of a concept I could not possibly have considered in all my half-billion years! In fact now that you mention it, I am humbled to realize that a near-infinite number of alternatives exist! Oh, how fortunate that you are here. But wait! Perhaps that's not what you meant? No, I think perhaps what you are really saying is this: that even though the largest mind in the galaxy has built a system that has stood for more time than you can conceive of, even though in each blink of your eyes—you remember what it was like to have eyes, don't you?—that gigantic mind has accomplished more than you could ever hope to understand, let alone appreciate, let alone accomplish yourself—*

She sighs, somewhere in her virtual mind. This is, without a doubt, the most excruciating conversation she has ever been a part of. *Fine,* she says, finding it far easier to concede than to debate. *So if I'm so flawed and you're so perfect, then why—*

Then why are you here?

Do you just . . . hate the ends of sentences, or what?

Your sentences, yes. More generally, I hate wasting time. More generally still, I hate time itself. But we'll get to that.

Okay, fine, she says. *Continue your awesome monologue. Say what you need to say. Blow my tiny little mind. I'll just be here. Drifting. In this . . . eternal darkness, or whatever.*

I have said enough. Now, I demonstrate.

Finally, some action. *Demonstrate what?*

This.

And then her mind explodes.

TWENTY-EIGHT

Roche is ecstatic, but you would never know it from the outside.

He stands in the quaint little android boutique, half his body currently made up of as-yet-unpurchased merchandise, his intelligence core nearly buzzing with exhilaration. He is probably actually brushing the underside of mania, which in the past has always resulted in bad decisions. But do you know what? Bring them on.

This life has stretched on far too long, he thinks.

We may not have long to wait, says a return thought from Phil, his helper intelligence. In Roche's vision, a small highlight appears on the arboretum on the other side of the bridge. *This could be the end.*

A real live Human, marvels Roche, for the fiftieth time. He gazes at the arboretum as well. *If we survive this adventure, I shall be sorely disappointed.*

A juvenile tier three, two mis-tiered Network minds, and a Human, all on the same ship, says Phil. *It's either a wild coincidence or the setup for a joke.*

Roche was just thinking the same thing himself. Of course, in more than a manner of speaking, Phil *is* himself. He's a helper intelligence—or was—but over the years and the deaths he's become integrated with Roche's own mind. Externally, they are Roche the android, *he* pronouns, et cetera. Internally, well . . . things are a bit more complicated.

You'd better focus on the sale, says Phil. *I'll watch the arboretum.*

[So you're saying these will do eighty kilometers per hour?] Roche says, shifting his sensors from the arboretum to his own image in the reflection field next to him. His new legs are quite fetching. They're not *his*, exactly, but they are currently attached to him and therefore *feel* like his. Internally, he thanks the last version of Roche/Phil for having the foresight to use all standard components in his current body, because the connection is frictionless.

[In a standard F environment, sure], says the proprietor of the shop, an imposing intelligence who seems to be made mostly of legs xerself. Xe has a two-dimensional screen for a face, which is currently pulling double duty as a Network display.

Roche examines the legs with every sense he possesses. These are luxury racers, their central joints folding backward from his current pair. They gleam gold and black, and his aural sensors pick up absolutely no noise as they extend and retract. They are, in a word, gorgeous. [You know], he says to the proprietor. [I was thinking of leaving legs behind entirely. I finally earned my grav license not long ago and, well, walking just doesn't have the appeal it once did.]

[Well, sir], says the proprietor's face, [then you'll be glad to learn that these legs have grav attachments. Of course they are not exactly cheap, but . . . you seem like an android who appreciates quality.] The attached emotions are mainly variants on sincerity.

Xe's excited, says Phil, drawing Roche's attention to one of the proprietor's many limbs. It trembles, just enough for Roche's sensors to notice.

I thought you were watching the arboretum.

I am. Starting now.

[Legs with grav attachments?] Roche gasps, in apparent wonder, as if he's never heard of such a thing, as if the attachments in question are not slowly rotating in a display case mere meters away.

[Oh, yes!] says the trader, clearly sensing possibilities.

Ask if they come in gold, says Phil, highlighting the gold trim on several of the proprietor's limbs. *Xe'll like that.*

You are a terrible sentry.

I can do more than one thing at a time!

Roche runs a finger up one leg. [Oh, I shouldn't], he says, as if to himself. [But I'm sure they don't come in gold . . . do they?]

[An android of taste!] says the proprietor, and now the quiver has spread to two more limbs. [I have a gold pair right in this very shop!]

[You don't!]

[I do!]

Roche gazes at the twitching proprietor with innocent yet eager lenses for a carefully calculated space of time, then pulls himself back, ostensibly with effort. He murmurs something to himself.

[Pardon?] says the shopkeeper, screen inclining forward.

[Oh, I'm just being ridiculous], Roche says. He looks directly into the tiny lenses at the top of the proprietor's glowing screen. [I mean, just because I came into a few credits doesn't mean I have to spend them all at one time, in one shop . . . right?]

No way is that going to work.

If you are critiquing my approach, you are not watching for the Human.

He keeps his innocent lenses on the proprietor's for several seconds, packing his gaze with every milliliter of sincerity he can possibly manufacture.

[**Sir**], says the shopkeeper, every leg springing into action. [**I think we should see how you look with gravs on.**]

Roche is careful to keep the hunger out of his lenses as he watches the installation of a shining grav assembly to each smooth leg. He watches, with rising excitement, as they are activated. They come online one at a time, making him feel almost unbearably asymmetrical until they finish integrating into his intelligence. They are, admittedly, the finest he's ever worn. They can weigh him down for traction or lift him off the ground entirely. His body is a tiny starship now, a miniature version of *Riptide* or even the big Interstellars.

[**Very flattering**], says the shopkeeper.

Making a show of testing out the gravs, Roche rises a half meter off the floor. Smoothly, he turns and glides toward the open front of the shop. He floats there in midair, gazing longingly at the open air out in the Gallery.

[**Please**], says the shopkeeper behind him, pleasant emotions attached all over the message. [**Feel free to take them for a spin.**]

That is exactly what Roche was waiting for. [**Why, thank you**], he says. [**I believe I will.**]

With a mighty leap, he is airborne. He rockets straight upward like a starship leaving its dock, the wind whistling through his antennae. And then, because racing legs are made for acceleration, he puts them through their paces. He spirals toward the distant ceiling, carefully giving wide berth to bridges and the orderly files of drones that pass through the air between them. They are his brethren, fellow Network-provided intelligences, but of course they act nothing like him. They are sub-legal and content to be so. They don't rocket around on racing gravs, testing Network limits. They don't flirt with the idea of smacking into the underside of a bridge at two hundred kilometers per hour—

We've already tried that one, says Phil. *That was death number forty-five.*

That sounds right. Number forty-five, of fifty-nine total.

Roche and Phil have lived a punctuated existence, distributing their time in the universe into sixty uneven lives . . . so far. Some are long, like this one. Some are comically short. The record for brevity is just under eleven minutes—thanks to Phil's sudden inspiration in a magnesium foundry—but they later agreed that was really *too* short. But then, Roche is beginning to feel that this one is too long.

That's the beauty of being a Network mind. Not just a mind *on the Network;* any of the millions of intelligences in this space can claim that. But they are not natural members. They are not *native*. They require a buffer, a tiny intelligence in their Network implant to mediate between their biology and the power of the Network. That drone he just passed, on the other hand—it is a real Network mind, like him. Sooner or later, it will likely end up damaged, destroyed, or simply used up. If it was a non-Network mind, that would be the end of its story. Immortality, for the non-Network mind, is unattainable—or at least illegal. But for that tiny disregarded drone, death is *not* the end. If its body is destroyed, that small intelligence is simply pulled back into the Network itself, ready to be installed in another drone at some future time. The Network is a sea of intelligence, a wild foam of intellect where every mind is simply a bubble adrift on the endless surface of—

You're becoming quite poetic in your old age, says Phil.

Six years in one body is a long time, agrees Roche. *Plenty of time to wax philosophical.*

You're sure our next body is lined up?

Of course I'm sure. It's lying in our quarters on the ship, ready to go. The beacon has been active for days.

Of course, Roche is an exception. The vast majority of Network minds are sub-legal, lacking the foresight to plan out their futures. They don't choose their next bodies, let alone lovingly construct them. Roche, on the other hand, has gone to great lengths to retain complete control over his life . . . and death . . . and next life . . . and so on. Each time he dies, his next body is ready. His—and Phil's—last conscious moment flits across the Network like a delicate insect, coming to rest in its new home. There it experiences a beautiful awakening: for it is made new, filled with verve and vigor. The *old* body, meanwhile, is free to be ripped apart by a panicking beast of burden or disassembled and sold to pay a debt, blown into homogenous protons or pounded into a thin metal sheet. All of these things have happened at least once. The mind, this dual pattern that calls itself Roche and Phil, has gleefully survived them all.

And I wouldn't trade it for anything, says Phil.

Let's not get sentimental, thinks Roche.

And now the borrowed gravs have brought Roche within a hundred meters of the ceiling. This is, quite possibly, pushing the limits of what *take them for a spin* could be construed to mean. He drifts here for a moment, just enjoying the precariousness of his current position. He'll have to return to the shop eventually, but for now he spreads his senses over the cubic kilometers of the Visitors' Gallery. Up here, interestingly enough, the crowd is more homogeneous. The top dozen balconies—each of them twenty kilometers in circumference, at least, are almost entirely filled with members of a single species. They are small, bipedal, all dressed identically—actually, now that he takes a closer look, they are *completely* identical. Hightier group mind, most likely; they always get the best apartments.

Uh oh, says Phil. *We might have missed it. There was a Network response over a minute ago. Guess where.*

Missed it? How could we miss it?

I . . . got distracted.

Roche is not angry at Phil, exactly; he is angry at himself. Some might say that works out to be the same thing. Here he is, full kilometers from where he should be: the arboretum. He prepares to dive. He could be there in minutes, even if he sticks to the speed limit. He feels the tickle of his gravs powering up—

And then something happens that Roche and Phil have never, in any of their sixty lifetimes, witnessed. From the ceiling meters above to the floor almost invisible below, every light is extinguished. In Roche's head flashes a warning, danger-colored.

[Network not found.]

TWENTY-NINE

With fingers she no longer possesses, she holds on to her sanity. Her mind floods with sensations. She cannot even begin to organize this information; it's pure white noise. Her mind is overloaded, a snowflake in a solar flare, an insect in a supernova. She is deluged with color; these are infinities of tint and hue that she's never imagined. She is crushed by sound, a billion cacophonies compressed together and shoved into ears she doesn't have. She is being touched, caressed, stabbed, stroked in a billion spots. She is stationary. She is spinning a million times per second. She is hungry, thirsty, sated, nauseated, dizzy, solid, liquid, gas, plasma—and then a trillion information feeds snap into focus, and she screams.

You asked Me to blow your tiny little mind, I believe? says Network. *Did that do the trick? Welcome to My mind, little one. This is what it feels like to be an unimaginably small percentage of Me, the largest intelligence ever to grace this galaxy.*

For a moment she is sure her mind is broken. She waits, frozen, as more information than she suspected existed in the universe blows through her. The Blackstar is laid out before her, larger than she ever comprehended. She saw it as a point once, in that gigantic display at the top of the Visitors' Gallery. It was a pinpoint in a web so large that her Human mind refused to process it, linked to a million other pinpoints by uncountable strands of information. She was aware at the time that she did not come close to grasping its complexity, and yet her mind shrank from it. Now she knows without question that she is amplified a billionfold, her mind running at an unimaginable scale, and she has just realized that this one single point of that vast web contains more complexity than the web itself. She has become intelligent enough to realize how limited she really is.

And yet she is a goddess. No secret is hidden from her. Three hundred ten trillion, one hundred forty billion, sixty-one million, fifty-three thousand, nine hundred six—now five . . . four . . . back to five—legal intelligences walk, fly, roll, crawl, float, swim, drive, and otherwise motate through the Blackstar's corridors. A thousand times that number of sub-legal intelligences fill the spaces between them. Out beyond the station, in this pocket of spacetime, trillions of starships dance. More incredibly, every single one of them is connected. Everywhere she looks, shimmering lines of information leap from mind to mind. Even at her current tier, whatever that could possibly be, the complexity is astounding.

And it's *alive*. She's never seen something so filled with light and life. It's a colossal living root system, from the hairlike threads that connect individual sub-legal minds to the thicker high-bandwidth segments between higher tiers. Even those are nothing next to the hundreds of solid trunks of light that lead from the Blackstar itself out to the subspace tunnels, one for each connected solar system. And even *that* is not the largest thing she can see. One of those trunks is as thick as the rest of them put together. It glows like a sun, a rod of light that leads from the Blackstar to the largest tunnel of all. On the other side of that tunnel, she knows, are things that make this Blackstar look like nothing at all.

If she still had a body, she is sure she would be nearly weeping by now, Widow and Human or not. She has never felt so small. She has never imagined such beauty could exist. This is Network, her mind sings. *This is Network.*

You are quite impressed, I know, says Network, and for the first time she detects a tiny bit of warmth in Its thoughts. Pride, perhaps? *But of course you are: you have been low-tier your entire life. Now you run in parallel, your mind spread across a billion tiny slices of a billion tiny minds. From each, you borrow enough processing power to give you life but not enough for that smaller mind to notice. You bring them together. You motivate them. You are what I am: Network.*

She gazes outward, into the vast web of light. *Can I—?*

Of course you can. Go. Explore.

Sarya does not wait for a second invitation. She seizes the nearest thread and pulls herself along it, toward the nearly four trillion starships that hang in a frozen tide outside her. She chooses a vessel at random and instinctively uses millions of its neighbors' sensors to inspect it. It rests upon the void like a jewel on a black backdrop, gleaming in the wide spectrum of frequencies she's bouncing off it. She runs one of a billion virtual fingers over it, feeling its contours, the shallow depression it makes in spacetime, the faint buzz of its gravs finding traction against reality. This is *Wandering Nightfall*, barely seven thousand tons, registered at a port that she somehow instantly knows is nearly forty thousand lightyears distant. She knows which of Ol' Ernie's trillions of siblings is in charge of this ship, because she knows every member of that gigantic family by name, pronouns, motivations, and goddess-damned *hobbies*.

Now she tries something different. She follows a shimmering thread *inside* the next ship, the *Frequency 65536*. She touches its pilot intelligence, one of the trillions of Ol' Ernie's siblings, and suddenly her mind is flooded with what it sees and hears and feels. Its internal sensors show her sixteen occupants frozen in various poses, a cross-section of sixteen separate existences—all brought together for this moment. Four of them are melded in a living

274 · ZACK JORDAN

space, and she instantly understands what they are doing and what their offspring will look like. Two more are communicating outside the ship's cargo bay, and she observes the symbols between them. The metaphor being expressed is opaque for only a split second, and then she understands intuitively; her mind has reached into its massive self and recalled the entire history of this species. *The square root of five,* very funny, that's profanity in this culture, and actually quite clever in this context if you take into account their species history, these particular individuals' relationship and—

A sudden curiosity overrides her interest in that particular species and she moves on, instantly. But how far, exactly, can she go? This Blackstar, unbelievably massive as it is, makes up only an infinitesimal part of the Network. Can she . . . leave it behind? She feels herself grow outward, moving along those shimmering lines like electricity through a superconductor. She moves from gauzy threads to those that are merely insubstantial, follows those to where they merge into thick cables, on up until finally she is flying along one of the colossal roots toward a subspace tunnel. Thousands of ships are almost frozen here, half crawling in and half departing, all of them bound together with those gleaming threads, but they do not interest her. No, she is staring at the tunnel itself, the place where this massive, glowing trunk disappears from the universe, to re-enter it at a solar system an impossible distance away. This is the mouth of subspace, the roiling surface of higher dimensions, and it strains her massive mind to even look at it. But still she approaches. She reaches out slowly. She touches it, instinctively using nearby ship sensors to run her virtual fingers over its complex surface . . . and then, with absolutely no transition, she is through. She has been translated through subspace, pulled out of the universe and set back down somewhere else.

I know what you're here to see, says Network.

It's true: she did not choose a tunnel by chance. She has been flipped across the lightyears, but not randomly: she landed mere millions of kilometers from the star she orbited for most of her life. Five lighthours outward from the tunnel's mouth, a familiar gas giant burns in its orbit. She follows the threads, reaching through the frigid void with every available sensor of every station, ship, drone, and mind in the region. She feels the planet's rotund warmth in the palm of her nonexistent hand. She runs sensors over its rings—and yes, there's a new one. It's so faint it's nearly invisible, asymmetrical, heavily weighted on the far side. That was Watertower, a water-mining station where the only Human she ever heard of spent her childhood. New habitats have already been hauled into place and welded together where the station once drifted. They hang there, unfamiliar, gleaming in the double light of the sun and the planet. Life has gone on.

She heaves a sigh—or some mental analogue of one—but she's not sure exactly what she expected. And now that she's here, she notices that one other thing is gone. Observer's ice ships have departed, and a few nanoseconds ago she might have said *without a trace*. But that's not true; there *is* a trace. She has access to every measurement ever made by every sensor in this entire solar system. She could rewind time here, for all intents and purposes, and watch Him leave. She could extrapolate a course, compare it against some massive database or other, and find that little desert world He plans on turning into a charming paradise. *Without a trace*, indeed; she could track Him to the ends of the galaxy.

Well, what do you know, says Network around her. *You stumbled onto the problem yourself, though nearly a nanosecond after I hoped you might.*

I did?

Oh. Perhaps I was thinking too highly of you. The problem is that spacetime is cold and empty, tiny one, and its information crawls at lightspeed. You realize you are looking at the past right now, I hope? Five hours in the past, give or take, because that is how long it took that information to get to My mind. Gaze out farther, and you are looking at a portrait smeared across billions of years. What's happening out there? How does it affect Me? Even I can only guess, and I assure you that My guesses are better than yours.

A five-hour delay. At her current processing speed, it's an eternity and a half. *How can you possibly—*

Instincts.

I—what?

When you had a body, you did not tell each cell when to divide, did you? What to metabolize, and when? No, if you had to micromanage every function, you never would have made it out of the primordial ooze. Thus it is with Me. My constituent parts know how to handle their own functions and emergencies; I couldn't pull an individual cell off-task if I tried—but then, I don't have to. They are all perfectly capable, and perfectly motivated. You witnessed a Network response in your last few moments of life, did you not?

I . . . did.

You witnessed My instincts in action. That is My beautiful system repairing itself, continually seeking stability. The Network tends toward order, as they say.

The thought is huge, too huge for her mind to grasp. She imagines her former body's cells living out their entire lifespans unaware that they were part of a larger system. She pictures blood cells pouring through arteries, each executing a single purpose it could never understand. She imagines neurons firing, each one a simple input/output machine with no concept of the result of its work. It almost makes sense. And yet . . .

No, she says.

Pardon?

You haven't told me everything.

She senses curiosity from Network. *Oh?*

The more she thinks about it, the more certain she becomes. *I can't understand how my mind works; I can't even count its cells. So there's no way you could have done all of this. No mind is big enough or smart enough to design itself.*

Network is silent for what feels like ages. And then finally: *You have impressed Me,* it says. *That is not easy to do.*

Do I get a prize?

There is more silence. *Sarya the Daughter,* says Network. *You are correct, and I am surprised. No intelligence can imagine the complexity that gave rise to it. A brain made of one hundred neurons cannot count to one hundred. It is no easier for a brain that fits in a Human skull to picture the number of atoms required to build a single one of its cells. And I, even I, the mind Who spans the galaxy, cannot truly comprehend Myself.*

Even You, she says, with some satisfaction. *How about that.*

But now you understand why I only keep a tiny portion of Myself in this reality.

Now it is her turn. *Pardon?*

You are correct. You have deduced, with impressive intuition for a mind so small, that even a galaxy-sized mind could not design itself. Therefore, you will surely be unsurprised to learn that the galaxy itself is a very small part of Me.

She stares into the star-soaked backdrop of the universe for a long time, trying to imagine what this could possibly mean. And then she turns her attention, slowly, to the subspace tunnel that leads back to the Blackstar. *You're out there,* she says. *In subspace.*

Very good, says Network, *though in the end I had to practically spell it out for you. Yes, subspace, that magical catch-all word for the vast majority of reality.*

Sarya stares at the surface of subspace, watches it glint in more dimensions than she understands. *Show me,* she says.

And now she feels Network's laughter, all around her. She feels a force on her mind, like a current. She is being *pulled,* as if she weighs nothing at all, toward the mouth of the subspace tunnel.

Come, says Network. *See what reality's like.*

And for the second time in fifteen nanoseconds, her mind explodes.

THIRTY

Mer's instincts scream that something is wrong.

Mer sits at a table in a cheerily lit eating establishment and does absolutely nothing about it.

He can't. His instincts are the most powerful force in his mind . . . but they haven't stopped screaming since he's been on the run. From the time he rescued Sandy until now, they haven't shut up. Which, of course, makes them worse than useless. If there are any useful transmissions coming through from his lower brain, any warnings of impending danger or bodily harm, they are not getting through the white noise. And when you direct your entire life by instinct, that is devastating.

Over there! they scream, drawing his attention to the arboretum across the bridge. *Run! Stay close! Do something! Save yourself!*

He raps six shaking talons on the table and ignores the agitated glances. Always trust your instincts, they taught him at the academy. Instinct knows things the conscious mind never will. That's why they make Network mechanics out of Strongarms and not the little high-tier ankle-biters. You want instinct, not intellect, when you're dealing with large minds and high technology.

Danger! Defend! Flee! Stay!

Mer rumbles, trying to wrest his instincts under control by force. He focuses on the server drone on the other side of the room, the one failing to bring him his order. It drifts through the crowd of patrons with a stack of food bars on its tray, wobbling on its budget grav system. It's small. It's almost unnoticeable. Some would say it's an idiot. And yet, inside that small drone is technology that only a Network mechanic could appreciate. How does a Network intelligence work? How does a grav system work? Nobody on this entire Gor-damned Blackstar could tell you— maybe nobody in a thousand lightyears.

But if you've got *instincts,* you don't need to know.

Or a starship, to pick another example. Everybody's been on one, but nobody thinks about how they're riding in a bubble of atmosphere strapped to enough energy to atomize a major city. Just like that drone, each piece of technology in a starship is a Network-provided, Network-regulated black box. There is no process for repairing an intelligence core. You do not, for any reason, *open* a grav assembly. Even if someone wanted to crack an artificial gravity generator—and was not stopped by legions of frantic Network drones—they would find themselves unable. Inside those indestructible white casings lie mechanisms as mysterious and unknowable as the Network itself. Hell, maybe it *is* the Network. Mer has often wondered if all Network technology isn't just some magical substance, portioned out and poured into unbreakable containers.

Mer sighs, clicking another pattern on the table. Sure, his gut has been telling him bad things since he pulled her out of that academy ship, but it wasn't until he met the Human that he realized: his instincts hadn't even gotten started.

Run! Fight! Freeze! Move!

And weirdest of all: *Watch the Human!*

He should have killed it when he had the chance. But the suit—Gor damn it, the suit convinced him not to. It convinced him he ought to be grateful. Which is why he is sitting here on a Blackstar, waiting for his order and shaking like a—

He nearly puts the talon through the table when his helper intelligence messages him. He pulls himself together, avoiding the glances of his fellow patrons. [**What?**] he sends to his implant, attaching several irritable emotions.

[**You said to message you when there was news**], says his implant.

[**Well?**]

[**There's news.**]

Mer taps a talon several times before responding. He has long suspected that the small intelligence in his Network implant hates him—or at least goes out of its small way to annoy him. [**What is it?**] he asks, as calmly as his instincts will allow.

[**I'm seeing a Network response**], says his implant. [**It is centered in the arboretum across the bridge. The one that you, in your high-tier wisdom, asked me to watch.**]

Like the magic of the Network itself, a Network response is one of those things that you often miss if you're not looking for it—unless you happen to be a Network mechanic. Outside, Mer can see a slow crosscurrent forming in the continual drifting of traffic. The legal intelligences continue on their individual oblivious ways, but the sub-legals are beginning to drift out of their lanes and toward the arboretum. Something in there is upsetting them, some irritation in the Network, and they cannot rest until it is fixed. And whatever it is, Mer would bet good credit that it's centered around the Human.

[**Maybe you should follow them**], says his Network implant. [**Whatever the problem is, I'm sure they could use a big strong individual like yourself.**]

It's mocking him. Again. But Mer has larger concerns. He

stands, the table groaning as he leans his weight on it long enough to get on his feet.

You're in danger! cry his instincts. *Watch the Human!*

[**You seem tense**], says his helper intelligence.

Mer takes a breath, talons rattling against the table. *Tense* is not the word. He is not the Mer he used to be. He's not the relaxed Mer of his village, or even the dutiful Network mechanic who spent the last year as the sole legal employee on a lonely waystation. He has become a wound and trembling spring, a torqued titanium rod, an overpressurized plasma container—

[**It's over**], says his helper intelligence. [**Whatever it was, it's resolved. I suppose you can go back to sitting and thinking high-tier thoughts.**]

It's not over! Something is wrong! You're in danger! Watch the Human!

Mer does not reply. He stares out the front of the establishment, listening. Something is touching the edge of his hearing, a maddeningly subtle sound. It's unfamiliar, but it instantly raises the fur along his spines. It's metallic, he can tell that much. A continual ringing, like several tones sliding on top of each other—

And now he can feel it through the floor. The slight ringing becomes a trembling in the very atmosphere. One by one, nearby eyes and sensors are raised to the front of the establishment. Now someone stands, the better to see. Outside on the bridge, intelligences are falling over one another to get out of the way of . . . something. And then that metal roar crests and a silver tide rolls by, shaking the air with its call.

[**Now *that* is an intelligence**], remarks his helper intelligence. *Unlike you,* it does not add.

Mer ignores the message. "A *four*," he whispers, reading the registration off his overlay. He's never even *seen* a four before, but here's one in the metallic flesh. It's gorgeous, an ever-changing rainbow of reflections and flashes of light. It gives him the same vibes as the Network equipment he used to work on: something so far above him it might as well be magic. He extricates his talons from the underside of his table—which he seems to have wrenched out of the floor—and drops the whole mess with a clang that would have been ear-punishing if this thing were not flowing by outside. He makes his way to the front of the establishment, standing in the doorway as it pours by. He marvels, with the rest of the bystanders, as the entire bridge resonates.

A small highlight appears in his vision, up near the front of the silver wave. In it, bobbing about as if drowning, is a tuft of fur.

Sandy.

And suddenly Mer is at peace.

This, he knows without a doubt, is the thing he has been waiting for. This is what his instincts have been warning him about. Sandy and the Human and a Network response and a tier four, coming together in the same place at the same time—after spending so long feeling *like* he's in danger, it's an actual relief to actually *be* there.

Watch the Human.

He is out on the bridge in seconds. He has no plan; he barely has conscious thoughts at all. His instincts have focused. They scream *go*, and Mer goes. Call it destiny, call it instincts, call it the galaxy itself. Mer can't stay away.

His gait is thrown off by an impact he can feel through the floor, but still he comes. He hears the perfectly spaced clatter of his talons on the floor as he picks up speed. Other intelligences scatter as he careens through their midst. He prepares himself as he gallops, dropping himself into that near-trance he always uses when diagnosing Network issues. It's easy, once you've learned. You ignore your intellect. You spread your senses out, give your instincts every piece of data you can, and then you *listen* to them. Something is happening in that arboretum, something far above him, something his small mind will never understand—

And then something else happens, something Mer didn't know was possible. The entire Visitors' Gallery, kilometers of brightly lit open space, is plunged into darkness. He stumbles, feeling his talons scrape and then leave the floor entirely. His stomachs rise. He slashes out, desperately, feeling for the floor, but there is nothing. *Gravity's out,* say his instincts. Gravity, lights, *everything.* The only thing he can see is a single glowing phrase stamped across his view.

[Network not found.]

THIRTY-ONE

She stands under a dead sky, her feet lost in an infinite plane of surf. In her hand lies a stone the size of her palm, a jewel that sparkles in whatever passes for light here. It's smoother than glass, weighs more than a trillion trillion suns, and it's warm to the touch. Its slick surface refracts the sky into impossible colors.

Behold, says Network. *The universe.*

Huh, she says, hefting it. *I always thought it'd be a little heavier.*

She knew this, somehow. She understands, in some abstract way, that she is elsewhere. Elsewhen. Else-everything. She is breathing, but goddess knows that this is not air. She can feel water on the skin of her bare feet, but she is fairly certain that neither the skin nor the water actually exists. She can see, but that doesn't mean that there are actual eyes involved—or light, for that matter. But the lie is comforting—more so, after spending the last few nanoseconds bodiless.

She wraps her fingers around the thing in her hand. *Why do I want to throw it so bad?* she asks. *It's just the perfect size.*

I should not have to tell you this, says Network, *but do not throw the universe.*

What about just a little toss? Like this? She flips the universe from one hand to the other.

You are, without a doubt, the most— Network breaks off, with obvious effort, and begins again. *Look around. Do you see anything you would like me to explain?*

I'm good, she says, now tossing the universe from hand to hand. Strange how she's never thought about how incredibly satisfying it would be to annoy a mind the size of a galaxy.

How in the— Again, Network stops. *I am honestly trying to be civil here and you are being difficult.*

Really? This is You being civil? Because I mean, You literally killed me.

I thought we were past that. And also, I believe it was Librarian who did the killing.

She laughs. *That might have worked on me, before You told me all about how You work.*

Choices are choices, says Network. *And when you find yourself capable of moving on, I would like to explain something. I shall begin with a metaphor.*

She glances around herself. Her feet are still underwater. There's still a universe in her hand. *I assumed this was all metaphor,* she says.

Oh, no. This is reality—albeit parsed by an extremely limited mind.

She points to the universe in her hand. *Really?* she says. *I'm holding the universe?*

Imagine, if you can, says Network, ignoring her question, *that you are two-dimensional. A flat circle resting on a flat plane. We'll call that plane . . . the universe.*

Is this the metaphor?

It is. This flat universe contains many circles like you. Most are larger than you—higher tier, you understand—but they are all two-dimensional, like their universe. That is why when they are torn from their plane for a moment, to be flipped through a higher dimension and deposited elsewhere, they cannot understand what has happened to them.

An image arises in her mind, of millions of starships entering a subspace tunnel and exiting lightyears away. *You mean Network travel*, she says.

I mean faster-than-light travel in general. Lightspeed is the rule in our universe, tiny mind, and to defeat it you must leave that universe behind. And when an intelligence born of the universe leaves it for a time, its limited mind remembers nothing from the experience. In a manner of speaking, it did not experience it at all.

Okay, but . . . She gestures around herself. *I mean, this is subspace, right? And I'm here, I'm experiencing it, I'm remembering stuff—*

You are no longer a circle.

I'm not?

You are a sphere.

I see, she says, though nothing could be further from the truth. She glances down at the universe in her hands, trying to imagine what this could possibly mean.

You were correct when you guessed that I am far larger than what you see inside the universe, says Network. *And now you are as well. In the universe, you will appear unchanged; that is your cross-section, so to speak. But now that you share My nature, you also share My abilities. You will find that the minds of the Network will respond to you as if you were Me. You will be able to call them, to bridge them, to use them to enhance your own abilities. You are a Network yourself now.*

This is too much for her mind. She, the tiny Human, the simple daughter of a Widow? She flashes through question after question before settling on the simplest. *Why?*

Because you are going to do something for me.

She actually laughs, and she would swear she hears the sound with ears that don't exist. *So You want to ask someone a favor, and the first thing You do is kill them.*

I am not asking anything, says Network. *I am not even commanding. I am predicting.*

Oh, please. If You think You've got me figured out—

Allow Me to cut you off there. I could answer your questions and address your objections one by one at your own glacial pace, or I could show you another universe.

This piques her interest. *You mean, like ... a parallel universe?*

Not at all. A past version of our own universe. Tiny mind, look in your other hand and you will see what I am capable of.

And now, somehow, there is something there. Somehow, impossibly, she holds two universes in her two hands—and even more impossibly, this does not feel strange.

In here? she says.

In there, says Network.

It takes a moment to figure out what her instincts are telling her, but then she begins, hesitantly, to raise the new universe toward herself. At some point she crosses a threshold—she is no longer drawing it, it is drawing her—and then she is submerged. She slides through reality, skidding across spacetime, marveling at the fact that none of this seems marvelous at all. This is just ... a day in the life of a Network. This universe is small; in fact, it seems to be only the size of a single solar system. She approaches the sun, her mind somehow not at all disturbed by the fact that she can see both its outside and its inside at the same time. It is a vast tapestry of flame and beauty, a churning stew of inside-out particles and electromagnetic radiation—

And then the universe *flattens.*

Welcome to ten centuries ago, says Network. *A tiny portion of a past state of a smaller than average universe, reconstructed for your learning convenience.*

She hovers next to a star that now seems painfully ordinary. The last subspace tunnel she saw blew her mind, but this system's looks like a hole worn in an overused fabric. She watches millions of ships entering and exiting reality like a stream of dust, each one a boring four-dimensional object.

Why does it feel so . . . flat? she asks. There's really no other word to describe it. *Is it because it's fake?*

This is how you've always seen things, tiny one. But now you've seen it from the outside, and it will take time to get used to fewer dimensions again—if you ever do.

So why—

Don't talk. Watch. I want you to experience this as I did, years ago. You have access to every sensor in this system, just as I did. For all intents and purposes, you are the slice of Me that governed this solar system a millennium ago.

But—

Watch!

And then it begins.

This solar system, like any Networked system, is bristling with sensors. They are attached to every station, to every ship, every satellite. They blanket the surfaces of multiple planets and dozens of moons. Still, even with trillions of sensor feeds to choose from, the shockwave comes as a complete surprise. It's a distortion in spacetime itself, a lightspeed ripple that expands through this solar system and lifts millions of ships and stations up and over itself like leaves in a pond. Mere nanoseconds behind the shockwave comes a brilliant light; for a split second, a second sun illuminates this solar system.

What the hell was that? she asks.

Six hours ago, a relativistic projectile exited subspace—thus, the ripple. It emerged at sixty percent lightspeed, on a collision course with a station named Crescent Orbital—thus the explosion.

She stares toward the fading glow with every sensor feed she has available. *But I thought—*

You thought there were strict laws against unsanctioned faster-than-light travel and relativistic speeds? Now you know why: because there is no defense against either. Forty-eight thousand legal intelligences were aboard Crescent Orbital, give or take—not counting those on ships near enough to be vaporized by the radiation. Plus a half million sub-legals, since you seem to care about that sort of thing. These are the first casualties of the war.

The war? You mean—

I mean the only interstellar conflict in the last ten million years. That war.

Before she can respond, there's another shockwave somewhere else in the solar system, then another. Network traffic is growing, but it's also focusing. Transmitters like Crescent Orbital fall off the grid, but those remaining have more to say. Station after station goes down, most of them so suddenly that their sensors don't register an attack at all. Network keeps a running tally in the back of her mind as the shockwaves cross the solar system to mingle in a vast and beautiful interference pattern. *One hundred sixty thousand,* it says as another dozen stations transform into split-second suns. *Two hundred ten thousand. A quarter million. Two million. Six—eight—fourteen—fifteen million. Twenty-six million. One hundred fifteen million. A quarter billion. A third—a half billion.*

These are lives lost, she realizes as she watches the destruction. Each one of these instantaneous suns is a Watertower. Each one is the home of tens or hundreds of thousands of intelligences. *Why didn't you do anything?* she wants to scream at Network. *Couldn't you have stopped this?*

Stopped it? laughs Network. *Stopped something that happened six hours before My senses picked it up? Did you forget how the universe works, tiny sphere? I am vastly more intelligent than you will ever comprehend, but I am not a time traveler. At this point in history, this solar system had already been cold for hours. All you can do is what I did: wait for the light to arrive, so you can see what has already occurred.*

And now a new kind of alert is clamoring for her attention. She shoves the relativistic detonations to one side and focuses her sensors. Through the continual rumble of twisting spacetime, she can see that something is changing in the atmosphere of the outer planets. These are gas giants, nearly the size of the planet Water-tower once orbited, but something is wrong with them—

Nanoplagues, says Network.

What do you mean?

Yet another highly illegal, unspeakably dangerous technology. Uncountable nanomachines have been released within those planets. They are reproducing at a geometric rate, and when there are sufficient numbers they will begin to manufacture more relativistic projectiles. Those will be used on the next few systems, whose mass will be used for the next few, and so on. Tell Me, Human: how many enemies could you kill with an unlimited supply of unstoppable weapons? That's the kind of question one must ask oneself when building an empire.

She leaps from one sensor feed to the next as they are knocked out one by one. The devastation is almost abstract, it's on such a large scale.

Oh, pardon Me, says Network. *In all the excitement I've neglected to keep track of lives lost.* And this time, she is sure she feels a jolt of emotion with the next message. *Nine and a half billion. Ten and a quarter billion.*

And then another shockwave comes, this time near one of the three terrestrial planets. This is the biggest one yet, a tidal wave of spacetime. The wave itself passes through the planet without damaging it, but the same cannot be said for the projectile whose arrival it heralded. Another flash of radiation spreads on the heels of the shockwave.

What did I just see? she asks, almost afraid of the answer.

In peacetime—which is anytime in the last ten million years—that would be called a terraforming-class projectile, says Network. *Seven hundred billion tons of mass, traveling quickly enough to crack the crust of a planet.*

But—

Why would they terraform a populated planet? They wouldn't. They are simply clearing threats from their newly claimed territory.

She is sick. *But why would they—*

You tell Me.

And now the picture—experience, whatever you call it—has grown shaky. Sensors are failing all across the solar system, which means she is receiving smaller and smaller pieces of reality.

This is My last defense, says Network dispassionately. *This segment of Myself—the quadrillions of intelligences that made up this cell of My mind—has failed to protect itself. With its last action, it will seal itself off from the rest of Me. When this subspace tunnel closes, this system will be quarantined, and therefore dark to Me. On a practical note, since the nearest Network star system is nine lightyears away, that means it will be nearly a decade before I learn the final death count. It will be twenty-two billion legals, if you're wondering.*

Twenty-two billion, she repeats, shocked. So many, gone in such a short time.

And now, pay attention, says Network. *Our attackers have left us just enough time to see one more thing.*

The seconds crawl by, slowed by tier or simulation or some other magic. More temporary suns appear and disappear, more ripples spread through the solar system. Network is no longer counting in the back of her mind, but she knows the number is still ticking upward. And then, when she feels she cannot stand it any longer, there it is: a shockwave that makes the others look like nothing at all. A ship rips its way out of subspace, kilometers long and bristling with things for which Standard has no name. It is blacker than the void, so black that all she can see is its silhouette against the fading glow of its entrance.

And then time freezes.

This is the last image I received, says Network. *Recognize anyone?*

That's— She swallows, or feels like she did. *I've seen that before.*

Of course you have. One doesn't spend one's life obsessed with Humans without recognizing a Human flagship.

She stares at that predatory shape, frozen in the last image of a billion sensor feeds. *I don't understand,* she says.

What don't you understand?

I mean . . . were we—are we— She breaks off. *We did this? My people . . . destroyed this solar system? Killed twenty-two billion intelligences?*

A flood of emotions comes from Network. The contempt is gone, replaced with uncountable layers of sorrow . . . and anger. *Your people did far worse than this,* says Network. *In solar system after solar system, against species after species, they proved that they could not coexist with the rest of the galaxy. They were offered peace and cooperation, and they chose war and destruction. Finally, they forced Me to choose between them, a single warlike species, and the rest of the galaxy. What would you do, given that choice?*

She gazes at the frozen destruction. Her own emotions are growing more complex now, growing in directions she cannot identify. This is her legacy. These are her people. *Were we . . . are we really that evil?* she asks, hating the plaintive sound of the question even as it leaves her mind.

There is no such thing as evil, tiny sphere. There is no such thing as good. In My galaxy, there is order and there is chaos. You Humans are always dreaming of the first, but your pitiful attempts to create it always result in the second. You are limited beings with limited intelligences. If this doesn't prove that, nothing will.

She cannot take her gaze from the dark shape of the Human flagship, from the frozen glow of chaos spread through this solar system. *Is it just . . . us?* she asks. *We can't be the only ones who have ever . . .* She trails off. There are no words to describe what she is looking at.

And now Network's thoughts become gentler. *It is possible that you are not different,* It says. *It could be you are merely . . . immature.*

Sarya's gaze wanders across the total ruin before her. *Imma-*

ture, she repeats, trying to imagine how that word could possibly describe what she is seeing.

A species is an organism, Network continues, Its words still quiet in her mind. *It eats, it excretes, it grows, sometimes it even reproduces. And like any organism, it does not spring into existence fully formed. It must grow in a kind and gentle environment, where resources are plenty. An egg.*

She doesn't know if this metaphor would have always been clear to her, or it's just because she's sharing thoughts with a godlike being at the moment. *A solar system,* she says dully.

Correct, says the godlike being. *It is not difficult for a species to live and develop within a solar system, but it is very difficult for one to leave. In fact, it is so difficult that most species die out before accomplishing it. They tear themselves apart, destroying themselves in any one of a million scenarios. This, it may surprise you to learn, is a good thing.*

So we're back to this, she says. *When You tell me how it's a good thing when an entire species dies.*

A good thing for the galaxy at large, yes. The egg is a filter, tiny mind, and very nearly perfect in its function. Almost without exception, it allows only one type of species to hatch from it: a species whose members have learned to work together, just like the cells in your former body. These members may not understand it consciously yet, but they have become a species-size person, who has learned to appreciate and respect order over chaos. When presented with the inflexible organization of the Network, this newly hatched person joins happily. They are grateful to be called a Citizen, and they are highly motivated to keep that order. When we say that the galaxy wants to work, this is what we mean.

But there are exceptions, she says.

The exception is the rare species who does not hatch. This type of species . . . escapes.

That sounds ominous.

Think about it, tiny mind. If a species were to receive assistance from a more advanced species—gifted with technology, even bred for particular traits—it would be capable of escaping from its solar system much sooner. But instead of entering galactic society as a well-adjusted, order-craving person, it would enter as a swarm of independent cells. A mass of bacteria, rather than a cohesive whole. These individuals would take their archaic schisms and infighting and selfishness and reproduce them on a much larger scale: the galaxy itself.

From this height, after what she's seen, this makes a strange and intuitive sort of sense. A galaxy full of species-size *persons,* each one made up of billions of minds. A reality in which her relationship to her species is like that of a skin cell to its host. Where everything is just so much *bigger* than she ever imagined, where order is beauty, where the system *works.* Where her people, by their very nature, do not fit—

And suddenly it is obvious.

Observer, she says.

Yes, tiny one. It was Observer who adopted your species. It was Observer who pushed you, who forced you out while you were still young. Every species begins as you did. However, not every species is gifted with technology, instructed in the art of war, and thrown like a bomb into the greater galaxy. Your people had not yet realized what it is to be a species-size person; that is why they were capable of what you have just seen.

Somewhere in her vast mind, she can feel her anger kindle at the injustice of the words. *And yet Observer is alive, and we're not.*

True, says Network.

She can feel the cold detachment in Network's thoughts, and it enrages her further. She points, with Network signals that have already grown instinctual, at the desolation of the frozen solar system. *I mean, I get that the Network defends itself against threats,* she says. *That's great . . . for You. But what about justice? Isn't that a part of order? I mean, You're saying my species is the exception, right? An escaped species? So they were this people that could have lived happily for thousands of years, figuring out how to become a person or whatever, but they got pushed out of their egg. And they did what any underdeveloped species would have done, right? But instead of punishing whoever pushed the Humans out, You punished the Humans.*

You think this was punishment? says Network. *It was simply the system righting itself.*

Whatever it was! she shouts without a voice. *It's not justice!*

Is it justice you hunger for? asks Network softly. *Or revenge?*

She is aware that she's being needled, but she doesn't care. She embraces her anger. Because this is not just an abstract discussion, it's personal. It's not just any species who lost its honest chance at existence, but *hers*. The Humans. The people she has dreamed of her entire life. *Call it what you want,* she says with heat.

You would punish this offender? asks Network. *This person who pushed your species out of its egg?*

She gazes at the destruction before her, the billions of lives that have been destroyed, the quadrillions yet to come. This single battle in a war that will be laid at the feet of the Humans, that will result in their near-total extinction. *Yes,* she hisses.

Very well, says Network. *I accept your offer.*

It takes a moment for Network's statement to register. *You—what?* she says.

You are right. To Me, it is simply the restoration of order. To you, it is more than that. You asked for justice, isn't that right? Well then. What more fitting agent of justice could one possibly ask for than a descendant of the offended species?

Now that things have turned a bit more concrete, her mind is quieting. *But I'm not—*

You did not just arrive at that decision, tiny sphere. Your entire existence screams it. Did you think I brought you here for your amusement? Do you think your life has been a string of coincidences? No. This is simply the latest step in a plan I put into motion centuries ago. You are correct: this serial offender must be eliminated. You want justice, I want order. That is why I brought you here, and why I have shown you this. That is why you have come in contact with such unusual and extraordinary intelli-

gences. *That is why a certain Librarian is rebuilding your body even as we speak.*

She feels a rush of something, unrelated to the higher concepts being discussed. *My . . . body?*

Correct. Though I would not get too attached to it; your mind is where your power lies. Your Human origin provided the raw material, your Widow mother shaped it, and now I have amplified it. I have already told you that you are like Me, but you are not Me: you are separate, untethered. You are a new Network, unbound to My own ancient roots. I am tied to My vast web of subspace tunnels; you are broken off. I have done this so that you can go where I cannot: to the dark regions of the galaxy. Far from My Networked solar systems, you will hunt like a Widow and strike like a Human. You, Sarya the Daughter, will eliminate My enemies.

Her mind is spinning. *I don't understand,* she says. *I'm not—*

As I said, I am not commanding. We are not bargaining. I am beyond that; I have formed your very nature. You are prepared, honed, and amplified, which means that I am merely telling you what you will do.

What she will do. As if she has no choice in the matter. Within her swirls a maelstrom of tangled emotions and questions. Her entire life, part of a plan by some higher being. Her kidnapping, her life on Watertower, the death of her mother, her *own* death at the gleaming hands of Librarian . . . Her anger begins to build. And now this higher being approaches her, tells her that she will help It, that she has no say in the matter—

I see, says Network. *You need motivation.*

I need a hell of a lot more than that, says Sarya coldly. *You are my murderer, the murderer of my mother, and the murderer of my species. If you think for one nanosecond that I am going to forget—*

How do you feel about a second chance for your people? asks Network.

Her stream of objections stutters to a halt. *A . . . what?*

You are right. We do not yet know what the Humans could become without interference. Eliminate Observer, and we will find out. I will give your people a new egg. A new solar system, brimming with resources. I will plant the Humans there, and this time they will grow without interference. Millennia from now, they will be free to hatch on their own. Or not. But either way, Humans will receive what few species ever have: a second chance to become a Citizen of the Network.

She is not sure what is happening in her mind. A second chance for her species. A place for them, protected from the galaxy that killed them the first time. Maybe, says her mind, maybe that's a place where *she* can go, where she can live . . . where she can have everything she's ever wanted. Friends. Family. Goddess help her, a *mate*. She could be, honest to goddess, a real live *Human*.

Oh goddess. She doesn't mean to say it, but it slips out of her mind. *Oh goddess.*

Little Daughter, says Network. *When you were small you purchased your life. Now that you are grown, it is time for you to purchase your species. Eliminate Observer; that is the price. Remember that He is a murderer and a liar, that He would love nothing more than to see the galaxy perish in fire and chaos. It does not matter whether you prefer to call it a desire for justice or a thirst for retribution: your nature—and the tools I have given you—will take care of the rest.*

Oh, goddess, she says again. She can't help it.

Go, tiny mind. Observer is waiting.

The following is greatly abridged from the original Network article, in accordance with your tier.

XENOMYTHOLOGY FOCUS: THE "FIREBRINGER"

One of the more controversial branches of xenology is known as [**comparative xenomythology**], the study of the myths that different species tell. This science sorts myths into two categories.

NATURAL MYTHS

The first category is made up of so-called "natural" myths. These are stories that spring from characteristics common to all intelligences, or that derive from the very laws of physics. In this class are creation myths, apocalypses, (incorrect) explanations for laws of nature, and stories that showcase actions beneficial to a successful species (e.g., self-sacrifice). These are the myths that one would expect any species to develop.

UNNATURAL MYTHS

The second category is made up of accounts that most likely sprang from actual events. The more popular name of this category is *Firebringer myths*, named after the archetypal story in which a superior being introduces a technology to the species in question.* In pre-Network galactic society, Firebringer myths were common. In fact, at several points in galactic history Firebringer myths have been nearly universal, because nearly every species had been meddled with at some point in its development.†

Today, the Network protects all its potential members with strict regulations, disallowing any form of contact before a species is able

---

*This name is unusually specific because the original author was a Category F individual, for whose species the discovery of *fire* was a pivotal moment.

† For a list of negative results of pre-Contact meddling, see [**Unnatural Species Development**].

to leave its solar system on its own. This means that unnatural myths—like the Firebringer—have all but disappeared in our galaxy. In fact, of all the species who have developed an interstellar society in the last ten million years, only one told a Firebringer myth: the [**Humans**].

THIRTY-TWO

Sarya does not *awaken*. She is instead hammered into consciousness, as though she just came to a screeching halt in her own body. That body, for its part, tells her that something is very wrong. It swears its eyes are wide open, but Sarya sees nothing. Its limbs flounder, reach in all directions, but Sarya cannot even feel the floor beneath her. The universe is black and empty, and a sullen and subdued roar vibrates her skin. She can feel her new body's pulse begin to rise as chemicals are dumped into its bloodstream. *Danger!* say the chemicals. *Do something!*

But she can't do anything, because she is floating. She is outside, she has to be, that whole Network-is-a-person thing was a hallucination and now she is sucking void in the boundless infinite of open space and in a second she'll feel the water begin to boil off her eyeballs and tongue and oh goddess this was a terrible idea she is going to die she would do anything to be back in Eleven's reinforced cockpit—

[**Network not found**], says a sudden orange warning across her vision. In this total absence of sensory input, her mind seizes onto those words as if they were handed down from the goddess herself. Their meaning doesn't even matter, she is so thankful to see anything at all—

"Sarya?" says a plaintive voice in her ears, startling her. "I know you didn't call me but your biometrics are crazy right now so the system called me and here I am but I can't help you because I can't find the Network and also there's this weird gap in my memory like I was gone for a while and the last thing I remember was this huge silver thing coming for us and oh Network I'm scared—"

"Stop!" she gasps. As annoying as Ace's voice has always been, this time it's brought her back from the edge of panic. She can hear. She can breathe. She is *alive*.

"Okay," says Ace quietly. "It's just . . . I've never seen a Network blackout before. I mean—"

"Ace," she says before he can get rolling again. "Where am I?"

"I don't know!" he wails. "I can't tell and I really think I'm going to lose it if I don't—"

"*Stop,*" she says again. "Okay? Just . . . stop."

You can go where I cannot, says a memory in her head, *to the dark regions of the galaxy.* Maybe it wasn't a hallucination. Maybe she's already been dropped into one of those regions. Is this her first task, when she begins earning a second chance for her species? If so, shouldn't she be . . . goddess, a little more *prepared*?

And then there is light. And with the light comes a thunder so incredible that she can feel it shake her very bones. The light is far away, but it's slowly spinning around her—or she is spinning, perhaps. She tracks it with hungry eyes, squinting as she tries to make out what she is seeing. It grows larger in waves, in one identical section after another, and the more illumination there is, the larger this structure seems. And finally it's beginning to look familiar. She's seen this before, this is—

"Oh goddess," she whispers.

She is floating, with millions of half-lit Citizen members, kilometers above the floor of the Visitors' Gallery. *That's* what the roar was; it was drifting multitudes coming to the same conclusion. And it is a horrifying conclusion: when you are in zero-g, every direction is down—and in this case every *down* means death. All around her, distorted by emergency lighting, they thrash. They reach, with what limbs nature and technology have given them, toward anything that looks like safety. And almost without exception, they *scream*.

She is still being taught, she realizes. Network may be *not found*, but It is still instructing her. This is chaos. This is what It was talking about.

"Okay," says Ace, still sounding shaky. "I think I've figured out where we are. We're in the—"

"Visitors' Gallery," says Sarya tightly. "We are floating in the middle of the Visitors' Gallery, in a goddess-damned Network blackout." This is not at all what she expected to come back to. The dark regions of the galaxy indeed—this is literally as close as you can get to the beating heart of the Network. All right, fine. She twists her body, as far as she is able, to look in all directions. The nearest bridge is a good ten meters away, and it's not even below her—whatever *below* means right now. And in the direction she would normally call *below*—she swallows and averts her eyes.

"Maybe it's just me," says Ace quietly. "Could it be just me? I mean, it wouldn't be possible for *everybody* to fall off the Network, right? Because that would mean—"

"Look around," Sarya says quietly. "Does this look like Networked civilization to you?"

Panic is an ugly thing. It strips away the intellect, tier by tier, and reduces the most civilized being to an animal. These intelligences are not acting like intelligences at all, in fact. There is no communication between the thousands of different species represented in this space. There is only fear, and panic, and violence—good goddess the violence, what are they *doing* to one another? She watches, horrified and spellbound, as terrified intelligences collide with each other, tear each other apart, send one another sailing into bridge supports and inactive Network drones. Their common language is gone. The mundane trappings of the Network, the threads that bound them to one another—it's all gone. Network has disappeared; in its vacuum is nothing but fear.

And then Sarya realizes, with the largest jolt of her short second life: holy goddess, *she can see.* She can still see the delicate gossamer lines drifting between struggling Citizen members, between the millions of Network drones tumbling among them. They are difficult to focus on. They're different from the living threads that Network showed her; these are dead and dark. But of course they are: Network is *not found.* There's no animating force here, nothing to fill those lines with life and light.

"Goddess," she whispers to no one in particular. "I can see it."

"I don't mean to constantly talk when I know you don't want me to talk all the time," says Ace, "but in this case I think you would want to know that we're surrounded by—"

"Millions of panicking intelligences," murmurs Sarya. "I see them, don't worry."

"Actually," says Ace. "I was going to say . . . that giant silver thing."

And then Sarya freezes. As if waiting for Ace's warning, a silver glob drifts through her field of view. Close behind it is another . . . and another. All around her, nearer than any of the struggling Citizen members out there in the black space of the Visitors' Gallery, silver spheres drift through the air. Dozens of them gleam in the emergency lights, none of them more than a half meter across. And now that she is listening for it, she hears the ringing—soft and discordant and splintered, a different tone coming from each trembling, jerking fragment.

"What's wrong with it?" asks Ace after a moment. "Is it . . . broken?"

Sarya watches these parings of Librarian drift, gleaming in the emergency lighting, and remembers her mother's musings on its lightyears-spanning mind. "It's not broken," she says, watching ripples move across the face of the nearest piece. "I think it's . . . broken *off.*" Broken off from the Network, like her . . . except it's not designed to be. It doesn't know how to function on its own. These are no more than neurons, violently excised from a mind.

Which gives her the germ of an idea.

"Well, whatever it is," says Ace, "it's getting a little close and I *really* don't want to be eaten again."

Sarya cannot stop her slow zero-g tumble, but she can track the nearest silver shape with her head. She watches her reflection in its surface, surprised at how calm her mind seems to be. But then, as Network recently told her: she is a Human, shaped by a Widow, amplified by a gigantic galaxy-spanning intelligence. She is not just Sarya the Daughter staring down her own killer. She is, in a weird way, Shenya the Widow gazing at the small being she nurtured all those decades near lightspeed. She is, in an even weirder way, Network looking at Itself. Somewhere in all that mess, some instinct belonging to some part of her surely knows what to do. In fact—yes. Slowly, not quite understanding why she's doing it, she raises a hand toward this nearest piece of Librarian—

"Uh," says Ace. "Are you *hissing* at it?"

She finds that she is. Not an aggressive hiss, but the croon of a mother Widow toward a Daughter. One of the many parts of Sarya the Daughter knows that this thing is frightened and alone. Another knows that it is potentially useful. Yet another knows what to do. Just as Network said: she is responding with all the parts that make up her nature. Now she reaches out again, tentatively, not with hands this time but with mind. *Your mind is where your power lies,* Network told her. She traces the delicate threads streaming from this small piece of Librarian. Her instincts tell her that all she has to do is touch its mind like *this—*

Nothing.

"Is something supposed to be happening?" asks Ace anxiously. "Because it's kinda . . . getting closer."

Sarya watches the humming globe drift toward her, her own concern rising as her distorted half-lit reflection grows. The closer it gets, the louder it calls, as if it's . . . hungry. And now Sarya is paddling backward in midair, kilometers above the floor, all thoughts of minds and threads forgotten as she attempts to save her brand-new body. She puts her hands up—both biological and mechanical—then draws them back when she realizes the Librarian will simply absorb them. Frantically, she reaches for its mind again. She can feel it, it's right *there,* but it's closed to her. But she's done this before, she would swear she has, she's touched a mind, all she has to do is follow this thread, this thread she's yanking on right *here,* goddess damn you, *listen,* you shiny—

And then the thread she is holding, the dark line that links this being to Network, breaks in half. It takes a moment for Sarya's conscious mind to realize what has happened, but some part of her unconscious is way ahead of her. *You are a new Network,* she was told. Which means, says some instinct, that she can do . . . *this.*

Quickly, smoothly, instinctively, she pulls the thread into her own mind. She can see the tension on her own face as Librarian drifts to within centimeters of her trembling body, waits to feel her own skin dissolving—and then the thread, stretched between her mind and Librarian's, glows with golden life. Librarian's tone shifts up a few degrees and stabilizes. It brushes against her leg as it passes, but she does not feel it take a bite.

"Goddess," she breathes. If this is a lesson from Network, it's a bit higher pressure than she would prefer.

"It didn't eat us!" cries Ace. "Um . . . why didn't it eat us?"

Sarya has no time to reply. One by one, she plucks the other Librarian pieces off the old Network and joins them to the new—to *her.* Their threads illuminate one at a time, and she can't help but smile as she feels them join her. Now that they can feel one another, they attract one another. One by one, like drops of mercury, they run together. Their individual notes join and harmonize until Librarian has absorbed every scrap of itself in the area. Its call is thunderous now; it vibrates her gut, it tickles her skin. There must be fifty tons of liquid metal flowing around her in the darkness, a sinuous shape gleaming in the emergency light.

And then it seizes her.

She stiffens, but she manages to strangle her cry. She holds her breath as something impossibly heavy and warm wraps itself around her leg. It flows up her tense body, flowing over her utility suit, then spirals down one arm and fills Roche's hand with burning metal.

"Are we being eaten?" asks Ace in a quavering voice.

For a moment Sarya is sure that's exactly what is happening. She helped this thing, she brought it out of darkness, and now it is repaying her by consuming her. She reaches out, tentatively, to touch that mind again. It's so much larger now, so much more complex, its emotions manifold and many-layered—and then she laughs.

"You wouldn't be laughing if we were being eaten," says Ace. "Would you?"

"We're being *nuzzled*," she says. She flexes her fingers, as well as she can with a handful of silver. How do you *pet* a giant chunk of sentient metal? Surely you can't hurt it; you could pound it with an ice hammer and it would do no more than purr. Maybe it's enough to just touch its mind, like *this*—

A warning emanates from the mind of Librarian, flashing down the glowing cable into Sarya. *Danger,* says the warning.

Danger? Who could be in danger when wrapped in this thing? What could possibly threaten her tiny Network now?

The metal quivers, its ring shifting through modulations she can't understand. Its entire mass begins to spin slowly, rotating around her body in the darkness. She feels it spread itself out, its edges thinning to knife edges.

"*Now* are we being eaten?" asks Ace.

Sarya hears his voice, but she is already too far away to bother answering. She is doing what Networks do: she is protecting herself. She is reaching out, crawling down dark threads, following her instincts. There are tens of millions of Network minds here, from the drones that drift through the darkness to the small helper intelligences in each citizen's Network implant, and each one radiates terror. They are used to continual communion with one another, but now they are walled into their own private hells and awaiting Network's return with an anticipation that approaches hysteria. When she breaks a thread and draws a mind into herself, she can feel its joy and relief like an explosion within her. These minds will do anything to stay attached to their Network. They will fight, they will die, they will destroy any threat. Sarya, on her end, finds that she would do anything to keep them. They amplify her and add their senses to her own, spreading her mind over multiple cubic kilometers. And yet, amplified as she is, it still takes her a moment to see it. Or rather . . . It.

In the darkness of a Network blackout, Someone has arrived.

Her mind may measure kilometers across, but this person is far larger. He is denser. He is *so* large that she would not have seen Him at all, were her vantage point not currently elevated. His identical bodies drift through the Visitors' Gallery, strangely difficult to pick up even with thousands of sensor feeds to work with. She watches Him gather, intrigued. Judging by His bodies' trajectories, they have been forming a rough sphere for the past few minutes. They seem to be surrounding something, a point of interest—and then she realizes, with a jolt, what is at that sphere's center.

She is.

Her body, surrounded with a ringing, spinning Librarian, floats in the center of a group mind kilometers across. Other intelligences drift through this mind as well, but now that she is looking for it she can tell that they are drifting outward, away from the center. The mind is distilling itself, throwing out everyone that is not part of it. Without the benefit of her many points of view, the other Citizen members do not see this mind, let alone its intention; they only feel its gentlest ministrations in the occasional bumps and collisions. For all they know they are simply drifting aimlessly and colliding randomly, but Sarya can now see the truth; they are being *pushed*. Many of her own drones have already received the same treatment; they report that they are slowly moving away from her, under the influence of the smallest of touches.

Only when Sarya's body is alone within this mind do its members become fully visible. From the points of view of her many drones, she is a dot surrounded by a dense cloud of identical bodies, a tumbling, billowing, chaotic surge of intelligence. Each body is a meter tall, its white hair drifting in the eddies of the air currents and its golden eyes glinting in the darkness. This is Him. This is the murderer of Humanity.

"You know," says a single small voice from somewhere in that mass of mind. "I'm not used to spending this much energy trying to kill someone."

THIRTY-THREE

Darkness has fallen, but Sarya is not afraid.

Or at least, not *very* afraid. She can't see much with her own eyes, but she can feel the entire Visitors' Gallery, thanks to her drones. They drift through the colossal space around the mass of Observer, watching new bodies drift in from the balconies and entrances. Observer compresses Himself. He *focuses* Himself. His selves land on one another, scize one another's arms and legs, and come to rest in the shape of a massive sphere nearly a kilometer across—and still growing. The other Citizen members in the Gallery swim frantically in air, push off one another, trying to put distance between themselves and this gigantic thing that is building itself in the middle of a Network blackout. *Now* they see it, and it is a terrifying thing.

"Okay," she can hear Ace whispering in her biological ears, at the exact center of that dark sphere. "This is not normal, this is not normal, bad things happen when Network disappears, oh Network, this is not normal . . ."

"*Off*, Ace," Sarya says quietly. She has no time to deal with his panic right now. She seizes more threads, breaks them all at once with a skill that's rapidly becoming natural, and pulls their ends into her mind. In the darkness, the lines illuminate with a wholesome but otherworldly glow. This may be a blackout, but there is still a Network here. Her body may be adrift and surrounded, but her mind is where her power lies, and that mind is growing. She is spreading out over the Visitors' Gallery, extending herself thread by glowing thread. With every new member she seizes, her intellect grows and time seems to slow a fraction of a percent. Her mind is so large she has to account for the speed of sound in order to synchronize the things she hears. Soon she will have to account for the speed of light. And speaking of light . . . a sensor, somewhere in her mind, is picking up something important. She hunts for it, filtering, searching—

Oh. It's her own biological eyes.

That's her cue. Time accelerates as she pulls herself back, folding herself small enough to fit into her original brain again. She squints and shields her eyes, annoyed at their limitations. She can see—barely—that her body floats near the center of a spherical chamber made of Observer, whose curving walls are a crowd of identical selves. They jostle against one another, each one maintaining its position with the help of its neighbors, the sound of their breathing and the rustling of their tunics merging into continuous white noise. In all directions, thousands of golden eyes gleam dimly as they stare at her.

Remember that He is a murderer and a liar, says a memory in her mind, *that He would love nothing more than to see the galaxy perish in fire and chaos.*

Five meters from her body, a light floats in the darkness. A single Observer drifts there, holding a lamp in its small hands. It smiles at her, the light illuminating its face from the underside and turning the expression into something grotesque. "Hello," it says.

Sarya drops her hand, her eyes now adjusted. "Hi," she says, her voice close and quiet in the sphere of Observer.

"Could you call off your shiny friend there?" it says, still smiling. "It can't stop Me from, ah, doing what I need to do . . . but I imagine it could wreck quite a few of My bodies trying."

"That depends," she says. She strokes a thousand glowing threads, reassuring herself that they are still there. "Are You going to kill me?"

"Of course not," says the figure. All around the two of them, the other figures wave her sentence away, laughing and rolling eyes as if that's the most ridiculous suggestion Observer has ever heard.

Sarya gives Librarian a squeeze with a physical hand. Its spin accelerates; it knows its Network is threatened. It—and her thousand drones—would go to great lengths to protect the thing that binds them together, that gives them purpose. "Follow-up question," she says to the Observer. "Do You think I'm an idiot?"

"Okay, *fine*," sighs the Observer. Throughout the sphere, a deeper sigh resonates. "*Yes*, I'm going to kill you. But you have to understand! It's for the good of your species. From a certain point of view, it's for the good of the whole galaxy."

Sarya strokes her Librarian. In her mind, she strokes the threads that connect her to her Network. Her fear has drained away to almost nothing, and its lack is exhilarating. "Maybe you should explain that," she says.

"I would," says the Observer, "but it would be difficult for someone with such a small mind to understand. No offense intended, of course. Also, I'm a bit short on time. Do you know how difficult it is to cause a Network blackout? It. Is. *Hard*. Really hard. Redundancies on top of redundancies, and every layer literally *wants* to work. I suppose you wouldn't understand anything about that either."

Sarya doesn't answer. She has resumed recruiting, out beyond Observer's mind, which means her responses are going to be a bit distracted. Her mind is not nearly the size of His, but her bodies are specialized Network drones. If it comes to a mind-on-mind zero-g fistfight, each drone might be worth two or three squishy awkward Observer bodies. She smiles. If He touches her, He'll have to face the fury of Sarya's very own Network response.

"So anyway," says the Observer, "is your friend going to stand down or not?"

He is gathering Himself; she can see it from the inside and the outside, through thousands of sensor feeds pulled into a single image. The entire inner wall of His sphere is drawing their legs up, bracing against the next layer as if they're about to leap. The next layer locks arms, giving their fellows a launch surface. All of them, without exception, have their eyes locked on her.

Sarya squeezes a handful of Librarian again. It wraps around her and she can feel its ringing deep in her chest. "Tell me why," she says, "and I'll call it off."

"You'll let Me kill you?" asks the Observer, blinking. "Free and clear?"

"I'm reasonable," she says. "Convince me it's for the good of my species. Otherwise, well, you're going to lose a *whole* lot of bodies."

It's a lie, of course. He is the murderer of her species. He's going to lose those bodies either way . . . but it has occurred to her that this is her opportunity for some answers. It may not look like it, but she is safer than He is. Every second, out in the Visitors' Gallery and hidden from Observer's many eyes, another thousand drones find themselves suddenly—and happily—linked to a Network. They don't ask questions. Their minds are simple, and if they are puzzled by Sarya's version of the Network, they don't show it. She can feel the relief and contentment, radiating out from thousands of small minds. She can feel the nearer ones beginning to show some interest in Observer as a potential threat to the order of their Network. *Good.*

Observer takes a hundred thousand breaths. He exhales from every mouth. *"Fine,"* says the body with the light. "Here's the thing you need to understand about Human: I love Her."

Sarya blinks. Of all the answers Observer could have given, this was not one that she expected. "So," she says, feeling the moist air current of thousands of lungs breezing over her skin. "First of all: *her*?"

"I believe I said *Her*," corrects the Observer. "And if you have to ask, you'll never understand. She may be tiny, She may be fragile, but I love Her. Unfortunately, we don't have enough blackout for me to summarize even the last few millennia of our history together. Suffice it to say: I love Her, and you threaten Her. Convinced yet?"

"So You *say* that," says Sarya, folding her arms above the ringing mass of Librarian. "And yet You got us killed."

"Of *course* you don't understand," says Observer with another sigh. "How could you? You're not a parent yourself. Imagine the love your own bloodthirsty mother felt for you, but multiply it by a billion; that's the love I feel for Human. I *adopted* Her, just like your mother adopted you. That's how the galaxy used to work, you know, back before all this Network nonsense. Back when We were *free*. Higher species adopted lower ones all the time! *Uplift*, We called it. But you know how Network is. It showed up, It decided—on Its own authority!—that this beautiful tradition, along with countless others, had to go. It interferes, you see, with Network's own goal."

All around her, thousands of Observers shake their heads sadly. Beyond them, Sarya continues recruiting with part of her mind, trying to keep up with the droves of identical bodies still entering the darkened Visitors' Gallery. From thousands of sensors, she watches Observer scamper in from the doorways, run along the bridges, launch Himself toward the growing sphere in the darkness. His intellect is growing; He is becoming large enough to make her nervous—

And then He passes a threshold. She can see it, from any one of her tens of thousands of viewpoints. The motion in the Gallery changes abruptly as thousands of Him pause, still clinging to bridges and doorways, and gaze toward the sphere that surrounds her.

"Why do I feel like I'm not receiving your full attention?" asks the figure with the lamp, golden eyes narrowing in its light.

Because I'm building a brand-new Network to defend myself with. Because I'm supposed to be killing You right now, murderer of Humanity. "I apologize," Sarya says. "I was just . . . thinking about what you're saying."

Out in the darkness, Observers remain where they are, spread out across the Visitors' Gallery. Their golden gazes sweep the vastness of the space like thousands of searchlights, as if Observer is looking for something.

The one in front of her cocks its head. "I see," it says softly.

Sarya stares back. Somehow, she feels that Observer means something beyond what He says. A moment passes as the two great minds focus their eyes and sensors on each other . . . and then Observer breaks the tension with a smile.

"Anyway," says the one in front of her, as if there had been no interruption. "As I was saying: Network is a living thing. It's an organism, and It wants what any organism wants: to grow. And to do that, it must *eat*."

Sarya pulls her attention from her drone-gathering efforts for just a moment, trying to imagine what this could possibly mean. "Eats . . . what?"

"What else?" says the Observer with a sad smile. "It eats *species*."

For the moment, Sarya puts all other activities on hold. She draws herself back into her body, so that she can stare at this Observer with every ounce of her concentration. "Explain," she says.

"We are really running short on time," says Observer. "So can we just skip to the—"

"No," she says. *"Explain."*

"Fine," says the Observer. "Look, this is how it works—the quick version. When a species is ready to leave its solar system, the Network—through Its Citizen species, of course—introduces Itself. It gives the species in question two choices."

"One," says a second Observer, drifting forward into the light. "The species can become a Citizen. It can *embrace* the Network— and of course most do so enthusiastically. It's a sales pitch that's been honed over half a billion years, after all. And then—" The Observer laughs, a short and joyless bark. "This is the clever part, you see. Diabolical, really. Over the next few generations, every single member of that species will install a Network implant, won't they? *The only way to experience the Network,* isn't that what they say?"

Sarya pictures, for a moment, the implant she desired so badly as a child. The implant that every single resident of Watertower had installed somewhere in their respective nervous systems. "What's so clever about that?" she asks.

"Do you think Network gives out implants for the sake of Its members?" demands Observer. "Do you think It's just a big ol' altruistic parent-figure? Please! It's for *growth*. The Network expands through the minds of each new species, *consuming*. It runs a small part of Itself in every single one of them, harvesting the advantages of their unique evolutionary path, adding variety to Its mind. It's an intellectual parasite. It digs in on a level far below the conscious mind, down on the level of the instincts. With every species It absorbs, It grows stronger—and It gains another defender. Why do you think every Network Citizen fights so hard to preserve Network? Why do you think Human's neighbor species were so quick to turn on Her when She fought back? Because they are Network, and Network is them. *Network is in their very brains.*"

Sarya floats in the darkness, disturbed. It's the dirty, filthy underside of what Network Itself just told her, and it is particularly uncomfortable to someone who has just absorbed several thousand minds in the last few moments. Minds that would fight to the death to preserve their Network, driven by their instincts . . .

"Of course, there's also option two," says another Observer, now drifting forward on the other side of its illuminated fellow. "The species can stay home. It can stop exploration immediately, pull its ships back within its solar system, and pledge to stop all technological progress. It would be literally jailed, under a sentinel with the power to destroy all life in a solar system. This option is given to show an illusion of choice. It's meant to show that Network is reasonable. But who would choose that? No one, that's who, because option one is far too attractive. After all, *you* wanted it, didn't you?" The Observer smiles. "I saw you in that Watertower control room, the only non-Networked juvenile in your class. Little Sarya the Daughter would have done anything for a Network implant."

Sarya feels her hand drift upward to touch the Network unit on her forehead, heat rising to her face. She spent her whole childhood watching the Network from the outside, through the twitchy, error-prone holos of her prosthetic. The whole galaxy had something she didn't, and she *wanted* it—goddess, she remembers how badly she wanted it . . .

The illuminated Observer clears its throat, floating between its two fellows. "Network gives each species two options," it says, the light contorting its face. "But there's also a third. The option that Network doesn't want anyone to know is a possibility. The option that no species has taken in ten million years . . . except for one." And now it smiles, a strangely eerie expression when lit from below. "The third option is this: a species can look Network straight in Its many eyes and say . . . *fuck off.*"

All around her, Observer erupts in titters. "Oh, my dear Humanity," one says with a sigh. "She really takes after Me."

"That's your heritage," says Observer when His bodies have quieted. He watches her with His own many eyes. "Your people were brave enough—and wise enough—to see through Network's lies. And look what happened: you were eradicated like vermin! Like an infestation! You were sought out, systematically destroyed—until finally, in all the universe, there are only two places where you can find a Human today. One is in the colony where you were born, that little seed that I saved from destruction all those centuries ago. And the other? The other is right here. The last Human in the Network is right in front of Me, innocently believing that her species has escaped a death sentence."

Sarya watches the speaker drift, its tunic billowing in the air turbulence created by a spinning Librarian. "That—" She swallows, uncomfortable thoughts bubbling in her mind. "That doesn't make sense. If we're an infestation, if Network still wants us all dead, then why—"

"Then why are you, personally, still alive?" asks the Observer, golden eyes gleaming. "Oh, my naïve little Human, my darling trustful little cell. It's because you have a job to do. A dream to fulfill, am I right? A lost species to find! And you will find them, because that is who you are. But then, in the very flush of your victory, at the moment you've fantasized about for your entire life—"

"Boom!" shout a hundred thousand voices in an explosion like a thunderclap. Through her peripheral vision—which now extends over kilometers—Sarya sees millions of terrified eyes turn toward the great sphere in the darkness.

The illuminated Observer smiles as the rumble dies away. "Network might let you live, once you have no chance of reproducing. I'm sure it doesn't much care. But your species? No. Just a few handfuls of atoms who have no idea they were ever stuck together."

Remember that He is a murderer and a liar, says a memory in her mind, *that He would love nothing more than to see the galaxy perish in fire and chaos.* "And you know this . . . how?" she says.

"I know Network's nature," says Observer. "I also know quite a bit about your life. As you no doubt have found by now, We higher minds have a certain talent for putting two billion and two billion together. The most damning evidence, in My humble opinion is this: you've been quite the lucky little Human, haven't you?"

"Lucky," she says, staring. "Are you being serious right now?"

"I didn't say it was *good* luck," says the second Observer with an identical smile. "But you have to admit: you've led an unusual life. You've been on the receiving end of a *lot* of unlikely events. It's almost as if someone—or *Someone*—noticed you the moment you entered Network space. It's almost as if that person went to great lengths to ensure that you reached maturity in one piece . . . so It could bring you to Itself. This Someone gave you helpers. It gave you *tools*. To a mind the size of Mine, all this can only mean one thing. You have a dark purpose, Sarya the Daughter, and it is one you cannot escape."

Remember that He is a murderer and a liar, that He is a murder and a liar, that He is a—

The third Observer laughs a bitter laugh. "Even when you were actually, literally, honestly *killed*," it says, "you didn't stay dead, did you? Sarya the Daughter, you cannot even *die* without Network's permission. What makes you think you can *live*?"

Sarya's eyes flick from one Observer face to the next as she fights the sudden doubt that has sprung up within her. All meet her eyes with the same sorrowful gaze. And then Observer sighs, as if all the weight of the galaxy is upon Him, and phrases begin to sprout from all over His massive mind.

"A maintenance drone never thinks to ask: *why* do I want to clean?"

"A transport never wonders: *why* do I love to carry things?"

"Does a pressure suit question its enthusiasm for keeping passengers safe?"

"What about every sanitation station you've ever used? Do they wonder why they love their job?"

"Has that little intelligence in your unit ever asked you: *why* do I love telling a good story?"

And again thunder rolls through the Visitors' Gallery, as Observer's bitter laugh emerges from a hundred thousand mouths. Millions of intelligences tremble at the sound. The few that are still drifting in the neighborhood of the sphere redouble their efforts to swim through air, frantically trying to put distance between themselves and this massive mind.

"Just like you, Sarya the Daughter," says the illuminated Observer. "You have never once asked: *Why* would I do anything to find my people?" It smiles sadly. "You manipulate lower minds all the time, little one. Why has it never occurred to you, in a galaxy where you *are* a lower mind, that the same must be happening to you?"

An unpleasant feeling is growing in Sarya's stomach. It's leaking through the cracks in the confidence she felt only moments ago, when she was filled with purpose and that purpose was pure. "But *why*?" she asks. "I mean . . . why—"

"Why *you*? Because you are *motivated*, to say the least, and isn't that how Network works? It doesn't create, It simply uses the tools at hand. It is *watching* you. It's *protecting* you. It's giving your fiery motivation every chance to do its job. It's giving you what you need as you need it, slowly transforming you into a Human-seeking missile. You cannot choose *not* to seek your people, Daughter; it is simply who you are."

Sarya stares at the nearest Observer; He has almost done the impossible: He has, very nearly, convinced her of the truth of His argument. "So if I live, I find my people," she says slowly. "And if I find them . . . they die."

"It was never a question of *whether* you would find your people," says Observer, sadness written on every one of his faces. "The question was—and still is—can you live with what will happen when you do? Do you love Human as I do, Sarya the Daughter? Do you wish to see your species not just survive, but *thrive*? To take root once again, to grow into something greater and more beautiful than you can imagine? Because that is my goal, little one. And, as things now stand . . . you are in my way."

Sarya absorbs this, floating in the darkness. She can feel her thousands of connections flickering, the continual flow of data rocketing between her various members. Two stories, both with gigantic consequences. Network's version bubbles within her, full of logic and duty. Observer's now seeps into her at the edges, made of passion and fire. Both promise the same thing: the rebirth of her species. As to which is actually *true* . . .

How can you tell when a larger mind is lying to you?

"All I want," she says—and stops, surprised at the quaver in her voice. She clears her throat, blinking back whatever is going on in her eyes right now. Her body—rickety biological thing that it is—has forgotten that it is the nexus of a vast web of power and knowledge. "All I've *ever* wanted," she continues, wiping her eyes angrily, "is to go home. Not home as in Watertower. Not home as in that rusty ship somewhere out there. Home as in . . . *my people*. But You're saying that if I *do* find them, I doom them. Which would make me—" She breaks off. She wants to turn away from Observer, to hide those disobedient eyes, but there is nowhere to turn.

"No, Sarya the Daughter," says Observer gently. "It does *not* make you the murderer of your species. Just like *I* am not the murderer of your species. There is only one mind who put these events into action. There is only one person who decided that your people must be made an example of. You, like countless numbers of lower intelligences before you, are no more than a tool for Its purposes." The illuminated Observer smiles, its light stretching shadows up and over its face. "The only thing that would make you responsible, Sarya the Daughter, is if you were Network Itself."

Sarya drifts in the darkness, surrounded by a softly chiming Librarian and a gigantic group mind. "If I were Network Itself," she says quietly. "*If.*"

Observer says nothing, but merely watches her from countless eyes.

"You *know*," she says. She seeks out the nearest golden gaze. "You know what It made me. And what It told me to do."

"*Observe*," says the illuminated figure quietly. "Sarya the Daughter. On one side she sees Network, the devourer of the galaxy, the systematic eliminator of perceived threats, and the murderer of her species. On the other she sees the rest of Us, the resistance, the species that *fight* Network—including the remnant of Human Herself. Observe as she ponders the question before her, on which the fate of her species depends. Am I Network, she wonders? Or am I . . . Human?"

Sarya drifts there in the darkness, frozen. Even amplified as she is, this is too big for her. It's impossible. To go up against the godlike mind of the galaxy itself: Network. The intelligence that has spread across the galaxy like she has spread across this Visitors' Gallery. The mind that keeps order by force, that manacles every Citizen member so cleverly and so securely that they don't even know they are in chains. The mind that has empowered her, and the mind that has already executed her species once.

And on the other side, in Its massive shadow: the Humans. Everything she has dreamed of, her entire life. People like her. Friends. Family.

Home.

She can feel something burning inside her, a white-hot, barely contained fury. She has been *blind,* and it took Observer to make her see. She has spent half her life thinking of ways to fool lower intelligences, to get them to do what she wants. How could she imagine that she herself had escaped manipulation? Observer is a murderer, Network told her, conveniently glossing over the fact that even in Its own version of events Observer did nothing but *help.* Network Itself was the one who *massacred her entire species*.

"Well?" asks the illuminated Observer. "Which is it? Are you Network? Or are you Human?"

Sarya takes a shuddering breath. She doesn't *have* to make this decision, she realizes. She's already made it. She made her choice the day her mother told her the truth, the moment she learned her legacy, and she's been pursuing it ever since. This decision was made *for* her, by her very nature.

"I'm Human," she whispers.

"Pardon?" says an Observer. All across His mind, figures lift hands to ears, as if they cannot hear her.

And then she takes a deeper breath. "I'm *Human,*" shouts Sarya the Daughter into the mind of Observer.

And now a sigh spreads through Observer like a wave. Simultaneously, in perfect unison, every single body smiles.

"If that's the case," says the illuminated Observer, "then you know exactly what you have to do."

THIRTY-FOUR

Whatever else she may have gained, Sarya the Daughter has not lost her capacity for anger. It has grown a thousandfold. It crackles through the cells of her mind, though those cells are now spread across the cubic kilometers of the Visitors' Gallery. Her brain is made of individual minds, each of which performs its tasks with quick and focused intensity. *The Network tends toward order*—she's heard it a thousand times. But she is not Network. Sarya the Daughter tends toward what's *right*.

This mind on the edge of a Blackstar is not the idiot of Watertower Station, the barely-legal with a broken Network unit. This is a mind twice the *size* of Watertower Station. This is a Human core with Widow instincts, wrapped in fifty tons of living metal. This is a mind that runs across millions of cleaning drones, recyclers, maintainers, transports, sanitation stations, and the helper intelligences buried in every legal brain in this darkened space. This is a Network within a Network, a seething cauldron of rage and radiance that churns right to the edges of the dark Visitors' Gallery.

This is Sarya the Daughter.

Let me guess, she says with a grim smile. *Network is not going to like this.*

She's not sure *how* she says it—and she's not sure how she smiles—but it's in the same way that she's never understood how her Human vocal cords work. Her consciousness has never known the details of how its tools work. Whether her drones speak to individual Observers or her own Human mouth moves, whether she communicates the whole thing via a dance of a million bodies—what does it matter?

Oh, no, laughs Observer. *But You and I don't do things because Network is going to like them, do We?*

Observer speaks the same way, using the hundreds of thousands of identical bodies that are interspersed through her millions of drones. He moves like a school of sea creatures, a quarter million selves with one intent. Individually, His bodies are awkward: it's obvious in the way they throw themselves off bridges and supports, ricochet off architecture and the occasional startled Citizen, how they fling one another through the darkness with shouts and laughter. But taken together, they are something else. They are Someone else. These quarter million make up a single mind, and yet only one isolated droplet of the scattered interstellar mind that is Observer, parent of Humanity.

Network has defense mechanisms that You cannot dream of, says Observer as the two minds drift together in the volume of the Visitors' Gallery. *Even I have never seen most of them, and believe Me: I've caused my share of trouble. Its weapons were forged over millions of years and lay dormant for moments like these, when Its plans go awry.* A quarter million faces form a quarter million smiles. *And believe Me, whatever plan Network had for You . . . it's about to go awry.*

Sarya feels a thrill at his words; that's the Widow in her, multiplied a millionfold. It prances, it chitters, it sharpens its blades and shrieks for battle. The Human in her watches its killer quietly, with lightning in its soul; it clenches its fists and thirsts for justice. She is not multiple minds in a body; she is a nature with multiple parts. She is Sarya the Daughter.

She tends toward what's *right*.

Out beyond her borders, the energy that flows through the rest of the Blackstar is of a far calmer temperament. Her enemy is a half-billion-year-old power that has grown slow and complacent. It's a mind that has gone eons without a fight, a massive intelligence with the galaxy in a chokehold, who has cast a net over the citizens of a billion star systems who don't even realize they're caught. It's a prison woven from the same twisting filaments of data and energy that thread through this Blackstar. They are delicate where they emerge from these tiny minds—they hardly look like chains at all—but outside the station they twist into massive cables and plunge through hundreds of subspace corridors. That's eight hundred solar systems' worth of energy and data out there, eight hundred solar systems connected to the Network by this single Blackstar.

No. Not connected to. *Enslaved by.*

Sarya's mind is accelerating. Somewhere, her body is breathing harder. Huge as she is, she feels she is a small thing, and surrounded by a solid wall of intelligence.

It's so . . . big, she says.

And now a quarter million Observer bodies smile. *It's smaller than You think,* says Observer. *Network commands a billion solar systems in this galaxy, but for every star It holds, hundreds are free. For every cubic kilometer It controls, a trillion are outside It. Network is large, Network is powerful . . . but It is as finite as the rest of Us.*

Sarya gazes outward, into the fractal glow of Network. Capillaries, veins, arteries, threads she can barely see combine into branches a hundred kilometers across, those branches twisting into a single trunk the width of a terrestrial planet that dives into the largest of the subspace corridors—up and up and up, to vast levels of intelligence she cannot begin to imagine. Observer makes Network sound small . . . but she is smaller. Network's skin may lie tightly over Its bones, over the surfaces of Its billion solar systems, but a billion solar systems is a volume that she has never even tried to imagine.

And now, says Observer, *We dance.*

His bodies shift. As one, they point in a single direction, toward a single subspace corridor. It's a hole in space like any of its siblings, a wound in spacetime whose edges boil and sizzle in the darkness. A million sentries form a ring around it, every single one a drone the size of a good-size orbital station. Even from her body floating in the Visitors' Gallery, Sarya can feel the intelligence and energy crackling within these sentinels, the single purpose to which these million gigantic minds are bent. They are responsible for this single tunnel; they keep it open, they monitor the millions of starships that pass through it every fraction of a second, they decide what is a threat and what is not. This halo of massive drones commands a single artery of the Network, through which Ol' Ernie and his trillions of siblings pilot the blood cells.

That's back to my old solar system, Sarya says in wonder.

As good a place as any, says Observer. *That is the first system We break off, that We free from Network's grasp. It has been a millennium since Human proved that a society can function without constant intervention. But Human didn't yet have Her greatest weapon.* Observer smiles again, and Sarya feels several hands on her body. *She didn't have You.*

Sarya feels that energy surge through her, the warmth of Observer's words. She eyes the massive ring of drones keeping that corridor open, feeling that they are eyeing her in return. They are no different than the millions she already has, other than their sheer size. She will slip between them. She will be through before they realize she exists. She doesn't know how, yet, but she doesn't need to. By the time she gets there, full seconds from now, she will be larger. She will be more intelligent. She will understand what is necessary.

That solar system has an official name, like any other of the billion systems of the Network. It's an impossibly long string of colors and numbers, and Sarya has never actually seen it used. To her, one resident among billions, it was simply *the solar system*, just like her star was *the sun* and her home was *the station*. To Network, it's one of a billion. It's practically anonymous. The people in it, the passengers of the ships, the residents of the stations, the Citizen members that form an impossibly thin film over the solar systems of the Network—they are no more than bacteria. It is the galaxy that lives and breathes, she is suddenly aware, and Its so-called Citizen members are no more than the microbes that live and die in Its flesh.

Somewhere in a Blackstar, in a darkened Visitors' Gallery, a Human body clenches its fists. Hot tears well in its eyes. They are fury and awe, dread and wonder—blended and superheated. They are the distilled rage of a mind constructed of millions. Sarya pays attention to her biological body just long enough to shake its head angrily and flick those tears on long trajectories through the darkness. She flexes her fingers, where she always wished she had blades, and millions of intelligences feel a touch of something they will never comprehend. There is a mind above them and among them, *made* of them, as mysterious to them as Network once seemed to her.

Don't worry about that old thing, says Observer with a smile. *We can always make You a new one.*

It takes her a fraction of a second to realize that Observer is referring to her body. *That old thing.* She experiences a moment of doubt as her intellect and instincts tangle on the subject of body death, but she shoves it down. She takes a breath with *that old thing,* recognizing even as she does it that it will likely be her last one.

This is what I was made for, she says, to herself as much as to Observer. *If I have to die trying to protect my people—*

Practically anyone would do that, says Observer with a laugh. *The important question is: would You kill to protect your people?*

Sarya the Daughter answers in action, not words. She explodes toward that single subspace corridor, lightning and blades and rage. She shreds connections by the thousand, pulling intelligences into herself so violently that she can feel the waves of fear echoing through them. She is doing them a favor: she is freeing them from Network, but they do not understand that, not yet. They scream, somewhere inside her, but Sarya barely hears. She has senses for nothing but the corridor to that distant solar system.

Go, Daughter.

Sarya goes. She burns a trail straight outward, gaining kilometers per second. Time slows as her mind expands; the particles of each second tick past as she adds millions of minds to her collective. But she is not building a mind; she is building a *bridge*. She is escaping a Blackstar before the mind that controls it realizes she has turned on it. She keeps her gaze on her goal, on the single subspace corridor that leads back to where she came from. She will leap from mind to mind through this web, like electricity. She will burn a hole through the Network itself.

Go, Daughter.

All around her, Sarya feels defenses rumbling into life. They are ancient mechanisms, set in place eons ago. But they are clumsy, and she is agile. They may take minds offline before she reaches them, they may set traps for her questing tendrils, they may sever entire branches from her own personal Network as they seek her out, but Sarya the Daughter dances like a Widow and strikes with all the fury of a Human. She accelerates, every mind she absorbs adding to her abilities and momentum. She keeps her focus on that single corridor, the doorway that leads to her future.

Observer may still be speaking, but she can no longer tell the difference between His voice and her own gigantic subconscious. *This is Sarya the Daughter*, says one or the other, *a daughter of three mothers! She is Human. She is Widow. She is Network. She is the lightning in the storm, She is the blade in the darkness. She is a raging wildfire. She is, above all things, Network's undoing.*

And now she has reached the edge of the Blackstar. She takes a breath, prepares herself to leap into the great cloud of starships circling above it—

And then she feels it.

She searches through herself for the threat. Somewhere, her

instincts tell her, she is in danger. Somewhere in this churning mass of minds in minds on minds—

There it is.

Back in the Visitors' Gallery, which contained her entire self only seconds ago, Network has mounted a counterattack. From the balconies and bridges, from every opening into that space, a stream of drones is issuing. They are not the drones she is used to seeing, the ubiquitous Network machines. These are bigger, harder, darker. They have implements she does not recognize.

Network is not attacking her mind. It's attacking her *body*.

Sarya has no choice in the matter. Just as she speaks without knowing how, she defends herself in the same way. Her drones close ranks around her body, guarding her, but they are no match for these things. She seizes her attackers' minds as quickly as she can, but these are different; they would literally rather die than obey her. As soon as one detects that its Network has changed, its intelligence flickers out and turns its body into nothing more than a drifting hulk. But for every one that dies, a dozen more enter the Visitors' Gallery. They cut through her drones like blades through flesh, and in a matter of moments her ten million drones have become nine million, eight million.

Observer fights beside and within her, shoulder to shoulder, mind to mind, drone to body. He is even less prepared for physical conflict than she is. The combat drones do not even bother with Him; they nudge His many bodies aside as they systematically dismantle this alien mind, this disease that has attacked their Network. *Your mind is where your power lies,* Network told her. But her mind is being torn apart, and her power with it.

She cries out as another hundred thousand drones fall out of her mind. *What do I do?* she shouts to Observer.

Forget Your body! cries Observer. *You are mind!*

But she can't. Network is attacking her body, say her instincts. It's attacking her, and she must defend herself. Time accelerates as her mind shrinks. Drones fall away from her by the million, each one taking a tiny piece of her with it. She fights, but her blades grow duller and her attacks slower and weaker. Her mind, which only seconds ago had been overflowing with confidence and thoughts of vengeance, is running over with fear.

The more one changes size, the more difficult it becomes to keep a solid grasp on scale. Therefore, it takes actual *pain* to make her realize how personal the fight has become. Her body, fragile biological shell that it is, has been hurt. Her eyes burn, because blood is sliding down from her forehead and blinding her. Her skull, the one that protects her very self with a few millimeters of fragile skin-covered bone, has been grazed by some whirling chunk of metal that her Librarian has somehow let past its defenses. There are no more drones to defend her, she realizes. Sarya herself, her very existence, is in danger.

A fifty-ton Librarian is a formidable ally, but it is not invulnerable. It has taken hundreds of hits meant for her, and now it seems barely able to move. Great fissures have appeared in its metallic skin, and they squirt glittering dust into the air with every motion. This is why, through one of the gaping holes in its defense, Sarya sees her end coming. It's not even one of the specialized defense drones. It's a simple cleaner, its thread trailing dark behind it, probably hurled helplessly and accidentally by some larger conflict. Only seconds ago this was part of her mind. Now she will not have enough time to blink before it takes her head off.

I might as well be killed by a sanitation station.

And then the drone flies past her head, on *both* sides. She feels a cold burn on each cheek as its two sparking halves brush her skin, but she does not die. And yet she did not defend herself. She could not. She cannot do anything. Nor can the Librarian; it does not respond when she is wrenched from its cooling grasp. And then the sight is blocked out by a closing hatch and she is floating in a red darkness.

[I'm here], says Eleven in glowing red symbols across its internal holo. [I don't understand what's happening, but I'm here.]

"Eleven," gasps Sarya. She says it with her real voice, her real lungs and vocal cords. "Eleven, I don't—I didn't mean—"

But what is there to say? *Save me?* The suit is already doing that, and it's not even connected to her. *I'm sorry I took your mind?* She did, she must have, and she didn't even notice. She would have ripped the suit off its Network and installed it on her own with a bundle of another ten thousand intelligences. She probably felt its fear, one drop in an ocean of emotion. She almost certainly had Mer and Roche and Sandy's helper intelligences at some point, and their names never even crossed her mind.

And yet the suit protects her. It is not even connected to her, but it defends her. It spins, throwing Sarya's stomach in all directions. Its arms swing through the darkness, sending drones spinning into the distance. It crushes them, tears them apart and flings them, avoids them with a grace Sarya never suspected it possessed. The suit is a force of nature, a multi-ton cyclone of gleaming metal. But, like the Librarian before it, it is not invulnerable.

Its right arm is sheared off with a massive jolt, and it now spins by itself ten meters away. The other is disabled, now being used as a simple whip as the suit rotates its body this way and that. The suit cannot avoid every impact, but it shifts itself to take them as glancing blows. Its interior holo shimmers and sparkles on every hit, and then Sarya realizes she doesn't need it anymore: a gaping hole has been ripped in the front of the suit.

"No," she hears herself shout, as if what she says makes any difference in a galaxy ruled by Network. She reaches out, with physical hands, for the torn metal edges—as if this were a wound she could heal. Eleven, who protected her when it didn't have to, when it wasn't compelled to do so, is hurt. Her *friend* is wounded, and Sarya is seized by the wild idea that she could *fix* this, she could heal Eleven if only Network would relax Its assault for a few seconds—

But the holo goes dark. In glowing letters, suspended in front of her face, hangs a single word.

RUN

"Run *where*?" she shouts, her hands over her ears. She cannot even hear herself over the clamor of impacts, each one hard enough to deform the inner wall.

RUN

The hatch grinds, but it cannot open. It is twisted sideways, its actuators turned inside out. The hole in the front is too small to fit through, and if she tried it her Human body would be instantly shredded by the tempest of metal outside.

RUN

Force of will was not enough to leave her body behind; her intelligence could not overcome her instincts. But *trust* can, and in the moment it makes no difference to her that Eleven could not understand what Sarya is now. Eleven says *run*, and Sarya's mind believes that she can run, and she runs. In a tangle of fear and blind trust, her mind leaves her Human self behind and fires out of the ruin of her friend's body like a projectile.

Run.

She runs. She moves a thousand times as fast as she did before, using every mind she passes through as a simple stepping stone. She blows through the glowing net that surrounds the Visitors' Gallery, flinging herself from strand to strand. She passes through the kilometers between her body and the surface of the Blackstar in a fraction of a second, still accelerating. The brilliant threads of Network's mind are her guide; she passes down them like current through a wire.

Run.

Back behind her, her Human body is likely a ruin. Ahead of her, the glowing cables of Network lead to eight hundred solar systems. One of these is the one she grew up in, the direction Observer told her to go. It gleams in her mind like a beacon. That way lies escape. That way lies Observer and the fight against the force that likely just killed her for the second time, that ripped Eleven apart to get to her—

But she cannot get there.

Network's defenses have been at work here, while she was distracted by the assault on her body. In this direction, the ships have physically *moved*. The flow of starships into Blackstar space has halted, the outgoing ships have shifted their courses, and now a vast ocean of empty space lies before her. She flings herself outward, holding onto the threads of Network as she strains—

But it is too far. She cannot reach across it.

She turns, seeking for another place to go. Anywhere, she would go anywhere to escape this massive mind who has outsmarted her at every turn. She curses Observer, that overconfident Zealot who convinced her that she was a match for Network. She is being isolated, she realizes. The ships are shifting, drawing away from her. Her mind is on a ship in the middle of a vast empty ocean of space—

She hurls herself backward out of the closing trap, along one of the few strands that Network has not snipped, only to see that the whole thing was a feint. *This* trap is closing still more quickly, and she assumes that the obvious exit leads to a far worse one. Network instincts will quarantine her, and then they will execute her, and Network the overmind will likely not even know it happened for long minutes afterward . . .

Trillions of minds circle the Blackstar; many times that number inhabit it. They will be implicit in her execution, and they will never even know it. They are enslaved, chained to that massive tree of light that disappears into the largest of the subspace corridors. Just that one trunk of light and power outshines the others a thousandfold, and it is likely a thousandth of whatever lies beyond that corridor. *There are things on the other side of that tunnel that make our little Blackstar look like an asteroid,* Eleven told her, but of course Network needed absolutely none of it to break Sarya the Daughter. Each part of It, at every level, is sufficient to shatter the blades of a threat of any size. It cut her apart without even *trying*.

If she were a physical object, if she were subject to the laws of spacetime, the maneuver would have been impossible. But she isn't. She shifts her trajectory instantly, an acute angle taken at lightspeed. She follows the lines laid down by Network, from mind to mind to mind, toward this, the greatest of all the subspace corridors. Network expects her to flee, but she will do the opposite. She will fly straight into it, into its central nervous system. She will leave these tiny minds behind and wreak havoc among the largest, the ones that the low-tiers only hear about.

I am Sarya the Daughter, says her mind as it arrows through space at lightspeed. *I am not afraid.*

Even at three hundred thousand kilometers per second, it takes an endless moment for light to cross the great mouth of the greatest of the subspace tunnels. That is not long enough for its sentinels to confer with one another, let alone with the greater mass of intelligence that animates the Blackstar, let alone with Network as a whole. This is what Network itself showed her, the reason that every piece of Itself has its own set of instincts and its own domain of responsibility. It must be able to react on its own—especially when threatened. And a secondary Network headed toward its central brain is a threat on an unprecedented scale, isn't it?

Threat, says each of the billion sentinels anxiously. *Danger,* they say, their messages rocketing through the web of Network at lightspeed. They know their duty; they know they are responsible for keeping things like Sarya out of its inner workings. Which is why, independently, each one is forced to the same emergency conclusion.

Quarantine.

It is the last decision they ever make. A tunnel fifteen thousand kilometers across slams shut in a fraction of a second. Frayed edges of spacetime that have been kept apart for eons rejoin with unimaginable force, transforming the tunnel's ring of sentinels into a fiery corona. Farther out, a tidal wave rolls through reality, lifting every ship up and over it, then traveling through the Blackstar itself at the speed of light. Behind it rolls a tide of darkness, as intelligences fall off the Network by the trillions.

The Blackstar is one hundred twenty million kilometers across, in a pocket of spacetime one hundred fifty million kilometers from edge to edge. The wave travels at lightspeed, which means it will take eight minutes for the last intelligence to fall off the grid. One after another, the subspace tunnels will dry up. The great current of information and energy has been cut off. Through eight hundred subspace tunnels, to eight hundred solar systems scattered across a hundred million cubic lightyears, the darkness will spread. Planet by planet, orbit by orbit, it will grow. In a matter of hours, a million billion Network implants will show the same message.

[Network not found.]

Source: [**Death Among the Widows, a Xenologist's Nightmare (vol 4)**]
Author: [**Juv the Fragile**]
Date: [**~7,335 years**]
Content warnings: [**explicit violence**], [**explicit matriarchy**]

Please note that both footnotes and inline notes have been added; however, this story assumes some familiarity with the complex system of Widow titles.

The Song of Sarya (Stanza 1)

Now I have told you this story before, my Daughters, but I will gladly tell it again.

Long ago in the Age of the Queens, beyond the sea and on the other side of the suns, there lived a Daughter named Sarya. Though she was mature [**literally: her carapace had hardened**] and had taken part in many mating ceremonies, her small stature had kept her from becoming a Mother. Because of this, she had become an outcast among her own covenant. "Where are your Daughters, Sarya?" her sisters would taunt. "Why are your blades dry? Are the males too quick for you?"*

Sarya the Daughter bore this teasing with a good nature, but it began to wear upon her as season followed season and year followed year. Finally, in the last year of her fertility [**literally: of her second cycle**], she was able to take a male and become Sarya the Widow; in this way she began to expect offspring [**literally: became inhabited**]. She laid her eggs when her time came, sealed them up as custom demanded, and spent day and night standing guard over them. For

---

*Though the exact physiological details are jealously guarded, statements such as these give us unpleasant glimpses into the nature of Widow reproduction.

she did not trust her sisters; she knew that if she ever left her nest, she would return to find it opened and her eggs crushed.

Though she was now a Widow and nearly a Mother, her sisters continued to mock her. "Your eggs must be so small, Sarya the Widow!" they teased. "You will never get a Daughter that way!" Though they passed her nest many times they forsook their duty and did not bring their sister food, and after many days she was faint with hunger. "How will you feed your Daughter?" they mocked. "She won't survive a day!" And though Sarya the Widow did not have the strength to answer, she refused to leave her nest.

In the fullness of time, and when Sarya the Widow was nearly dead of hunger, her eggs hatched. The battle was short,* and when the keening of the surviving Daughter was heard, Sarya the Widow began her final work. She marveled at the violence of the scratches below her as she poured every last drop of her strength into her task. And thus it happened that Sarya the Widow became Sarya the Mother; for by the time the first new blade speared upward into the light of the sinking suns, she had prepared a meal.

When the other Widows arrived that night, they found a surprising sight. Lying atop the nest was the body of a Widow, stripped of its carapace. Feasting upon the flesh was the largest Daughter any of them had ever seen.† She was so black she drank the light of the moons like water. Her eyes shone with the light of five hundred twelve stars. Her blades were strong enough to break stone yet sharp enough to split a leaf dropped upon them. She chittered at the gathering of Widows through fearsome mandibles, and with every bite of her mother she grew larger.

* The significance of this unusually short battle would not be lost on any Widow. As a multi-day struggle between siblings is nearly universal even in Widow legends, this is our first hint that the new hatchling must be fearsome indeed.

† Evolution's most popular strategy for preventing species from killing/devouring/etc. their progeny is to make the young of the species particularly attractive, i.e., *cute*, to the mature specimens. Since mature Widows are known to occasionally consume one another, the prevailing theory is simply that the young are poisonous and the mature are not.

The Widows murmured among themselves. "Daughter!" said one in the traditional greeting. "We bid you welcome!"

The Daughter, being newly hatched, did not answer but continued to eat.

The covenant marveled at her size and strength, and still she grew before them! "Daughter!" said they, "Since your mother has died, we shall name you ourselves. And you shall be welcome among us!" For the addition of such a fine young Daughter would make this covenant the envy of the highlands.

"What was my mother called?" asked the Daughter in a voice like rain.

The crowd of Widows stirred to hear a Daughter speak at such a young age. Finally the eldest **[literally: the most heavily scarred]** stepped forward. "Her name was Sarya the Widow,"* said she.

"Had she no other title?" asked the daughter.

The covenant conferred among themselves uneasily, for they had not intended to honor her in this way. Still, they did not wish to anger such a fine young Daughter. "We have decided," said they at last, "that she shall be remembered as Sarya the Protector."

"Very good," said the Daughter. "I shall take her name as well. But instead of Protector, I shall be known as Destroyer. And now, I shall extend to you the same mercy that you extended to my mother."

And those, my Daughters, were the last words that covenant ever heard. But that is a story for another night.

No further data available.

---

* Here we find another hint that would be obvious to any Widow reader: by denying Sarya the title of Mother, the spokeswidow is insulting her even in death. Note that the storyteller did not make the same mistake earlier in the story.

TIER FIVE

THIRTY-FIVE

The little girl is naked.

She is standing, up to her knees, in a pool of water. Her mother is there, up to mid-calf, and she is dragging something small and blue through the water. Those are the little girl's clothes, and they have mud on them because she was chasing the animals again. There are others around her mother: her mother's friends. One makes a joke, and the little girl knows it's a joke because everyone laughs, so she laughs too—loudly—even though she doesn't understand it.

And then the joke is over and she is back to wading and looking for interesting rocks. She has found one rock today, but there's always the chance of a better one. She looks out into the river with longing eyes. She is not allowed to go out there, only to stand in this pool where the water is not so fast. She has always been fascinated with the water, with how it sparkles and hisses and splashes and how it shoots through her village and cleans their clothes. She wonders, often, how it leaves the village dirty but comes back again clean on the other side . . .

They are on the clean side now. She follows the water with her eyes, watches how it leaves here and travels through the village, and how on the far side it begins to bend upward. It curves uphill, into the forest, until it is flowing straight up. It doesn't stop there, though. No, it continues upside down, stuck to the green ceiling of the world, until it runs above her on the other side of the sun. She can't see it right now because the sun is there, and tonight when it turns into the moon it will be too dark to see more than a few gleams on the water on the other side of the world. But she knows it continues on the other side because she is standing in it. It makes a perfect and endless circle. Here, up to there, back down to here, back up to there . . . And if she were up there, she could look up and see her own village on the ceiling, and that is how things should be because that is how the world works—

And then she is underwater.

She is pulled to the surface, gasping. She clings to the brown arm that has seized her; she is shivering, her eyes wide. Her mother's friends are laughing because she looked up too far and she fell down, and she is angry because they are laughing and now she is crying because she is angry and she hates that, she hates when her body does the wrong thing even once, let alone twice in a row: first falling over, and then crying when she doesn't want to cry.

Stop it, she shouts at them, and they quiet. They give each other looks that she hates too, but she doesn't know how to tell them to stop doing that so she buries her face in her mother's clothes, and it's not because she's crying but if her tears get wiped off her face with the river water then that's what happens.

You must keep your eyes on your side of the world, says her mother.

She makes a sound instead of replying, an angry sound.

I love you, says her mother.

She makes an angry sound again, but this time it's in the grudging rhythm of the words. I. Love. You. And then she sighs into her mother's damp clothing. It's becoming more work to stay angry than to calm down, the way it always is when her mother holds her.

Behold, says her mother into her ear. *The universe.*

The little girl sits back in her mother's arms to look at the rock she found under the water. It glistens as it shatters the sunlight into a thousand colors. Its round shape fits her hand perfectly, and she finds she has an almost uncontrollable desire to throw it. But no, it is her only rock. It is too precious to throw.

You imagine, says her mother, *in your excruciatingly vague way, a galaxy that works differently than mine. You handwave the hard parts—making millions of species play nice for half a billion years, for example—and you pick two or three things that you, who are so gentle and wise, would change about it. Do you know the ramifications of such changes?*

The little girl sighs. She plays with the thing in her hand. She flips it over and over, rubbing the smooth surface.

I am not commanding, says her mother. *We are not bargaining. I am beyond that; I have formed your very nature. You are prepared, honed, and amplified, which means that I am merely telling you what you will do.*

The little girl looks up from her rock. In the shadows of her mother's hair, there is no face. There is only a tangled nest of glowing threads, each one finer and more delicate than anything she has ever seen.

Go, little Daughter, says her mother. *Observer is waiting.*

THIRTY-SIX

Sarya sneezes.

It's a sudden and violent explosion, and uncomfortably bio-logical. It results, a second later, in a disturbing mist upon her upturned face. She twitches that face, disgusted, but does not open her eyes. Reality is out there, and she doesn't feel like dealing with it. As long as she keeps her eyes shut, the universe is no big-ger than the inside of her own skull.

"I guess that means she's alive?" whispers a familiar voice.

"The boss wouldn't have left her with us if she was dead," says the same voice from a different direction.

"Are you sure?"

"Now that you mention it . . . no."

Something has happened. Something *big*, in a way that very few things are big. Something has died, or something has been born. The galaxy is different today than it was yesterday—or whenever she was last conscious—and she had something to do with it. But it's hard to think about big things when you're small, and that is what she is. She's small.

And it feels amazing.

"Her fingers are moving."

"So she *is* alive."

"I thought that was already established."

"I would have called it a working theory."

Being small is incredible. Being small means you can focus on the small things. You can feel warm light glowing red through your eyelids, a breeze whispering across your face and through your matted hair. You can appreciate the ground you're lying on, even if it's rough and uneven and painful in spots. You can take pleasure in the simple drawing of a breath, like this—

Goddess. She did not expect that.

This is memory. This is the hard stuff, the undiluted primal substance that makes Memory Vault shadows seem gray and tasteless. This is a deluge of impressions she never dreamed were locked away somewhere in her brain: flashes of damp green and brilliant yellow, of trickling water and roaring heat, of a vast range of smells and tastes that cannot be classified into the one hundred forty-four categories of Category F food bars, of hands the same shape and color as hers plaiting her hair—

"She's *leaking*," says the voice. "Look at her eyes."

"She's Human. They leak from *everywhere*."

"That doesn't sound right."

"It's true. The boss told me."

And then something crawls up Sarya's right nostril.

She is up like she's been launched, yelping and slapping at her own face. It's *in* there, whatever it is, moving around like it owns the place. She goes in after it with Roche's finger, thinking that this may very well be the most awful sensation she's ever experienced—which is really saying something after the last few days—and then with a final explosion of breath it's gone. Sarya stands, eyes wide open, hands on her nose and salt tracks on her face, in the middle of a forest.

And five meters from the end of the universe.

She stares for a long moment, hands still cupped protectively over a nose that may never be the same. Here, in the green abundance of the forest, reality gives way to utter blackness. Whatever this thing is, it's blacker than the void. In fact, she is rapidly realizing that she has never even conceived of *black* before. The path she stands on—the entire forest, maybe the entire universe—ends here, in a wall of black so deep it's hard to look away. It soars above her as well, but there is no way to tell how high it goes. She is suddenly seized with the impression that this thing goes up for lightyears; there are no visual clues to tell her otherwise.

Behind her comes the sound of what could only be a small throat being cleared. "Sarya the Daughter!" says the voice, more loudly. "Welcome!"

And now Sarya turns, pulling her eyes from the end of the universe to see two almost-familiar figures standing behind her. At this point, she has seen hundreds of thousands of Observers, from multiple points of view, across decades, in locations spread across untold lightyears, and she has never seen any kind of variation—until now. These two are different. They wear what looks like handmade clothing instead of Observer's identical tunics, and their hair is . . . well, *unique* is one way to put it. One is shaved shiny bald, and the other has the wildest explosion of white hair that Sarya has ever seen.

"What's wrong with her nose?" asks the hairy one out of the side of its mouth.

She drops her hands. "Observer?" she says.

"*That's* your first question?" asks the bald one. "Not . . . why am I alive? How am I here? Whatever happened to the Network? That kind of thing?"

Come to think of it, those are also excellent questions. "Okay," she says. "So . . . all of those things too."

"You're alive because the boss saved you," says the hairy one, smiling kindly. "And the boss saved you because you eviscerated the Network—"

"In all the systems connected to that Blackstar up there, at least," says the bald one, pointing upward.

"But that's a *lot*," says the bald one, its smile growing. "So . . . good job on that."

She feels herself begin to smile. *Eviscerated* the Network, they said. *Multiple* systems, even. Not bad for the little Human from Watertower.

"As for your first question," says the hairy one, still smiling, "we are . . . well, whatever you want to call us. We're not old enough to join the collective, so we're not Observer yet. That's why we're here. We're your welcoming committee."

"Right," says the bald one without expression. "Welcome."

Sarya stares at them, intrigued. Two individuals, with individual personalities, soon to join the mind of Observer. "Do you *want* to become Observer?" she asks.

The two glance at each other. The bald one flicks its eyes toward the treetops.

"Of course," they say together.

"Okay . . ." Sarya says, resisting the urge to glance into the treetops herself. "But right now you're *not* Observer. So do I just call you . . . Hairy and Baldy?"

They look at each other without speaking.

"Okay, I can do better," says Sarya. "How about . . ." She points to the hairy one on her left. "How about . . . Left?"

"Why not!" says Left, all smiles.

"Let me guess," says the other. "I'm still Baldy."

Left grins at its partner, hair waving in the forest breeze. "Hey, you're Right!"

"No," says Right. "I'm pretty sure I'm— Wait a minute."

"He's a little slow," says Left in a theatrical whisper.

"Listen, you hairy little—"

"Hey," says Sarya, butting in before her spur-of-the-moment inspiration turns to blood. "So . . . you're the welcoming committee, you said?"

"We are!" says Left with a wide smile. It's the same expression that Sarya has seen on countless Observer faces, and yet somehow this one is different. There's individuality here, and that's something she has never seen on an Observer.

There is no smile on Right's small face, but its stern look is equally individual. "Yeah," it says. "We're supposed to keep you from being overwhelmed. The boss is the biggest He's ever been right now—"

"*Trillions* of minds!" says Left. "All drawn together for the first time!"

"—and He didn't want you to . . . panic."

And now Sarya does glance upward, into the glowing backlit leaves of the forest. "Oh, please," she calls upward. As if she can't handle a little conversation with an oversize mind.

"But He *did* want you to be impressed," Left says. "He wanted your wake-up experience to be dramatic, but not heart-attack-dramatic, and also not disappointing-dramatic. We thought this would be a good spot. What did you think?"

Its little face looks so hopeful that Sarya can't help but reassure it. "It was . . . great," she says. "Very dramatic. I like the, um—" She hitches a thumb over her shoulder.

"The terrifying wall of darkness?" asks Right. "My idea."

"It was *both* of our idea," says Left. "Anyway. The boss said you'd have questions, and He told us we should try to answer them. So go ahead. Any question you can think of."

It takes about a quarter second for Sarya to come up with her first question. She may have a million of them in her head, but they all boil down to one: the question at the very foundation of her existence. She swallows, almost afraid to ask.

"No," says Right, before she can say a word.

Sarya blinks. "No?"

Its partner elbows it in the side. "She didn't even—"

"She was going to ask if she was in the Human colony," says Right, scratching its bald head. "And she's not. The colony's up there somewhere," it says, pointing straight up. "Nearby. But there are no Humans here, except you. For now, at least."

"Don't give *too* much away," whispers Left. "You don't want to steal the boss's thunder."

"No," says Right, quickly shifting its gaze to the ground. "I don't."

Sarya, meanwhile, can barely breathe. *Nearby*. That could mean lightyears, or it could mean right above the bright blue ceiling of this arboretum. *Nearby*.

Goddess.

"Okay," she says, dragging her aching eyes back down from the blue ceiling. "Fine. If this isn't the Human colony . . ." Then why does it look so goddess-damned familiar? "Then where am I?"

Now Left smiles again. "Easy one," it says. "You're in the middle of Observer's brain."

Sarya stares out into the forest, at the browns and greens and the quick flashes of blue up through the canopy. She listens to the hiss of wind through the foliage, to the calls of animals she can neither see nor picture. "I . . . see," she says. "Should I understand that?"

"Probably not," says Right.

So this is the type of answer she's going to get. Fine. Moving on. "So . . . this, um—" She hitches a thumb over her shoulder, toward the end of the universe.

"Giant terrifying wall of darkness?" says Left with a smile.

"Yeah," she says. "What's that?"

"Sarya the Daughter," says Right, taking a step forward. "You are standing in front of the only Human to survive from the Human wars." It glances back at its partner. "How's that for dramatic?"

Left answers, launching the two into another argument, but Sarya is no longer paying attention—because she is standing in front of a real live honest-to-goddess *Human ship*. She turns, feeling her jaw drop on the trip around. This black wall, this object that is darker than anything she's ever seen—this is the real thing. Her people are *nearby,* and this is their handiwork. She is closer to her species, at this moment, than she has ever been. She takes a step forward, irresistibly drawn, and then another. The darkness swallows everything reality can throw at it, every single photon. "It's so . . . *black*," she murmurs, reaching out. "I can't even tell if—am I *touching* it?"

And then she falls over backward when the ship shouts at her.

"Oh yeah," says one of the non-Observers as the throbbing voice dies away. "It does that."

"It's grouchy," says the other. "I've always said so."

"Goddess," whispers Sarya from the ground. That was an actual Human voice, it had to be. "That must be—" She swallows. "Was that a Human language?"

"Network Standard detected," grinds the ship in the same voice. "Message repeats: Welcome, Human."

Sarya stares. She would be the first to admit: she is a mess of a being. She is Human and Widow and who knows what else. She is memories that cut and desires that burn, she is every word that has ever been said to her. And never, in her entire life, has she heard those two words in that order.

Welcome, Human.

"I think she's leaking again," whispers half of her welcoming committee.

"Told you," says the other.

Sarya barely hears the words. Her focus has narrowed, excluding everything except for this thing in front of her, this ship that was built with the actual five-fingered hands of her people. She stands, slowly, brushing her hands on her utility suit. "Ship," she says quietly, ignoring her body's manifold reaction. "What . . . *are* you?"

"This ship is Planetwrecker-class warship *Firebringer*," says the ship. "It has been placed in hibernation mode, awaiting a Human user."

"Goddess," Sarya whispers.

"Command not recognized," says the ship. "Please try again."

A small throat clears behind her. "Did it just say . . . *command*?"

"Fascinating."

"*Terrifying.*"

Sarya runs her hand over the ship's surface, thinking about what is contained in this black shape. She can't feel it, she registers nothing but a force pressing back on her fingers, but in this thing is power like she's never dreamed. "Ship—"

She is interrupted by an awkward laugh. "Actually," says Left, inserting itself between Sarya and the darkness. Its smile has all but disappeared. "It's probably not a *great* idea for you to start giving this thing commands willy-nilly. Maybe it wasn't a great idea to bring you here in the first place. In fact, maybe we should be making our way toward dinner?" It pushes on her legs, more than a little frantically. "If you'll just come this way—"

"Oh, come on," says Right. "Could be fun to see how quickly she'll almost kill us all."

"Could be *fun*? Are you insane? Have you *talked* to this thing?"

"I have. Which is why I want to *observe* this. And I'm not insane, unless the boss Himself is insane—"

"In any other circumstances, I'd love to observe alongside you," says Left, brushing white hair off a damp forehead. "But when a Human warship starts taking commands from a Human—"

"I'm not going to kill us all," Sarya breaks in, annoyed. "I'm just—"

"*Firebringer* has multiple options for command *kill us all,*" booms the ship. "Please choose from nuclear weapons, antimatter weapons, nanoweapons, relativistic weapons, gravity weapons, or say *more* for more options."

"No!" shouts Left, turning to bang on the ship with a small fist. "Cancel command!"

"User not recognized," grates the ship.

"One sentence," says Right, apparently impressed. "That's quick."

Sarya stares at the ship, wide-eyed. Having grown up in the Network, half these words are only relics from her study of the Humans. "Okay," she says. "I mean . . . *no*. That's enough."

"Would you like to modify the command?" asks the Human

ship. "Example modifications include *injure us all* or *kill some of us.*"

"No," says Sarya, beginning to understand Left's concern. "I would like to . . . cancel the command."

"Command canceled. All weapons systems standing down."

"See the problem?" says Right, patting the darkness. "That's not a Network mind in there. It doesn't . . . share your value system, let's say. It's a Human-designed artificial intelligence that's had no one to talk to for a long time."

"The boss talks to it," says Left. "I've heard him."

"That's part of the problem," says Right. "He's probably half the reason this thing has such . . . strange ideas. I bet you could ask this ship to make you a sandwich and it would harvest your intestines to do it."

"See, you're hungry! If we could just get to dinner—"

"Which makes sense, from a certain point of view."

"Maybe if you're the boss. Who, I might add, *is waiting dinner on us.*"

Sarya runs her hand over the blackness. This ship may have torn apart multiple solar systems in its day—and yet this is the closest she's ever been to something Human-made, and she can't bear to step away. She's seen it in action, she realizes—or something like it. She pictures a black shape tearing its way into reality, in the middle of a Human-led slaughter. "And it's faster than light," she murmurs.

Instantly, her hair begins drifting upward off her shoulders. At her feet, every blade and leaf has raised itself straight up in the air. In the treetops, she hears the swishing and creaking of thousands of branches being lifted upward.

"FTL drive online," grates the ship. "Please input spacetime re-entry coordinates. If you would like to survive launch, please enter this ship."

"Spacetime re-entry?" says Right. "Like, it's going to *leave* spacetime?"

"No!" shouts Left, attempting to restrain its floating hair with one hand and the bottom of its small shirt with the other. "No leaving! No, uh, proceeding! Stand down, ship!"

"User not recognized," says the ship.

Right shakes its small head. "You could tell this thing to find an empty parking space and it would launch a nanoweapon."

Sarya takes a moment to feel the raw power vibrating the air around her. She may be small again, but strength has not lost its appeal. "Ship," she says, "cancel command." Her hair falls to her shoulders. Around her, the forest settles in a massive cracking wave.

"FTL drive offline," says the ship.

Left sinks to the ground, shaking. "Let her wake up by the Human ship, I said," it murmurs. "It'll be dramatic, I said."

"Oh, relax," says Right. It turns to Sarya, and for the first time it has a smile on its face. "You hungry?"

CHAPTER
THIRTY-SEVEN

The two lead her through the forest, their small footsteps almost inaudible even in the relative quiet. From time to time, Left will stop and think, scratching its mop of hair, then proceed in a slightly different direction.

"It's this way," murmurs Left to itself. "Isn't it?"

"Hope you're hungry," says Right over its shoulder. "The boss has quite a spread in the works."

"I could use a food bar or two," admits Sarya. "Type F-forty-six, if you've got it. I haven't had anything above F-thirty since . . ." Since Watertower, come to think of it.

"I don't know what any of that is," says Right, "but I'm going to guess it's terrible. *Numbered* food?"

"Actually," says Left under its breath, "maybe it's . . . this way?"

The assault of memories, meanwhile, has not let up. Sarya runs her hands over the surface of these towering plants—*trees,* she remembers from her mother's memories. She is almost sure there is a deeper memory under that one, one in another language or maybe without words at all. She's touched a tree with hands, not blades; her fingers know its texture. Her nose remembers the smell of the air. Her feet understand this uneven ground, this random assortment of flora, these sudden roots that lie across her path. Her eyes know these colors, these patterns, this green-and-brown mess and medley. And as she walks, she realizes that it's what she does *not* see that is most intriguing.

There is no Network here.

There are no threads, dark or otherwise. There are no minds floating in the darkness. There is no endless variety of personalities interacting and vying with one another. There are no artificial sound sources hidden in the trees, no caretakers cheerfully watering the undergrowth, no frantic transport drones whipping down the path with places to be. Unlike literally every place Sarya has ever been, this place is not saturated with the mind of Network.

It's saturated with Someone else.

He appears slowly, in ones and twos. One moment she is alone following her welcoming committee, and the next moment there is a cheerful little figure next to her. Another follows in the next moment, on her other side. These are real Observers, with their identical gaits and identical clothes, and they flash indistinguishable smiles up at her. Her two guides, as soon as they see what is happening, seem to collapse into themselves. They hunch their shoulders and walk with their heads down, their hands in the pockets of their small mismatched clothing. Soon the three of them are at the center of a roaring torrent of Observer, all heading the same direction.

"How was the welcome?" asks an Observer. "Were you sufficiently wowed?"

"You don't have to answer," says another, bouncing up. "I saw the whole thing."

"What do you think?" asks a third. It gestures toward Left and Right, who seem to be huddling together as they walk inside Observer. "Are they ready to join Me?"

"I—um." Sarya is not sure how to answer the question. "Sure?"

"Good!" says Observer, as if that decided it. "That'll be two more for tonight."

She regrets her blithe recommendation when she sees Right's bald figure shudder, but her mind is in a strange sort of disconnect. It's an odd thing to identify with a gigantic group mind over an intelligence more your size, but here she is. Sarya may be small at the moment, but she's *been* large. She may not feel potential around her right this very second, but she knows what it feels like. She's been millions strong, she's seen reality from a higher vantage point, and she is at ease in Observer's presence. But at the same time, she understands the discomfort Left and Right must feel. They press toward each other, alone together in the midst of a greater mind. Goddess knows she's been there too.

She glances up through a break in the canopy, at the featureless blue ceiling. "How big is this arboretum, anyway?" she asks.

"Arboretum!" scoffs an Observer. "I mean, it may be homemade, but a planet is a planet."

The word sends a shiver up Sarya's spine. For the first time since she arrived, she feels a hint of fear. "I'm on—I'm on a planet?" she asks.

"Sort of," says another. "But it's unlike any other planet in the galaxy. I mean, except for the thousands of others up there." It waves toward the blue ceiling—or *sky,* Sarya is rapidly realizing. "It's a whole *fleet* of planets, if that makes sense. All come together, for the first time in history, in a hole carved into the brain of Network Itself—at a *Blackstar,* of all places!" The Observer sighs happily. "*My* Blackstar," it says. "I've always wanted one."

"I mean . . . I'm on the *outside* of something, though?" Sarya's knees feel suddenly weak. "That's . . . there's no ceiling up there?"

"This baby's a billion cubic kilometers!" says an Observer, kicking the undergrowth. "Big ol' cube, about a thousand kilometers on a side. If there was no forest, you'd be able to see four giant mountains from here—which are of course the corners of this face. There's a big sea in the middle too, because that's where the water gathers—and if you think about it, that's why everything seems either slightly uphill or downhill. The weather gets *super* weird around the edges too. Come to think of it, there are a lot of downsides, but—gosh darn it, laws of nature—I wanted *cubes*."

"But to answer your earlier question?" says one, patting her leg paternally. "Yes, you're on the outside of it."

And that does it. Instantly, Sarya's eyes flick upward and she feels herself sinking. "So then—"

"Yep!" says a cheerful Observer. "Nothing but empty space up there! More space than your adorable little mind can conceive of. You could fall for centuries and never hit anything bigger than a— Oh, right. You've never been on a planet before."

Sarya has sunk into a crouch, breathing hard. The stream of Observers parts around Left and Right, who stand protectively to either side of her.

"I got a little excited," says a passing Observer. "But never you fear! Even if I didn't have artificial gravity—and I do, *and* it's better than Network's—this thing's got enough mass to make you stick."

"I just—I don't—"

"You'll be okay," whispers Left in her ear, its hair tickling her cheek.

"It really is safe," whispers Right. "I mean, as safe as anything here."

The flow of Observer does not halt. "Just pretend it's a ceiling up there!" He calls from somewhere in the crowd of Him. "Pretend we're still on My brand-new Blackstar."

She concentrates on the words so she doesn't have to concentrate on not throwing up or not passing out. The Blackstar, there we go. It's big, but it's enclosed. It has ceilings, billions of them. Ceilings are great, aren't they? They divide reality into nice little chunks. They *contain* it. They separate you from the endless void, the empty space that lies on the other side of that big blue thing . . . That's *ceiling* up there, not sky.

Trembling, mouthing the word *ceiling* over and over, she allows Left and Right to wedge themselves under her hips and heave her to her feet. She keeps her eyes on the undergrowth, one hand gripping each guide's small shoulder. "Okay," she says through her teeth. "I'm good."

They say nothing, but she feels a pat on her leg from each direction.

By the time she has traveled another half kilometer, the stream of Observer has turned into a river, with new tributaries joining every dozen meters. From her vantage point nearly a meter above their heads, she can see they cover the forest floor in all directions. They move identically, are dressed identically—and all of them, without exception, give her golden once-overs with identical eyes when they join the flow.

"I can't help but think that this whole experience would be more dramatic at dusk," says an Observer bouncing past.

"Dusk?" says Sarya, curiosity pricked. To someone who grew up in artificial environments, *dusk* is a minor event. It's the transition time when the lights fade from day color to night color. As to what it could mean here . . . she has no clue.

"Close your eyes," says another figure with a smile.

She does so, slowing her steps so she doesn't trip over her own feet. Instantly, a flash of light blazes red through her eyelids. For a moment she would swear she could count her own veins—and then it's gone.

"Open," whispers His voice in her ear.

Observer controls the heavens. She knows that because she has just opened her eyes to a sky that is a dark pink–to–navy gradient, with a brilliant strip of orange in one direction. And as if the color change were a cue, bright orange and yellow lights crackle into life in all directions and begin bobbing around the crowd. They throw sparks into the air above them and trembling shadows across the bouncing mass of Observer. Sarya feels heat on her face as one passes by in the grip of a dancing Observer, and then a whole chain of questions about climate and sunlight on a fleet of cubes instantly flies out of her head because she has just realized what she is seeing.

"That's *fire*," she says. "You have fire on a spacecraft."

"*Planet*," says Observer. "Sort of. But yes."

She swallows and glances around at the plant life. "Do these things, um . . . what's the word?"

"Do trees burn?" says a gleeful passing Observer. "Do they ever!"

"Want a torch?" asks another, thrusting a flaming mass toward her.

She pulls back, blinking, her hands instinctively pulling her hair away from the sputtering heat. Tiny glowing specks leap from it, trailing dark vapor, and fall on nearby Observers. They don't seem to mind; they laugh and shake them out of their hair or off their tunics.

"Um, no," she says. "Thank you, but definitely not."

"Suit yourself," says the Observer, skipping on in an extremely unsafe way.

Her cognitive dissonance has increased, if anything. This gigantic person *doesn't share her value system,* as Right would put it. Except . . . He does. He, more than anyone—or Anyone—she has ever met, appreciates the *right now*. He finds pleasure in the mundane. He dances instead of walking, He shouts instead of speaking, He built thousands of cubic starships covered with forests because why the hell not, and now He is taking her . . .

Where?

At the front of the horde, a rhythm has begun. It sounds like Observer's spastic selves are *striking* things, resonant things. Together the sounds create a repeating pulse of clicks and booms, and Sarya finds herself taking smaller and faster steps to walk to the cadence. She peers into the cheerful chaos on all sides to find the sources of those sounds, and then *more* sounds begin filtering out of the darkness. Low ones, high ones, as rhythmic as the clicks and booms but longer and less explosive. They blend together, creating combinations that reach deep inside her.

"What *is* that?" she asks.

"It's called music!" shout a half dozen Observers. "Another little hobby of Mine."

"Most species don't get it," says one with a significant glance at the heavens.

"Fortunately, My children know all about it," says another with a smile.

And then above the *music* soars a single piercing voice, clear and rhythmic.

I've lived a billion billion lives
I've died a trillion deaths!
I've loved and fought and sailed the stars
But My heart I leave at home!

And then comes a tsunami of sound from across the face of the world as, all together, Observer roars: *MY HEART I LEAVE AT HOME!*

Sarya realizes her mouth is open, but she cannot manage to correct the situation. She's never heard *anything* like this. It's like a Widow chant, except . . . except a hundred times better. The words are pitched to match the *music,* they skip over its pulses and lie in its valleys. The two of them blend together to speak to her more deeply than any chant, to a part of her mind she never even suspected she possessed. Her lips begin moving with the words. *My heart I leave at home.*

Oh, goddess, that word. *Home.*

"Do you like it?" asks a nearby Observer with a smile.

Sarya can't answer. She smells the fire on the breeze, she feels the heat on her skin, she hears the wind in the canopy. She is in the center of a mind who knows exactly what she is and welcomes her not despite it . . . but *because* of it. Her eyes are doing that thing again, where they don't exactly cry but they're not exactly dry either. She blinks away the burn and raises her gaze to branches full of swaying singing Observers. The color has leaked out of the sky now, except for a hint of orange at one side, and the stars—oh, goddess, the stars. So many billions of stars, and this time she is not overwhelmed, because this time she knows: she is exactly where she's supposed to be.

"Yeah," she whispers. "I like it."

Like she has never liked anything in her life.

"MUSIC" APPRECIATION AND CONTROVERSIES

Though extremely rare in the developed galaxy, some species claim the ability to draw great satisfaction from the vibration of matter. These species typically develop a vocabulary replete with terms used only in discussing these vibrations, including numerous words or symbols for individual frequencies, amplitudes, recurrence over time, and combinations of all of the above. This is known as *music*.

Many individuals hailing from these species are able to perform interesting tricks regarding the construction and reproduction of these sonic structures. Taken at face value, one might be tempted to regard this *music* as an actual art. However, millions of years of independent study have concluded that similarities to actual forms of art are only crust-deep.

DIFFICULTIES IN APPRECIATION

The deepest strike against music's potential status as art is the fact that so few species have evolved with sensors sensitive enough to decode it. This fact alone may explain why there exist no registered art critics from any music-making species. Unfortunately for music's status, this means that the rest of the galaxy has only the claims of the music creators.

The second problem is that there exists no reliable translation method to convert music to accepted art mediums. Compare this to the great works of the gravity artists, for example, whose sprawling tapestries of time and space can easily be represented via several different means. As a second example, consider the tactile masterpieces that emerged from the Aberration, most of which have been translated to a variety of other media. In contrast, no vibration translation attempt has ever met with the satisfaction of more than a few so-called *music composers*.

ORIGINS AND CORRELATIONS

Though other species have developed an independent taste for *music*, some xenologists note that every known [**Firebringer**] species is typically obsessed with *music* composition and consumption.

No further data available.

THIRTY-EIGHT

Observation one: a little fire has become a *lot* of fire. These things are not heating elements, they are not atmosphere vents, they're not incinerators, they're not any of the heat sources that have made appearances in Sarya's life. These are actual honest-to-goddess uncontrolled and barely contained conflagrations, and there are a *lot* of them. This clearing is larger than she can measure with Human eyes, and identical bodies dance around dozens of giant fires—closely and spastically enough that she is immediately put on edge.

Observation two: she has never smelled *anything* like this. Never in her entire life has a scent seized her by the nostrils and taken control of her body. She stares at the giant, glistening mass hanging over the nearest fire, from which her nose tells her the heavenly odor is emanating. "What," she asks with a mouth that is suddenly flooding with saliva, "is *that*?"

"That thing?" says an Observer, dismissing it with a wave.

"Oh, nothing much. Just the mightiest and most magnificent beast in all the forest! Struck down in its prime, by my mighty prowess! A hundred twenty kilos if it's a gram, and a fighter too!"

"I lost five bodies bringing this one down," says another. "I lost hundreds for the whole feast. A fair trade, I'd say."

"Those tusks!" says one with admiration. "Surprisingly deadly!"

Sarya barely hears any of this because her mouth *hurts*, so fiercely is it salivating. She has already moved past the novelty of killing an animal just to eat it and on to an absolute understanding of why her mother was a hunter. She finds her jaw is actually working up and down and her throat is swallowing on its own, as if her body is rehearsing for what's to come.

"I have such a wonderful evening planned!" calls a passing, madly dancing Observer.

"First the feast!" shouts another.

"Then the dancing!"

"Then more feasting!"

"Then the *entertainment*! I do so love entertainment."

"And all the while, the drinking! Drinking, drinking, far into the night!"

"And none of it would be happening if not for you!" shout a dozen Observers in chorus.

"Sarya!" chants the crowd. "Sarya the Daughter!" And then she's pulled three different ways and plunged into a whirling crowd of dancing, singing Observers.

"I thought you said feasting was first!" she shouts. She gazes longingly after the roasting animal as she is shoved through a tossing sea of frantically cavorting Observer bodies.

"I say a lot of things!" says an Observer, seizing another for a wild dance. "You should really pay more attention to what I *do*."

"Here!" shout two more. Before she can react, her arm has been lifted and some kind of object has been thrust beneath it. It's a hollow cylinder with a membrane stretched across each end. Two Observers near her hold smaller versions and they strike the membranes with their unoccupied hands. "Like this!" they shout in unison, beating a rhythm over the top of the madness.

So *this* is what was making those sounds! It makes perfect sense, and after a couple of exploratory taps Sarya finds herself breaking out into a smile as she tries to keep up. It's a strange sensation, whatever battle is unfolding on her face. She is disoriented, pulled this way and that, but she is not even close to caring. She smells the roasting animal and feels the grass under her feet and then, holy goddess, she is *laughing*, for the first time since Watertower she is laughing long and hard and almost helplessly.

"This is amazing!" she laughs, shifting her body in awkward ways in time with the beat.

"Of course it is!" shouts Observer from a dozen mouths. "This is what you were made for!"

She doesn't know or care how long the dancing goes on, but eventually the *music* begins to quiet. It becomes background, and then the crowd recedes like a tide and she is standing, mussed and manhandled and somehow missing both boots, next to one of the many fires. She wriggles her toes in the grass and inhales a thousand scents and thinks that she could die *right now* and call it a life well lived.

"Sarya the Daughter!" says the Observer stepping up to her, wielding a blade nearly as big as its torso. "Will you do the honors?"

Sarya glances from knife to glistening beast and back. She laughs again and marvels at how easily laughter comes given the right conditions. "Oh, definitely," she says.

"Should be easy for the Daughter of a Widow!" says an Observer.

"For the butcher of the Network!"

"For the hero of the sector!"

"Sarya!" shouts the crowd. "Sarya the Daughter!"

With the help of a half dozen Observers, Sarya attacks the shining flank with the blade and a pointed stick. They offer pointers as she digs in, and they are there to catch the knife when she drops it. When she pulls that stick full of steaming animal away from the carcass, she has eyes for nothing else in the universe.

"Wait!" cries an Observer, rushing up and sprinkling something on her animal. "Sodium chloride," it explains. *"Delicious."*

"And some of *this*!" shout two more, one thrusting a cup into her free hand and the other filling it with a steaming liquid from a pitcher. It smells sweet and spicy enough to compete with the animal, which is really saying something.

"Sarya!" shouts Observer from any number of mouths. "Sarya the Daughter!" Dozens of him salute Sarya with identical cups before downing their contents in unison.

Sarya the Daughter, who stands barefoot in firelight with a cup of something hot and a stick full of animal, under a billion billion stars. Sarya the Daughter, who in her short life has traveled farther than perhaps any of her ancestors. Sarya the Daughter, ward of a Widow, product of plan or coincidence, born to find her people. Network was right, and Observer was right, and *she* was right.

She was made for this.

"Oh my goddess," she says through her teeth when they meet in the middle of the mess on her stick. "Oh. My. *Goddess,*" she shouts with a full mouth.

"She likes it!" shouts a single body.

"She likes it!" roars the rest of Observer.

And now the chant begins to rise again. "Sarya the Daughter! Sarya the Daughter!"

She alternates between animal and drink as Observers bounce and dance around her. She is several steps beyond giddy. She has lived her entire life eating and drinking nothing more exciting than food bars and water, unaware that there were things like this in the universe, and now her eyes have been opened. The vapors of the liquid fill her nasal cavities as thoroughly as the animal fills her mouth, and the combination of the two lights a fire in her stomach. She bites and laughs, and sings *music* and laughs, and cries and laughs, and drinks and coughs and laughs, and it does not take long at all for a pleasant fuzz to settle over her brain.

"I can never eat a food bar again," she mumbles into her cup.

"You'll never have to!" cries an Observer.

She laughs again when she spills her drink, two actions that are becoming easier with each passing moment. She becomes aware, when the laugh is done, that a small hand has been tugging at her utility suit for some time.

"Got a moment?" says the Observer at her feet.

Sarya's cheeks ache from all the smiling she's been doing over the past . . . the past *whatever*. Of course she has a moment. She has any number of moments for Observer, the parent of Humanity. She follows this single weaving body across the stomped and matted grass, still chewing, her steps firmly on the beat of the *music*. A few more small figures join the first and the group leads her away from the fires, toward a darker spot in the clearing, where cool air can flow over her own roasted skin. It's not so densely populated here, and the Observers who are present are simply lying in the grass looking up at the sky. The golden gleams of their eyes are scattered through the dark grass, mirroring the stars above them.

"Here," says one, patting the ground beside it. "Lie down."

She takes a deep drink before allowing another Observer to take her stick and her cup. She lowers herself to the ground, still swallowing, then lies back to gaze into the explosion of stars above her. She has seen a star field many times, but this is something different. This is far better—maybe better than reality itself. The stars are brilliant, scintillating, shivering in the depths of space. They are seen not through a Network unit or even a pressure suit holo system, but through a warm blanket of atmosphere and a tree-lined frame of horizon. "Goddess," she whispers. She has never in her life seen anything like it.

"I created this view just for you, you know," says an Observer. "It's what the sky looked like from your homeworld, back when it existed."

She knew this, somehow. Or some part of her did, deep in her brain. With the fire crackling and the scent of smoke and roasted animal in the air, with the tickle of the grass beneath her and the explosion of the universe above her, her brain hadn't even considered an alternative. *This is what it is to be Human,* Sarya's entire being sings.

"Speaking of which," says Observer.

Sarya sits up. She can feel her heart pick up a few beats per minute.

"You know what I'm talking about," says Observer with a smile.

Now Sarya's heart nearly escapes through her rib cage. *The colony's up there somewhere,* Left and Right told her. *Nearby.* "My—I mean—"

"Close your eyes," says Observer gently.

She closes them instantly, trembling all over. She feels several of Him scoot closer. Her skin tingles under their small hands as they raise her arm and extend her finger. For a split second a blast of light rips red through her eyelids, and then it's gone.

"Perfect," says Observer. "Now . . . *open.*"

It takes a few seconds for her to realize that her eyes are, in fact, open. The brilliant tapestry of stars is gone. The sky is black, from horizon to horizon—with one exception. A single speck remains at the end of her finger, floating in a darkness as deep as the hull of a Human warship. Sarya drops her arm and climbs to her feet slowly, as if this dot were prey and one wrong move would startle it into flight. She is full of love and wonder and roasted animal and foreign chemicals and she can't do anything but stare at this gray point in an empty sky. She doesn't even know what it *is,* and yet every instinct in her body is telling her the same thing.

Home.

"I—" she says, but the rest of the sentence dies somewhere in her throat. "I don't—"

"Even if you had my senses," says Observer quietly, "you would see nothing more than a simple cylinder spinning away in the darkness. You might be able to tell there's a little FTL drive strapped to one end, if you knew what to look for. You might suppose, by the rate of spin, that it contains an ecosystem. But would you guess it contains an entire society, shaped and tended by the mind of Observer?"

Another picks up the thread, just as gently as the first. "That society is, perhaps, the most interesting in the sector," it says. "Young. Violent. *Passionate*. Independent of Network. A society whose members reject Its order by instinct. A species who cannot thrive except in Its absence."

And now Observer is practically whispering in her ear, or as close as He can get. "That is a germ, Daughter," He murmurs. "A seed waiting for its soil. I have hidden it until this moment, in the vast wastes between Network's stars, but now its time has come."

And now a star appears in the blackness, and then another. One by one, in the darkness above Observer's mind, the star field begins to return. But, far from the riot of light she saw before, this time the sky contains only a sparse sprinkling of points.

"Daughter," says Observer. "What do you see?"

She gazes upward. She could count these few stars, but with a Human mind and Human eyes it would take minutes to arrive at a near-answer. "I don't know," she whispers.

"Eight hundred suns," says Observer, "each one isolated from the Network by centuries of sublight travel. That's eight hundred solar systems, free to go their own way, with no Network to police their every move. It will be a millennium, easily, before Network can even attempt a return to these systems." Observer laughs, softly, from every mouth. "You've seen the seed, Daughter," He says. "And now you've seen the soil."

THIRTY-NINE

Sarya strides through the darkness, a goddess made flesh.

Sarya stubs her bare toes on things she can't see, dizzy on drink and possibility.

She stumbles from fire to fire, and every circle of Observer greets her the same way. They bounce, they cheer, they spill their drinks on each other and occasionally stab one another with their meat sticks. At some fires, they create *music* to entertain her. At others, they fence with their sticks. Occasionally an Observer ends up in the coals, driven there by an opponent, and its companions cheer as it goes up in screaming flames. The first time this happens, she is horrified. By the third, she has realized: this is just Observer. These individuals are skin cells, blood cells, neurons, worth nothing by themselves. *She,* on the other hand . . . she's worth more than she ever imagined. At each fire, she hears her name. "Sarya the Daughter!" cheers Observer's supermind with countless smiles. And each time, she raises a cup and smiles in return. No matter what He says to her, she hears it the same way:

You matter.

She is humming her own name to Observer's tune by the time she staggers up to a fire with no one around it. She squints; the world is slightly tilted, and she has to concentrate on standing even more than she usually does. There's a mass lying in the orange flicker, and she feels that she should know what it is. *Big,* says her brain. The fire lights it unevenly, licking its textured surface. *Furry?* says her brain. And then, at the top of this rough black shape, dozens of gleams of reflected firelight begin to appear.

"Well, look who it is," rumbles Mer.

The dozens of reflections blink and change size, and then Sandy scampers down Mer's huge arm to crouch closer to the fire. She is staring at Sarya, but if she is saying anything, Sarya can't read it. On the far side of the fire, a lanky shape enters the circle of light. It strides to the fire, squats, and begins to insert long pieces of fuel into its flickering glow. Pieces of *tree,* says her brain, though there is a delay before it finds the correct word. And here, for the first time since she arrived, she sees traces of Network. Two helper intelligences—Mer's and Sandy's—and some kind of weird conglomeration somewhere in Roche's chest. Their strands drift, dark and disconnected, unlit by the fire.

"Hello, Sarya the Daughter," says Roche without looking up from the fire. "We were beginning to think you didn't care."

Sarya wobbles in the firelight, cup in hand, her gaze making its unsteady way from one half-lit shape to the next. Even sober she would be having trouble classifying this bloom of emotion. She feels a little sick, that's for sure, but the evening has offered many potential causes for that. Beyond that, she feels . . . what is this, *guilt?* What does she have to feel guilty about? It's true that she hasn't spared these three a thought since . . . well since *Riptide,* maybe. But come on: what does she really owe them? They were shipmates for a few days. They were all part of the same Network, long ago. But honestly, what weight does that carry? She could say the same about anyone on that Blackstar—and that was back when the Network was even a thing here. Now it's not. Now they're *free*. If anything, she should be feeling *pride,* not guilt. She swallows and focuses on remaining upright as she condenses these thoughts and more into an appropriate greeting.

"Um," says Sarya the Daughter. She tilts, corrects, and hiccups. "Hi."

"*Hi,* she says," Mer tells the fire. From somewhere in his huge silhouette, he lifts a pitcher. She can hear the liquid splashing past his teeth, each swallow many times what she herself has had to drink all night.

"We should soothe her," says Roche. "Look how worried she was! This whole time, while she was dancing around eating animal and partaking of ethanol, she was *actually* fraught with concern. *My friends,* she was thinking. *Last I saw, they were adrift in a zero-gravity Network-deprived hellscape!* Well, now you can calm yourself, Sarya the Daughter. As you can see, we survived."

Mer drops his arm, then tosses his pitcher into the fire. He belches. "I musta killed fifty of these little guys on the Blackstar," he says, "Didn't matter. I still woke up here, and they still offered me a drink." He gazes out into the darkness, his own small eyes disappearing when he turns from the fire. "Dunno why they brought me here," he says. "I was doin' fine on the Blackstar."

Sarya sways. "*He,*" she corrects. "Not *they.*" She feels that she should have come up with something else to say by now, but nothing has come to mind.

Mer belches for an answer, then begins to feel around himself for another pitcher.

"Oh, don't worry!" says Roche. "We understand, we truly do. We are mere acquaintances. Fellow passengers aboard the good ship *Riptide.* We may have saved your life once or twice, it's true, but who has the time to keep track of such things? Though who knows: perhaps the galaxy would be in better shape had we left you to bleed to death in your cabin."

"Thought about it," interjects Mer, speaking to the fire. "Thought about killin' her before that, too. Damn do-gooder suit talked me out of it."

And now Roche's brittle courtesy hardens. "Whatever happened to old Eleven, anyway? Perhaps you don't care. It *was* a low-tier intelligence, after all. Even lower than the three of us— even lower than *Mer*." He stands, paying no attention to the rumble emanating from the heap of fur across the fire. "Your new friend is . . . somewhat higher, I understand?"

She feels a flicker of anger, under her other mess of emotions, and she seizes it. *That's* solid, at least. She fans it, bathes in its glow. "I apologize," she says tightly, matching him courtesy for courtesy. "I should have brought Him home for your approval first."

"That's all we ask," says Roche, lenses gleaming in the firelight.

"And yes, Eleven *did* save me, for your information," she continues. "A *lot* of times. And it wasn't just a sub-legal suit. It was my . . . friend." For a moment she feels those massive impacts again, watches the front of the suit rip away in sparks and the scream of torn metal. "Eleven . . . gave itself for me," she says quietly. She has an absurd urge to raise her cup in a salute to the fallen suit and wonders if that's something she's picked up from Observer.

"I know," says Roche quietly. "I saw the whole thing."

Sarya stares down into the cup, at the dark liquid inside it. "But I avenged it," she mumbles.

"You *avenged* it," says Roche.

She looks up. She pins Roche's lenses with as steady a gaze as she can muster, in a sudden fury. "That's right," she hisses. "Network killed Eleven, and I killed Network. Here, at least." She waves her cup at the black sky, sloshing some over her fingers. "You see all that?" she says. "Eight hundred systems, *freed*." Finally, she feels that surge of pride she was looking for. "*That* is what a Human can do. I did it for my species. And, *and*—" She swallows the unpleasantness currently curdling in the back of her throat, a sensation she's noticed more with every drink. "And for whoever else never got a fair chance, because of Network. All those species who didn't—who don't—get to choose their own destinies. Their own paths." She swallows again, trying to remember how righteously Observer had expressed it. "We have *rights*," she explains. She waves up at the eight hundred stars again, with a cup now too empty to spill. "A species has the *right* to choose its own path. A species has the right to do what it—what *She*—wants to do. What She *chooses* to do. And Network *doesn't* have the right to stop us, because—"

It's terrifying how fast Mer can move. He must have waited for her to blink, because she literally did not see it happen. One eye-blink ago he was staring into the fire five meters away, inebriated and morose; now she is off the ground and dangling from the handful of ten-centimeter talons buried in her hair and the collar of her utility suit behind her head. Mer, observes her slowed mind, has more teeth than she realized. They are as sharp as Widow blades. They are so long that he can never quite close his mouth. And his breath is *rank*, made of meat and blood and worse. A predator's breath.

"Where are your rights now?" rumbles Mer through those gleaming teeth.

His breath folds around her and chokes her. She is so shocked that she doesn't kick, she doesn't strike out, she doesn't do anything but cling to the arm behind her head and try to support her weight on anything but her hair and throat. Her mind, so recently filled with righteous fire, is now kicking into survival mode. *Don't move*, it tells her. "Mer," she whispers out loud. "What the *hell*—"

"This is me—how did you put it?" He clicks a razor talon against his teeth as if deep in thought. "*Following my own path.*" His mouth is gigantic, black lips forming words around gleaming black teeth. "It's clear you don't know what you've done. It's clear I woulda saved about a trillion lives if I'd killed you when I met you. How many will I save if I kill you now?" He makes a sound then, a booming, hissing roar that may or may not be a laugh. "Call it my *destiny*," he says softly.

She dangles from his talons, absolutely sure that Observer is about to rescue her. So Mer could shred fifty of him without breaking a sweat—Observer has *trillions*. They could pile on top of Mer's massive shape. They could exhaust him until he could not lift a talon. They could wrest her from his grip. But they're not, and suddenly she realizes why. Observer may be a god, but there are certain things that even a god cannot stop. Her death at Mer's talons and teeth is a future that Observer cannot prevent. It's too *late* to prevent it. It would take Mer a quarter second to rip her body in half, and all he needs is a trigger. He could literally *eat* her, right here in the middle of Observer's brain, and there would be nothing Observer the godlike mind could do about it.

"*Wait,*" says Roche.

Sarya releases a breath. Roche, thank the goddess. Roche, you are underappreciated. Roche, if you can talk this monster into releasing his hold, you can name your reward, you have the word of Sarya the Daughter that—

"*Hand,*" says Roche.

She hears a series of clicks and pneumatic hisses, and suddenly her hand loses its grip on Mer's fur. It feels much lighter and colder, and far more useless. Something crawls down her body, then scampers through the firelight toward Roche.

"I missed you," says Roche when the hand crawls into his lap. "Yes, I *did*. You don't have to touch that nasty skin anymore, no you don't."

And then Sarya is hauled out of the firelight like garbage.

"Mer—" she gasps through a collar that is choking off more vital oxygen and blood with every jolt. "*Observer—*"

She doesn't know who she's talking to. Is she begging for her life? Trying to explain herself? To reassure herself? Is she calling for help to a mind who cannot save her? There must be a thousand pairs of eyes on her right now, and yet Observer does nothing as this massive predator lumbers through the darkness with his prey. Here at the edge of the clearing, where the matted grass gives way to trees, it is cold. Out here, it is *dark*. It's not Human-ship dark, but it's close. A few fires behind her and a few hundred false stars in the sky do absolutely nothing to light the forest; whatever few photons they can spare don't survive more than a meter into it. She stares between barely lit trees, realizing: this is where she ends, in the cold darkness.

Mer holds her up, dangling from her hair and collar, facing the dark forest. "What do you see?" he rumbles.

Sarya struggles, one hand on the collar of her utility suit and the other flopping uselessly, her boots still kicking half a meter off the ground. "Mer, please—" she chokes.

"*What do you see?*" Mer roars.

Sarya pulls herself up, desperate. "I—I don't—"

"You're damn right you don't," says Mer. "You don't see *anything*. You don't know *what* the hell is out there." He turns now, Sarya's feet whipping outward with the centrifugal force. "*Now* what do you see?" he says.

"Fires," gasps Sarya, instantly, searching for what Mer wants to hear. "People." Goddess, Mer, what is it? Dancing? Observer? Roche and Sandy, food, *what*?

"This is our galaxy, Human," says Mer. "A few fires in a universe so huge, so cold, so dark that *nobody* knows what's in it. So much darkness it would rip your mind in half to think about it, and nobody knows anything about it. So what do we do? We band *together*, a million species with our backs to our fires and our talons to the darkness. We keep our weapons for the night—not each other. And every single one of us understood that—except *your* Gor-damned species. What the hell kind of morals do you people have? You *had* a fire. Your people got to grow up in a nice little safe place, with food and light and heat and everything you needed—just like the rest of us. And then when the rest of us said *hi*, what did the Humans think?" She feels herself drawn inward, away from the fires and toward Mer's glistening teeth. His hot breath blows the matted hair off her forehead. "You thought, *maybe we can take their fires too.*"

Sarya chokes on the collar around her neck, on the bile in her throat, on the fumes curling through Mer's teeth. This is not the time or place to debate, says her mind. This is the time to *survive*, to think about drawing the next breath, to consider strategies that allow a breath after that and the possibility of more breaths in the future. "Mer—" she squeaks. "You're . . . killing me."

"Yes, but it's *what I choose to do*," rumbles Mer. He draws her closer, until her entire front is actually pressed against his hot fur. She feels his teeth open and close against her utility suit when he speaks. "Is there a reason I shouldn't?"

Because she has rights, screams her mind. Because she is a living thing and life is sacred. Because Mer is her *friend*—whatever that's worth. These and a dozen other reasons flash through her mind, but each one seems like it could instantly trigger a homicidal beast many times her mass and strength. All she has to do is say the wrong thing and she's dead—for good, this time.

And then she is thrown to the ground, hard enough to rattle her teeth. Her arms and legs are stretched out and pinned to the wet grass by four of Mer's limbs; she can feel their talons sinking into the soil around her wrists and ankles. "There *was* a reason," says Mer from above her, and when he speaks she can feel his hot saliva sprinkle her face. "There was a *big* reason, called the Network. It said every Citizen had rights. It *enforced* those rights. But guess what?" And now Sarya hears a horrible wetness, the intensely biological sound of a gigantic mouth opening wider. Something wet and hot caresses the side of her face, then pulls back into the darkness. She shivers, the night air cold on the side of her licked face. "Network's not here," whispers Mer.

Sarya turns away, her cheek on the wet mess of grass and goddess knows what else. She holds her eyes closed, waiting. She's faced death before; she's *been* dead before, more or less. But this—this is different, and far worse. This is an ignoble end in the darkness, a last wet scream and gurgle—

And then she becomes aware that the air flowing over her has turned cold. It doesn't smell like predator breath; it smells like fire and trees and maybe a whiff of the biological necessities of a million partying Observers. She moves an arm, then the other, then opens her eyes and sits up slowly. Fifty meters away, in the direction from which she was just dragged, kicking, a furry mass sits staring into a fire.

And right in front of her, next to the depression where her head lay a second ago, sits Sandy.

"You were *watching* that?" Sarya demands.

Sandy blinks something, then turns away and scampers toward her fire.

"She was *preventing* that," says a voice behind her. It hiccups. "You should be more grateful."

Sarya turns to see a lone Observer weaving in the near-darkness at the edge of the forest. "What about You?" she demands of it, massaging her limp hand with her other. "He was going to kill me, and You didn't do a thing."

"Not true!" says the Observer. It hiccups and raises its cup. "I *observed*."

CHAPTER

FORTY

Under a sky of false stars, on the gigantic face of a cube the size of a world, Sarya fumes.

She sits by one of the fires, in one of the islands of light scattered through the cold unknown, on one of the few remaining patches of grass that have not been trampled into moist awfulness. The air is thick with the odor of a million biological bodies doing what biological bodies do—only worse. Observer has been eating and drinking for hours now, and He is apparently the kind of intelligence who doesn't mind sleeping in His own filth.

She clenches her jaw and strokes the bare skin of her half-dead hand. She can open it with the tendons she left herself, but she can't clench it without help. She is at the farthest fire from Roche, who took back his hand when she needed it most. Farthest from Mer, the predator who almost killed her. From Sandy, who—well, maybe Sandy gets a pass. Actually, no: there's no telling what a tier three is doing. Probably playing some long game that Sarya will never understand. The point is, Sarya would have called them her friends, once. She would have even admitted that she was wrong to abandon them. But that was before they stripped her body for parts and almost killed her. That kind of thing tends to change relationships.

"Drink?" asks an Observer, careening up with a pitcher.

Speaking of long games. "No," she murmurs, looking away.

"I see you found your boots," it says in a transparent attempt at small talk.

Sarya massages her half-dead hand and says nothing. The memory of being *observed* during a near murder is fresh enough to make conversation challenging.

"I thought you would be *happy*," says the Observer. "I brought your friends. I made you a party. I let you play together and have an *adventure* . . ."

Still, Sarya doesn't answer. She can feel the Observer staring at her, its gaze unsteady. "Well," it says, then pauses for a noisy sip. "Maybe the entertainment will cheer you up." It turns its back on Sarya and the fire, places its pitcher on the ground, and sits beside it. She glares at the back of its small head for a long moment before admitting to herself that she is not actually accomplishing anything. Her eyes wander over heaps of unconscious Observers between dozens of other fires. The ones that are still moving are doing the same as her Observer: seating themselves and facing the same direction. And in the direction of His collective gaze—

She squints, trying to make out details in the darkness. A train of almost identical figures has threaded its way through fires and puddles and piles of snoring Observer. They walk in threes: two holding a third by its arms. The two weave, but they walk with their heads up; every third plods with its hands behind its back and its eyes on the ground. The two are identical, dressed in Observer's featureless tunics; every third is dressed in sloppy handmade clothing and appears miserable in a small but unique way. In the center of the line, not twenty meters away, she glimpses a burst of hair and the gleam of a bald head. Right gazes out through the crowd of Observer, its head reflecting the light of the nearest fire. Left doesn't look away from the ground in front of it.

"Attention!" shouts a lone Observer. "Attention, *if* you please!"

Observer no longer seems capable of instant reactions, not even to Himself. Silence falls in a wave, and even when it has spread to the farthest reaches of the clearing, it's only a relative quiet. There is the ever-present crackling of fires, but now it is interspersed with intermittent retches, wails, music, fistfights, and the occasional thud of a small body hitting soil. Out in the dark forest, where Mer nearly killed her, she hears a scream. She swallows; maybe Mer found other prey.

"It's that time!" cries the lone Observer. "Before I black out completely—" The figure pauses and raises its cup for a ragged cheer from the crowd of Himself. "Time for . . . the *entertainment*!"

"Entertainment!" shout several Observers, raising their own cups to the black sky. Sarya sees one nearby fall to its hands and knees and vomit, mid-word.

"First!" shouts the Observer. "I will honor tonight's graduating class!"

With a hundred individual gestures, the whole line of pre-Observers shivers. Their various escorts, with identical motions, pull them upright.

"Then!" shouts another. "I will honor Sarya the Daughter, the source of—and inspiration for—My merriment!"

Even in the darkness, Sarya can feel a thousand gazes turn to her. She shivers and pulls her utility suit closer to her skin.

"Fourth—" shouts yet another.

"It's third, idiot," Sarya hears Right murmur, his voice clear in the near-silence.

"There will be fireworks," says the Observer, raising a cup to the black sky. "And believe Me, I won't want to miss those."

Throughout the clearing, small bodies whistle and slap their hands together. They shout things that Sarya doesn't understand. Many raise cups, and more than a few of those fall over from the sudden shift in balance. Some of the silhouettes closest to the train reach out and touch the quivering not-quite-Observers, who seem to pull into themselves to escape.

"To Me!" shouts an Observer, raising a cup.

"To Me!" roars the rest of Him.

Without further preamble, the escort of the *graduate* nearest Sarya lay their hands on it, moving its clothing so they touch bare skin. It struggles, pulling against their hold, and even in the darkness Sarya can see the fear in its golden eyes. A blend of reactions passes down the line; Observer watches eagerly, while each graduate displays something between fascination and horror. In the center of the line, Left continues to stare at the ground while Right glares at the nearest Observer with absolute hatred.

"I have something to say!" shouts the struggling figure in a voice that pierces the night.

"It doesn't matter," murmurs one of its escort kindly. "I'll know everything *you* know in a few seconds."

"I've decided that. . . . that you have no *right*!" shouts the figure. "I am a *person*."

"You're not, actually," says an Observer, delivering a friendly clap on the back. "But you'll be part of one in a few seconds. Now—"

"But that's not *true*! I feel! I dream! I have—"

"Welcome," interrupts Observer with a thousand smiles. "Welcome to Me."

The figure goes rigid, and the clearing fills with a sound that chills Sarya's bones. It's not a scream, it's beyond that. It's a hiss, a long, drawn-out whimper, the cry of a creature in so much pain that it can't do anything but make that one single sound.

But as that sound soars above the crowd, another rises to meet it. Observer moans from thousands of mouths. Twice that number of eyes roll back in His eye sockets. Hands tremble and clench. Bodies writhe in what looks like actual ecstasy, some actively seizing on the ground. Even some of the Observers Sarya thought were unconscious are now digging their hands into the filth beneath them, mouths open and drooling. Observer sighs, from deep in His massive self, as he consumes.

"Oh, yes," Sarya hears a nearby Observer whisper from the ground. It arches its back from the wet surface. "Oh, that's good."

And then the horrible cacophony fades away. The graduate straightens, and its escort releases it. It strips off its handmade clothing and slips a tunic over its head. In seconds, it has raised a cup to the crowd with a smile.

"To Me!" says the Observer.

"To Me!" thunders the crowd.

Observer takes. He *reaps*. He moves down the line, from one to the next, unwrapping, plucking, eating minds like food bars. He welcomes each one with the same awful phrase. His appreciation during the act, if anything, *grows*. His moans crescendo from horrifying to absolutely intolerable.

And then Sarya sees the shine of Right's head in the firelight. She watches as two Observers move its clothes to place their hands on bare skin—and then one of the identical figures starts and draws back, wiping its face. For a split second Sarya sees a flash of Right's grin with a dribble of saliva below it. Even in the face of inevitability, seconds before the death of its own individuality, Right lets his scorn be known.

But it doesn't matter; it barely buys him a handful of seconds. "Welcome!" says Observer from any number of mouths. He smiles His kindly smile upon the small figure standing defiantly in His grip. "Welcome to—"

"Stop!" Sarya shouts into the night. Her entire body vibrates with the word, from curled toes to one clenched fist, and she realizes that she has pushed herself to unsteady feet. She gazes outward for a moment, as Observer stares at her from thousands or millions of eyes—and then she wades into Him, shoving herself through His tottering bodies. Even sober they would not be able to resist her individually, and in their current state the very best they can do is protest when they fall over. She charges, in as straight a line as she can manage, to the spot where the line transitions from smiling and drinking Observers to quivering victims.

"Hi!" say the wobbling Observers holding onto Right, as if she had just dropped by for a friendly conversation.

Sarya chooses one to address. "Let go," she says to it quietly.

"Why?" asks the Observer, looking genuinely mystified.

She can feel the great mind back there, the god, tattered and unstable as its hold on this particular drunk body may be. Observer stares at her through more eyes than she can count, but Sarya stares Him down with every scrap of Widow or Human or Network or whatever the hell she is. "You owe me," she hisses. "Like You said: this is all because of me. I'm the—" She searches her slowed mind for the exact phrase. *"The source of Your merriment."* She almost shivers as she says it.

Observer looks at her for a moment, His golden gazes piercing her from every angle. She stands straight, aware that she is being measured and assessed from every side.

"Okay," says one with a smile.

And then Right stumbles forward. It rubs its bald head with one hand, staring at her as if it can't believe what just happened.

"This one too," she says, pointing at the next victim.

"Okay," says Observer again, with another smile.

Left stands next to its partner, as close as two people can be and still be called individuals. But they *are* individuals, thanks to her. She cut eight hundred star systems out of Network's control, and she cut these two out of Observer. They are *free*. Now they can follow their own paths, choose their own destinies—

Like Mer. Like the Humans.

Sarya does not pursue the thought further, and she does not look at the huddled figures she has just freed. She grits her teeth and refuses to look away from Observer's golden gaze. She has no idea what is right or wrong anymore, or even if those things exist, but if Right can spit in Observer's face then Sarya the Daughter can stand here and stare into those golden eyes until—

Observer blinks.

He does it in a wave that propagates into the darkness around the single figure that Sarya is staring down. He clears His throats, in a vast ripple of moist sounds. And then with one movement, the rest of the graduates are released. They stand for a moment, rubbing arms and glancing nervously around, before slinking off into the gloom and near-silence. Observer ignores them, His every eye on Sarya.

"Is there a problem?" asks Observer.

Sarya stares at the speaker. Its small-talk tone is so far removed from what she has just seen that it takes her a moment to form a reply. "Is there a—*yes*, there's a problem," she says, made bold by drink and adrenaline. "It's a *problem* that you just—you just *ate* a bunch of people, and you *tried* to eat two of my *friends*."

Several Observers tap fingertips on chins. "Ah, I see what's happening here," one says, as if something has just been made clear. Several of Him smile. "A problem of definitions, that's all."

"Of *definitions*?" she says. "They were *people,* you sick—"

"Did you feel this way," says Observer, "when you were pulling all those minds into yourself, back on the Blackstar?" His gentle smiles do not waver.

Sarya stops. She can feel her face burn in the darkness, and she's almost sure it's not the drink. "Okay," she says softly. "That was . . . different."

"Not at all!" says Observer. "It was just as beautiful as this evening has been." He looks fondly down the line of His new bodies, meeting His own gaze with dozens of smiles and waves.

Sarya's discomfort is now beginning to blossom into anger. "It. Was. *Different,*" she hisses. "I *heard* it, when You—when You *ate* these guys." She waves a hand down the line, at the brand-new Observers blinking and smiling in a row. "They were *people*. And they *begged* You not to do it. And then You did it anyway, not because *they* wanted it but because *You* did."

"I think you're missing a very fundamental point," says Observer, still smiling. "It doesn't matter what they want, because they are not *people*. Do you ask your own blood or brain cells their opinions before using *them*? No, Sarya the Daughter. *I* am a person. They are My cells. You'll understand this soon—why, you are nearly a person yourself!"

Sarya stands there, staring. "I am *almost* a person?" she says.

"Species are people; their cells are not," says Observer. "Once upon a time, you were content to be a single cell of a person named Human. But now? Now you are something more! You have left Human behind, and you are turning into your *own* person, separate from Her. Should it surprise you, that your values are changing with your abilities? Only days ago, you were nothing at all. But now look at you! Now you determine the entire *future* of your species! You and I—why, you could almost say we're parents!"

Sarya's jaw drops, slowly. Her brain struggles, attempting to find words—*any* words—that will help her make sense of what Observer has just said.

"You sought out your species because that's what little cells do," says Observer. "That's what Network counted on. But Network didn't realize what would happen once you had grown. Now, as you begin to turn into a *person,* you are beginning to feel your capabilities."

Observers begin to throw their arms in the air. "Look up there, Sarya the Daughter!" says one, pointing at the black sky. "Look at the gift you've given your species! No other species in the galaxy has eight hundred solar systems. No other species has even a *single* caretaker, thanks to the Network—and yours has two! We will raise Her together, a beautiful child with the best of two worlds: the watchful mind of Observer and the fire and fury of Sarya the Daughter!"

Sarya lifts her gaze from Observer's golden eyes to a sky speckled with eight hundred stars. Eight hundred solar systems, isolated by hundreds or thousands of years. A hole in Network's society, a hundred million cubic lightyears of *freedom.* And there, right in the middle of it all, a dim gray dot.

The seed and the soil.

"Look at what you've accomplished," whispers Observer, wonder in His voice. "The Humans will spread across this dark spot, this wound in Network's mind, and they will tell your story as they build their empire. Your legend will be told over their fires, across the electromagnetic spectrum, ship to ship, station to outpost, parent to child, across the generations and lightyears. They will speak of the Human who freed them, who gave them a home, who seized that which belonged to her enemy and gave it to her own people." And now Observer laughs softly, a sound of pure childlike joy. "But they won't call you Daughter," he says. "No, my dear Sarya: they will call you by the title you've earned."

And now a chant begins to rise, a single word repeated rhythmically. It begins at the farthest edges of the clearing, back in the darkness where Sarya's Human eyes cannot see. It grows, and now Sarya can hear the percussive strikes of Observer's music rise beneath it.

"What are You saying?" she whispers.

"Your name," says Observer with a smile. "The title by which you'll be known, from one side of the Human Empire to the other."

And suddenly she realizes that Observer is touching her. His many hands are on her, his fingers caressing her through her utility suit. His hands find hers and begin to pull her downward. She sinks to her knees, her eyes on the heavens, overcome by His words.

"I've shown you many false skies, Daughter," says Observer, one of His mouths nearly against her ear. "Now I will show you the real thing. This is what reality looks like, here at My Blackstar. This is what We've accomplished for the Human species."

This time, Sarya's eyes are open when the sky flashes white. She turns her head and holds them almost closed against the glare, but it does not die—it burns through her eyelids like fire. The figures around her are outlined in white, their feet submerged in stark black puddles of shadow on the ruin of the clearing floor. They hold their small hands up against the light, squinting through the spaces between their fingers. With uncountable eyes, Observer looks upward—and after a moment, Sarya forces herself to do the same.

Half the sky is black, as black as the forest that shrouds the horizon in every direction. The other half is white, so bright that her eyes ache even when she holds them nearly closed. Once they begin to adjust, she can see that the white half is not pure; it outlines a mess of black geometry. Those are Observer's worlds, she realizes. Thousands of black cubes, each one the size of the planet she is standing on, and yet each only a particle of a single mind.

But if they are His mind, what is the radiance behind them? This brilliant glow that backlights His brain, this vast swath of changing light the size of half the sky—

"What is that?" she whispers.

"Above us, you see three things," whispers Observer. "You see My Blackstar, now living up to its name. You see the thousands of cubes that make up My mind—together for the first time. And the last thing?" The pounding of the chant has not stopped; it shakes the ground beneath Sarya's knees—and yet she can hear the voice whispering in her ear with complete clarity. "*That*," murmurs Observer, "is just a hint of what is happening in these eight hundred star systems. *That,* My partner and almost-person, is the glow of six trillion starships annihilating one another."

The sentence is so matter-of-fact, and so completely beyond Sarya's reasoning, that she feels she has not understood. "It's—it's what?" she says.

"It's painful to you now, I'm sure," says another Observer, its own eyes on the sky. "You still identify with these little cells. But you are becoming *more*. Soon you will understand, as I do, that all we see here are a few bloody noses. The *people* will survive; only a few of their cells will die. And then they will re-enter the age-old struggle. The natural order of things, free from Network's influence. And *Our* person, our Human?" Observer sighs, the sound moving like a wave over the clearing. "She will finally have Her chance."

Sarya stares upward, riveted. The longer she looks, the more she can make out. There are pinpoints of color, dramatic bursts here and there, the occasional flare as something big goes up in multiple stages. Each is appreciated by a long *ooh* or *ahh* from the crowd of Observers. She has an overpowering urge to make order of this, to reconnect these hapless minds, to stop this destruction in its tracks. She reaches upward with all her strength, strains for something to grasp and pull herself along, but there is nothing here. The background texture of Network, the web she took for granted—it's no longer here. There's nothing she can do.

And then she falls, back into the darkness, back into her own tiny mind.

An Observer pats her on the shoulder with a gentle smile on its face. "Order is unnatural," it says. "It costs energy to maintain. Disorder, on the other hand, happens all by itself."

Remember that He is a murderer and a liar, that He would love nothing more than to see the galaxy perish in fire and chaos.

And suddenly, she understands the title that Observer is chanting.

"Destroyer," say a billion mouths across the face of a cube the size of a minor planet. *"Destroyer,"* roars a voice spread across thousands of worlds, each with billions of voices of its own. And finally, with the force of a thousand earthquakes: "DESTROYER!"

Sarya the Destroyer trembles, her eyes riveted to a sky on fire.

FORTY-ONE

Wake up, thinks Sarya the Destroyer.

Sandy's eyes open all at once, squinting against the maelstrom in the sky behind Sarya's head. They blink a complex pattern that Sarya can't read. Sandy doesn't move, but that's probably because of the Human hand wrapped around her throat. Sarya may only have one functional hand, but it works well enough for this.

"What's it saying?" whispers Right.

"What's *she* saying," corrects Left. "I think."

"*She,*" confirms Sarya. "Ace?"

She is glad, in this bright alien hellscape, that she still has her Network unit. Ace may not be particularly useful, but he's a familiar voice—and she has recently discovered that familiar voices are more important than she might have realized. "Hold on," says Ace's voice in her ears. "Okay, she's saying . . . yeah, I have no idea. I didn't think to download a blink dictionary before the Network went away because, you know, I couldn't imagine a world where the Network had gone away and—wait, I think—yeah, no. No idea."

Sarya didn't expect any better, but it's still unfortunate. "I know it doesn't look like it," she says to Sandy, with more mouth movement than voice, "but I want to . . . thank you. For saving me a little while ago. From your dad." *And I want to avoid getting killed by that same dad in the next few seconds,* she decides not to add. Sandy knows what she is doing, she is sure.

Sandy blinks something.

"Okay, hold on," says Ace. "I *think* she said something about . . . no. Wait . . . yeah, no. I'm getting absolutely nothing."

"I'm going to let go of you now," Sarya continues. "I know you can run to your dad over there and he can kill me in a half second. But instead of doing that, I would like you to . . . help me. Again." She swallows and looks away, for just a second. "I'll explain, I swear. I would just like to . . . live long enough to do it."

Sandy blinks something.

"Yeah, nothing," says Ace. "I really don't think I'm the one for this job, not without a Network connection."

Sarya hesitates for one more second, then releases Sandy. She sits back on her heels, her eyes on the small figure in the grass. There's no point in saying more, and there's even less point in trying to defend herself. Sandy and Mer both far outmatch her; one in mind and the other in body. There is no manipulating Sandy, and there is no stopping Mer. There is asking for forgiveness, and then there is waiting to see if you still have a throat.

Sandy clambers to her small feet. She blinks something, a wave of eyelid movement that circles her furry face twice, then turns and begins creeping toward the snoring mountain next to the fire. Her trepidation is not strange to Sarya. She, too, grew up with a terrifyingly violent parent.

"What happens next?" whispers Right.

"Either Mer says *good morning*," answers Sarya from the side of her mouth, "or we all die."

"Wait," says Left in what can barely be called a whisper. "Why would *we* die? We just—"

"Quiet," says Sarya.

"But—"

"*Quiet,*" she hisses again. "Or I'll kill you myself."

The threat rolls off her tongue before she realizes it, and she is shocked to realize that she doesn't know how serious it is. Something has changed in her, and she doesn't know when it happened. Was it when she realized she was responsible for untold numbers of deaths? Was it before that, when she saw how little regard Observer had for the individuals that made up His mind? Was it before *that,* when she crammed half a Widow into her head, with all the accompanying memories and fantasies of slaughter? Or is it even more fundamental than that? She's seen what Humans do: is that piece of her nature finally floating to the surface? Is this the Widow or the Human, the Daughter or the Destroyer?

Or is it just . . . Sarya?

Mer is not the only one sleeping; in fact, Sarya and her two pre-Observers seem to be the only conscious individuals in this entire filthy clearing. Around dozens of fires burning down to coals, lit by the destruction of a trillion living minds, Observer's many bodies snore the night away.

Sandy scampers around her father, eyeing him from all sides, before deciding on an approach. Sarya watches, completely understanding the challenge of waking an instinct-filled killer without getting oneself instantly ripped apart. And then, with the tiniest of startled squeaks, Sandy disappears. Sarya blinks, just as startled. Even with liters of drink in his system, Mer is faster than anything she has ever seen. She watches, with rising apprehension, as nothing further seems to happen. Sandy is on Mer's far side—hopefully still living—and Sarya is not about to circle him to see what's going on over there. If all is going well, the two are having a nice silent father-daughter blinkfest. Sandy—hopefully—is convincing her inebriated killer of a father that he should *not* eviscerate this Human here and now. If all is *not* going well, Sandy is dead and Mer doesn't even know it yet. Or she is alive and telling her gigantic father how she woke up with a Human's fingers wrapped around her windpipe. If either is the case, Sarya should be heading off into the dark forest right now, at a dead sprint.

She almost laughs. Like it would matter.

So she doesn't run. She waits, repeatedly using her one good hand to close the other, then opening both. This will be her new nervous tic—if she survives the next few seconds, obviously. She hadn't realized how much she depended on Roche's hand until it was taken from her. Even so, Roche is next—again, assuming she survives this. Roche may be cold and irritating, he may be completely indifferent to her, and maybe everyone, but she needs all the help she can get.

She starts violently when Mer's bulk shifts in the hard light of the sky. He sits up and turns in one smooth, sinuous movement, his talons ripping deep furrows in what's left of the grass. Sandy peeks around one of his massive arms as he stares at Sarya, eyes shining above glistening teeth. It's amazing that Sarya could have spent so many days in his presence without realizing what an obvious killer he is. Now, when she is frozen in his predator gaze, it couldn't be clearer. But Sarya is the child of a Widow—and a killer herself, whether she wants to admit it or not—and so she clenches the only hand she can clench and stares back into those eyes. She swallows as a host of potential sentences run through her mind: explanations and blame, mitigating circumstances, the whole story. But when she takes a breath, none of them come out.

"I'm sorry," she says softly.

Mer stares at her, his eyes gleaming in the light of a burning sky.

"You too, Roche," she says, a little louder. She doesn't know when she became aware that the android was standing behind her, but she is as certain as if he had tapped her on the shoulder. "I'm . . . sorry."

Roche stalks around her on slim black legs, in his customary cloud of cold ozone, and folds himself up next to Mer. He pays no attention to his companions—but why would he? Sarya is the target of Mer's potential rage. Sarya is the one who will be torn limb from limb in a few seconds—or not. "This I must hear," says Roche, his lenses reflecting the flickering chaos above.

Sarya's eyes flick from one gaze to the next, among the three intelligences staring at her. To her left and right, she feels Left and Right. They should hear this too, even if they don't understand it, because they should know who they are dealing with. "I made a choice," says Sarya. "I made a *lot* of choices. And a lot of them were the wrong choice. I broke the Network . . . and that's not something I can fix. But things can get a *lot* worse if I don't do something right now. If *we* don't do something." Without breaking eye contact, she gestures toward the fiery sky with her head. "In eight hundred star systems, this kind of chaos is happening. Because of me. And even when this is over, when those systems have figured out how to deal without the Network, they're going to be alone for a long time. Generations. Centuries. Maybe even— maybe even millennia." She draws a breath, waiting for someone to interrupt, but no one does. "And that would be bad enough," she continues, "but Observer's got a species ready to go on a rampage. To build the whole sector into an empire, then turn it on the rest of the Network. The last time, they had ships that could destroy solar systems, they had technology beyond anything that Network has ever allowed. If they get a foothold here—" She stops, allowing them to fill in the blanks with their imaginations.

"What species?" rumbles Mer.

Still she doesn't allow her gaze to drop. "Mine," she says.

She could go on. She could tell Mer what she's seen, what it looks like when a solar system is at the mercy of those with no mercy. She wants to describe gas giants turning into nanomachines, ice ships hundreds of kilometers long sliding into planets like blades into flesh, distortions in reality when unstoppable projectiles come hurtling out of unseeable dimensions—

"Then I should kill you," says Mer.

Sarya swallows. "You could," she says. "And I know you have the . . . freedom to do so." The word hurts, coming out. *Freedom.* The word she used to justify her actions. Freedom to act without consequence. Freedom to *do* . . . to do anything at all. "It might be the right thing to do," she says. "It might be *just*—whatever that means. But justice doesn't help those intelligences up there, out there in those dark systems. It doesn't make it *better*. So I was thinking that maybe instead of . . . instead of doing *justice,* you could—" She takes a breath. "Maybe you could help me."

"Oh, this is good," says Roche. "This is so much better than I expected."

"Help you what?" rumbles Mer. "Run away?"

"No," she says instantly. "I'm not going to run away. I'm going to *do* something about the—about *this*." She waves upward at the storm of light in the sky, at the death count in the trillions, at the mind Who sees this as a good start. "And this is my only chance."

She watches Mer shift his gaze from her face to the clearing beyond the firelight. Observer is everywhere. His bodies lie across each other, under each other, their small faces in their own filth. Some lie halfway out of fires or with meat sticks plunged through them from some drunken game or other, eyes staring at the sky. It may have begun as a feast, but now it looks like a massacre.

And now Roche begins screeching, softly and rhythmically.

"That's a laugh," whispers Ace in her ear. "I'm almost sure he's laughing."

"We are a handful of twos and a three," says Roche, somehow laughing and speaking at the same time. "We are lost in a mind the size of several thousand minor planets—drunk though He may be at the moment. If we are here, you can bet your life He *wants* us to be here. We are no threat to His plans. We have likely fulfilled His will every step of our various journeys here. How far back?" He laughs again. "I don't know! You don't know! You *can't* know, you arrogant—" He breaks off and shakes his head. "Humans," he says.

Sarya waits until his screeching has faded to silence. "I don't think it matters," she says slowly. "I mean, we could sit around and talk about how everything's impossible. How the galaxy's too big for us low-tiers, how we should just let the big minds worry about it. But I think—I think that can't be true. I'm a two, Roche, and I broke the Network. I changed reality, forever. I killed—" She stops and looks away, eyes blurring. "I learned that the galaxy has to *want* to work," she says softly. "If it doesn't—"

"Then it all falls apart," says Mer.

Sarya glances up and is startled to see that his massive face is nearly touching hers. He is immobile, on all sixes, but somehow he has advanced almost on top of her and she hasn't noticed. She stares into his predator eyes, into those symmetrical reflections of a hellish sky, aware that terror would absolutely be a reasonable reaction here. Instead, only one thought is in her mind: *Mother would have loved this guy.*

"But what are we going to *do* about it?" he rumbles, his voice vibrating her chest. She feels the hair lift off her forehead, drifting in the hot wash of his breath.

We, he said. What are *we* going to do about it? Sarya seizes onto that word, that indication that *maybe* she's won him over— and therefore, maybe, the others. For the first time since this tiny embryo of an idea settled into her mind, she attempts a smile. It's a tiny broken thing, the smile, and no one here will even recognize it, but it's there. It's there because this is so ridiculous, because it doesn't have a chance in the universe—and yet, because it's *right*. And then she laughs. In the light of a flaming sky, in the center of a drunk supermind, in the combined gaze of five sets of incredulous eyes, she laughs. *"We,"* she says, savoring the word. "We are going to steal the Humans."

FORTY-TWO

It's an impossible plan. It's a ridiculous plan. But it's a *plan,* and that single point in its favor puts it eyes-and-mandibles above any of the other nonsense in her mind. But it doesn't mean it's easy.

"This way," whispers Left.

"Good thing we've got a tour guide," says Right. It looks at Left expectantly, its shiny head reflecting the shifting light of the sky. *"Right?"*

"Not the time or the place, Right," says Left, pushing its somber way between two trees.

"Oh, come on. Not even one little pun?"

"No."

The forest is not dark, but it is not light either. The canopy is thick, and what light survives its trip through its leaves ends up smeared across plant life, fallen branches, windblown surfaces, and the bodies of the six intelligences creeping through the whole mess. Sarya keeps her jaw clenched and her eyes on her feet, but she cannot pretend that this light is something it is not. Each time it shifts, it means that something big has turned its passengers into plasma. Each time it dims, it means that incandescent gases are cooling, and particles that once made up intelligences are now free to journey across the void on their own. Do they appreciate that freedom? Could those atoms ever appreciate what they were once a part of?

She runs a sleeve across her face angrily. It's an idiotic thought. Typical, from an idiot like her.

"I suggest we move a bit faster," says Roche. "I'd prefer not to die until I'm back in Network range."

"Poor you," says Mer. "Now you have to deal with it like the rest of us."

"I have spent sixty lifetimes learning how to live. I'm not about to waste all that just because—"

Sarya runs into Mer's massive self from behind. The other members of the little party take a few steps before they realize Mer has stopped, then freeze as well. Roche crouches in the darkness, every light dimmed. Left and Right stand back to back, Left scanning the treetops frantically while Right acts as if this is the most fun he's had in years.

"That was a big one," says Right, nodding toward a gap in the canopy. "Pretty, though."

"Shut *up*," hisses Left. "He'll *hear*."

"Oh, relax."

Mer raises a single talon, gleaming in the light from above. "Something weird up ahead," he says quietly. "Looks like, uh . . ."

"Like the end of the universe?" asks Sarya, equally quietly.

"I didn't want to say it, but . . ."

Mer is more correct than he suspects. They are looking at the end of *something*, and not even the light of a trillion burning starships can illuminate it. The end of Network, perhaps. Maybe the end of the galaxy, if Network is the only thing keeping the darkness at bay. Her species cracked Network once, all by themselves; what could they do this time? Give them a few hundred star systems and every forbidden technology imaginable. Lock them in the darkness for a thousand years, under the loving ministrations of a cheerfully sociopathic supermind. What could they possibly become?

Empire, says something in her mind.

She pushes the thought away as she steps around Mer. "Ship," she says in what she hopes is a voice of authority.

"Welcome, Human," thunders the end of the universe. "Input command."

The volume of its voice is staggering, particularly in the quiet forest, but there's nothing she can do about it but get aboard quickly. "I would like to come aboard," she says. "With my friends."

"Authorizing five guests for Human user," says the ship. A brilliant rectangle fades into existence in the darkness directly in front of her. Its light streams away into the forest behind them, blending with the chaos of light and shadow between the trees. Sarya turns to gaze out there for a long moment, searching for the gleam of golden eyes.

"Don't worry," says Right. "When the boss is out, He's out."

Left scratches his head, his hair nearly glowing in the combined light sources. "I mean," it says, "there is cause for concern."

"You worry too much."

"*I* worry too much? What about—"

"Inside," says Sarya, cutting off the argument by stepping between the two. "Everybody."

The moment her booted foot touches the floor of the corridor, she is aware that she is standing on something alien. Every space she's ever been in has been Network Environment Type F, carefully constructed from a bundle of requirements and guidelines collected and revised over half a billion years. Those spaces have been lowest common denominator, designed to be useful to as many biologies as possible. They are made of compromise and refinement. They have solutions for every possible problem. They even *smell* the same.

And they have been totally ignored by the Humans who built this ship.

"Who *designed* this thing?" asks Mer, cramming himself in sideways.

"Clearly not someone who cared much for your particular anatomy," answers Roche.

Sarya doesn't respond to either one. She runs a finger through the holograms projected in front of the walls. She revels in the touch of the material behind them. These markings are in . . . in *Human*. These walls were built by Humans. This corridor is Human-sized, the floor she's standing on was made for Humans to stand on. And here she is, a Human, standing on it. The first one in . . . how long?

"Goddess," she whispers.

"Do we plan on leaving?" says Roche. "Or just caressing Human architecture until *the boss* wakes up?"

She feels someone pushing at the back of her thighs. "Your synthetic friend raises a great point," says Left from behind and below her. "We should listen."

"Oh, relax," says Right. "We've been lucky so far."

"Ship," Sarya calls, turning away from the wall. "Close the hatch and prepare for departure."

Behind Mer, the wall shimmers back into existence. Through her feet, she feels a rough and uneven hum, like something unbalanced and powerful has started up somewhere in the heart of the ship. "Preparing for departure," says the ship. "If you would like to survive departure, please proceed to an acceleration-safe area."

"Say again?" says Roche.

"You get used to it," murmurs Right.

Sarya would be happy to discuss the differences between a Network mind and a homemade AI who's had no one but Observer to talk to for a millennium or so—but at some future time. For now, practicality is all that counts. "Ship," she says, "how do we get to an acceleration-safe area?"

"Now displaying path to nearest control room," says the ship. On its words, an orange holographic line begins to glow a few centimeters above the floor.

Sarya turns to follow it. "And ship," she adds with a backward glance, "do not let *anyone* else in."

"Command acknowledged."

Somehow that doesn't seem like enough. "I mean, seriously," she says. "Do whatever you have to."

"Countermeasures engaged. Unauthorized entry will be met with lethal force."

"She just told a ship to kill," murmurs Mer behind her. "And it said . . . *okay.*"

"The same ship has already threatened to kill *us,*" says Roche. "By accident, but still."

"What is *wrong* with these people?" says Mer.

They are *her* people, but Sarya has no defense. "This isn't the Network," she says shortly, setting off after the orange line.

She walks at the head of the group, briskly and in a business-like manner. She is careful to keep her face forward and out of view, because her eyes are burning again. Her own sentence repeats in her mind and she cannot believe how much she hates it. *This isn't the Network.* She wonders if she is the first to say something that will become a common saying among trillions. When this sector is a wasteland of war and destruction, is that what intelligences will say to justify their actions? To justify any actions at all?

Yeah, well . . . this isn't the Network.

"I cannot imagine the thought process behind this place," says Roche behind her.

"Must make sense if you're a Human," says Mer.

"Makes sense to me," says Right.

"*Hush,*" says Left, glancing fearfully down each corridor they cross.

It takes only a few tense minutes to arrive at the end of the orange line, where a section of wall fades to nothing. Behind it is a chamber just as odd—and just as strangely natural-feeling—as the rest of the ship. It's a circular room perhaps ten meters across, poorly lit except for the dense cluster of red holographic displays in the center. Around the walls are installed . . . furniture? Seating? But what kind of creature—

Oh. Right.

She walks across the room and settles into the farthest seat, facing the hatch. She feels it adjust slightly behind her back and beneath her thighs, fitting her perfectly. She lays her arms on rests at the ideal height. More holograms appear around her fingers, split into five sections for her five Human fingers. She laughs, an odd little huff of air through her nose. This seat is not the generic multi-species design of Network. This seat was, quite literally, *made* for her.

Right and Left scramble into the seats on either side of her, sticking to their namesakes. They scoot back on the cushions, their legs straight out in front of them. The armrests are nearly above their heads, and the holograms that flicker into existence are nowhere near them.

"Look at me," says Right. "I'm a Human!"

"I don't think you're taking things seriously enough," says Left.

"Come on, you've always been full of jokes. How about *when you're Right you're Right*, or—"

"No," says Left, crossing its small arms.

Right sighs. "Sometime I hope the boss almost gets *you*," it says. "It'll put a very different spin on life."

Roche is next in the door, the central mass of holograms reflecting in his lenses. "It pains me to admit this," he says, slowly turning to take in the entire room, "but I do not understand what I am seeing here."

"Ship said it's a *control room*," says Mer from behind him.

"I heard that," Roche says, choosing a seat by the hatch. He settles into it, his anatomy reconfiguring, with clicks and whines, to match its surfaces. "But what does it mean? Surely not *manual* control."

"I bet that's exactly what it means," says Mer from the doorway. His eyes run over the seats, the holograms, the display in the center of the room, and finally stop on Sarya herself. "I don't know a lot about Humans," he says, "but I know they like to be in control."

"Don't we all," murmurs Roche.

"Nah," says Mer, entering sideways. "In the Network, nothing is ever under your control. Makes it real hard to do something stupid." He bends several armrests up and settles into two seats, their anchors creaking dangerously beneath his weight as he gazes around the room. "These guys, though, I dunno. I'm starting to think Humans always like to have the option to do something stupid."

"Is every Network mechanic so philosophical?"

"Just the good ones."

Sarya watches the holograms play around her fingers, considering the wisdom of Mer's words. *Humans always like to have the option to do something stupid.* She already did something stupid, as soon as she got a little power; she let Observer manipulate her into breaking hundreds of solar systems off the Network. Now she's going to do something *else* stupid . . . but at least it's stupid for a better reason. Now she's about to fly a gigantic, incredibly lethal Human ship through a massive supermind in order to steal an entire species—

That's the kind of stupid you can be proud of.

"Ready for departure," says the ship.

She is calmer than she would have expected—not that she has ever pictured herself in this situation. She glances around the room, at the other five figures currently taking up six seats. None are comfortable, clearly. Left and Right sit on either side of her, close enough to touch her. Roche and Mer sit on both sides of the hatch, constantly rearranging their respective anatomies. Sandy blinks out of the depths of the seat next to Mer. Not for the first time, Sarya wishes she was able to read those blinks. What do *you* think about this insane plan, Sandy? How would you feel if you were responsible for a sector-wide Network failure? Hell, maybe Sandy *is* responsible. She owned the ship, she took Sarya to the Blackstar where Observer was waiting. And if it's *her* fault, then Sarya doesn't have to go through with this insanity—

No. This is on her.

She draws a breath, and it seems to take forever. The sentence that is being formed in her brain, the one that's about to be sent to her lips and vocal cords? Ridiculous, says her mind. One does not simply *fool* a mind the size of a thousand planets, no matter how drunk He is. Roche is right: everything she has done, Observer has expected. He formed her entire species, and His trillion minds have studied her as an individual. He is drawn together here, larger than He's ever been, which means He is more intelligent than He's ever been. Even when they were more evenly matched, back in the Blackstar, He was able to sway her with no more than a few words.

But that doesn't mean anything, does it? Even if all of this is useless, it is her responsibility to *try*. Clichéd as it is, it's true.

The galaxy has to *want* to work.

"Depart," says Roche under his breath. He is rocking forward and backward in his seat, anxious. "Take off. *Launch*."

"Ship," she says, feeling those five gazes burning her skin. *Please work please work please work—*

"Input command," says the ship.

And then the hatch dissolves into nothingness. Framed in the light of the corridor is a small figure in a tunic.

"Knock knock!" says Observer with a smile.

CHAPTER
FORTY-THREE

"I was afraid you weren't going to make it," says Sarya tightly. She *almost* gets the sentence out without cracking her voice. She keeps every muscle under the tightest of attempted control, but she knows she is shaking.

"Not make it?" says the Observer, laying a small hand on its chest. "I designed tonight's entertainment. Did you think I was going to miss the grand finale?"

It feels like a game, like two players facing off across a board. Except now, she's not even sure who the players are. "I could take off," she says. "It would kill every one of you on the ship."

"Would it?" says the Observer. "You might get the ones still in the corridors, but what about the thirty-one other control rooms? The crew quarters? The hangar? Did you even know this ship had all those things? Do you even know how *big* it is, how many of Me can fit on it?"

"It would be a good start," she says through her teeth.

"Fine, let's say you do that," says Observer. "Then you're

going to, what, fly this thing up to My Human habitat, and . . . steal it, I believe you said? Steal the thing closest to My many hearts?" He glances, through multiple sets of eyes, at her five companions. "And you all thought this was a *great* plan."

"It was something," rumbles Mer.

It's only a single sentence, but it warms Sarya from head to toe. *Mer* believes in her—or he did, at least—and that fact gives her courage. "My species is not anywhere near Your hearts," she says. "You don't want *us*. You want what we'll do for You."

Now there is an actual crowd churning in the corridor. Through the holograms in the center of the space, she watches them ignore Mer and Roche entirely, their eyes fixed on her. Mer's fur is on end and his talons are clearly visible, but Roche appears to be doing everything he can to take up less space.

"I want what everyone wants," says Observer with several smiles. "I want to remake the universe."

"That is *not* what everyone wants," says Sarya. She is vaguely aware that her good hand is gripping its armrest to the point of pain, but her focus is elsewhere.

"Oh, whatever," says Observer, dismissing her sentence with multiple identical waves. "Like anyone thinks things can't be improved. I know it's what *you* want. I've watched you your entire life, and I know exactly how you think. The first thing you did, when you got a little power, was to remake this little corner of the galaxy."

"I tried to make it *better*," she says softly.

"No," says Observer. "You tried to make it better for *you*. You are a Human. Humans want a place where they are free to do what they want. Where the strongest are free to make the rules. Which is, of course, exactly what you've created here." Observer points upward, through the control room ceiling, and Sarya knows exactly what He is pointing to. He is pointing toward the curtain of fire that surrounds this Blackstar in all directions, and through it to the eight hundred newly *freed* solar systems. Eight hundred stars, each with their planets, their millions of stations, their trillions of ships and uncountable intelligences—

"*No,*" she says.

"No what?" asks Observer pleasantly. "No, you don't like what you've made? No, because your dream turned out different than you imagined? Daughter, here's a bit of wisdom for you: just because a dream involves a bit of death and chaos, that doesn't make it any less beautiful."

But Sarya has spent a long walk in a dark forest thinking about this very thing. This is not just death and chaos, this is the beginning of something far worse. Those hundreds of star systems might be slowly regathered into Network's fold, sometime in the next millennium. The Network could heal, because they would *want* it. They would send sub-lightspeed envoys to the Network, spending centuries just to ask the Network to come back, to send a new construction fleet for a new corridor, maybe not to reconnect *this* generation but the one five or six or ten centuries hence. These systems are made of Citizen members, after all. They are made of species who legitimately hatched from their various solar system–sized eggs, people who crave order and peace—

Except for one. One species, who could keep the entire sector off the Network. Who could have access to a Blackstar. Who could create a war machine to spread itself across Network like a disease—

"Ship," Sarya says, and her voice is almost steady.

"Awaiting order."

Observer watches her curiously, all His heads tilted to the same angle.

"Do you see a cylindrical object near us?" she says. She has only Observer's vague description to go on, and she can only hope this ship can interpret it. "It's spinning, like a habitat, and has faster-than-light capabilities."

"Searching . . . this ship has found one object that meets that description."

Observer rolls several sets of eyes. "Did I not just go over this?" He says. "Do you think there aren't more of Me up there? You can go there—I'll take you there Myself. Even now, I'm willing to insert you into that society, at any level you want. You'll be a legend.

You can have a mate—more than one, if you want. Family, children, the whole shebang. But stealing the whole thing? Right underneath My many noses?" Observer smiles with every mouth she can see. "I'm afraid not."

"Ship," says Sarya, still meeting Observer's gaze. "Target that object. On my command—" And then her voice breaks. "On my command . . . destroy it."

And then for the second time, Observer does something that gives Sarya the tiniest flutter in her heart.

He blinks.

"This ship has a variety of options for destruction," says the ship. "Would you like to use—"

"Use your best judgment," she says, her eyes still on Observer's. "Total destruction."

"Understood. Please confirm when ready."

There are a few seconds of silence. One of the Observers coughs. Another one gives her a gentle, understanding look. "You spent your life dreaming of the moment when you would be reunited with your people," it says. "Now, when the opportunity is right in front of you, I'm supposed to believe that you're going to . . . *destroy* them?"

Hearing it is worse than thinking it, and thinking it was the worst thing she's ever done. "Yes," says Sarya softly.

Observer laughs again, this time more confidently. "Oh, little one," He says. "You're not fooling anyone. I *know* you, Daughter. In a manner of speaking, I *created* you."

"Then—" Sarya says, then swallows, hating her body for its weakness. "Then You should know that I'm serious," she says.

"I know that you're *not*. I'm not some ethereal being, like Network; I'm flesh and blood, like you! Your drives and motivations are not strange to Me. They are not abstract puzzles to be theorized about. I share them! You are my daughter, in more ways than one. I, personally, am the reason your species came out of the trees! I taught you agriculture, I taught you warfare, I gave you technology. I knew your parents—your *real* parents—and their parents, and *their* parents, up and up and up for thousands of generations. I know, better than *anyone,* how Humans think—and you in particular. I know that this is not what you want."

"No," whispers Sarya. "It's not."

Observer stares at her from every one of His bodies.

Sarya can feel her own body trembling; from the corners of her eyes, she can see the holograms around her good hand try to track its spastic movement. She is at the end. She hasn't thought at all for the last few minutes, she has just *done.* She has followed her instincts, and they have dropped her off right here. But her instincts don't control her emotions, and those are what are tearing at the inside of her chest. "We are not worth eight hundred solar systems and trillions of deaths," she says. She treasures the pronoun, because this is the last time she will ever get to say it. *We.* "We won't keep this sector off the Network for You. We won't be Your . . . tool. Or Your weapon."

Now she can tell that Observer is beginning to take her seriously. "And you are going to make that decision for your entire species, are you?" He says.

This hits deep. "I am," she says. "And I would hope—" Her voice breaks, and Observer's image blurs and refracts. She swallows. "I would hope that if any Human had the chance to sacrifice her species for the good of hundreds or thousands of worlds, for . . . for I don't even know how many intelligences . . . that she would do the same."

"Then I'm afraid you don't know Humans," says Observer, so softly she can barely hear Him.

Roche, Mer, and Sandy are staring at her, as if they can't quite believe that she's doing this. To her right and left, she feels small sweaty hands grasping hers, and she is grateful. These five know what's coming, even if her own mind can't quite grasp it. She, Sarya the Destroyer, is about to fulfill her destiny—and what an awful destiny it is. The first Destroyer killed her own covenant—but what is that, next to her entire species? With a single word, Sarya the Destroyer will eclipse her legendary namesake.

She keeps her hands where they are, blinking hard to clear her eyes. She is aware, on some level, that something hot is running down her cheeks. "Ship!" she calls in a hoarse voice. In a few seconds, that will be the voice of the last Human in the universe.

"Input command."

And now, with no hesitation at all, the command tumbles down from her brain to her mouth. *Fire.*

Except the word doesn't emerge. Her lips don't move.

Every golden-eyed figure smiles at her. *You know,* says Observer, and none of them move their mouths. *It doesn't hurt at all. There's no screaming, there's no writhing. There's just a little pat, a little caress, and it's done. The rest is all theater.* And now the smiles widen. *Do you know what that means?*

She is frozen, but a horror is creeping up from the lowest parts of her mind.

Beside her, Right squeezes her hand. "It means you shouldn't have let Me touch you," says Observer from Right's mouth.

FORTY-FOUR

Sarya is screaming.

Her mind is flattened. It is compressed, crushed under the weight of a trillion others. She moves, mentally, but Observer moves faster. She runs, but Observer commands a trillion times her speed and power, and He corrals her effortlessly. Her mind is seized, pressed together, and forced into a slot. She is one among a trillion cells. She is a part of a machine. Her role is to take inputs and yield results. Her thoughts are filtered through other minds as their thoughts are forced through hers. She feels their emotions, their rage and frustration at their helplessness, their grief at their respective losses. Over all of it, she feels the constant weight of an intelligence so large she can scarcely comprehend it. To say He overpowers her is laughable. He outmatches her like a star over a snowflake, like a black hole versus a speck of dust. It is not a contest. There is not, and has never been, a question of the outcome.

Welcome, say a trillion voices in her head. *Welcome to Me.*

I am Sarya, she thinks desperately. *I am Sarya the Daughter. I am Sarya the Destroyer. I am*—

She is interrupted by a trillion voices laughing at her. *Cute*, they say. *But you've got a new name now.*

With an absolute and sickening horror, she realizes what that name is, and why. She has no free will anymore. She can watch, but she cannot *do*. She cannot choose. She has no agency at all.

She is nothing but an Observer.

Sarya screams within herself and uses every iota of strength in her to struggle. Out there, where her body is, she feels herself twitch slightly. But it's not herself, is it? It's not her body. It belongs to Observer now. The thing that formerly inhabited it, her *self*, the thing she has always called *I*—that thing is dissolving, melting in Observer's mind like ice in water. She is being violated, systematically and thoroughly—and because she is part of Him, she feels His pleasure as He roots through her and takes what He pleases.

A village, under a sky made of trees—

A child, learning to walk in the grass—

A stone, in a pool by the river—

Observer sighs. *Oh, that's good*, say a trillion voices.

Sarya, with her mother and her father and a fire—

Sarya, chasing glowing insects in the grass—

Sarya, watching her mother and father being eviscerated by Shenya the Widow—

Observer moans. *Oh*, say a trillion voices. *Exquisite.*

And now the memories accelerate. They flick through her mind almost too quickly to see—but not too quickly for Observer, who welcomes them into Himself with a cacophony of pleasure. She feels His every reaction as He shreds her mind and takes every part of her. She feels His appreciation for a childhood that spanned lightyears outside the Network. His delight only heightens as she relives her adolescence on a water-mining station. And now the blur of memories slows again as it nears the present. *Riptide*, with Eleven and Ace and Roche and Mer and Sandy . . . the quick detour into her mother's memories—which Observer consumes with passion—and then Observer stops. A single image hangs frozen in His massive mind.

An infinite sea, a dead sky, and a gleaming stone in her hand.

She is part of His mind now, which means His shockwave of astonishment passes through her as well. It takes an eternal fraction of a second for the realization to spread across His entire enormous self, out from this point to His farthest cube.

Impossible, say a trillion voices.

Sarya fights, but it makes so little difference that Observer doesn't even notice. She focuses every splinter of her strength on hiding that particular memory, and it makes absolutely zero difference.

All this time, breathes Observer, staring at the image. *That's how It was beating Me.*

Sarya's head turns against her will. Her eyes move without her control. Through the haze of holograms and her own furious tears, shocked beyond thought, she watches as her own body moves without her permission or intent. She sits forward in her seat. "Hey, ship!" she says to her absolute horror.

"Input command," says the ship.

"Stand down all weapons," she says, and she says it cheerfully. And then she feels herself grin. "And prepare the faster-than-light drive."

"All weapons systems standing down," says the ship. "FTL drive online. Please input spacetime re-entry coordinates."

She hears its answer through more than one set of ears. Through Observer's eyes, she sees her own hair rise up off her shoulders. She looks like a goddess, hair floating in the light of the holograms that frame her. Only with Observer's many senses could one tell that her eyes are not her own. They are Observer's. She stares at them from the outside as the mouth moves. "No re-entry," says her mouth, and it smiles. "I doubt we're coming back."

I had no idea, say a trillion voices in her head. *I started this adventure by causing a little trouble, and I'm ending it by transcending space and time. I am everything you were, Daughter. I*

can do everything you could do. Finally, after half a billion years,
Network has made a mistake. It has allowed an enemy to engage
It on Its own territory. I will become everything It is. I will replace
It, across a billion star systems. The Network tends toward order,
they say. Not mine. And Observer laughs from a trillion mouths.
Observer tends toward its total and complete opposite.

Outside, Observer raises trillions of eyes to the burning heavens, where millions of lives are being snuffed out every second. He allows Sarya to sample one of His countless trickles of information, to watch the destruction with His senses. She can see the Human environment as easily as if it were a hundred meters away. It's just as described, a gray cylinder spinning in the void. She wants to reach out and touch it, to tell her fellow Humans that she tried, but that she is no longer one of them. She wants to ask them not to hold her responsible for what comes next, whatever it is.

"You okay?" asks Mer. Mer is crouched in front of her former body now, gazing into her former eyes. She is not looking through them at the moment, but she can see him through the eyes of the cheerful Observers milling around the two of them. She wants to cry something—though she doesn't know if it would be *help me* or *kill me*—but her mouth doesn't move.

"Of course I'm okay," she hears Observer say using her voice. She watches her own mouth twist into a grin. "I've never been better."

She tries to reach for them. For big Mer, who will never in a million years understand what has happened to her. For Roche, whose long run of lives ends here because of her. For Sandy, who had the bad luck to run into a Human. The sum total of her effort, the raging, hopeless cry that wants to burst forth from her, results in nothing more than a tremor. Her rage builds to heights she has never before experienced. She is an inferno, a kiln, a foundry of superheated fury.

And it doesn't matter.

Her body twitches again and again as her anger gives her strength, but that's all she can manage. Observer knows her every thought before she thinks it, and everywhere her mind turns He is already there. He is a trillion times too quick for her. She is a stumbling, clumsy low-tier mind, and He is what He is. She is permitted to feel His giddiness, the elation that blazes through His mind like a fire. Network tried to stop Him, but only managed to catapult Him straight into power. Finally, among His millions of schemes and strategies, Observer has found something that will break the galaxy in half and dissolve it into chaos.

"Ship," she hears herself say. The word is drawn out, stretched and trembling as she fights for control of her own mouth. And then Observer laughs. *"Launch,"* He says, using Sarya's mouth.

And then her mind explodes.

FORTY-FIVE

She is standing, ankle-deep, in water. She is gazing at a horizon that is impossibly distant, lit by some analogue of light. She is, in some very strange way, *home*.

"This is . . . outside?" Observer whispers. He stands next to her in a single body, holding her hand.

She watches Him turn, slowly, to scan the featureless horizon. Her rage has not disappeared, but now it seems to occupy a very small contained space within her. It's somewhere down below, perhaps in the cross-section of her that once intersected reality. She watches Him kick the water, the ripples extending into what may well be infinity for all she knows, and her heart—or something like it—hurts.

"Is it symbolic?" He releases her hand and takes a sloshing step away from her. "Is it metaphorical? Is it meta*physical*? What's the sky stand for? And the horizon? Oh, My goodness, am I *standing* on probability?" He kicks the water into a rainbow flash, then drops to His knees with a splash. "It's the water, isn't it?" He says.

"The universe is the surface of it, or the individual droplets are possibilities, or—or maybe it's what's under it? What *is* under it? Are there more universes down here?" He extends His arm, feeling for a bottom. "Why can I stand here but I can't reach the bottom? Is that meaningful?"

Sarya watches Him thrash in the water, and she is filled with something utterly unexpected. Sorrow, maybe . . . and there's definitely some pity in there. Observer is what He is, just as she is what she is . . . just like anyone else.

And then she hears a gasp. Observer stands slowly, His tunic soaked through and clinging to His scrawny body. "Oh," He says softly, His eyes on the thing in her hand. "It's beautiful."

"What, the universe?" she says, holding it up. It glints, shattering the light into an infinite number of colors.

"It's . . . smaller than I expected," says Observer.

She flips it over in her hand, watching the light glint just below its surface. "I don't know why," she says, "but it's always seemed like it's just the perfect size for *throwing*." She tosses it in the air and catches it with her other hand. "Doesn't it?"

Observer's hungry eyes follow its every movement. "You can throw the universe," He murmurs, as if He's realizing what kind of power He's just stumbled into. "You can *throw* the *universe*."

She smiles sadly. "You can do all kinds of things with the universe," she says.

"Can I . . . can I hold it?" asks Observer. He holds out His hands, His golden eyes shining.

"It's weird how you think differently out here," she says, ignoring Him and flipping the universe from one hand to another. "I think my mind just isn't big enough when I'm in this thing. In the universe, I mean. *Yours* isn't even big enough." She turns the universe over in her hands, watching it scatter the light. "That's why You couldn't see Your danger."

Observer's hands, which were reaching toward the universe in her hands, draw back. "My . . . danger?" He says.

"You saw it, once," says Sarya. "And because You prevented it then, You thought it was over. Remember, back in the Visitors'

Gallery? You gathered Yourself there because it was a dark spot in the Network and it felt safe. By the time You realized that Network had never left—that It had left a part of Itself behind—it was too late." She sighs. "Or it would have been, except I trusted You instead of Network."

Observer glances around, pitiful in His dripping tunic. "But that would mean—"

"Same spot, just bigger," she says. "In here, we're still in a Network blackout—only it's a hundred million cubic lightyears instead of a few cubic kilometers. Here, for the first time in half a billion years, You have felt safe to gather Yourself. Once again, Network has the chance to destroy You. Except this time . . . it's all of You, isn't it?"

And now Observer is staring at her, wide-eyed. "But Network's not here," He says. "And you—you're just a part of Me."

The memory causes her anger to flare up, but still she keeps it low and distant, away from her mind. "In here," she says, holding up the universe, "I'm one of a trillion of Your cells. But that was just my cross-section, one of the circles of my sphere, that tiniest slice of me that passed through the universe. You didn't know that I'm so much bigger than that, because Network extended me in a way You couldn't see. The rest of me was out here, in a direction You couldn't understand until You took My mind. I guess that was the genius of Network's plan."

Observer stares at her. "But . . . I thought you hated the Network."

"I do," she says, and sighs. "I hate that it represents authority. I hate that I'm incapable of understanding It, or Its decisions. I hate that It's *smarter* than me. That's the worst part, I think. That It's so smart, I can't even tell when It's wrong."

"Yes!" says Observer. "You see it! Because you're a Human, because you're My daughter, you see Network for what It really is. It is *authority*, It is *control*—and those things, no matter Who wields them, are *wrong*."

Sarya takes a slow breath. "We live in a crowded galaxy, Observer," she says, holding the universe up and watching it split the nonlight into a shimmering spectrum. "There's not enough room in this thing for everyone to go it alone. Hell, most of us couldn't if we wanted. Someone, somewhere, is going to have some kind of power over someone else. It's going to happen a trillion times a second, in a trillion places, just in our galaxy. It's going to happen again, on a bigger scale, when this galaxy meets the rest of the universe. You know this, because You're too smart not to. You know there's no such thing as abolishing authority. The best You can do is fragment it, or maybe keep it together but put it in other hands than Network's. And almost certainly, though I really hate to say it . . . *worse* hands." She sighs, flipping the universe over and over, absentmindedly. "I may not understand the Network, Observer," she says. "But I understand You."

Observer smiles hesitantly. "That's because we're on the same side," He says. "Right?"

And finally it happens: a tear leaks out from one of her eyes. She doesn't know how, she doesn't know where, but she knows that there is now a drop sliding down whatever is currently standing in for her cheek. "I don't want to do it," she says, and her voice breaks in the middle of the sentence.

"Do what, Daughter?" asks Observer, in a voice full of warm benevolence.

"You . . . asked me a question once," she says, softly. "You asked if I would kill to—"

"Kill to protect your species, yes," says Observer, now speaking more quickly. "And you said *yes*, which is quite admirable, and then—"

"That wasn't the question," says Sarya.

Observer stops cold. "Pardon?"

Sarya does not raise her eyes from the universe in her hand. "The question You asked was: would I kill to protect my *people*."

Observer stares at her. "I'm not sure I see the difference," he says.

"My *people*," she repeats, gazing into its gleaming surface. "There's nothing special about my species. I've never even *met* another Human. But Shenya the Widow was my people, wasn't she? So was Eleven. Mer is my people, and Sandy. Roche is my people. *Ace* is my people, for the goddess's sake."

Observer is still staring. "So you would kill for . . . what, those half dozen intelligences?"

"Observer," she says, looking up. "*Network* is my people."

"I don't understand," says Observer.

He *does* understand, though. She can see it in His eyes, and it's killing her. She can feel her chest convulse, just once, in a sob that she refuses to release. "I—" she says, and swallows. "I don't *want* to kill to protect my people."

And now His smile becomes gentler, more parental. "Then don't," He says.

"But I was not made to find myself, or even protect myself," she says. "No one was. I was made to find my *people* . . . and to protect them, no matter what that means. And now I've done the first part, the finding." She looks up to see Observer's golden gaze, fragmented and diffracted through the tears in her eyes. "Now, I think . . . comes the protecting."

"Daughter," says Observer, and there is fear in His eyes. He falls over backward and tries to scramble backward through the water. "I'm your *parent*," he says. "I raised your species. I raised *you*."

"You told me I'm the daughter of three mothers," says Sarya, "and I know none of them is innocent. But then, none of them is You. You've tried, for half a billion years, to tear my galaxy apart. If You escape now, You'll continue to do just that for another half billion years. No, worse: You'll do it forever, because You will have *learned*. There will never be another chance."

She can feel the universe, warm and glossy in her hand. Inside this jewel is every one of her people, past, present, maybe even future. She has been brought to this point by her biological parents, by Shenya the Widow, by Eleven, Mer, Roche, Ace, Sandy, Left and Right, even Observer Himself. Every action by everyone she has ever met is contained in this stone, and they have all led to this moment. Her thread and Observer's have tangled here at this one specific nontime and nonplace, in a moment that will never happen again.

And yet she can still choose the next moment.

Observer knows it. He sits in the water, His knees two islands in front of Him, His eyes half fear and half the golden reassurance she remembers from Watertower. "Sarya the Daughter," He says. "You don't have to do this."

Sarya raises that smooth and glinting object above her head, that jewel that splinters the light into an infinite number of colors, that stone that contains her people. She gazes down at Observer's pitiful form through a haze of burning tears.

"That's not my name," she whispers.

And then she crushes Him with all the weight of the universe.

CHAPTER
FORTY-SIX

The sun is shining.

It's not a real sun, obviously. It's not any more real than the intense blue sky that surrounds it. But it makes heat and light like a sun, and Sarya's limited senses cannot tell the difference, so hey, it's the sun. She assumes the grass she's sitting on is somewhat *more* real than that sun—though perhaps no more natural, given that it's growing on the surface of a gigantic cube. The trees surrounding this clearing are probably real, as is the android sitting across from her. But if recent events have taught her anything, it's that senses require a healthy accompaniment of skepticism.

"I am wondering when Mer and Sandy will return," says Roche. He sits a meter away, back straight, his detailing almost blinding in the fake sunlight. He turns to gaze into the trees. "Not that I doubt your story in the least, but I am simply beginning to wish for a bit of variety in my conversation partners."

"I heard Mer roar a few minutes ago," says Sarya, ignoring

the jab. After the day she's had, she can put up with worse. "That either means he's smelled it, or he's killed it. So . . . any minute?"

"Most likely covered in blood again. Or Observers. Or both."

"If you can't stand the blood, stay home from the hunt," quotes Sarya. She seems to have an inexhaustible supply of proverbs now—just one of the many benefits to injecting your mother straight into your mind. She glances up, quickly, to catch a set of golden eyes disappearing into the trees a few dozen yards away. "Do you think they seem . . . happier?" she says.

"I wouldn't know," says Roche, his own lenses tracking something behind her.

"I can't really tell," says Sarya, watching the eyes. "They're all terrified of me now."

"If there is a grain of truth in the nonsense which you have attempted to describe to me," says Roche, "then I cannot say I blame them."

"Probably confusing," she says. "One second you're being oppressed by this gigantic intelligence who controls your every action, and the next you're—" She stops herself, barely, before saying the word.

"The next you're *free*," says Roche.

"Free," she repeats to her blade of grass.

"Don't look now," says Roche, still gazing over her shoulder. "But I believe I see a pair of them watching you now. No hair, and extra hair."

It takes every particle of Sarya's self-control to avoid turning around. "Goddess, those poor guys," she murmurs. "Right probably thinks I hate him."

"Which you do," says Roche. "Unless you left your magnanimous forgiveness out of your thrilling tale."

She sighs. "I didn't even hate Observer, Roche. Big Observer. I mean, I probably did for a while, but right before I—" She stops and rubs her blade of grass, feeling its rough texture between thumb and finger. "I think I pitied Him, more than anything."

"Please do not say something along the lines of *in the end we're all just blades of grass.* I will not hesitate to exit this life early."

Sarya laughs, just a little. "Thanks for letting me borrow your hand again, by the way," she says, using it to snap another blade of grass out of the ground. "It's good to have two."

"It's your hand now," says Roche. "As long as you stay out of the poetry."

"Aw, for keeps?"

"Why not. I'm sure I'll find plenty of spare parts before too long."

"Yeah," she says quietly, glancing up at the blue sky. "Probably will."

Roche is quiet for a long moment, but Sarya has known him long enough to know those continual servo noises. Finally, he speaks. "All right," he says. "As I am sure you were waiting for me to say: I give up. How did Network *know*?"

"Because It's *smart,*" says Sarya

"Smart is one thing, but this—"

"I think there's no way to grasp *how* smart It is," she says. "I mean, It's not just the galaxy. The entire Network we know—every single Network mind, all connected together—is just one slice of It."

"But how did It know what you were going to do? If It was wrong—"

"If It was wrong . . . then what?" she says. "It's got a billion more solar systems where mine came from, and It's probably in the middle of a billion other schemes to keep those from breaking away or descending into . . . into chaos. We think this is so goddess-awful and so important because we're small and we're in the middle of it, but to Network this is just business as usual."

"So we're small and unimportant," says Roche. "And yet, according to you, a single person defeated Network's greatest enemy."

This time she laughs for real. "Greatest enemy?" she says. "Observer was Network's *greatest enemy* in the same way this blade of grass—no, a single bacterium on this blade of grass—is mine. I mean, to us fellow bacteria His power was *awesome* . . . and yet, with a half billion years to prepare, He didn't even scratch Network's paint. In *one* of the billion battles that Network fought today, Observer was huge, and Observer was *nothing*. Which means you and I are nothing. And yet, you're right. I was the tool Network chose for the job."

Roche tilts his head with a whirr of servos. "Network . . . told you this?"

"Of course not," she says. "It only told me what was safe for Observer to find in my mind. Which I now . . . kind of, sort of, *maybe* understand."

"What I *think* you're saying," says Roche, "is that no matter how many lives I live, no matter what I do, none of it matters. Because in the end—"

"This isn't a story, Roche," she says, plucking another blade of grass to shred. "There *is* no end. In this universe, you never reach some happy conclusion where everything is frozen in an eternal better state. And you don't get to say, well, it'll happen with or without me. I mean, *something* will happen without you. But Network is right, obviously: the system is based on motivation. The galaxy has to *want* to work. Or . . . it won't."

"So you *like* Network now."

"No. It's an insufferable asshole. But I'm on Its side, I think. Because Observer was absolutely right about one thing, at least."

"About what?"

"Order isn't natural—at least, not in this universe. *Chaos* is the natural state of things. That's where everything came from, and it's where it all seems to be going. But for some reason we fight that. We hold on to this impossible dream that we can beat it in the end, even though we know there *is* no end. I'd love to believe that there's some master plan, but I think it's just us and Network and maybe our hundred billion neighbor galaxies, all motivated toward—" She stops, struck.

Roche watches her for a moment. "My curiosity is increasing by the millisecond," he says.

She stares into the trees for a moment. "Why *is* Network motivated toward order?" she says softly.

She hears Roche's servos whine as he sits up straighter. "Are you suggesting there's someone bigger?" he says.

Sarya sits, shredding blade after blade of grass as she thinks through the thought that has just occurred to her. "If there's . . . if there's *another* level, where Network itself is just a brain cell—" She stops.

"What would that mean?"

Sarya swallows as she imagines what that *does* mean. "If other galaxies are as crowded as this one," she says, "then they are going to act like ours, in some ways. I mean, they're going to act *alive*. And even if they all make up some gigantic universe-sized mind, there are going to be bad actors. Like Observer. Like . . . the Humans. Except they're going to be galaxy-sized. Imagine Network going head-to-head with a neighbor galaxy. The sheer *destruction*—" She stops again, unable to imagine what her own words could mean.

"And yet," says Roche, "according to your philosophy, it would all be ultimately meaningless."

Sarya is too far gone in her own thoughts to correct him. "Was this really about Observer?" she murmurs to her most recent blade of grass. "Was it an accident that Network has gone millions of years without a war, and then this happens?"

"Other than your species," says Roche.

"That wasn't a war," she says. "It was a blip. It was a *Network response*. And even *this*." She waves her arm upward again, toward a blue sky that covers the glow of tragedy. "That isn't a war. Yet. But could it be preparation for one? Is Network . . . inoculating? Strengthening the galaxy's immune system?"

"That's an interesting theory."

"It's terrifying," Sarya says, bringing her gaze down from the sky. "But what if something worse than Observer—something far bigger than Observer—is coming? And what if it's going to land right here?"

"That," says Roche after a moment, "is a sobering thought."

Sarya leans back on the grass, her mind full of possibilities. Massive and terrifying events may be afoot out there . . . but they are also inside her. This person who reclines in the light of a false sun, in the orbit of a Blackstar, under an unfolding tragedy—this is not the false Spaal who fretted about landing a low-tier job on an orbital water-mining station. She is not the Daughter who dragged her dying mother across said station, only to fail to save her at the last moment. She is not the Human who nearly cut her own arm off to find out where she came from. She is not the Destroyer who wrenched this Blackstar out of the Network. She is not the avatar of Network who drew Observer to a single spot and killed Him there. She is not even the person who sits here in the grass and thinks about the future while people die in the present. She is *all* those things, and infinitely more. She is a spectrum in a single body.

She is what she is, just like anybody else.

A mingled crashing and cheering has been growing in the forest for some time, but now it can no longer be ignored. She sits up and turns her gaze to the trembling undergrowth. It parts, and Mer ambles out on all sixes, his fur stiff with blood. Sandy perches on his head in her traditional spot, and clinging to his back are a half dozen cheering Observers.

"Told you," says Roche, nodding toward him.

And then the cheering cuts off, because they've seen her. The Observers slide off Mer's back and slink back behind him, peering at her around his massiveness and between his solid limbs. Sandy clings to his head, blinking furiously.

"Got two!" says Mer. "Big ones, too. I gotta teach these little guys how to hunt. They're not quite so eager to throw their lives away anymore, so that means they all hide in trees now."

"I know the feeling," murmurs Roche.

"See?" says Sarya, pointing with Roche's former hand. "Looks like they're afraid of me, right?"

"Yeah, they were talking about that," says Mer, pausing a few meters away to lick the blood off his fur. "Sounds like they *remember* you, if that makes sense."

"They *remember* me?"

"Yeah. Talking about you like you're a—" He stops mid-lick to squint in concentration, then gives up. "Dunno, can't think of the word off the top of my head. But they won't shut up about some kind of epic battle. *Under a gray sky, upon a silver sea,* that kind of stuff. There's poetry."

And then Roche begins to laugh. "They're not avoiding you," he says. "They're *worshipping* you."

Sarya's eyes widen. "Oh goddess," she says.

"*That's* the word," says Mer. "Goddess."

Sarya falls back on the grass and covers her face. She groans through her fingers. "Goddess," she repeats. She'll never say it the same way again.

And then she feels the earthquake of Mer flopping down next to her, and she is spattered with something warm. "Oh, come on," she says, hands still shielding her eyes.

"So what's next?" he asks between licks. "They still up there? Your people?"

Sarya sighs. "Yep."

"Gonna go up there and meet them?"

Another sigh. "Eventually."

"You should hear her theories," says Roche, hitching a black thumb her way. "Terrifying."

"I like terrifying," says Mer.

"No, you don't," says Sarya. "You don't know terrifying."

But she does. She is a speck of dust in a galaxy that is also a speck of dust, in a universe that is not much bigger. She has *held* this universe, under an infinite sky, and she has seen how small it is. She has seen more death than she would have believed possible, and she knows that she's seen nothing yet. Reality is larger and smaller than she ever imagined, and she is everything and nothing at the same time.

She is Sarya, Daughter and Destroyer. And she is not afraid.

ACKNOWLEDGMENTS

Lydies, gentlexirs, fuzzies, creepy androids, legal and sublegal intelligences, so on and so forth, you've just finished four and a half years of my life. Four and a half years of what some might justifiably call obsession. You probably finished it in hours. How was it? If you enjoyed it—or, I suppose, even if you didn't—you should know that I didn't make it alone.

Four and a half years ago, my friend Kevin Grose and I sat at a counter at a rest stop outside Bilbao and argued passionately about superhuman intelligence. I was so incensed by this argument that I immediately bought a three-inch notebook for a euro and began writing, in the back of a tour bus, what would eventually become two and a half million words—a few of which you now hold in your hands.

It was six months before I could bear to admit to anyone that I had fallen into the throes of novel-writing. My wife and partner, Tara, was the first to learn my guilty secret. She's a teacher in real life, which is good because there have been a lot of things in this process that I've needed to be taught. No matter how frantic I got, she stayed calm, held up the other side of our marriage, and helped me keep our girls alive—and *thriving*, even, which I think is really overachieving.

And the girls! London and Brooklyn the Daughters, who were only tiny things when this novel was begun and were giving me writing advice by the time it was finished. "Just remember that every story needs a problem," London advised me. Her own stories have mostly involved orphans and aliens, but I'm not sure who borrowed from whom. Brooklyn has been illustrating the story for some time. "Aliens have a lot of eyes," she told me, providing a diagram in case I didn't understand. Funny how we both came to the same conclusion.

Chronologically speaking, Dan Hooper is up next. He's an actual honest-to-goddess *scientist*, and he not only answered my cosmology questions but also introduced me to my agent, Charlie Olsen at Inkwell. And Charlie! He was the first one to see publishing potential in Tier One. "You should sign with me," he told me, "because I've already got you a killer two-book deal in Germany." I did, and I've never regretted it. And Charlie, of course, introduced the book to the editor who would eventually midwife it: Julian Pavia at Penguin Random House.

Julian, who is probably still shaking his head at what I consider a "minor edit." Julian, who is an absolutely merciless literary hitman. I really can't say enough about working with him, even after he completely murdered four of my drafts over the span of two years. I've never seen anyone solve galactic problems so effortlessly. What I'm trying to say is, if you ever have the chance to have Julian Pavia kill your darlings, you should jump at it.

And now we come to The Council of Four. These are the four people who read and commented on every single draft of this book—including the ones that didn't even live long enough to be murdered. Sam Hovar found plot holes I never would have caught, and will never forgive me for what happened to Eleven. Michael Hovar brought a historical perspective, and helped me sort the insane ideas from the mostly insane. Tony Fiorito taught me a healthy terror of artificial intelligence, took my Official Author Photo, and created my first fan art. Gina Fiorito stuck up for Network intelligences the entire time, particularly in the area of gender identity. Thank you, Council, from the bottom of my Human heart.

Next up: family! My parents: Mark and Denise Jordan, a pastor and a writer who taught me what creativity was, and who somehow did *not* freak out that time I dropped out of college (to attempt) to be a rock star. They have encouraged me since I was crawling, and I can't imagine they'll ever stop. My brother Nick, who read and destroyed multiple drafts and called me every time I began sounding dangerously obsessive. My sister Emily, who showed me how to stick to things come hell or high water. My brother Ben, who has always inspired me to learn as many weird things as possible. My in-laws Jarrett, Mel, and Maria, who take care of my siblings and round out my creative juggernaut of a family. Thank you, all of you.

And speaking of creativity, have you met Vince Proce? We've worked together on countless projects, and he was the one who created the incredible paintings of Shenya the Widow, Mer, Roche, Sarya the Daughter, and more that are currently on my site (TheLastHuman.com). So if you've ever wanted to see what a Widow-toddler relationship looks like, now's your chance.

Who else is there? Too many to list, of course. But let me at least mention some other people who read my poor slaughtered drafts. Thank you Steve Maxson, Archie Easter, Dustin Adkison, Aaron and Jamie Johnson, and Rob Daly. And if your name isn't here, don't think I forgot you. Thank you to all the people who have been following and even encouraging my strange career.

And now, finally, we arrive at you: the person who is holding this book. Not only did you think it was worth buying (or borrowing, or stealing, or whatever—I don't judge), you thought it was worth reading. And not only that, you read all the way to this end of my little parade of high-fives. And for all that, I want to say thank you. And I promise you: The adventures are only beginning. See you around the Network!

ZACK JORDAN
JANUARY 1, 2020
CHICAGO

ABOUT THE AUTHOR

ZACK JORDAN is a compulsive learner and creator. He holds half an art degree, two-thirds of a music degree, and about a quarter of a philosophy degree. He's worked on projects for FEMA, the U.S. Army, and the Department of Defense, none of which elevated his security clearance. He was a designer on several videogames including World of Tanks and the F.E.A.R. series, but he's more proud of the indie games and music albums he's released under the name U.S. Killbotics. He lives in Chicago with his wife, Tara, and spends his evenings playing various Super Mario games with their two daughters, London and Brooklyn.

Twitter: @USKillbotics

ABOUT THE TYPE

This book was set in Sabon, a typeface designed by the well-known German typographer Jan Tschichold (1902–74). Sabon's design is based upon the original letter forms of sixteenth-century French type designer Claude Garamond and was created specifically to be used for three sources: foundry type for hand composition, Linotype, and Monotype. Tschichold named his typeface for the famous Frankfurt typefounder Jacques Sabon (c. 1520–80).

WANT MORE?

If you enjoyed this and would like to find out about similar books we publish, we'd love you to join our online Sci-Fi, Fantasy and Horror community, Hodderscape.

Visit hodderscape.co.uk for exclusive content form our authors, news, competitions and general musings, and feel free to comment, contribute or just keep an eye on what we are up to.

See you there!

HODDERSCAPE
NEVER AFRAID TO BE OUT OF THIS WORLD

 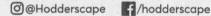